Neil Jordan, Author and Screenwriter

Reimagining Ireland

Volume 113

Edited by Dr Eamon Maher,
Technological University Dublin – Tallaght Campus

PETER LANG

Oxford • Bern • Berlin • Bruxelles • New York • Wien

Neil Jordan, Author and Screenwriter

The Imagination of Transgression

Bertrand Cardin

PETER LANG

Oxford • Bern • Berlin • Bruxelles • New York • Wien

Bibliographic information published by Die Deutsche Nationalbibliothek. Die Deutsche Nationalbibliothek lists this publication in the Deutsche Nationalbibliografie; detailed bibliographic data is available on the Internet at http://dnb.d-nb.de.

A catalogue record for this book is available from the British Library.

Library of Congress Cataloging-in-Publication Data

Names: Cardin, Bertrand, author.
Title: Neil Jordan, author and screenwriter: the imagination of transgression / Bertrand Cardin.
Other titles: Neil Jordan écrivain-scénariste. English
Description: Oxford; New York: Peter Lang, 2023. | Series: Reimagining Ireland, 1662-9094; vol. 113 | Includes bibliographical
references and index. | Identifiers: LCCN 2022050516 (print) | LCCN 2022050517 (ebook) |
ISBN 9781800799233 (paperback) | ISBN 9781800799240 (ebook) | ISBN 9781800799257 (epub)
Subjects: LCSH: Jordan, Neil, 1950---Criticism and interpretation. | English literature--Irish authors--History and criticism. | Motion
picture plays--History and criticism. | Screenwriters--Ireland--Biography. | Authors, Irish--Biography.
Classification: LCC PR6060.O6255 Z6413 2023 (print) | LCC PR6060.O6255. (ebook) |
DDC 823/.914--dc23/eng/20230103
LC record available at https://lccn.loc.gov/2022050516
LC ebook record available at https://lccn.loc.gov/2022050517

Cover image: Bertrand Cardin – 'Angel of the waters', fountain sculpture designed by Emma Stebbins (1868), Bethesda Terrace, Central Park, New York City, July 2018.
Cover design by Peter Lang Ltd.

ISSN 1662-9094
ISBN 978-1-80079-923-3 (print)
ISBN 978-1-80079-924-0 (ePDF)
ISBN 978-1-80079-925-7 (ePub)

© Peter Lang Group AG 2023

Published by Peter Lang Ltd, International Academic Publishers,
Oxford, United Kingdom
oxford@peterlang.com, www.peterlang.com

Bertrand Cardin has asserted his right under the Copyright, Designs and Patents Act, 1988, to be identified as Author of this Work.

Acknowledgements

It has been my good fortune to work with Peter Lang. I am especially grateful to Eamon Maher for his generosity, enthusiasm, advice and support. I would like to thank Dyana Jaffris and Tony Mason for their assistance and hard work. I do not forget the help of my colleagues and friends from the *Université de Caen Normandie*, in particular Marie-Laure Bouté, Alexandra Maclennan, Catharine Mason, Penny Starfield, Amy Wells and Jeremy Elprin and thank them for feedback and inspiration.

Contents

Abbreviations

BLECS   *The Ballad of Lord Edward and Citizen Small*
C   *Carnivalesque*
DB   *The Dream of a Beast*
DD   *The Drowned Detective*
M   *Mistaken*
NT   *Night in Tunisia*
S   *Shade*
SSM   *Sunrise with Sea Monster*
TP   *The Past*

Introduction

"Ye Powers
And Spirits of this nethermost Abyss,
Chaos and ancient Night, I come no Spy,
With purpose to explore or to disturb
The secrets of your Realm, but by constraint
Wandering this darksome Desert, as my way
Lies through your spacious Empire up to light,
Alone and without guide, half lost, I seek,
What readiest path leads where your gloomy bounds
Confine with Heaven"

– John Milton, *Paradise Lost*.[1]

At the boundary between land and sea, on the Northwest coast of Ireland, county Sligo is a harsh territory. Its rugged windswept coastline offers grandiose panoramas. The town of Sligo, nestled at the end of the bay, is not without charm. The landscape of the inland county is made of imposing hills overlooking the ocean, of steep heights on which flat tables have been added by mythical giants or spirits, of large plains littered with standing stones, but also holy wells or buried mounds. Of course, these fascinating, mysterious monuments developed popular imagination and aroused many legends; on this moor, local gods, the Firbolgs, were defeated by invaders, the Tuatha Dé Danann. Maeve, the queen of Connaught, who incited western men to fight against the troops of Ulster, rests forever below a huge cairn; whoever might attempt to desecrate her tomb would be under a curse, according to old superstitions. Nearby, the peaceful churchyard at Drumcliff is the final resting place of William Butler Yeats who is commonly regarded as Ireland's greatest poet. The latter makes Co. Sligo the backdrop of his inner life.

---

1   John Milton, *Paradise Lost*, 1667, Book II, 969-977.

He draws his inspiration from this part of Ireland which is, as he puts it, "a locale unusually rich in fairy lore and tales of hauntings, ghosts and eerie happenings".[2] Such a supernatural universe, which may be the realm of the dead, is intermingled with our own visible real world. There is constant interaction between them both. As a matter of fact, it is also in this region, at Rosses Point, a coastal village sitting a short distance from Sligo town, that Neil Jordan was born on 25 February 1950.

Neil was the second child of Michael and Angela Jordan. His father was a teacher, his mother a painter. The family appreciated artistic disciplines – painting, literature or music. Michael was an amateur violinist and occasional choirmaster. He encouraged his five children to play a musical instrument. The family circle is described by Neil as relatively strict, particularly concerning Christian values. Michael and Angela Jordan were Catholics and their sons were members of the choir in the local parish.

A few years after Neil's birth, the family left Co. Sligo to settle in the suburbs of Dublin, in Clontarf, next door to the house in which Bram Stoker lived as a child. Neil was educated at the local primary school in Belgrove; there, one of his teachers was the writer John McGahern. He received his secondary education at St Paul's College, Raheny, where he won a prize for a short story he wrote. Neil Jordan read a lot and started writing fiction when he was 15. Television was unavailable at home, but visits to the cinema were facilitated once every two weeks. He went to University College Dublin (UCD) where he staged shows and plays with his friends Jim and Peter Sheridan who, like him, subsequently won fame in Irish cultural life.[3] At university, Neil Jordan studied English literature and medieval history; his minor thesis was on the lives of the saints. He graduated with a Bachelor of Arts degree in 1971. That year, he married Vivienne Shields, a law student with whom he later had two daughters,

---

2   William Butler Yeats, *Writings on Irish Folklore, Legend and Myth* (London: Penguin, 1993), xx.

3   Jim Sheridan is a film director. With the producer Noel Pearson, he adapted Christy Brown's autobiography, *My Left Foot* (1989), which won two Academy Awards (for Daniel Day-Lewis and Brenda Fricker). Richard Harris featured in his next film, *The Field* (1990), which was followed by *In the Name of the Father* (1993). Peter Sheridan is a writer, playwright and scriptwriter.

Sarah and Anna. Due to the severe economic recession of those days, the couple migrated to London where Neil worked as a manual labourer while writing short stories. On his return to Ireland in 1973, he was a teacher and night watchman. Once his wife became a lawyer, Neil stayed at home to raise their two daughters. In the course of his life, he had three other children with two other women.[4]

Neil played the guitar and the saxophone in a showband which gave public performances in pubs and theatres. He also wrote a radio play – *Miracles and Miss Langan* – which was later broadcast on RTÉ and the BBC. This play was also made into a television drama in 1979; it was directed by Pat O'Connor from Jordan's script. Other television work by Jordan includes writing four of the thirteen episodes of the RTÉ production *Sean*, based on Sean O'Casey's autobiographies. As some of his short stories were published in magazines, his first collection appeared in 1976: *Night in Tunisia*. This set of ten stories brought Jordan to the attention of film director John Boorman, who, like many others, highlighted the literary style and visual quality of Jordan's writing. He subsequently invited him to collaborate on the script of his film *Excalibur* in 1979. In view of the success of the film, two years later, Neil Jordan directed a documentary about it, *The Making of Excalibur: Myth into Film* (1981). In between, Jordan published his first novel, *The Past*. From then on, his books alternate with films, which confirms the hybridity of his talent.

So far, Neil Jordan has been the director of about twenty films, the screenwriter of fourteen of them and the author of nine books. His fame experienced a boom with successful movies such as *The Company of Wolves* (1984) and *The Crying Game* (1992). It reached its peak in the early 1990s when Neil Jordan directed great actors such as Sean Penn and Robert de Niro in *We're no Angels* (1989), Brad Pitt and Tom Cruise in *Interview with*

---

4   Vivienne Shields and Neil Jordan separated in 1982. From 1983 until 1993, Neil Jordan lived with the American actress Beverly D'Angelo who acted in two of Jordan's films, *High Spirits* and *The Miracle*. He had a son – Ben – with the Irish architect Mary Donohoe, then embarked upon a relationship with Brenda Rawn, the Canadian assistant of several of his films. Together, they had two sons – Daniel and Dashiel – and married in 2004. As a result, Neil Jordan is the father of five children.

the Vampire (1994), Liam Neeson and Julia Roberts in *Michael Collins* (1996), Jeremy Irons in the TV series *The Borgias* (2012), Isabelle Huppert in *Greta* (2018), or Diane Kruger and Jessica Lange in *Marlowe* (2022).

Neil Jordan is an important figure in contemporary Irish cultural life, but his twofold creative output is not equally recognized. His literary career is overshadowed by his film activity. The artist is mostly known as a film-maker, a producer and director as various websites, articles and interviews show. He is not spontaneously identified as a man of letters. And yet, he has been a screenwriter, a short story writer and above all a novelist for over four decades. This focus on one part of his artistic production is noticeable among critics and interviewers to whom Neil Jordan feels sometimes obliged to remind: "You've got to realize I'm also a novelist".[5] Similarly, a certain number of Irish writers do not consider him as one of them, as if his Hollywood blockbusters had effectively expelled him from the Irish literary world.

This lack of interest is also observed in the small number of academic works dedicated to his fiction. As Neil Jordan's cinema is the subject of a variety of monographs, his literary work is not much studied. The critical apparatus is very limited: *The Fictional Imagination of Neil Jordan, Irish Novelist and Film-Maker* by Marguerite Pernot-Deschamps (2009) deals with the way Neil Jordan explores human condition. It adopts an essentially stylistic approach to the work.[6] Paul McGuirk's short book, *Neil Jordan: The Literary Fiction* (2016), summarizes each text of the author and sets it in the context of the twentieth-century literary movements, particularly modernism and postmodernism.[7] These studies are interesting,

---

5   Mario Falsetto, "Conversation with Neil Jordan", 1997; Carole Zucker, ed., *Neil Jordan. Interviews* (Jackson: University Press of Mississippi, 2013), 29. In May 2009, in a television interview with Gay Byrne, Jordan was eager to talk about fiction, making repeated reference to writing, but Byrne focused on filmmaking and mentioned writing only once ("Neil Jordan in conversation with Gay Byrne", *The Meaning of Life with Gay Byrne*, broadcast 24 May 2009, produced and directed by Roger Childs).

6   Marguerite Pernot-Deschamps, *The Fictional Imagination of Neil Jordan, Irish Novelist and Film-Maker: A Study of Literary Style* (Lewiston, NY: The Edwin Mellen Press, 2009).

7   Paul McGuirk, *Neil Jordan: The Literary Fiction* (Leipzig: Limanaki Books, 2016).

but they use a very specific approach to Jordan's literary fiction. In the latest academic book published in 2022, *Neil Jordan: Works for the Page*,[8] Val Nolan examines how readers and critics see Jordan's work. It contemplates fundamental questions of Irish history and identity throughout the author's career. This study, while definitely a significant contribution to the exploration of Jordan's fiction, does not pay tribute to each of the novels.[9]

Through textual studies, analyses and interpretations, the present book aims at giving Neil Jordan's talent the recognition it deserves. Its objective is to bridge a gap in academic research by studying Jordan's fiction with an open-minded attitude, combining various approaches insofar as a literary work is a whole world in itself that deal with the events of a lifetime, with a subject's dreams, desires and fantasies, with the social and historical determinations of a particular period and milieu, the use of language. Neil Jordan's texts are read and interpreted here by employing these approaches, which are considered as the mirrors of the writer's personal life, but also the expression of an era and a society. Their motifs and images provide sensations which make it possible to perceive the artist's creative imagination. Besides, their structures and rhetorical figures allow us to circumscribe the aesthetic specificities of the writer's poetic language. There is something polyphonic about Jordan's fiction insofar as it gathers a diversity of voices and refers to the works of other writers, particularly Irish writers, but also other texts by Neil Jordan himself, even if it is impossible to mention them all. Generally speaking, focusing on specific details implies leaving aside some others. Interpretation necessitates some choices which are inevitably subjective. Besides, Jordan's texts are sometimes read and explained in tune with his film activity, which cannot be ignored, all the more so as there are many connections between his books and films. Each of Neil Jordan's books is the subject of a dedicated chapter here, but two chapters also deal with the scripts he wrote, the latter involving cinema and fiction writing.

---

8   Val Nolan, *Neil Jordan: Works for the Page* (Cork: Cork University Press, 2022).

9   Nolan's study deliberately ignores Jordan's 2016 novel *The Drowned Detective* because it "did not achieve significant impact" (Nolan, *Neil Jordan: Works for the Page*, 225). Similarly, although it refers to Jordan's latest novel – *The Ballad of Lord Edward and Citizen Small* – it does not examine it at all. By the same token, it studies only three stories of *Night in Tunisia*.

These two artistic fields vouch for the fact that one of Neil Jordan's favourite topics is an interest in the irrational and supernatural. This is a specificity which can be connected with the "materialization of reveries" fuelled by his native land and the famous local figure – William Butler Yeats – for whom Co. Sligo is an extraordinary territory. Indeed, in *Water and Dreams*, Gaston Bachelard writes:

> The region we call home is less expanse than matter; it is granite or soil, wind or dryness, water or light. It is in it that we materialize our reveries, through it that our dream seizes upon its true substance. From it we solicit our fundamental color.[10]

Literary creation has certain similarities with the world of dreams. This may be the reason why realism and the supernatural are not incompatible for Jordan or Yeats. In their works, which demand a "willing suspension of disbelief",[11] this world and the other are not generally sundered. There is even interaction between them both. As a result, Neil Jordan's work – films and books – is realistic, fantastic, gothic and above all, uncanny. Indeed, according to Freud, "an uncanny effect is often and easily produced by effacing the distinction between imagination and reality".[12]

These inspirations contribute to rendering Neil Jordan's work complex and postmodern. Hybridization, a distinctive feature of postmodern aesthetic, implies a mixture of different things and styles. It suggests exchanges, borrowings and border crossings.[13] This specificity can be spotted in the way Jordan's work summons and includes other artistic means of

---

10 Gaston Bachelard, *Water and Dreams. An Essay on the Imagination of Matter* [1942] (Dallas: Dallas Inst Humanities & Culture, 1999), 15.

11 (Willing) suspension of disbelief is the intentional avoidance of critical thinking or logic in examining something unreal or impossible in reality, such as a work of speculative fiction, in order to believe it for the sake of enjoyment. The concept was first mentioned in 1817 in a text by Samuel Coleridge, *Biographia Literaria*. A character of Neil Jordan's fiction uses the expression when, seeing a clairvoyant, he says he is ready to suspend his disbelief (*The Drowned Detective*, 22).

12 Sigmund Freud, *The Uncanny* [1919] (London: Penguin, 2003), 251.

13 "Contemporary critical debates on [...] postmodernism often advocate necessary clarifications about different modes of border crossing" (Roberta Gefter Wondrich, 'Exilic Returns: Self and History Outside Ireland in Recent Irish Fiction' in Anthony Roche, ed., *Irish University Review*, 2000, 1).

expression – music, painting, cinema or theatre – or diverse social sciences – history, geography, philosophy, psychoanalysis, religion – but also in the way it builds bridges between fiction and reality,[14] imagination and verisimilitude or between different genres or subgenres.[15] As a result, it seems relevant to approach the work from the postmodern perspective of magic realism. The term is however refuted by Neil Jordan as it only applies to Latin-American literature, according to him.[16] Maybe it would be more appropriate to consider his work as falling into the category of fantastic realism. After all, there is nothing stranger than Irish reality, as Jordan himself reckons: "I grew up in Ireland in the fifties. I grew up in Dublin, was born in Sligo, that rural-urban background. I knew that small, strange world quite well [...]. If you stay here too much you can get very strange, very weird. It's a strange country".[17]

Fantastic realism implies both the precise observation of reality and the will to discover another mythical or poetical dimension. Neil Jordan's texts partake of this aesthetic when they blend the political issues of our world with some elements of myth, fantasy and magic of the Celts' Otherworld. By the interaction between these two spheres, they revive the Irish tradition of Celtic Renaissance which, similarly, establishes a mixed universe inspired by contextual reality and the local mythical past.

The destruction of barriers between the real and the marvellous is characteristic of the Celtic world. Indeed, many western intellectuals of the nineteenth century, who identified the specificities of that world and its literatures, enhance this duality. Matthew Arnold considers that the Celtic passion for nature comes from a sense of her "mystery". It adds "charm and

14   Fiction and reality converge when the texts mention people from the real world: Lord Edward Fitzgerald, Franco, Mussolini, de Valera, Gorbatchev or Putin.

15   "Borders between literary genres have become fluid" (Linda Hutcheon, *A Poetics of Postmodernism, A Poetics of Postmodernism. History, Theory, Fiction* [New York & London: Routledge, 1988], 9).

16   "I hate that term (magic realism). That's a very bad term. It's a very dangerous term. It only really applies to Gabriel Garcia Marquez. It doesn't apply to anyone else. And people who have tried to emulate that voice have failed miserably – particularly when people talk in cinema of magic realism" (Neil Jordan, *Sorrento Terrace Interview*, 17 May 2002, Appendix: 06.3).

17   Zucker, ed., *Neil Jordan. Interviews*, 93, 71.

magic" to nature, and the Celtic imaginativeness and melancholy that he considers as Celtic characteristics are alike "a passionate, turbulent, indomitable reaction against the despotism of fact".[18]

Similarly, Ernest Renan gathers imagination, mystery, magic and Celticism when he writes that "the Celtic race has a love of Nature for herself, a vivid feeling for her magic, commingled with the melancholy a man knows when he is face to face with her, and thinks he hears her communing with him about his origin and his destiny".[19] Last, William Butler Yeats's work is rooted in a special political context and, at the same time, in fairy lore and legends, thus reviving a neglected cultural identity and affirming his unconditional love for his birthplace whose dignity he kept on defending. Yeats has a gift for using the real and the fantastic in just the right amounts. He shows that reality can be apprehended and understood only if it is enriched with less rational components. As a result, the real is an integral part of mystery and strangeness.

In the wake of his famous predecessor, Neil Jordan depicts Ireland as he perceives it, a strange "country formed from ghosts".[20] Consequently, it is hardly surprising that his artistic universe is haunted by all kinds of fantastic creatures. Spirits, angels, fairies, monsters, chimeras and vampires turn up in his prose because they no longer depend on the laws of time and space which rule physical bodies. They appear on the border between two worlds, dream and reality, and work their ways into the human conscience without being always admitted there. They are no or no more humans, only inhuman or superhuman beings. This state of affairs results from the appropriation of another different identity, from escape from our human condition and extra-human experience.

Their haunting is similar to the process of memory. It often goes with the return of the interdict, the resurgence of repression. The vagaries of their appearances and disappearances establish a connection between the

---

18   Matthew Arnold, *The Study of Celtic Literature* [1867] (London: Bibliolife, 2007), 29.

19   Ernest Renan, *The Poetry of the Celtic Races and Other Studies* [1854] (London: Walter Scott, 2014), 268-269.

20   "Ireland is a country formed from ghosts", according to Neil Jordan (Zucker, ed., *Neil Jordan: Interviews*, 98).

past and the present, life and death, presence and absence in the reflection of the lost thing. Those monstrous, ghostly, angelical characters are transgressors: they go from a state, a place or a time to another with impunity. They are on one side of the mirror, in a world different from the one of the other characters, which creates hesitation among the latter and plunge them – together with the readers – into uncertainty and confusion. They are anchored in an evanescent universe where characters are split or doubled, where they get out of the shade to come to light, although they are supposed to have remained hidden,[21] which provokes an uncanny feeling.

Transgression is the leading strand of Neil Jordan's work: as we have seen, his fiction denies any limits and constraints. On the one hand, the dividing line between the visible and invisible, between the real and the dream is porous; on the other, the crossing of boundaries – whether they are geographical, historical, cultural or sexual – is the main theme of Neil Jordan's creative output. Rules and laws are cheerfully infringed: the limits between exogamy and endogamy are ignored; the triangulation of desire leads to unions which are condemned by the moral code; religion could feel outraged. Neil Jordan's work is not blasphemous for all that: true, it highlights that the religious sphere is weakening, but it also shows a return to the power of the sacred, and a new relation of a literature replete with symbols. As it is depicted in the work, nature itself proves to be transgressive when the sea submerges the coastline: the last pages of *Shade* or *The Drowned Detective* relate the encroachments of the sea which herald a new era.

The idea of the border is particularly significant for an Irishman,[22] considering the natural delimitations which determine the surface area of the insular territory, but mostly the artificial division which splits it up. The establishment and maintenance of this absurd partition between two Irelands is an issue which bothers Neil Jordan, whose artistic output shows

---

21   "Everything is uncanny that ought to have remained hidden and secret, and yet comes to light" (Freud, *The Uncanny*, 222).

22   "The novelists of the 1980s and 1990s are having to engage with a proliferation of possibilities in which the idea of the border – defined geographically, sexually, or culturally [...] – is becoming increasingly important" (Gerry Smyth, *The Novel and the Nation: Studies in the New Irish Fiction* [London: Pluto Press, 1997], 146).

an interest in this crucial period of his country's history which is the Anglo-Irish War and the Irish Civil War. As a result, it is justified to wonder if the motif of transgression, which is so present throughout his work, does not come from a will to break all dividing lines, to transcend old disputes and go beyond the national debate. This motif can indeed be conceived as a desire to appropriate an area of liberty, to explore alternatives according to the wish of the philosopher Richard Kearney who imagines the notion of a mythical "fifth province",[23] that is an area of free expression opened by *Crane Bag,* the journal cofounded by himself and Mark Patrick Hederman in 1977. In a similar development, three years later, the *Field Day Theatre Company* created a cultural centre, the goal of which was to go beyond the idioms of political and religious sectarianism. The latter appropriated the same concept imagined as "a fifth province of mind" through which another way of looking at the nation could be devised. This other possible Ireland could express itself in different ways, particularly through fiction. Such a cultural debate, opened and shared when Neil Jordan was about to start his artistic career, most probably gave him food for thought and modelled his view of how his art might develop. From then on, it is hardly

23   "The journal the *Crane Bag* [...] in the early 1980s explored the possibility of pluralist politics in a new way. It sought to move beyond the predictable categories of national debate, sponsoring the notion of a mythical fifth province as a kind of free space in which new accommodations of the old quarrels could be imagined. Writers, artists, academics, intellectuals from the North and South, and from opposed political perspectives, twice a year were given the opportunity to consider, in themed issues, the questions the editors had posed in the journal's second issue in 1978: 'Is there an alternative way in which Irish people can develop a sense of identity? Can we go beyond the idioms of religious sectarianism, nationalist self-righteousness and bourgeois preoccupation with the 'greasy till'?'" (Terence Brown, *Ireland. A Social and Cultural History 1922-2002* [London: Harper Collins, 2004], 348). In 1980, the Field Day Theatre Company appropriated the concept of a fifth province "as a province of mind through which we hope to devise another way of looking at Ireland, or another possible Ireland ... one that must be articulated, spoken, written, painted, sung" (*Ibid.,* 349). This notion was taken up ten years later by President Mary Robinson who, at her inauguration, declared that she hoped her presidency could be a symbol of a "fifth province – a place within each one of us, that place that is open to the other – this reconciling and healing fifth province" (*Ibid.,* 361).

surprising that his texts free themselves from the constraints of representation and ignore any boundaries.

Transgression means the abolition of norms, together with the fulfilment of desires. It shows a predominance of fantasy, a withdrawal from the real to access the unreal. In Jordan's fiction, some characters seem to come from another world and provoke hesitation in the reader: are they "natural" or "supernatural"? Do they belong to the dream or are they part of reality? It brings us to the very heart of the fantastic:

> In a world which is indeed our world, the one we know, a world without devils, sylphides, or vampires, there occurs an event which cannot be explained by the laws of this same familiar world. The person who experiences the event must opt for one of two possible solutions: either he is the victim of an illusion of the senses, of a product of the imagination – and laws of the world then remain what they are; or else the event has indeed taken place, it is an integral part of reality – but then this reality is controlled by laws unknown to us ... The fantastic occupies the duration of this uncertainty. [...]. The fantastic is that hesitation experienced by a person who knows only the laws of nature, confronting an apparently supernatural event, [...] a phenomenon which contradicts the laws of nature.[24]

The fantastic is an experience of limits that it does not ignore, but maintains "in order to furnish the pretext for incessant transgressions".[25] If Neil Jordan's fiction crosses gates and thresholds so easily, it is not because it shocks or offends readers, but because it confuses the issues, ignores boundaries and creates a hybrid, ambivalent space from spheres which are generally distinct from each other. It goes beyond an area which is familiar to readers, moves further than what they are used to and oversteps a dividing line in order to venture into an uncanny universe.

Doesn't Neil Jordan ignore the marks of traditional realistic fiction when he debunks a famous historical politician? When his characters change into monsters, are reduced to a mere head cut off from the body which recounts the story or are kidnapped by a supernatural people and substituted for a double? When they reappear after their deaths suffused

---

24   Tzvetan Todorov, *The Fantastic: A Structural Approach to a Literary Genre*, trans. Richard Howard (London: Case Western Reserve University, 1973), 25.

25   *Ibid.*, 116.

with a mysterious aura or haunt the minds of the living as long as they are not granted the sleep of the dead?

Neil Jordan's literary work does not aim at arousing the reader's fear, but at initiating further thought to the deceptive nature of our perceptions. It invites us to distance ourselves from the world that surrounds us. It testifies that death can be overcome, that it is possible to revive the dead, that our daily lives are both ordinary and extraordinary since they are also made of irrational components. Neil Jordan's fiction invites readers to let themselves descend into hallucinatory territories, to give themselves up to the surprises of the subconscious and let the narrator be their guide and leader in accordance with the point of view of Freud who notes that a quality storyteller, like a magician, will always be able to take us by the hand to lead us to an enchanting world:

> The story-teller has this license among many others, that he can select his world of representation so that it either coincides with the realities we are familiar with or departs from them in what particulars he pleases. We accept his ruling in every case.[26]

Since the writer himself invites us to go with him to faraway places, let us follow him.

26   Freud, *The Uncanny*, 259.

PART I

Putting Realism to the Test

Night in Tunisia and Other Stories: A Mysterious Collection between Tradition and Innovation

Like many of his peers, Neil Jordan launched his literary career with a collection of short stories. *Night in Tunisia and Other Stories* was first published in 1976 by the Irish Writers' Cooperative, a collective founded a couple of years before, of which Jordan was a member.[1] *Night in Tunisia* is very much in the tradition of the twentieth-century Irish short story insofar as it does match the technical presuppositions of realism, such as organic development of character, historic plausibility, significant episodes or temporal framework. In this case, characters – whether they are historical figures from the real world[2] or fictitious individuals, couples or families – are in line with the tenets of realism. The same can be said for place names: they refer to stable semantic entities and produce an *effet de réel* – or reality effect – that underpins the verisimilitude of the narrative. The author thus preserves the illusion of reality. In his writings, visual images predominate. They lead the readers to visualize the scenes as if they unfold before their eyes through the medium of a camera.[3] This specificity heralds Neil Jordan's double artistic career. Although visually distinct, his characters are not for all that totally transparent for the readers from whom many details are concealed. They remain secretive and mysterious, which is a typical feature of Jordan's fictitious universe.

1   The others including Ronan Sheehan, Steve McDonagh, Desmond Hogan, Leland Bardwell, Lucille Redmond and Jimmy Brennan.

2   Elvis Presley, Charlie Parker or Eamon de Valera.

3   It is worth noting that Neil Jordan's film *The Miracle* (1991) is based on his short stories "Night in Tunisia" and "A Love". Indeed, the three works are set in a seaside resort during the summer holiday and are focused on the awakening of a teenager who loses his virginity with the woman who marries his father. This experience reactivates the Oedipal crisis, which is a recurrent theme in Jordan's films and books.

The publication of a first book is an initiation rite, and it is certainly significant that the word can precisely be found in the title of the first story, "Last Rites". It is however ironic to title one's very first text "*Last Rites*", when its publication is a baptism of fire which, in this case, introduces a newcomer in the Irish literary world. Irony is a major component here; it plays an essential part in the collection.

Neil Jordan says: "When I started writing I felt very pressured by the question: How do I cope with the notion of Irishness? [...] How to write stories [...] without being swamped in the language and mythology of Joyce?"[4] Surprisingly, as he emphasizes how difficult it is for young Irish writers to start a literary career without being influenced by overwhelming national father figures, Jordan gives his first text a title referring to the last rites which are precisely given to the priest in the first story of his famous predecessor's collection *Dubliners*.[5] And yet, unlike this text – "The Sisters" – in which a priest is actually anointed before dying, Jordan's story refers to the last rites in a very ironic way. True, the protagonist also dies, but his last actions are rather unorthodox: contrary to what its title suggests, the short story relates an Irish labourer's masturbation and suicide in the cubicle of a public shower in London. Right from the first story of the collection, Neil Jordan seems like an ironist who uses elements of surprise and paradox. He takes up words referring to tradition, but means something different.

"At a cultural level", Jordan goes on, "the only identity that I could forge was one that came from the worlds of television, popular music and cinema which I was experiencing daily".[6] That is why *Night in Tunisia* repeatedly refers to rock culture, but also jazz music.[7] Although it is not properly

---

4 Richard Kearney, ed., *Across the Frontiers – Ireland in the 1990s* (Dublin: Wolfhound Press, 1988), 196.

5 In Joyce's "The Sisters", the narrator and his aunt visit "the house of mourning" and pray near the priest's body. Eliza, Father Flynn's sister, tells them: "Father O'Rourke was in with him a Tuesday and anointed him and prepared him and all" (James Joyce, "The Sisters", *Dubliners* [1914], in *The Portable James Joyce* [Harmondsworth: Penguin, 1983], 25).

6 Kearney, *Across the Frontiers*, 197.

7 The collection notably mentions songs by Elvis Presley and films in which he played.

speaking "popular music", "A Night in Tunisia" is a musical composition written by Dizzy Gillespie and performed by himself and saxophonist Charlie Parker, whose name is mentioned in the eponymous story. Here again, such a title is out of step with what is expected: there is something exotic about a title such as *Night in Tunisia*, which contrasts with the place where the story is actually set – a seaside resort on the mouth of the river Boyne, north of Dublin. The promise of a faraway charming, attractive place fails to meet the reader's expectations. Here again, Neil Jordan makes good use of irony and instils a personal touch to his prose.

If a literary work reflects a type of reality, in this case, it shows the experience of a determined young man who, in the career which opens before him, intends to follow in his predecessors' footsteps, without being too much influenced by them. He does not want to get caught in some old ways which would not allow him to express freely what he means. This first book shows Jordan's intention of writing an original, personal work. This is why *Night in Tunisia* is both traditional and innovative.

***

About fifteen years before Neil Jordan's collection was published, literary critic Frank O'Connor wrote *The Lonely Voice*, an essay in which he considered that realistic short stories are characterized by "submerged population groups".[8] They depict the slices of life of isolated, marginal, subaltern characters who are not really involved in community life. These anti-heroes are real or potential victims, which is typical of the genre. The lonely protagonists of *Night in Tunisia*, whether they are teenagers or immigrants, wives or spinsters, perfectly illustrate this stereotyped characterization. They have no power, no authority. And yet they are not resignedly submissive; they do not bend beneath the yokes imposed by others. Their silence is not a sign of obedience, but of resistance and contention. Indeed, teenagers rebel against their fathers, wives defend themselves by their own device against their husbands' diktats; as for the immigrant builder's labourer, he chooses his own fate, as his radical decision at the end of the story shows. True, the protagonists of Neil Jordan's

8   Frank O'Connor, *The Lonely Voice* (London: Penguin, 1962), 16.

collection belong to minority population groups, but they are not "submerged": they are able to hold up their heads and face up to their difficulties. What Frank O'Connor could observe in the fiction of his time is not always characteristic of the literary output of the following generation to which Neil Jordan belongs.

A cubicle is the décor of the first story of *Night in Tunisia*. This location is a private, enclosed space where each bather conceals himself from other gazes. Each cubicle is thus a mystery. This noun comes from the Greek *mysterion*, meaning "secret rite" or "sacred secret". It refers to "what is inside the walls of the sanctuary".[9] As the title of the story suggests – "Last Rites" – there is something sacred and ritualistic about having a shower in a public building at the end of a working week. This activity implies a break with the profane everyday world, an isolation in an enclosed space and a symbolical death that the protagonist makes real. A cubicle is obviously much more mundane than a holy place. It parodically suggests an initiatory rite of passage, an introduction to mysterious, forbidden knowledge. As he is walking to the public baths, the young builder's labourer anticipates a "revelation", a "secret victory". He *knows* what is going to happen, as the recurrence of the verb stresses:

> *He knew* he anticipated something, approaching the baths. *He knew* that it wasn't quite pleasure. It was something more or less than pleasurable, a feeling of ravishing, private vindication, of exposure, of secret, solipsistic victory. Over what he never asked. But *he knew*. *He knew* as he approached the baths to wash off the dust of a week's labour, that this hour would be the week's high-point.[10]

This weekly ritual stimulates his imagination. As he is usually a silent, passive,[11] reserved man, racked by melancholy and boredom,[12] who does not let his emotions show,[13] he seems to take a great interest in being in

---

9   Pausanias, *Guide to Greece: Central Greece* [160-180 AD] I, 38 (London: Penguin, 1971), 7.

10   Neil Jordan, *Night in Tunisia* [1976], *A Neil Jordan Reader* (New York: Vintage International, 1993), 5-6. My emphasis.

11   His passivity is implied by many perception verbs, such as "see", "hear" or "listen" (11).

12   There are five occurrences of the word "boredom" on one page (*Ibid.*, 10).

13   "he was silent, his face was immobile" (Jordan, *Night in Tunisia*, 6).

the public baths on Friday nights. He considers this shower as "the week's high-point", which proves how empty his life is otherwise. In this cubicle indeed, he can give vent to his fantasies:

> He heard splashing water, hissing shower-jets, the smack of palms off wet thighs. Behind each door he knew was a naked man, held timeless and separate under an umbrella of darting water. The fact of the walls, of the similar but totally separate beings behind those walls never ceased to amaze him; quietly to excite him.[14]

His imagination wanders in space as he tries to break the barriers of this compartmentalized building and penetrate the mysteries of the other cubicles, but it also wanders in time:

> He walked slowly to the shower, pulled aside the plastic curtain and walked inside. The tiles had that dead wetness that he had once noticed in the beach-pebbles. He placed each foot squarely on them and saw a thin cake of soap lying in a puddle of grey water. Both were evidence of the bather here before him and he wondered

14   *Ibid.*, 7. The "umbrella of darting water" is reminiscent of Saint Sebastian's martyrdom. *Sebastianus* was an early saint who, according to traditional belief, was killed in Rome during the Diocletianic persecution of Christians (c. AD 288). He was initially tied to a post or tree and shot with arrows, though this did not kill him. According to a witness, "the archers shot at him till he was as full of arrows as an urchin is full of pricks". Shortly after his recovery, Sebastian went to Diocletian to warn him about his sins, and as a result was clubbed to death. Saint Sebastian is venerated in the Roman Catholic Church. In medieval times, he was regarded as a saint with a special ability to intercede to protect from plague, and devotion to him greatly increased when plague was active. In 1976, the British director Derek Jarman made a film, *Sebastiane*, which caused controversy in its treatment of the martyr as a "homosexual icon", and indeed, a few years later, with the AIDS epidemic, Sebastian was still venerated. In 1996, American author Richard A. Kaye wrote that "Contemporary gay men have seen in Sebastian at once a stunning advertisement for homosexual desire (indeed, a homoerotic ideal), and a prototypical portrait of tortured closet case" ("Losing His Religion: Saint Sebastian as Contemporary Gay Martyr" in Peter Horne and Reina Lewis, eds, *Outlooks: Lesbian and Gay Sexualities and Visual Cultures* [New York: Routledge], 105). Sebastian is an enduring homoerotic icon. A combination of his strong, shirtless physique, the symbolism of the arrows penetrating his body, and the countenance of rapturous pain have intrigued artists (gay or otherwise) for centuries. The protagonist of Jordan's story here can be perceived as Sebastian's spiritual heir.

> vaguely what he was like; whether he had a quick, rushed shower or a slow, careful
> one; whether he in turn had wondered about the bather before him. (*NT*, 9)

After the shower, he looks at himself in the mirror, a narcissistic experience which reflects a fellow creature's image, as if another man was there with him:

> He wondered at the fact that there were sixteen other cubicles around him, identical
> to this one, which he couldn't see. A man in each, washed by the same water, all in
> various stages of cleanliness. And he wondered did the form in the next cubicle think
> of him, his neighbour, as he did. Did he reciprocate his wondering. He thought it
> somehow appropriate that there should be men naked, washing themselves in ad-
> jacent cubicles. (*NT*, 12)

Such visual thoughts represent the fulfilment of desire. He seems to long for somebody's presence and begins to masturbate: "The thought came to him that somebody could be watching him. But no, he thought then, almost disappointed, who could, working at himself harder" (*NT*, 13). Once he has ejaculated, he makes another liquid spurt out of his body by slashing his wrists. The life instinct of the sex drive is immediately followed by the death instinct of the suicidal impulse. Eros is replaced by Thanatos. The labourer's body is found on the tiled floor, behind the locked door of his cubicle.

The motif of the door has the symbolical value of the threshold between life and death. A bather, eager to have a shower, knocks at the door: "Hey, you rass, not finished yet? [...] Well move that corpse, rassman. Move!" (*NT*, 13) The remark is ironic, the word *corpse*, referring to a dead body, being particularly appropriate in this case: the labourer proves to be unable to "move that corpse".

The narrative is careful not to reveal the reasons why the protagonist makes such a drastic decision. It does not explain why the man slashes his wrists in the cubicle. The reader can however suggest a possibility from textual clues provided by the above-mentioned quotations. These extracts allow us to understand that the character's malaise is not due to his migration or homesickness, to his hard work or precarious living conditions. It rather seems difficult for him to have an ordinary social life[15] and, above all,

15   The reader does not know anything about the protagonist's living conditions: does

to come to terms with his sexual orientation, which is still considered as un-conventional in the 1970s when the book was published.[16] The protagonist obviously feels drawn towards males, but this attraction remains a fantasy. He is confronted with partitions which prevent him from blossoming. On top of the walls of indifference characteristic of the impersonal metrop-olis, there are the barriers of a society which condemns and represses any behaviour considered as deviant. Even in this relaxing hour – "the week's high-point" – the protagonist is separated from his peers by doors and partitions which isolate each man in his own cubicle. These demarcations seem impassable to him, each man being "a foreign country to the other" (*NT*, 17). They eventually cost him his life.

Each character is an unfathomable mystery for others, including for their spouses. Indeed, many husbands and wives come up against a wall of incomprehension with their own partners. In the short story titled "Outpatient", the woman is unwell: she gets thinner and thinner. She has just gone on a pilgrimage to Saint Brigid's Well where cripples who have been cured leave their crutches. Once home, she wonders about the amazing miraculous nature of these events: are these mysterious recoveries intended for initiates? Like the disabled of the gospels, are these people cured by Jesus? Is it a sign of God? She asks these questions to her husband, but gets no answer: the latter, preoccupied with much more material considerations, informs her that they are to look over a house for sale on the following day. She is dumbfounded:

> I've just come back from a place where people walk three miles to see the miraculous crutches and the rotting mass-cards and he –. Her thoughts stopped here, blocked by something deadening, momentous, stolid. (*NT*, 61)

She gives up trying to say what is on her mind, because it seems unspeak-able to her. She prefers not to reveal the end of her sentence. The process is

---

he live on his own or in a community? Is he in touch with other workers? Does he go to the pub with other men?

16   The hypothesis of the labourer's homoerotic sensual and sexual orientation is confirmed by the story's presence in Mark Henry's anthology of gay fiction, *Chasing Danny Boy: Powerful Stories of Celtic Eros* (San Francisco: Palm Drive Publishing, 1999).

called reticence. The sentence then suggests more than it says. It starts with a few words which are interrupted by a break, like a moment's hesitation, then the second part of it is abruptly ellipted. The predicate is hushed, repressed, held back and replaced by a dot. Reticence is, as Jankélévitch puts it, halfway between silence and allusion. It is both a syntactic break and semantic failure.[17] In this instance, the female protagonist's reticence reveals her hard feelings and strong aversion to her husband. She is aware of the gap between them: "there's a space between you and me" (*NT*, 61), she manages to say when she is invited to comply with her conjugal duties: "She determined to disappoint him and lay flat and rigid. She knew he was disappointed but felt the dome of a great heavy bell around her" (*NT*, 61). The bell is an ambivalent metaphor: on the one hand, it is a protective bubble which symbolizes woman's spirituality and obedience to the Word of God; on the other, it is also a sexual symbol with its "brass tongue falling with a threat", a detail mentioned further down in the text and confirmed by the man's initiative. In his presence, his wife feels like a piece of meat. According to her, she is nothing more in her husband's eyes. This is why, later in the night, her dream is reminiscent of some of Francis Bacon's paintings: the couple makes love under the meat carcasses of a butcher's stall. The husband's attraction to the carnal and his wife's to the spiritual reinforces the wall of incomprehension and incommunicability between them, as the recurrence of the verb revealing unexpressed emotions emphasizes: "Somewhere inside him he *felt* obscurely angry at her [...]. He *felt* cheated. He also *felt* virtuous, accepting as he was her flawed self, and only a little ashamed".[18] On the following day, in the house for sale, she withdraws into total silence:

17   « A mi-chemin entre le silence et l'allusion se situe la *réticence*, qui est une active collaboration du silence et de la parole, une parole refoulée ou ravalée [...]. On se tait quand on pourrait parler. La réticence, c'est le discours expirant, le passage de l'explicite au tacite [...]. [Cette] « figure de silence » est une interruption expressive, une espèce de valeur sonore » (Vladimir Jankélévitch, *L'Ironie* [Paris : Flammarion, 1964], 89).

18   Jordan, *Night in Tunisia*, 59. My emphasis.

> He drove her to the house, positively angry now at her silences [...]. They drove up
> to it and parked on the opposite side. Its façade, she saw, was a large rectangle, half
> red-brick, half pebble dash. What do you think, he asked. She nodded her head.
> You'll get nothing better under eight thou, he said. She didn't answer. She suddenly
> hated him for that abbreviated word [...].
>
> What do you think, he asked. She had her back turned to him and she felt the great
> bell descend on her, its brass tongue falling with a threat she only dreamed of. She
> turned to his voice, which was tiny and distant, and saw his horror of silence in his
> set face [...]. She heard him say: we'll look at the garden. [...] She walked towards
> him down the calloused garden wanting to tell him that this house had nothing to
> do with miracles and trumpets, knowing she would not. (*NT*, 62-63)

Silence is used as a means of defence, a weapon and a shield: their marriage turns into a single combat. By chewing things over in her corner, the woman thinks she can overcome her "opponent". Her behaviour is a sign of tension and protest. It is both a strategic withdrawal and a way out. When silence persists, as is the case here, the relation deteriorates. The husband is furious that his wife so loftily ignores him. His exclusion is mirrored by the narrative process of dramatic irony. Indeed, the husband has no access to his wife's thoughts since they are not expressed, whereas the reader knows them. This confidentiality arouses frustration and suppressed violence, and reveals the mystery that everyone can be for others.

As in most stories of the collection, the characters of "Tree" are nameless. Anonymity may be a narrative device to attract the reader's attention to nothing else but the strained relationship within the couple. Here again, the woman's mysticism conflicts with the man's rationalism. As she is driving the car, the wife suddenly brakes because she spots a flowering whitethorn tree by the roadside. "That's impossible", her husband says, furious that his head struck the windscreen, "it's the end of August" (*NT*, 65). And yet, for his wife who has faith, everything is possible. She starts up again and silently retreats into her thoughts.[19] Later, they stop at a pub. He orders a tonic for her, whereas she would have preferred a whisky. She talks with the barmaid and tells her that she drives the car because of her husband's bad leg:

19   "She thought of ..." is repeated four times in page 65.

> "There are two things he can't do. Get out of a car, and drive a car. But otherwise everything's fine. Isn't that right, John?"
>
> He had already gone towards the door. She fumbled in her pocket to find fifty pence. She couldn't and so she left a pound. He was standing by the door of the car.
>
> "Why did you have to jabber on like that?"
>
> "Why did you order me a tonic?"
>
> "You're impossible".
>
> "Nothing's impossible". (*NT*, 67)

The man cries, humiliated by his wife. And yet he still loves her and tells her. On their way back, she parks the car near the tree, gets out and says ambiguous words: "I'm leaving" (*NT*, 68). He tries to hold her back.

> "I don't –" she began, but her words were drowned by the sudden blast of the horn. His hand was on it [...]. She could hear the awful blare in her ears and could see his lips moving, saying something. (*NT*, 68)

Obviously, they do not get along any more. She walks to the tree to note that there are no flowers, but only scores of tiny rags and holy pictures, tied to the branches. They express the believers' hopes, requests and gratitude. As the horn goes on wailing, the woman tears a picture off and reads: "To Brigid for favours granted, August 1949" (*NT*, 69). The story, which is set in August, coincides with the anniversary of an encounter, a union, maybe theirs, and is focused on bitter disillusions towards their relationship: like the picture in her fingers, their marriage is crumbling and falling apart.

One of the few characters in the collection who bears a name is also humiliated on an anniversary. The eponymous protagonist of "Mr Solomon Wept" gets drunk to alleviate his despair and loneliness. His wife left him just one year before, during the annual horse-race on Laytown beach: "He remembered her as if she had died [...] He began to think of her as if she had died" (*NT*, 29). The few words he utters are with the barman: to keep up appearances and mask his mortification, Mr Solomon claims he has been a widower since the previous race day. He drinks all day long and broods over his grief, separated from other people by the pub window. Here again, the lack of communication reinforces the invasion of thoughts. Mr Solomon cannot disregard his own feelings and resentments:

> The street was packed with people. Mr Solomon began to *feel* for the first time a hatred towards them, en masse. He *felt* a malignant sameness in them. He *felt* they laughed, in their summer clothes. He *felt* they didn't know, in their summer clothes. He *felt* like a cog in the mechanism of holidays, of holiday towns, he *felt* somehow slave to their bright clothes and suntans. [...] He *felt* his grief burning inside now.[20]

Nothing is expressed. The protagonist is worn down, eaten away by his sorrow. Drunk by the middle of the afternoon, he cuts himself off from the crowd of his peers that he perceives "like a wall against him" (*NT*, 32). He proves to be filthy and gets thrown out like a waste, apart from the community. At the end of the story, he is not only deprived of company, but also excluded from society:

> He felt himself lifted then, carried a small distance off and thrown in the sand. He lifted his face and wept in the sand and saw the horses churning the sea-spray into a wide area down by the edge. He heard a loud cheer, somewhere behind him.[21]

The jubilant crowd contrasts with the man's sadness. They cry out in joy, while he bursts into tears. They jump and leap in a state of great excitement, whereas he is lying on the ground, literally humiliated and reduced to nothing. Considering the protagonist's name, the end of the story is once more particularly ironical: unlike his namesake, the biblical sensual king always surrounded with many wives and lovers,[22] who remained famous for the greatness of his aura and kingdom, Mr Solomon,

---

20　*Ibid.*, 30-31. My emphasis.

21　*Ibid.*, 32. 'Solomon' is not an Irish name, but refers to a Jewish identity. As a result, the protagonist's exclusion can be interpreted as the reaction of a xenophobic, anti-Semitic community who systematically rejects the Other, whoever he is, as the first story "Last Rites" also shows.

22　"Solomon had seven hundred wives, who were princesses, and three hundred concubines" (1 Kings 11:3).

abandoned by his wife, rejected by the whole community, is reduced to biting the dust like a common beggar, in the most absolute isolation.

Emptiness also characterizes the life of a middle-aged Catholic house-wife who fades away because of her daily routine, because of "the vacuity that suburban dwelling imposes, the same vacuity that most likely inhabited the house next door" (*NT*, 52). In a women's magazine, the protagonist of "Skin" reads that some women in Sweden offer themselves to strangers in orgies in the middle of the day so as to break the monotony of their humdrum lives. First disgusted by such practices that she immediately considers nothing less than the sin of fornication, she gradually fantasizes about a possible love affair and, in a fit of despair, gets into her car and drives "mechanically" to the seaside. There, she walks in the ice-cold sea water, notices that a man is watching her from the strand, tucks up her skirt, with the currents running about her thighs, "rivers of puffy white foam surrounding her like a bridal wreath" (*NT*, 56). Here again, Neil Jordan proves to be a master of irony.

These adult protagonists are steadily characterized by their apathy, mel-ancholy and deep malaise. They suffer from boredom and isolation. They are lonely hearts in search of sensual and sexual relationships. They silently brood over their frustration and the absurdity of their lives. They are iso-lated whatever their lifestyles, since couples are dislocated or dislocating. They are deeply affected by what they experience but never express their feelings. Their emotions remain secret, impervious to the other characters. Nevertheless, parts of the mystery are disclosed to the reader by the reve-lation of private details of their lives. The narrator thus establishes a close connection with the narratee. The latter has the feeling of being initiated to the mysteries of the depths of the characters' existence. Hidden, secret details are shared by the narrator, narratee and protagonist and remain unknown to the other characters. By dramatic irony, reinforced by the narrator's presence inside the narrative, whether the story is recounted in the first or third person, a close link is established between them.

The adolescent characters of the collection are not any happier. They turn out to be also obsessed with sensual and sexual experiences. In "Seduction", two boys spend their summer holiday in the guest house of a seaside resort. They fantasize about the chip-shop woman's fat body: "There was something mysterious, hard and tired about her, some secret behind those layers of make-up which those older boys shared" (*NT*, 16). For them, as Freud put it, woman is an unknown territory to be discovered.[23] This is why they station themselves on the beach at nightfall in order to see one of them strip off and go swimming. Jamie claims he has seen a woman, but the narrator knows he is a liar. Eventually, Jamie has to admit he is only deluding himself. He mourns for his lost innocence and falls asleep, snuggled up in his friend's arms. The narrator tells him later that a woman bathed in the nude while he was asleep. Jamie makes a fool of him; they laugh at themselves who both have similar dreams which incite them to make up the same stories. They have a swim together and embrace in the water "the way lovers do it": "I felt his mouth on my neck but I didn't struggle" (*NT*, 21). Ironically, the "seduction" put forward in the title does not so much refer to the influence exerted by women over male teenagers, as to the boys' attraction for each other.

There is also an element of flirtation between boys and women in "Night in Tunisia". The teenage protagonist and his peers are lying face down, in order to hide their erections: "They lay on the raft, watched women on the strand, their eyes stared so hard that the many shapes on the beach became one, indivisible" (*NT*, 37). The figures they spy on are reduced to one single entity which remains a mystery to a male teenager: woman. The protagonist is however particularly interested in one of them, Rita, who is 3 years older than he is. She lives in a small chalet with her alcoholic father. Marks on her wrists suggest that she has been assaulted. Among the teenage Peeping Toms, rumour has it that she is a prostitute: "They passed her once, on the same side, like an exotic and dishevelled bird, her long yellow cardigan coming down to her knees, covering her dress, if she wore any" (*NT*, 34). The protagonist's habit of going out at night to watch that

---

23   In 1926, in *The Question of Lay Analysis*, Sigmund Freud compares the sexual life of adult women to a "dark continent": "We know less about the sexual life of little girls than of boys. But we need not feel ashamed of this distinction; after all, the sexual life of adult females is a dark continent for psychology" (New York: W. W. Norton, 1969, 36). Freud borrows this phrase from J. R. Stanley (1841-1904) who was famous for his exploration of Central Africa and its dark hostile forests. Freud also considered himself as an explorer of female sexuality.

"exotic bird" justifies the title of the story which, as said above, is misleading, as the reading of the text confirms. Besides, it parodically distorts the title of the famous jazz composition.

This piece is precisely what the protagonist listens to with delight on the radio. He tries to play it on the piano in Rita's presence. His father, a saxophonist, irritated by his son's lack of practice, offers to pay somebody to teach him lessons. The boy agrees. He absorbs Parker's music, plays day and night, acquires experience and forgets his pals on the beach: "He imagined childhood falling from him, coming off his palms like scales from a fish" (*NT*, 47). His interpretation of "Night in Tunisia" appeals to his father who notes that his son has made great progress. As the development of the story could give the reader the feeling that the discovery of the artistic world favoured the boy's maturity – the jazz standard being a real revelation to him – the end of the narrative is ironical: at a tennis match during which Rita watches the players, the young man hears that she has been saved from drowning after two suicide attempts. The mental image of the mouth-to-mouth resuscitation given by the rescuer to the girl, together with the forward and backward motion of the tennis ball on the court lead the young man, at the end of the game, to make overtures to Rita. As he has money now, he can overcome his shyness and make the girl his "instrument", like the man who gave her the kiss of life: "he put his lips to her lips and blew".[24] Ironically, the protagonist agreed to be trained and paid by his father not to improve his musical skills, but first and foremost, to enjoy a girl of easy virtue's favours. He does not prove to be a born artist, but a venal and lustful man.

Sexual initiation is also a central motif in "Sand". There are three teenagers in this story: a boy, his sister and a tinker. The latter is totally naked when he meets the two others. He blames the boy for riding his own donkey and asks him to let go of it. Then, he changes his mind and suggests he gives the boy half an hour with the donkey for half an hour with his sister. Without asking the opinion of the girl who has gone away,

---

24   *Ibid.*, 49. Val Nolan highlights the fact that jazz is "a non-native musical form evoking sexual and imaginative freedom" (Nolan, *Neil Jordan: Works for the Page*), 29.

feeling uncomfortable in front of a naked boy, the careless brother accepts the deal, finding it to his own advantage. But the ride on the donkey stops short, interrupted by the girl's screams. The boy hurriedly dismounts, rushes to help his sister and settle his score with the assailant. The beginning of the story suggests that the girl feels superior to her brother to whom she talks with words "picked up from grown-ups" (*NT*, 24), but a reversal takes place at the end, since the boy who protected her does not seem to be under her influence any longer:

She was crying, great breathful sobs.

"You won't –" he asked

"I will", she said. "I'll tell it all –"

"Nothing happened, did it". (*NT*, 26)

He does speak very firmly like an adult now. When he fights hand-to-hand with the naked boy, he can feel the hardness of the tinker's penis in his groin, which recalls the donkey's impressive erection he witnessed just before. These initiatory experiences are associated with the lost paradise of ingenuous childhood. Initiation implies an acquisition of knowledge. The naïve boy first accepts the tinker's suggestion, because he sees no harm in the deal, but his sister's tears and screams, which express her shame and anger, open his eyes and brutally introduce him to the *res naturae*. He realizes then that nakedness and sexuality are connected, just like physical promiscuity and potential risks. The girl is humiliated by a concupiscent boy, but she is not dishonoured for all that. She has no reason to make a drama out of it. This is why she is rebuffed by her brother who incites her to regain her self-control and carry on, regardless of the incident.

In "A Love", the last story of the collection, the young narrator – significantly called Neil – happens to come across the woman who introduced him to the joys of sex. She is still the owner of a boarding house where he used to live with his father. Now, she has cancer. They meet again by chance in a Dublin café on the day of President de Valera's funeral, a few months

before *Night in Tunisia* was published.[25] The woman is old enough to be
Neil's mother, but she was his lover. Having an affair with her was a way for
him to assert himself in the presence of his father and supplant him. Indeed,
the man – a widower – was not impervious to their landlady's charm and
regularly invited her for dinner or to dance under his jealous son's watchful
eye. Neil, a motherless boy, suffered from exclusion and loneliness, like most
characters of the collection who are somehow orphans. The desire he felt
as a teenager for that woman was superimposed to the desire to find his
mother again. In two particularly long sentences, the narrative mentions
a vast number of images and memories which assail the young man. He
shares them with the one with whom he lost his virginity and innocence:

> I remembered the nights lying in your old creaking bed that looked out on the sea,
> our movements like a great secret between us, silent, shocking movements, our si-
> lence a guard against my father who had the room down below, our lovemaking a
> quiet desecration of the holiday town, of the church at the top of the hill, of the
> couples you fed so properly at mealtimes, of my embarrassed adolescence, the guilt
> you tried to banish in me, the country, the place, the thing you tried to hit at through
> me you taught me to hit through you. And all the time for me there was my father
> lying underneath, cold most likely, and awake and I wanted him to hear the beast I
> was creating with you, I wanted him to hear it scratching, creaking through to him
> from above, for your body was like the woman he must have loved to have me, I
> had seen her in those brown faded photographs with a floppy hat and a cane, in a
> garden, like you but fatter, with a lot of clothes that came off, the coloured dresses
> and blouses first, then the white underclothes, dampened under the armpits, be-
> tween the legs. (*NT*, 73)

Sexual experience with a middle-aged woman reactivates the teenager's
Oedipus conflict, leads him to visualize the primal scene and to fire several gunshots at the door of the bathroom where his father is locked
one night when, drunk, his hatred for him is at its peak. Years later, Neil
and his first love, happy with this unexpected reunion, decide to flee the
crowd gathered for the statesman's funeral and go to the west coast, to
Lisdoonvarna, where their affair starts again.

25   President de Valera's funeral was held in Dublin on 2 September 1975.

Characters do not go a long way to look for history, but history comes to them: De Valera's funeral is held in Dublin, where the two lovers meet. And here they go as far as possible, up to the ocean: they turn their backs on the historic event in order to have a moment's peace. Their attitude clearly challenges the glorification of the national past and the feelings of patriotism and gratitude towards a symbolical figure of traditional values. Neil Jordan's short stories depict new relationships between the citizen and the nation, between man and the world and this is probably a generation specificity.

Most characters of *Night in Tunisia* free themselves not only from the fetters of nationalist tradition, but also from the teaching of the Catholic Church. The labourer of "Last Rites" does not feel guilty about acting as he does: he is not at all preoccupied with sin or damnation. The practice of masturbation and the radical decision of putting an end to his life do not seem to torment him. He just feels he is confronted with absurd emptiness and considers that there is nothing more significant than the old red-bricked walls of the Victorian Baths. This is why he lets himself pass away "to whatever vacuum lay beyond" (*NT*, 5), with a cut-throat razor in his hand. The narrative is the reflection of the protagonist's frame of mind and never alludes to any element of Judeo-Christian doctrine that the Irish short story writers of the preceding generations would not have avoided.

Jordan's collection is the mirror of a new Ireland. It reflects the changing values of a young generation. When it was published in the mid-seventies, there were new developments in the country. The traditional image of a farming, Gaelic, Catholic, ultra-nationalist society, focused on the bitter memories of misery and oppression, gave way to a more open, confident, forward-looking country, industrialized, urbanized and determined to claim the whole national heritage as its own. True, the rates of inflation, unemployment and debt were still high, but the economic expansion, together with the subsidies of the EEC increased the population's standard of living and fuelled the requirements of young Irish people who were eager to turn the page of the past.

This intention of shaking up traditions is mirrored in Neil Jordan's fiction not only through its themes or its characters' behaviour, but also its very writing. This collection of short stories partakes of realism insofar as it reflects the global view of many of Jordan's contemporaries, in particular the rejection of traditional values. The author, however, also undermines some conventions peculiar to the realistic archetype. He adopts a partial and parsimonious kind of speech which deliberately creates a space of informative vacuum, which goes against realistic discourse. Indeed, the characters' anonymity is a way to distinguish itself from realism and proves that the collection does not comply with the traditional conventions of the genre.

Realist novelists pay particular attention to exact documentation. An instance is provided in the first name and surname fictional characters are given. The titles of realist novels often mention them, as *Robinson Crusoe*, *Silas Marner* or *Eugénie Grandet* show. Realism requires a fictional character to bear a name. And yet, here, out of the twenty-one protagonists of the stories, only five are given a name. Besides, they are incompletely identified: they are given either a surname (Mr Solomon) or a first name (Rita, Jean, Jamie, Neil). Two others are referred to by the relationship which unites them (father, sister); two are just mentioned by a generic term – "the man" or "the child"; one of them is identified by his trade (a young builder's labourer), another by the community he belongs to (a tinker). On the other hand, ten protagonists, that is almost 50 per cent of the characters, are referred to by a mere personal pronoun, reduced to some anonymous, translucent "I", "he" or "she". This minimalist reference makes them unidentified characters who move in a world where nobody seems to show the slightest interest in them.

Similarly, works of realism give an acute, detailed description of their characters. This denotes fidelity to the truth in depicting the inner workings of the mind, the analysis of thought and feeling, the presentation of the nature of personality and physical features of characters. For example, the reader of John McGahern's short story "Like All Other Men" – which is relatively contemporary of Neil Jordan's collection – is informed of the characters' first names and surnames. Their introduction is directly followed by a paragraph which describes their physical appearance, the colour of their eyes, their clothes, but also their psychological character, social position, geographical roots, etc.[26] It is noteworthy that John McGahern

---

26   The protagonists of John McGahern's short story are called Michael Duggan and
     Susan Spillane. The latter in particular is minutely described: "She wasn't tall or

belongs to a generation of writers who do not distinguish themselves from the conventions of traditional realism. This is not the case of the following generation of whom Neil Jordan is a member. The latter is no portrait painter: the few physiological details he gives about his characters concern a "frail body", "thin arms" or "hair that curled and dripped with oil" (*NT*, 8, 13, 15). Facial appearances are never really described. Interestingly, the protagonists of *Night in Tunisia* seem to have no faces, but only genitals: the narrative seldom deals with physiognomy, but it is focused on the bottom part of human bodies. Indeed, the male protagonists refer to their "limp member", "occasional erections hidden", "violent motions of [their] pricks" (*NT*, 13, 35, 37); they specify that "my cock sprang to attention in my tight trousers", that "there was something hot, hard against his stomach" (*NT*, 84, 25). Similarly, the only physiological detail we are given about the tinker is his pubic "patch of hair" (*NT*, 23), an implicit indication of the threat he represents for the girl. These male characters produce more flows of sperm than words. Therefore, these protagonists are reduced to their genitals by the narrative and otherwise seem to be deprived of everything since they have no names, no faces, no plans or passions.

If the young male is so much focused on his penis, it may be to deny the castration threat and assert his manliness. He seizes a symbol of power and authority to take his father's place and confront him without being afraid of rebelling against him and assuming his own sex. From then on, the son acquires his father's prerogatives and thus moves towards his personal, social and sexual maturity. Symbolically, Neil Jordan does the same with his literary predecessors: he has to "kill his father" in order to identify with his self. This symbolical parricide is an accreditation to reach power.

---

beautiful [...] She seemed quietly indifferent [...] She flashed no smile [...] When he did cross to ask her to dance, she followed him with the same unconcern on to the floor as she had showed just standing there. She danced beautifully, with a strong, easy freedom. She was a nurse in the Blanchardstown Chest Hospital. She came from Kerry [...] She had close curly black hair, an intelligent face, and there was something strange about her eyes [...] 'One eye is brown, the other grey'" (John McGahern, "Like All Other Men", *High Ground* [London: Faber & Faber, 1985], 59-60).

It is a test of maturity which implies counting on himself and working his own way, instead of following the one shown by others.

Obviously, Neil Jordan cares about writing a personal, original literary work. His fiction is based on the conventions of realism, but all the better so to undermine them.[27] It takes up elements of the past to make something new. Jordan does not want it to repeat the traditional forms of realism, which would be pointless to him. He aims at going further; his interest is elsewhere. Instead of dedicating himself to the faithful portrayal of life, he wants to create his own form. "A mere face-painter copies what he sees, and minutely traces every feature and odd mark. It is otherwise with men of invention and design",[28] notes Shaftesbury at the beginning of the eighteenth century. Obviously, Neil Jordan is a man of this calibre.

When his film *Byzantium* came out in 2011, Jordan declared that his contemporaries long for a life which is different from the one they have in the real world: "People basically hate reality and want something else".[29] Jordan shares this dissatisfaction with the real, and thus implicitly with realism. How can he blossom in an artistic movement which pretends to be a copy of nature and concentrates attention on the lot of the common man? Neil Jordan does not consider that artists should concern themselves with everyday events. It is of no relevance for him. He feels ill at ease with this traditional approach that he perceives as a dead end. This is why he strives to free himself from any oppressive form of imitation. It is significant that his stories insist so much on the absurd monotony of the daily routine, the disappointing, suffocating nature of everyday life, as if the

27   This is the sign that Neil Jordan's fiction is postmodern: "for postmodern fiction always works within conventions, in order to subvert them" (Linda Hutcheon, *A Poetics of Postmodernism. History, Theory, Fiction* [New York & London: Routledge], 1988, 5).

28   Anthony Ashley Cooper – Earl of Shaftesbury, *Essay on the Freedom of Wit and Humour* [1709] (Oxford: Palala Press Blackwell, 2015), 147.

29   "Why are people so interested in vampires in 2011?
      It's because it's that whole yearning for some kind of life other than the world we live in [...]. If the audience has the appetite to see a movie about the minotaur or Pan or the Irish fairy division or something like that, you know, it's all the same need, the same kind of dissatisfaction with the real world. People basically hate reality and want something else" ("Interviews with Neil Jordan" – *Byzantium* DVD).

disillusion and frustration of his characters expressed what he feels about the faithful recording of reality, as if their dissatisfaction was fundamentally the reflection of his own.

The way he turns his back on realistic conventions heralds a still greater liberation: in his later work, his characters even free themselves from their human nature. Progressively, Neil Jordan gives free rein to his fantasies to open the floodgates of his dreamy imaginative world and produce a fantastic, hallucinatory effect, thus giving another dimension to his output and accentuating its mysterious component.

CHAPTER 2

"There's a kind of truth in fiction, isn't there?" Family Memory and National History: *The Past* and *Michael Collins*

At the end of the twentieth century, a great number of literary critics acknowledged that a characteristic of much cultural production in Ireland was a curious obsession with the past. True, the encroaching millennium encouraged retrospection, but there was something excessive and neurotic about it. As Augustine Martin puts it: "Irish writing has been almost morbidly fixated with the past".[1] This "anomaly" is strong evidence that Irish society was still struggling to face its past, and that it needed to rethink what happened to reach a deeper understanding of its national identity. As Terry Eagleton remarks: "It is not a question of debating whether 'literature' should be related to 'history' or not: it is a question of different readings of history itself".[2] This preoccupation with the past and its contested meanings was accompanied by a vigorous debate about the practice of history itself as an academic discipline with national implications.

This cultural controversy was made of revisionist, neo-nationalistic and postcolonial versions. Some favoured a revision of history. For example, Roy Foster or Edna Longley[3] were outspoken promulgators of revisionism in Ireland; on the other hand, academics such as Seamus Deane or Declan Kiberd published major works of cultural nationalism and postcolonial criticism.[4]

---

1   Augustine Martin, *Bearing Witness. Essays on Anglo-Irish Literature* (Dublin: UCD Press, 1996), 95.

2   Terry Eagleton, *Literary Theory. An Introduction* (Oxford: Blackwell, 1983), 209.

3   Edna Longley, *The Living Stream. Literature and Revisionism in Ireland* (Newcastle: Bloodaxe Books, 1994).

4   Major works of postcolonial criticism, such as *Inventing Ireland* by Declan Kiberd, *Rethinking Irish History* by Patrick O'Mahony and Gerard Delanty or *Hidden*

In the minds of the former, it was time for Irish literary criticism to adopt the "revisionist" approach that characterizes the writing of Irish history, to denounce the spectrum of radical nationalism that goes with violent Catholicism and challenge some historic foundations, such as the absolutely negative influence of Britain's presence in Ireland or its responsibility for the Great Famine trauma. The past, as it had been envisaged to that point, had to be rejected, adapted, revised and transformed.

This approach derives from the rhetoric of colonialism and imperialism, according to the anti-revisionists for whom a moderate nationalist discourse is legitimate. If nationalist voices are marginalized, Ireland is condemned to amnesia. And the nation must not forget that its history is painful mainly because of the colonial condition the Irish people have endured for centuries. Although it is England's neighbouring island, and a nation of Europe with a White population, Ireland is a former colony, "a white colony", as Edward Said puts it.[5] And there are some who may consider that, unlike many postcolonial territories, independence has not been totally acquired yet, since British troops are still present in Northern Ireland. No one can deny that the Province, where the conflict was focused remains a potential trouble area. It is, however, the entire island, including the Republic, and more generally the British Isles as a whole, which is concerned by this issue. Such is the opinion of Field Day, the theatre company and cultural association founded in 1980, whose members agree that art has a crucial role to play in the resolution of what has come to be known as "the Troubles". Field Day played a major and often controversial part in the critical debates of the period over the redefinition of Ireland's cultural identity. According to its members, it was a necessary step because Irish identity had for so long been obscured and concealed by colonial policies. Field Day members consider that violence in Ulster is a persistent effect of colonial domination. Seamus Deane, one of the board's figureheads, states: "Field Day's analysis of the Irish situation derives from the conviction that it is,

---

Ireland. Reassessment of a Concept by Louis Cullen often use a recurrent prefix which highlights a re-reading of history.

5　　Edward W. Said, *Culture and Imperialism* (London: Chatto & Windus, 1993), xvi.

above all, a colonial crisis".[6] Maybe this is the reason why colonial thought and discourse, which are so present in the texts published in decolonized nations, are all the more so in the territories which are not totally liberated. This experience gives rise to a certain number of questions about national specificity and makes the search for identity more vivid:

> Because it is a systematized negation of the other, a frenzied determination to deny the other any attribute of humanity, colonialism forces the colonized to constantly ask the question: "Who am I in reality?"[7]

This question is the one the narrator asks himself in the novel eloquently entitled *The Past*. His anonymity, respected from the beginning to the end of the narrative, may be justified by the fact that his questioning is shared by many young Irish citizens who feel the need to be tied up to their origins, their present being obviously the result of their past. His individual quest mirrors the collective reflection of his contemporaries who, in the 1980s, revised their approach of history. Memory is at the heart of the novel, whether it is individual or collective memory, whether it deals with family or the nation, and its very nature is questioned by the text itself.

In 1980, when he published *The Past,* his first novel, Neil Jordan was a 30-year-old man. That very year, Field Day was created. Doubtless, the writer was conditioned by the society in which he lived and the issues that emerged then, particularly the contrary debates about the role of memory, the diverging interpretations of the big events of national history or the controversies over the way history should be taught at school. Such a context ultimately influenced the writer's vision of the period he chose to describe in his novel, that is the 1910s, 1920s and 1930s.

***

The narrator, who tells the story in the first person, explores the past like a detective. He tries to retrace the lives of his parents and grandparents to

---

6   Terry Eagleton, Fredric Jameson and Edward W. Said, *Nationalism, Colonialism and Literature* (Minnesota: University of Minnesota Press, 1990, introduction by Seamus Deane), 6.

7   Frantz Fanon, *The Wretched of the Earth* [1966] (New York: Grove Press, 2007), 182.

find out what lay behind the great mystery which shrouded their past. He does his best to establish the truth of his parentage and identity.

His narrative is a work of detection across the breadth of time. It is characterized by chronological progress punctuated by a series of events in which some characters are involved. He tries to understand causes and intentions, attempts to answer the following questions: "What happened? Why did it happen?" This work of back-tracking can be considered as a saga, a family's story which is told over several generations.

The Past is a complex work of fiction evoking throughout its pages the atmospheres of past times and places. Each section of the book is prefaced with a setting and a year, from 'Cornwall 1914' to 'Dublin 1921', from 'Bray 1922', and 'Sandymount Strand 1928' to 'the Provinces 1934'. Across this itinerary, the narrator traces the movements of his parents and grandparents in times past.

Drawing from old postcards and photographs, visits to the spots and witness accounts, the narrator endeavours to establish a coherent order of truth and, as far as possible, determine to what extent the past makes sense. For indeed, as Neil Jordan himself said when the book was published, "The contemporary dilemma for an Irish person growing up today is that the past has no meaning any more".[8] This statement by the author leads us to the understanding that his novel – with its symptomatic title – is anchored in the process of collective searching.

The narrator quickly realizes that the fragments, bits and pieces that he somehow manages to gather, hinder his access to the past: the places captured in the photographs are no longer the same; there are, in fact, a limited number of photographs; most of these are unexploitable, and the only witness he can meet – Lili,[9] a friend of his mother's – is losing her memory. The veracity of her narrative is uncertain and the information she gives is limited. As a result, she admits with fatalism: "But, then I could be wrong, we could all be wrong. All I can really tell you is that they went

---

8   Niall Williams, "Time Past. Imagine and Remember: A View of Neil Jordan's Novel *The Past*" (Lille: *Gaeliana* 3, 1981), 167.

9   The choice of this name is no matter of chance: indeed, Lili spontaneously recalls her namesake – Lily – in James Joyce's short story "The Dead". In both texts, these elderly ladies remember the dead people they knew in the past and feel nostalgic.

there".[10] In similar fashion, she often qualifies her narrated episodes and descriptions with "from what I remember" (*TP*, 26). Lili is, however, the only link in the chain to the past. With the events she portrays, she allows the narrator to excavate large portions of his own family's story and establish connections with the present. The young man is yearning for details about the previous generations while there are a number of matters that his informant cannot remember or piece together. Her lapses of memory account for numerous questions and speculations that run through Jordan's narrative. Such guesswork is frustrating for the young man who acknowledges: "I would petition her for memories like these" (*TP*, 5). When some aspects remain unclear, he can only surmise what happened; when her memory fails, his imagination takes over.

From the very first pages of the narrative, the old postcards raise questions which simply cannot be answered: "I extend the picture on the postcard beyond the serrated edge" (*TP*, 8). And so the narrator resorts to his imagination in order to fill in the gaps. He puts forward likely hypotheses to try to establish the facts of the past and relations of cause and effect. He qualifies his gap-filling with "one can surmise", "I have to imagine you, Rene, since he took no photographs", "I picture her wearing a bulk coat" (*TP*, 1, 51, 256). By the same token, the narrator inserts adverbs such as "maybe" and "perhaps" (*TP*, 23); use of the conditional perfective such as "They would have pronounced [...] or would they have walked" (*TP*, 23); modal auxiliaries expressing probability as in "there must have been", "she must have known", "It must be soon after this that..." (*TP*, 2, 2, 61). All of these formulae highlight the major part that imagination plays in the reconstruction of the past.

The narrator's freedom to form images creates a work of fiction which compensates for the limitations of the old lady's memory. The boy's narrative describes what *could have been* – whether he refers to places, characters or context – considering that his representation is plausible. For after all, the narrator justifies himself: "There's a kind of truth in fiction, isn't there?" (*TP*, 185). By definition, the past is out of reach and becomes attainable only through the medium of creative fiction. The old photograph viewed

10   Neil Jordan, *The Past* [1980] (Berkeley: Soft Skull Press, 2012), 7.

by the character immortalizes what is only a punctual moment, thereby representing the impenetrability of the past. It places the chronological background of the event in the shade. In this way, a picture gives rise to a work of fiction in which visual images predominate.

***

One of these postcards was written in Cornwall. Dated 1 June 1914, the narrator's grandmother, Una, informs her parents that she will soon be home in Ireland. On the reverse side of the other card, sent seven months later, sometime after the Archduke Ferdinand had been shot in Sarajevo, Una announces the birth of her daughter, Rene, the narrator's mother. Una, an actress, had left Ireland and gone to England to avoid a scandal: she had married a law student, Michael O'Shaughnessy, to legitimize her pregnancy. This event is the starting point of a fictitious story, which is fuelled by Lili's memory and the narrator's imagination.

Back in Ireland, Una plays Cathleen Ni Houlihan.[11] Her theatrical career begins to take off, but she is not satisfied with her married life: her husband, Michael, is unfaithful. The latter, a member of the IRA, happens to be murdered in a Dublin street in 1921, within a month of Rene's first communion.

The third section of the novel – 'Bray 1922' – takes place in a property owned by an Anglo-Irish Protestant family of three men, the Vances. James, a widower, lives there with his son, Luke, and his father, an eccentric painter. James Vance is a very cultured man who enjoys talking about mathematical theories and Cartesian philosophy with Father Beausang, a friend of his late Roman Catholic wife's. James Vance also has a passion for photography: he takes pictures of 13-year-old Rene, who is instructed by her mother in playing Rosalind in *As You Like It*. He also takes pictures of her when she gets a job modelling silk stockings for a newspaper advertisement. James is not impervious to Rene's charm. He repeatedly approaches

---

11   *Cathleen Ni Houlihan* is an overtly nationalist and controversial play by William Butler Yeats (1902) in which Maud Gonne played the title role. It is one of the early plays which show Yeats's artistic effort to engage with national affairs.

her and suggests that she might give his son Irish lessons, without realizing that Luke is now a man.

In the following section, 'Bray 1933', Rene is expecting a child whose father can be either James or Luke, since she has had an affair with both of them.[12] Her pregnancy, however, does not prevent her from going on tour with a company throughout Ireland. She still plays Rosalind in *As You Like It*, and takes to the road with Luke who gets a job as assistant stage manager for the troupe.

Informed of Rene's pregnancy by Father Beausang, James Vance leaves Bray and sets out for the west with a view to tracking down the wandering group. He follows the company's posters from town to town, ultimately finds them and attends a performance of Shakespeare's comedy in Lisdoonvarna. That night, Rene gives birth to a child, the narrator who, years later, retraces the path followed by James Vance (who could be his father or his grandfather) from Ireland's eastern coast to the western one in 1934.

That year, Eamon de Valera also stops in Lisdoonvarna in his election campaign. The posters of the theatrical company are next to the ones of the political parties. Father of the nation, de Valera not only takes part in the creation of the Irish State, but he also witnesses the birth of the narrator. The latter, whose father is not clearly identified, comes into the world under the authority of a patriarchal trinity, the Father (James), the Son (Luke) and the Spirit (de Valera, a symbolical father): "It is no coincidence that when James and Luke ploughed through the road [...] de Valera followed soon after" (*TP*, 231). Like the Magi who set out to contemplate the newborn child, the three men are protective father figures. Moreover, their number is a good omen, as Father Beausang remarks in his abstract, mathematical reflection:

---

12   This incestuous configuration recalls Eugene O'Neill's play *Desire Under the Elms* (1924) in which father and son share the same partner who gives birth to a child. Desire, enhanced in the title, but also hatred and jealousy lie at the heart of this threesome to such an extent that the child is ultimately killed by his mother. It is quite different in Jordan's novel in which James, Luke and Rene seem to have peaceful relationships.

> A triadic base gives quite different, exciting results than that of the binary code. [...] Two, after all, is an oddly unsatisfying concept. With two one has the dialogue, the linear, but with three one has the conspiracy of space. And thus the triangle, perhaps even more than the circle, is the symbol of harmony; of definition within unity rather than just unity itself. (*TP*, 234)

This triple divinity is closely associated with de Valera whose major work, the 1937 Constitution, is established "in the Name of the Most Holy Trinity, from whom is all authority and to whom, as our final end, all actions both of men and states must be referred". The individual and the collective are superposed in the text and the spheres of private and public lives are intermingled – "nothing is distinguishable", as the narrator puts it (*TP*, 250). The ordinary citizen "sees the tide of history, and people simply washed" (*TP*, 87), as shows the untimely death of Michael, the narrator's grandfather murdered on the street because of his involvement in the Irish Republican Army.

Similarly, the child's birth, like the creation of the State, results from an "act of union":

> Because that was the first month and it would have still been a honeymoon month [...] and their bodies just might have made those shapes on the dampish bed like those maps in which the larger island envelops the smaller one, backwards admittedly, but expressive of an act of union rather than one of buggery or rape. (*TP*, 16)

The Act of Union bringing together Britain and Ireland in 1801 establishes a superficial sort of parallel with the heterosexual act of sex. Indeed, from the viewpoint of the dominant culture, Ireland is often personified with the features of a female, and specifically as Cathleen Ni Houlihan, the Shan Van Vocht or Roisin Dubh, whereas Great Britain is endowed with the authority of the rough stronger sex embodied by John Bull. This caricature is typical of the colonial discourse in which, as Ania Loomba describes, "sexual and colonial relationships become analogous to each other".[13]

---

13   Ania Loomba, *Colonialism-Post-colonialism* (London and New York: Routledge, 1998), 73. Similarly, a character of William Trevor's fiction highlights this metaphor: "When you looked at the map Ireland and England seemed like lovers. 'Don't you think so? [...] Does the map remind you curiously of an embrace? A

This embrace, symbolical of patriarchal *and* colonial domination, is considered by the narrator as an "incongruous union".[14] This phrase implants a revealing ambiguity: what union is he talking about? His grandparents' marriage or the relationship of two neighbouring countries which are so different that their association is absurd?

When he considers the union as such, the narrator implies that such a misalliance is no source of pride. The way he visualizes this intimate, inappropriate "act of union" even leads him to dissociate from his roots and consider himself as an illegitimate child, all the more so as his mother's identity is clearly established, but his father's is not. Just as the "Act of Union" between the woman, the embodiment of Ireland, and the man, the symbol of the English colonizer, painstakingly creates a small hybrid bastard state immobilized between them, bound never to develop or become independent, the misalliances in his family incite in the narrator feelings of illegitimacy. He does not, despite all, try to replace his father with a man of higher standing. He does not create an ideal filiation for himself, nor does he portray himself as the son of "the father of the nation". On the contrary, he proves to be sceptical about the politician's paternal qualities.

The novel exploits the theme of paternity in a variety of forms: the narrator's father whose identity is uncertain; the writer's father, who is clearly identified and to whom the novel is dedicated; and the father of the nation, whose designation "the father of us all" (*TP*, 268) is used here in an ironic way, insofar as Eamon de Valera has no reason, as the narrator implies, to be considered as such.

Metaphorically, this Irish statesman's parental function conveys notions of proximity, security and protection, and succeeds to the paternal function of the British occupier, the authoritarian colonizer who imposes the respect of order. De Valera's emblematic figure is the reflection of decolonization, de-anglicization. It lies within the scope of a re-creation of history, a reinvention of the father, as Declan Kiberd puts it: "This generation of Irishmen and Irishwomen fathered and mothered themselves,

---

most extraordinary embrace to throw up all this'" (William Trevor, *Fools of Fortune* [London: Penguin, 1983], 162).

14   "that incongruous union" (Jordan, *The Past*, 248).

reinventing parents in much the same way as they were reinventing the Irish past".[15] The allegory is particularly significant: on the paradigmatic axis, the political leader is a *pater familias* whose major function is to provide the ones who are under his authority with comfort and well-being. The nation is thus perceived as a family whose heads are like parents. Such a metaphor reinforces a sense of belonging in the population for, as Kiberd remarks: "the family is the one social institution with which the people can identify".[16] Anxious to be close to his fellow citizens, de Valera attempts to be "the father of the nation" when he delivers speeches in praise of family virtues. He states: "we can have our own people united as a family – a nation of brothers each working in industrial harmony, not for himself only but for the good of all".[17]

Therefore, when the narrator depicts his own family in the grip of the vagaries of life – births out of wedlock, conjugal infidelities or unhappy married lives, not to mention doubts about the identities of fathers or a common partner shared by father and son – doesn't he demolish the ideal conception of family and marriage according to the 1937 Constitution of Ireland which was supervised and introduced at the instigation of de Valera? This official text indeed writes that "the State pledges itself to guard with special care the institution of marriage, on which the family is founded, and to protect it against attack".[18] There is clearly a discrepancy between the official fundamental text and the novelist's family story.

***

De Valera is neither the main protagonist of the novel, nor even a minor character, but a mere figure moving past discreetly in the background. Indeed, he only makes brief appearances in *The Past*. The narrative mentions his unusual physiognomy, his long, gangling, horselike silhouette,[19]

---

15   Declan Kiberd, *Inventing Ireland* (London: Jonathan Cape, 1995), 7.

16   Kiberd, *Inventing Ireland*, 380.

17   Quoted by J. P. O'Carroll and J. A. Murphy, eds, *De Valera and his Times* (Cork: Cork University Press), 1983, 47.

18   Constitution of the Republic of Ireland 1937, Article 3-1.

19   "his long frame upright" (Jordan, *The Past*, 260), "his gangling unlikely bearing" (47), "there is something horselike in the features which only adds to their allure" (115).

his short-sighted eyes or his sullenness.[20] De Valera is also depicted under the features of an elusive enigmatic being.[21] This is why he is described in a hazy, misty, vaporous aura which accentuates his status as the incarnation of the Ireland of the past:

> His glasses are *mist*ing now with the *vapour* which, despite the closed windows, seems to seep through every crevice of the bodywork. Or is it just the heat he generates? Does his body *steam* with its own logic, embodying as it does generations of effort, the doctrines of eight centuries? This *steam* has the smell of hay, that musty, incongruous feminine smell as if, nourished on the peat of generations of the fallen, its inherited heat rubs, *steams* and oxidises. He is considering a scheme for turf-fuelled power stations. The *steam* on his glasses gathers, forms two separate tears which drop to his cheeks, as if his eyes had shed them.[22]

Similarly, the text mentions his determination to forge ahead and his ambition for the future of the nation, as shown by the path which opens in front of him:

> His profile etched against the afternoon haze, tilted slightly upwards, looking *forward*. The *line* of his nose, strong and almost elegant, is what seems to pull his body *forward*, echoed by two deep *lines* falling downwards to the curve of each lip. Were there ever *lines* deeper than those and is it the sense of smell that pulls him *forward* with the profile of his nose, towards some distant future?[23]

He is depicted as "the chief, whose light step straddles the past and whose profile points towards any number of possible futures" (*TP*, 260). In the mirror of the pools of sulphurous waters in the spa town of Lisdoonvarna, he seems to anticipate that he will soon come to power:

20   "He passes Rene, but of course he doesn't notice since his sight, bad at the best of times, has become clouded with her vapour, condensing into tears again on his rimless glasses" (258), "The corners of the mouth sweep downwards" (115), "The mouth is turned downwards without a hint of sourness, but in a contemplative moral curve" (254), "two deep lines falling downwards to the curve of each lip" (260).

21   "The eyes reflect his own abstraction" (115), "His face is abstract and expressionless" (254).

22   (254). My emphasis. Significantly, a new occurrence of the adjective "incongruous" can be picked up here.

23   (260). My emphasis.

> De Valera comes to the sister *pools*. He compares the motive *powers* of water with the combustible *powers* of turf. He *lowers* his lips to one, then the other. He sees his own face reflected, his spectacles like *pools* themselves. The curve of his mouth loses its strictness in the water's ripple. He sucks with extraordinary *power*.[24]

The mirror effect is not only established by the pool waters or the glass of his spectacles, but also by the poetic style of the excerpt, with the recurrence of the words 'pools' and 'powers', the latter introducing a rhyme with 'lowers'.

The man is bound to become a powerful politician, but his elusive figure which is just passing through the diegetic universe is only the reflection of himself, a weakened representation of his public personality. As a matter of fact, there is no possible comparison between the major part he plays in the history of his country and his minor role in the novel. For indeed, no one can deny that Eamon de Valera is a founding father of Irish democratic independence. He is an inevitable figure on the political stage of twentieth-century Ireland. As a result, the choice of minimizing his place in the narrative is quite significant.

***

When the question of Home Rule arose again in 1912, one British MP proposed that any new Bill should not apply to the most prosperous parts of Ulster. Within a few years, the debate centred on the question of whether a separate Northern Ireland should be composed of six or nine counties and whether this division should become permanent. The debate raged, triggered an outburst of violence, anger and hatred, and pulled Ireland apart. Then the First World War intervened. Home Rule was suspended and the question of partition temporarily dropped.

As the Great War ended, Ireland quickly descended into the chaos of the Anglo-Irish War. Police auxiliaries recruited by the British government were sent to troubled areas. They gained a reputation for harsh methods. The questions at stake revealed the deep divisions between parts of Ulster and the rest of the country. The separation of the island into two distinct territories was once more on the agenda. It was even voted in the

---

24   (263). My emphasis.

Westminster parliament in the absence of the Irish MPs. While the violence continued, King George V travelled to Belfast and called for a truce.

To make this peace lasting, it was necessary to negotiate with the British government. Eamon de Valera, the president of Sinn Fein, a political group that rose to prominence, declined to participate in the talks but sent a delegation to London. A team led by Arthur Griffith and Michael Collins went there with orders to accept only a treaty that included either a full break from the British Empire or full unity for Ireland. In the end, they got neither.

For nearly two months, the Irish representatives debated the issue with Winston Churchill and Lloyd George. Exasperated, the latter – the then British PM – finally offered the Irish an ultimatum: sign the treaty or face a resumption of war. On 6 December 1921, Arthur Griffith, Michael Collins and the other Irish delegates signed the Anglo-Irish Treaty, which established the Irish Free State as a dominion of the British Empire. The North of Ireland would be given the option of joining the Free State or remaining independent. In the latter case, a special "Boundary Commission" would be established to redraw the border between the two states.

When Griffith and Collins returned to Dublin, they were blasted by de Valera and other Irish Nationalists who felt betrayed: not only was Ireland divided, but the Irish would still be required to make an oath to the King. Despite de Valera's objection, the Dail ratified the treaty. The Anglo-Irish War was over, but the divisions left in its wake soon tore Ireland apart and plunged the country into a civil war. The Irish Republican Army once again vowed to take up arms and fight until Ireland was fully free of the British Empire.

Michael Collins had authority over the IRA, but not over all of its members. Upon returning from London to Ireland with the treaty, he became chairman of the Provisional Government formed to administer the twenty-six counties of "Southern Ireland" until the formal establishment of the Irish Free State. In this position, he led the battle against the IRA Republicans who threatened to reduce his fledgling state to chaos and anarchy. While on a tour of duty in his native West Cork, Collins was killed in an ambush at Bealnablagh, near Macroom on 22 August 1922. His men managed to return his body to Dublin City Hall where it lay in state for three days. Tens of thousands of mourners paid their respects.

Killed at 31, martyr of the Republican cause, Michael Collins is an almost mythical figure in Irish history. To some, he is the greatest hero since Brian Boru, a ruthless patriot, whose single-minded devotion and determination greatly advanced the cause of Irish statehood.

The man is a source of inspiration for Neil Jordan who, from 1982, two years after *The Past* was published, wrote the script of the film he dedicated to him. Nevertheless, *Michael Collins* would only be released fifteen years later.[25] The way Collins and de Valera are portrayed in the film is captured in the latter's remark as he refused the erection of a memorial on his rival's tombstone: "It is my considered opinion that in the fullness of time history will record the greatness of Michael Collins and it will be recorded at my expense".[26] Indeed, Jordan's film does not make de Valera out to be a national hero. On the contrary, it shows that the man can be blamed for some of his actions. In an interview, Jordan states:

> De Valera was the villain of that period in a strange way. I tried to not make judgements on de Valera. Alan Rickman gave a magnificent performance and we tried to use many of de Valera's original speeches and as much of his actual dialogue as I could find but we are talking about a figure who did send these untried ruffians, who the British press called gangsters and murderers, to negotiate a treaty with the people who ran three quarters of the world at that time. [...] That is a decision which is utterly puzzling to me. He disagreed with the treaty Collins brought back, which is acceptable in a way, it was put to popular vote, de Valera lost that popular vote and then gave that 'rivers of blood' speech and in a way was responsible for the Civil War. [...] De Valera alone was not responsible for the Civil War but he was a pivotal factor in the fact that there was a civil war. They weren't his best years. The movie chose a villain and it found him.[27]

---

25   Emer Rockett and Kevin Rockett, *Neil Jordan. Exploring Boundaries* (Dublin: The Liffey Press, 2003), 271.

26   Tim Pat Coogan, *Michael Collins* (London: Arrow Books, 1990), 432.

27   "Neil Jordan: de Valera was 'villain' of Collins biopic", RTÉ (28 February 2016), <https://www.rte.ie/entertainment/2016/0227/771221-neil-jordan-still-hasnt-forgiven-de-valera/>.

This reference to the 'rivers of blood' echoes de Valera's speeches in some parts of Ireland in March 1922. In Thurles, for example, he declared:

> If the Treaty were accepted, the fight for freedom would still go on, and the Irish people, instead of fighting foreign soldiers, will have to fight the Irish soldiers of an Irish government set up by Irishmen. The IRA would have to wade through the blood of the soldiers of the Irish Government, and perhaps through that of some members of the Irish Government to get their freedom.[28]

Such words may explain why English actor Alan Rickman not only looks, acts and speaks like de Valera, but also bears an uncanny resemblance to Dracula, as some critics observed.[29] As soon as it was released, the film, "based on real facts" as the credits put it, was the subject of violent criticisms concerning a number of unrecognized events, anachronisms or inaccuracies, and mostly a biased re-reading of history.[30] A fierce controversy flared up about de Valera's possible involvement in his rival's elimination. When Collins was killed, de Valera was in the region, and probably knew that an ambush was brewing. This does not prove, however, that he was behind his assassination. He could even have tried to prevent the ambush, according to Tim Pat Coogan, his least indulgent biographer who claims that de Valera considered it was the opportunity for him to start peace talks with Collins.

It is highly likely that Collins's murderers were untamable extremists, whereas the film implies that they could have been supporters of de Valera who is portrayed as a politician for whom it was inevitable to cause bloodshed, even among his own fellow citizens. De Valera's personality remains barely penetrable. True, he proved to be able to fight against the British – and the film glorifies the rebels of the 1916 Easter Rising he was part of – but unable to resolve the Northern Irish problem. Many of his critics

28   Perhaps this reference to the 'rivers of blood' inspired some scenes of the film Neil Jordan made in 2012, *Byzantium*. Indeed, the characters discover a cursed island where the high black cliffs are covered with cascades of blood when human beings are changed into vampires.

29   Rockett, *Neil Jordan. Exploring Boundaries*, 169-170.

30   *Ibid.*, 174.

blame de Valera for the decisions he made in the early twenties, and Neil Jordan, who attended one of his meetings forty years later, is among them:

> I once heard de Valera speak, actually. My father brought me to hear him speak outside the GPO. I think I was about 10 and I hadn't a clue what all these weird people were doing or talking about. I suppose I grew up in de Valera's Ireland and I didn't like it that much. He was a fascinating figure, like a schoolteacher with that whiney voice that every schoolteacher or Christian Brother seemed to have. That period was his worst period, particularly towards the end of the War of Independence and during the Treaty negotiations. He made a whole series of decisions that had consequences people had to endure for the next 50, 60 years.[31]

Neil Jordan criticizes de Valera for making unfortunate choices to put an end to the Anglo-Irish War, but also for shaping a conservative nation, withdrawn into itself, hostile to modernization, the one he was born and raised in.

In *The Past*, the question asked by Father Beausang in 1922 – "Can de Valera enlighten us?" (*TP*, 108) – remains in suspense, which implies that an affirmative answer is unlikely. The writer himself is obviously doubtful: he refuses to put de Valera on a pedestal. In his novel, it seems that he wishes to curb the enthusiasm of those who fuel hagiographic narratives of national history and praise the public figure to the skies. This is why de Valera is not portrayed in his true historic greatness, but only as a simple figure stealthily sketched out in the background of the story. He is described with his virtues and qualities, but also with his faults and weaknesses. Neil Jordan calls into question the part played by de Valera in history only implicitly in the novel, but much more explicitly in the film. His challenging approach may be interpreted as a relativist, if not revisionist, reading of the past.

***

With this first opus, Neil Jordan's ambition is not to write a historic novel. On the one hand, he strives to establish a link with the past which sheds

---

31   Tara Brady, "Neil Jordan: Michael Collins Was Conventional – Apart from the Guerrilla Warfare", *The Irish Times*, 17 March 2016. <https://www.irishtimes.com/culture/film/neil-jordan-michael-collins-was-conventional-apart-from-the-guerrilla-warfare-1.2569575>.

light on the present of the society he belongs to; on the other hand, he endeavours to show that history is a construction. Two kinds of past – the domain of the history-book and the one of personal emotion – are recalled and recreated side by side. Both of them are somehow remembered and reshaped in order to make an incomplete narrative more comprehensive. By this binary approach, Neil Jordan draws a parallel between the way historians make facts of times-gone-by and the way a family views its own history. Whether it relates to Irish history or the footnotes of history, the past is no more than just another fiction. It can be fit together like a jigsaw puzzle some pieces of which are lacking and must be created to form a homogeneous whole. No less than forty-three occurrences of the verb 'imagine' in the novel, as Elena Cotta Ramusino observed, are suggestive of the novelist's consciousness of the role of the creative process in historical narration.[32]

Without the fervour of most revisionist intellectuals, Neil Jordan revises history in his novel to challenge and re-assess what some tend to consider as the naked truth. His vision of an iconic politician, a symbol of the power of the State, is not mythologized at all. As a result, *The Past* is a counterpoint to the hagiographic biographies, published a few years before, which considered de Valera as the man Ireland needed to shape its destiny. The diegesis of the novel, which – it must not be overlooked – is set between 1912 and 1934, plays down de Valera's part on that period. In the way he is depicted, the politician is neither a hero nor a saint, but a mere candidate in an election campaign, trying to find his way in a foggy spa town.

Neil Jordan's first novel challenges ideological approaches of national history. It dares to revisit the past critically. It is a postmodern work which practices "incredulity towards metanarratives",[33] to use Lyotard's definition. *The Past* illustrates what Linda Hutcheon calls

---

32   Elena Cotta Ramusino, "Neil Jordan's *The Past*: A Journey in Time and Memory" in Sean Crosson and Werner Huber, eds, *Towards 2016–1916 and Irish Literature, Culture & Society* (Trier: Wissenschaftlicher Verlag, 2015), 147.

33   Jean-François Lyotard, *La Condition postmoderne* (Paris : Editions de Minuit, 1979), 7.

"historiographic metafiction",[34] or a textualized ironic rethinking of history. It contests the tenets of dominant ideologies, questions what constitutes historical knowledge and challenges all that "goes without saying".

Historiographic metafictions are highly prized at the end of the twentieth century, as if the interest in the past was a way to turn a page, to better understand the present and prepare the future. In this process, tradition is not a nostalgic museum, but a door open to the future, as Declan Kiberd puts it: "how to build a future on the past without returning to it?"[35] The return to the past makes it possible to (re)discover some forgotten or unknown parts of it, to reshape history and create an opinion which is often different from the official discourse. Such an attitude is a sign of resistance. It challenges the traditional versions and ideologies of history books, reveals the limits and powers of historical knowledge, and favours a different, more subjective approach of past events which may resort to fiction. From then on, no wonder the novel uses a figure of speech which makes it possible to 'speak otherwise'[36]: "allegory may often be a prominent aesthetic in acts of resistance", according to Kevin Barry.[37] *The Past* can be read, understood and interpreted at two levels: there is a primary or surface meaning and a secondary or under-the-surface meaning.

In his childhood and youth, Neil Jordan witnessed the authority of de Valera who was the *Taoiseach*, and later the President of Ireland. The story of the novel ends in the 1930s, but de Valera remained on the political scene for four more decades. He passed away only five years prior to the publication of *The Past*. In those days, the nation took stock of the politician; Neil Jordan sought to do the same, and to give his opinion about

---

34   "Historiographic metafiction represents a challenging of the (related) conventional forms of fiction and history through its acknowledgement of their inescapable textuality" (Linda Hutcheon, *A Poetics of Postmodernism. History, Theory, Fiction* [London and New York: Routledge, 1988], 11).

35   Kiberd, *Inventing Ireland*, 292.

36   The term 'allegory' derives from Greek *allēgoreïn*, "speaking otherwise".

37   Kevin Barry, "What Have You in Your Hand? Some Critical Notes on Post-colonial Aesthetics", in *L'Irlande : Identités et Modernité* (Villeneuve d'Ascq : PU Lille, 1997), 19.

the situation. By doing so, he was, in fact, the spokesman of many fellow citizens of his generation.

The narrator of *The Past* is an ordinary, anonymous citizen who can be perceived as the writer's *alter ego.* The internal restrictive point of view tends to confirm this identity. Indeed, both of them share the same age, gender, ideology, perhaps the same dreams and desires, thwarted by a protectionist state which offered no decent future to its talented youth who had to emigrate to start a new life abroad.

Neil Jordan was only 30 years old when he wrote his first novel. He could not express himself freely in this book for fear of being banned. Nevertheless, his personal opinion can be discerned. His use of indirect statement is telling and makes it possible to question the implicit and clarify the deeper meanings of the text. According to the French critic Philippe Hamon, absence is a key concept in the relationships between text and ideology.[38] In this case, Neil Jordan interweaves the history of his nation with the stories of his characters, thus establishing powerful connections between text and context, and giving place to social unconscious throughout the text.

About fifteen years later, when his film *Michael Collins* was released, Jordan had become much more mature, and had risen to international fame. He could write and say openly what he was thinking about the past events of his country. By doing so, he was still somehow his generation's spokesman. Indeed, in plain language, he claimed that this great figure of Irish history was a man of extremes, a questionable decision maker: "There was an element of fanaticism in de Valera's character that I would find unpleasant".[39] Such remarks, made when the film was released in 1996, the year of the eightieth anniversary of the Easter Rising, and thus in a period particularly favourable to a thoughtful approach to history, complete, clarify and make what was only implicitly evoked much more explicit.

38 « Le concept d'absence est un concept clé dans le discours théorique sur les rapports entre texte et idéologie » in Philippe Hamon, *Texte et idéologie* (Paris : Presses Universitaires de France, 1984), 11.

39 Zucker, ed., *Neil Jordan. Interviews* (Jackson: University Press of Mississippi, 2013), 86.

***

The Past and *Michael Collins* are "works of creative interpretation".[40] And yet, there is no comparison between the publication of his first novel in 1980 – when he was an unknown young man – and the media hype caused by the release of his film sixteen years later. *Michael Collins* was a great success, but also the object of an intense critical debate. It was particularly lucrative too, since it took more than €5 million at the Irish box office.[41] Such popularity, together with undeniable profitability, aroused a lot of jealousies.

The film reinforces the visual aspect of the novel, whose story is based on old photographs, pictures from newspapers and theoretical views. *Michael Collins* is not a screen adaptation of *The Past,* but it shares with it a critical look at the major events of Irish history. Visual scenes are common in both works.

Surprisingly, Lord Longford and Thomas O'Neill's biography, *Eamon de Valera,* also starts with the description of a picture showing a big room in a New York apartment in 1885: a man is sitting near a fireplace; his wife is playing on the floor with a young boy. The latter is Eamon de Valera. His father is dying; his mother, an Irish expatriate, says her farewells to the child who is to be sent to Ireland where he will be raised by his grandmother and uncle. According to his biographers, "this snapshot of the past is all that de Valera remembers of his American origins".[42]

If the man he was to become proved to be so attached to family links, it was probably because he never really experienced them personally: born in America, raised in Ireland by other relatives, de Valera inevitably felt he was abandoned by his parents when he was a child. Such living conditions probably gave rise to questions which remained unanswered. The way he looked at this picture – the last remnant of his first years – certainly shaped mental images and fictitious scenarios in his mind. It allowed him to visualize his past, as the narrator does in the novel. De Valera's biography

---

40   Brown, *Ireland. A Social and Cultural History 1922-2002*, 409.

41   Rockett, *Neil Jordan. Exploring Boundaries*, 175.

42   Frank Pakenham Longford and Thomas P. O'Neill, *Eamon de Valera* (London: Arrow Books, 1970), 1.

was published in 1970 and it is highly likely that Neil Jordan read it. He may have even been inspired by this book insofar as *The Past* starts with a similar scene. What is certain is that the novel becomes more personal when it expresses implicit reservations about the part played by de Valera in twentieth-century Ireland.

To conclude, whether dealing with a key figure of international politics or an ordinary family, the past is always conditioned by the way it is approached. In the words of John Banville, "the past doesn't exist in terms of fact. It only exists in terms of the way we look at it".[43] In his novel and film, Neil Jordan shares this view of the past. Obviously, history had become a highly contested matter in 1990s Ireland, as the release of *Michael Collins* indicates. The critical debate it aroused also showed that historical writing is one discourse among many and that it cannot escape its imbrication with ideology, insofar as a totally objective approach without any prejudice is nothing more than wishful thinking.

---

43 John Banville with Ronan Sheehan and Francis Stuart, 'Novelists on the Novel', *Crane Bag* 3/1 (1979), 84.

PART II:

Zoomorphoses

CHAPTER 3

Demons of Darkness at Work: *The Dream of a Beast* and *The Company of Wolves*

The Dream of a Beast raises a number of questions. The title itself is somewhat ambiguous: is the beast the subject or the object of the dream? In other words, is a beast dreaming or is a man dreaming that he is a beast? The literary genre of the text is also problematic. *The Dream of a Beast* is made of about one hundred pages, divided into 33 sections and can be considered as a short novel, a long story, a novella[1] or even maybe a tale since it depicts an alternate, paradoxical universe. It also partakes of the bestiary, as the paratext[2] indicates: on the one hand, the title refers to "a beast"; on the other, the epigraph – a quotation from a poem by William Blake – confirms the dominating role of animals in the story:

> Kill not the moth nor butterfly,
>
> For the Last Judgment draweth nigh.[3]

The Dream of a Beast shows that borders between literary genres have become fluid. It accentuates the elusiveness between realism and fantasy and tries to reach the dark layers of the subconscious.

1   Seventeen years after its original publication, *The Dream of a Beast* was published again in a cross-section of Irish short fiction by John Somer and John J. Daly, *The Anchor Book of Irish Writing* (New York: Anchor Books, 2000).

2   Literary theorist Gérard Genette defines paratext as those things in a published work that accompany the text, things such as the author's name, the title, preface or introduction, or illustrations. He states: "More than a boundary or a sealed border, the paratext is, rather, a threshold" (Gérard Genette, *Paratexts: Thresholds of Interpretation* [Cambridge: The University of Cambridge, 1997], 1–2).

3   William Blake, "Auguries of Innocence" in *Selected Poems* (London: Penguin, 2005), 48.

***

Published in 1983, *The Dream of a Beast* relates a Dublin commercial's sur-real nightmare in an apocalyptic world.[4] The unnamed narrator witnesses strange phenomena around him:

> It was during a summer that it all quickened. There was the heat, first, that came in the beginning and then stayed. Then fools who for as long as I had known them had been complaining about wet Junes and Julys began to wonder when it would end. The pavements began to crack in places. Streets I had walked on all my life began to grow strange blooms in the crevices. The stalks would ease their way along the shop-fronts and thick, oily, unrecognizable leaves would cover the plate-glass windows.[5]

The four occurrences of the words "begin" or "beginning" emphasize that a new era is on its way. On a more personal plane, the narrator notices that his senses become highly acute, particularly his sense of smell, but also his sights and sounds.[6] He feels trapped inside a body that is under-going some transformations and changes him into a monstrous beast. This physical metamorphosis leads him to cut himself off and move only by night. In the daytime, he remains aloof, in a drowsy state and gives himself up to dreaming.

Although he does not understand the grotesque transformation of his body, the narrator seems to accept it with resignation. And yet, he is aware of the revolting image of the mirror:

> I hardly recognized the stranger who stared back at me. Had I not looked for so long, I wondered. I stared for a long while and concluded that I mustn't have. Certain moods of self-loathing had in the past kept me from mirrors, but never had the gap between what I remembered and what I eventually saw been so large. (*DB*, 94)

4   The city where the story is set is not explicitly mentioned, but the names of the streets make it possible to recognize Dublin.

5   Neil Jordan, *The Dream of a Beast, A Neil Jordan Reader* (New York: Vintage, 1993), 89.

6   Considering the following metamorphosis, there is obviously here a parodic echo of "Little Red Riding Hood", and more particularly of the girl's remarks in front of the beast which pretends to be her grandmother: "What big ears you have. [...]. What big eyes you have!".

He is not repulsive for everyone though: indeed, his new body leads him to embark on an affair with the female representative of a perfume company. They give vent to their bestial nature and have sex in the Dublin Zoo. He is however ostracized by Marianne and Matilde – his wife and daughter – who become closer to Ambrose, an old friend of the family's. As a result, the narrator has to leave the marital home. He finds refuge on the roof of a public building[7] where he meets a bat who teaches him to try out his wings and fly in the air.

***

In an interview, Neil Jordan observes:

> I'm attracted to the fantastic ... the level of the fantastic in things, whether it's baroque or whether it's horror. It's a huge strain in Irish literature. If you look at Laurence Sterne, Flann O'Brien, Sheridan Le Fanu, Bram Stoker, there's a huge strain in Irish literature, in Irish theatre, that has to do with the baroque, the fantastic, the absurd and the surreal.[8]

With *The Dream of a Beast,* Jordan connects the fantastic to the morbid state of conscience which produces images of terror, nightmare and delirium.[9] The fantastic makes a breach in everyday reality and yet introduces verisimilitude, hence the reader's feeling of hesitation. It breaks boundaries, overlooks barriers, gates and doors, upsets time and space, disturbs identities. The fantastic is transgressive, but also suggests a regressive return to instinct and disorder, a descent into archaic fears and anxieties. In this case, it is perceived "from inside", under the beast's skin, as in

---

7   The building that the narrator scales – "square shaped, beetling over the tiny streets around it... the seat of some power" (104) – is possibly the Central Bank in Dame Street in Dublin city centre.

8   Neil Jordan, *Sorrento Terrace Interview* (17 May 2002), 6-1 in McGuirk, *Neil Jordan: the Literary Fiction*, 51. Baroque literature does not exist as such. Neil Jordan uses the adjective to lay stress on the strange, marvelous themes of some literary forms which are considered as unexpected and bizarre.

9   « Le fantastique est lié aux états morbides de la conscience qui, dans les phénomènes du cauchemar ou du délire, projette devant elle des images de ses angoisses » (Pierre-Georges Castex, *Le Conte fantastique en France de Nodier à Maupassant* [Paris : Corti, 1951], 11). My translation.

Kafka's *Metamorphosis*, whose narrator – Gregor Samsa – is a prisoner of a body that he cannot recognize any more.

The Dream of a Beast and *The Metamorphosis* have a lot in common. Both novellas have similar lengths. Their male protagonists undergo some transformations which give them a great deal of trouble: their voices change into grunts; their words are unintelligible; their physical appearances fill others with disgust; they are doomed to stay aloof, in the dark, and yet remain capable of emotion. However, although Kafka's protagonist is stuck on his back and unable to get up, Jordan's character moves about quite easily. Besides, a major difference is noteworthy: the first sentence of Kafka's text makes it clear that the metamorphosis is factual: "As Gregor Samsa awoke one morning from uneasy dreams he found himself transformed in his bed into a gigantic insect".[10] The narrator insists further down: "It was no dream". Kafka repeatedly denies the dreamlike nature of his story. On the contrary, Jordan's protagonist changes into a beast in his dream. This specificity is clearly pointed out by the title of the novella.

According to Todorov's distinction, we can therefore consider that *The Metamorphosis* is marvellous insofar as the fantastic event must be accepted as such, whereas *The Dream of a Beast* is rather uncanny since the supernatural episode is explained by the last sentence of the text,[11] which reports a kiss between the narrator and Marianne who is also changed into an animal:

> The kiss was long, long enough for the sun to cross the dial, for the moon to traverse it and for the sun to rise once more. I saw the globes of her eyes and in my visage reflected there saw something as human as surprise.[12]

10 Franz Kafka, *The Metamorphosis* [1912], in Nahum N. Glatzer, ed., *The Complete Stories* (New York: Schocken Books, 1971), 89.

11 The seminal project of *The Dream of a Beast* can rationally be explained: indeed, in an interview on the RTE arts review programme *Rattlebag,* twenty years after the publication of the book, on 27 February 2003, Jordan said that when he was writing it, he was suffering from psoriasis and that may have had something to do with the image of the beast. He joked that it was not so difficult for him to put himself in the skin of a lonely creature who sparked off hostile reactions among his peers (Cf. McGuirk, *Neil Jordan: The Literary Fiction,* 49).

12 Jordan, *The Dream of a Beast,* 175. It must be noted that Marianne's eyeballs merge with the globes of the sun and the moon.

The narrator's awakening next to his wife goes with a moment's surprise, a return to the real world and the progressive awareness that the whole story is nothing but a dream, that his metamorphosis is only the fruit of his imagination. This ultimate sentence refers to the beginning of the narrative, when the couple went to bed the previous evening:

> We made love of course. I watched her undress and thought of all the words to do with this activity [...]. We seemed to twine round each other as if our limbs had lost their usual shape. We made the beast with two backs. (*DB*, 96)

This popular phrase – first occurrence of the word "beast" in the story – referring to a couple engaged in sexual intercourse introduces the image of a beastly creature in the narrator's mind and gives rise to his dream. It takes up the sixteenth century's ribald vocabulary. Indeed, it was used by Rabelais to describe the origins of his hero Gargantua:

> In the vigour of his age, Grandgousier married Gargamelle, daughter to the king of the Parpaillons, a jolly pug, and well-mouthed wench. These two did oftentimes do the beast with two backs together, joyfully rubbing and frotting their bacon 'gainst one another.[13]

A few decades later, Shakespeare used the same phrase in the first scene of his tragedy *Othello* in which Iago gives Brabantio, Desdemona's father, the following information:

> BRABANTIO: What profane wretch art thou?
>
> IAGO: I am one, Sir, that comes to tell you your daughter and the Moor are now making the beast with two backs.[14]

In Jordan's text, the narrator's mental activity which consists in listing the different ways of referring to sexual intercourse is directly followed by the dream and makes it possible to interpret it. Dreams give vent to

---

13   François Rabelais, *Gargantua and Pantagruel* [1532-1534], Ch. 3 (New York: Barnes & Noble Books, 2005), 98.

14   William Shakespeare, *Othello* [1622], I, i, 126-127 (London: Penguin Classics, 2005), 27.

fantasies, produce a release of energy and reveal the strangeness of desire. The material of dream symbolism is often sexual, as Freud showed. For example, the openings of the protagonist's house symbolically represent the entrances into the body cavities. Similarly, the staircase is connected with the sexual act because of the rhythmic climbing. The scene when the beast climbs the façade of the building on the roof of which it finds refuge can be sexually interpreted: it corresponds to the erect human body.[15] In the field of intertextual echoes, such an episode also revives the Irish fantastic tradition, and more particularly Bram Stoker's work, mentioned here above by Jordan. Is not Dracula caught by his visitor in the act of climbing the outer wall of his castle? There are many allusions to the Count of Transylvania in the text. Like him, the protagonist of *The Dream of a Beast* is a lycanthrope: he notes that he becomes very hairy, that his mouth is getting wider, his teeth longer, his hands harder. His voice is breaking and his set of muscles developing.

In one of Ovid's *Metamorphoses*, Lycaon, an irreligious cannibalistic tyrant, is punished by the gods and excluded from humankind:

> He begins to howl, trying without success to speak [...]. He delights in blood. His clothes have disappeared, changed to hair, his arms to legs. He is now a wolf and still retains some vestiges of his old form – the same grey colouring, the same violence in his expression, the same glare in his eyes, the same savagery in his appearance.[16]

If "he delights in blood", there is nothing surprising about Dracula's capacity to be transformed into a wolf. This precision also leads to think that male adults can be predators, on the look-out for virgins to deflower, a seemingly bestial act. And as a matter of fact, the narrator's dream is not without ambiguity when it deals with his daughter Matilde:

> She came towards me and kissed me. The kiss was a brief one, but in the quick withdrawal of her face from mine I sensed a torrent of emotion. I looked into her eyes and saw them at once angry and pleading for kindness. I knew then she was in love,

---

15   "It is apparently not unknown in this connection that the sexual intercourse of many of the larger animals requires a mounting, a climbing upon the female" (Freud, *A General Introduction to Psychoanalysis*, 143).

16   Ovid, *Metamorphoses* [760] (Harmondsworth: Penguin, 2004), 231-235, 48.

> she had been in love and felt mishandled. I felt pity, but even more, a sense of great misplacement that her body had touched another's, her soul had met another's. She called me by a name then, not my own, and it dawned on me that she was in love with me. (*DB*, 142)

A shade of Freudianism spreads throughout the story. Matilde is in the dream because she caught her parents in the heat of action. Her father narrates:

> We made the beast with two backs then and somewhere in between our cries another cry was heard, a little more urgent. Matilde was standing in the doorway, still in her dream.
>
> You go to her, Marianne said, turning over. I rose from the bed and took her in my arms, which seemed no longer pliant, but heavy and cumbersome in every movement. Matilde whispered parts of her dream to me as I carried her to bed.
>
> Marianne was asleep when I got back. I looked at my body in the dark and saw all the tiny hairs glistening in the moonlight. (*DB*, 96-97)

Like a wolf baying at the moon, the father is aware that he can be a potential danger in the heart of his familiar universe. He is standing by the window, on the boundary between the inside and the outside, which implies that a borderline state has been reached, that there is a fight between desire and guilt. The oedipal love that his daughter is allegedly feeling for him leads him to think about what he feels for her. But is the narrator trustworthy? Is he a protecting father or a perverse demon? How can his metamorphosis be interpreted? Later, when, under the appearance of a hideous beast, he wants to enter Matilde's room, he is not allowed in. His wife tells him: "Don't come up [...]. Say goodnight from the doorway" (*DB*, 127). The couple's sexual relation, interrupted by their daughter's irruption into the room, is resumed in the erotic dream in which some incestuous components interfere. There is a mirror effect between the dream world and the real world, the former showing a reversed image of the latter, that is the dark side of the human soul. *The Dream of a Beast* can be read as a variant of "Beauty and the Beast", about which Bettelheim remarks:

This tale foreshadows by centuries the Freudian view that sex must be experienced by the child as disgusting as long as his sexual longings are attached to his parent, because only through such a negative attitude toward sex can the incest taboo, and with it the stability of the human family, remain secure.[17]

The father's possible "unmentionable sexual behavior"[18] towards his daughter is symbolically embodied by his repulsive look whose transformation may be an imaginary punishment he inflicts on himself. In his monstrous dream, he teams up with a huge bat who teaches him how to fly. And, according to Freud:

> The dream has another far more expressive way of symbolizing erection. It makes the sex organ the essential part of the whole person and pictures the person himself as flying. [...] The dreams of flying, often so beautiful, and which we all have had, must be interpreted as dreams of general sexual excitement, as erection dreams.[19]

The bat is traditionally recognized as equipped with erotic and libidinous powers. It is a symbol of impurity, a blood-sucker often represented with an open jaw. It is no chance if it plays so prominent a part in the story, just like the wolf who, by its devouring mouth and lustful ardours, is very good at causing bloodshed. The bat and the wolf are precisely the two animals into which Dracula is metamorphosed[20]: he can indeed become a wolf or a vampire bat at will. In Stoker's novel, Mina Harker reports in her journal what Professor Van Helsing said:

> There are such beings as vampires [...]. This vampire which is amongst us is of himself so strong in person as twenty men [...] he is devil in callous [...] he can, within limitations, appear at will when, and where, and in any of the forms that are to him; he can, within his range, direct the elements; [...] he can command all the meaner things: [...] the bat – the moth [...] and the wolf.[21]

---

17   Bruno Bettelheim, *The Uses of Enchantment* (New York: Vintage Books, 1976), 356.
18   *Ibid.*, 418.
19   Freud, *A General Introduction to Psychoanalysis*, 140.
20   "He can transform himself to wolf [...]. He can be as bat" (Bram Stoker, *Dracula* [1897] [Ware: Wordsworth Classics, 1993], 214).
21   *Ibid.*, 212.

Because it is also associated with the night, the moth is mentioned in *Dracula*'s bestiary. Its link with the bat refers to this episode of *The Dream of a Beast* when the narrator hears shrill cries in a grim concrete underground corridor which seems like a tomb to him. He can see a bat tracing a moth: "Their paths merged into one then, the bat's mouth opened, then closed, and the bat flew on alone" (*DB*, 151). This cruel scene brings tears to his eyes. He does not forget it when later, the bat asks him if he can fly: "I remembered the death of the moth" (*DB*, 157). The phrase echoes the short story "The Death of the Moth" by Virginia Woolf, whose surname symbolically refers to the animal too. This name, in its Germanic form – *Wolf* – is repeatedly mentioned by "Wolfman", a patient of Sigmund Freud's, who was traumatized because he had witnessed a "primal scene" – his parents having sex "from behind" or "doggy style" – at a very young age. Like him, will Matilde have a phobia about wolves all her life?

The death of the moth, together with the mentions of the wolf or the bat[22] also refer to the epigraph of *The Dream of a Beast,* an excerpt from Blake's poem already conjured up here:

Kill not the moth nor butterfly

For the Last Judgment draweth nigh.

This quotation, an invitation not to damage what is fragile for fear of being cursed, is particularly significant when it is connected with the theme of incest. The very title of the poem, "Auguries of Innocence", is also relevant in this regard. By the same token, Virginia Woolf's story whose plot amounts to the incapacity of "an insignificant little moth [...] with his frail and diminutive body" to fight "against a power of such magnitude"[23] – that is death – is symbolically meaningful in the context of an incestuous relationship between father and daughter.

---

22   "Every wolf's and lion's howl / Raises from hell a human soul. / The bat that flits at close of eve / Has left the brain that won't believe".

23   Virginia Woolf, *The Death of the Moth and Other Essays* [1942] (Boston, MA: Mariner Books, 1974), 88.

Matilde disturbs the beast with two backs made by her parents and gives a scream which is superimposed on theirs. She is dreaming of her father[24] who, in his turn, introduces her into the world of his dream. All of these details are associated with old taboos. They create an impression of strangeness and transgression. Borders are crossed on many occasions insofar as the narrator is thrown out of his working place, expelled from his home and even excluded from humankind. His dream establishes a corrupt world of vice and sex where there are no limits or safeguards. Ambrose is a silent character who plays a major part there. He could be the narrator's dark side, his evil counterpart, the personification of his incestuous instinct which attracts him to Matilde. It is worth noting that the names of these fictional characters are not chosen by chance: they refer to the protagonists of a famous Gothic novel, *The Monk*, by Matthew Gregory Lewis.

In this sensational story of temptation and depravity, the respected monk Ambrosio is overwhelmed with desire for Matilda. Once having abandoned his monastic vows, he begins a terrible descent into immorality, violence and horror. His appalling fall embraces blasphemy, torture, incest, rape and murder. At the end of the novel, Ambrosio is brought before the Inquisition, imprisoned and sentenced to death. Lucifer appears in his cell without any deceptive appearances: "Over his huge shoulders waved two enormous sable wings".[25] With these wings, Lucifer carries Ambrosio into the sky and drops him onto the rocks of the wilderness where he dies alone, damned for eternity. Like Lucifer, the bat is the enemy of light. Its specificities can be applied to the demon himself. They are confirmed by Freud when he deals with a patient suffering from "demonological neurosis",[26] and also characterize Dracula whose name means "son of the dragon" or "son of the devil".

***

24 "I was dreaming of you, she murmured" (Jordan, *The Dream of a Beast*, 94).
25 Matthew Gregory Lewis, *The Monk* [1796] (Harmondsworth: Penguin Classics, 1998), 295.
26 Sigmund Freud, "A Seventeenth-Century Demonological Neurosis" in *The 'Wolfman' and Other Cases* (Harmondsworth: Penguin, 2002), 287.

Introduced to the joys of flying by a bat, the monstrous narrator passes his know-how on to a boy who is kind enough to feed him:

> He told me of Jack, who had planted a stalk that made a ladder to the skies, of how the story never told him what Jack found there. I would dearly love to fly, he said, turning his face to me. We will wait till evening, I told him. (*DB*, 167)

Like Daedalus and Icarus, the beast and the young man fly around together, but the flight is fatal, as in the myth. Nevertheless, the boy is bound to live on in his "father" in this case: "The boy was dying. I wrapped myself fully round him, assumed him into myself" (*DB*, 173). Such a gesture is ingestion, incorporation of the other, as the following episode confirms:

> I came to a pool [...] I saw a reflection there, no less terrible than mine. A hand rubbed white sand away from a mouth. It was like mine in its shape and texture [...] I raised my head and the boy inside me leapt [...] I recognized Marianne. (*DB*, 173)

There are some who may see here a grotesque parody of the Visitation, this scene of the gospel when Mary visits her cousin Elizabeth, who is expecting a child, John the Baptist: "And when Elizabeth heard Mary's greeting, the baby stirred in her womb".[27] The Scriptures are undermined by mock-heroic debasement here since the meeting of the immaculate Virgin with a holy prophet's mother is replaced by the confrontation of two monstrous creatures. And the narrative goes on:

> Matilde, [Marianne] told me, was inside her now. I put my arms down to her waist and felt her. The boy kicked with pleasure at the touch.
>
> Once a large beast flew above us and her hand gripped mine. (*DB*, 173-174)

The beast flies away, together with the fantasies of the dream. The couple becomes human again. Darkness is disappearing to give way to "an eternity of light" (*DB*, 174). The long languorous kiss that Marianne gives her husband, heralded by the one she previously exchanged with Ambrose, helps him come out of the dream and wakes him up. Still half asleep, the

---

27   Luke 1:41.

narrator regains consciousness, reincorporates his male body and contemplates the possibility of a sexual relationship with the woman who is lying next to him, that is without breaking any taboos. As for his daughter, she can transfer the oedipal love she felt for her father onto a male partner whose "beanstalk" allows him to climb up to the gates of heaven.[28]

***

The fairy-tale universe is well and truly present in *The Dream of a Beast*. There are many allusions to its characters. When Neil Jordan wrote his novella, the fairy tale as a genre was the object of a renewed interest in the anglophone cultural sphere, particularly in the wake of the publication of Bruno Bettelheim's *The Uses of Enchantment* (1976). For example, the British writer Angela Carter translated Perrault's tales into English, then published a revised version of them, *The Bloody Chamber and Other Stories* (1979), "to extract the latent content from the traditional stories",[29] as she put it. Her collection of short fiction is both original and innovative. On the one hand, most of her stories are narrated by teenage girls; on the other, they target an adult readership. They are subversive and obviously take a meaning which is very different from the original tales that inspired them. Carter's stories deal with the corrupting aspect of marriage, but also with women's relationships with men. They openly refer to sex. One of the ten stories of the collection, "The Company of Wolves", was adapted by the writer into a radio play which was broadcast on BBC Radio 3 in 1980. This adaptation highlighted the oral, popular heritage of the genre. As the revision of the tales is focused on their textual dimension, in accordance with the project of the author whose stories challenge the way women are represented in the traditional tales of the past, the radio makes it possible to value the art of telling and establish a magical world.

Angela Carter and Neil Jordan met in 1982 at a writers' festival in Dublin marking the centenary of James Joyce's birth. Jordan felt "The

---

28   The tale to which the boy refers is indeed "Jack and the Beanstalk".

29   John Haffenden, "Angela Carter" in *Novelists in Interview* (New York: Methuen Press, 1985), 80.

Company of Wolves" had the potential to become a full-length feature. They discussed producing a film adaptation and decided to write the screenplay together. Jordan's second film, *The Company of Wolves,* is therefore essentially inspired by Carter's anthology, but also by his own text that he had just finished, *The Dream of a Beast.*[30]

Straightaway, the audience of the film is introduced into a dream world: an estate wagon is speeding down country roads carrying an English couple home. In front of their big house, they emerge from the car to greet their eldest daughter, Alice. She informs them that her sister, Rosaleen, is locked in her room. The latter – a teenage girl – claims her stomach hurts but, according to Alice, she must be sulking. As a matter of fact, Rosaleen is asleep in her bed. She wears red glistening lipstick, rouge on her cheeks. She is no longer an "innocent child", but is obviously discovering the adult world of desire and eroticism. Her sleep is restless. The camera gets closer to her face and lets the audience enter her dream: in a distorted forest, Rosaleen looks disorientated, dressed in a hooded coat, the scarlet colour of which symbolizes her indisposed state:

> She has just started her woman's bleeding, the clock inside her that will strike, henceforward, once a month. [...]. Her breasts have just begun to swell [...]. She stands and moves within the invisible pentacle of her own virginity. She is an unbroken egg; she is a sealed vessel; she has inside her a magic space the entrance to which is shut tight with a plug of membrane; she is a closed system; she does not know how to shiver. She has her knife and she is afraid of nothing.[31]

The brave girl walks across the woods to her grandmother's house. She meets a handsome hunter who makes a deal with her: whoever can get to the house first wins, and if the hunter wins she owes him a kiss. The narrative specifies that "gleaming trails of spittle clung to his teeth".[32] The girl is determined to let the hunter win because she wants to kiss him. Once

---

30   "I drew a lot of images from my novel *The Dream of a Beast*, which I'd just finished" (Zucker, ed., *Neil Jordan. Interviews* [Jackson: University Press of Mississippi, 2013], 47).

31   Angela Carter, "The Company of Wolves", in *The Bloody Chamber and Other Stories* [1979] (London: Vintage Classics, 1995), 64.

32   *Ibid.,* 66.

arrived at his destination, the man tricks the old lady to let him in and gives vent to his savagery:

> He strips off his shirt. His skin is the colour and texture of vellum. A crisp stripe of hair runs down his belly, his nipples are ripe and dark as poison fruit but he's so thin you could count the ribs under his skin if only he gave you the time. He strips off his trousers and she can see how hairy his legs are. His genitals, huge. Ah! huge.
>
> The last thing the old lady saw in all this world was a young man, eyes like cinders, naked as a stone, approaching her bed.
>
> The wolf is carnivore incarnate.
>
> When he had finished with her, he licked his chops and quickly dressed himself again, until he was just as he had been when he came through her door.[33]

In the film, this scene is an opportunity for bold experimentations: the werewolf's tongue unrolls in an impressive way; his golden eyes fix the grandmother with a piercing, threatening look; his face exhibits a monstrous creature. He grabs the red-hot end of the poker, screams in pain and uses brute force to behead the old lady with the back of his hand.

A few moments later, the girl comes in, surprised to note that her grandmother is not in the house. The strange visitor confirms: "There's nobody here but we two, my darling".[34] When a pack of wolves howl around the place, he says:

> "Those are the voices of my brothers, darling; I love the company of wolves". [...].
>
> "It is very cold, poor things", she said; "no wonder they howl so". [...] Since her fear did her no good, she ceased to be afraid.[35]

She proceeds to seduce her guest, strips off her clothes, throws them into the fire, then, "dazzling and naked", joins the man in bed:

33   *Ibid.*, 68.
34   *Ibid.*, 69.
35   *Ibid.*, 69-70.

"What big arms you have."

"All the better to hug you with." […].

"What big teeth you have!"

"All the better to eat you with."

The girl burst out laughing; she knew she was nobody's meat. She laughed at him full in the face, she ripped off his shirt for him and flung it into the fire, in the fiery wake of her own discarded clothing. […].

Carnivore incarnate, only immaculate flesh appeases him.[36]

The repetition of this phrase – "carnivore incarnate" – already used in a previous quote, insists on the taste of these beings who prove to be voracious when they are confronted with young flesh, either because they feed on raw meat or because they strive to satisfy their physical needs through fornication. The girl laughs at the man who treats her like a piece of meat to let him know that *she* can also consider him as a means of enjoying the pleasures of the flesh. *She* can also become the seductress and take control of the situation. Indeed, she proves to be able to defend herself, level the rifle and shoot at the visitor who, howling with pain, is metamorphosed in front of her with spectacular special effects: a thick fur covers the man's body; his skin cracks to give birth to a strong beast whose jaw stretches in a sharp muzzle. When she is bitten, Rosaleen recoils; she gives a grimace of pain. Obviously, she is no longer "an unbroken egg" or "a sealed vessel". On the screen, the change can only be suggested: a white rose becomes soaked with blood.

First initiated to the thrills of sensuality, the girl discovers the exciting joys of sex. She does not intend to become a wife or a mother, and thus clearly distinguishes herself from the heroines of traditional fairy tales. In the wake of a savage marriage ceremony, she has now all that she could wish for, and "sleeps in granny's bed, between the paws of the tender wolf".[37]

36   *Ibid.*, 70-71.
37   *Ibid.*, 71.

In Carter's stories, females are triumphant, not only because they seize the males' traditional weapons, but also because they are bold enough to become their lovers' equals, and no longer their terrified victims.

In the original tale, the girl is afraid of the wolf; on the contrary, she finds him very attractive in its postmodern variants such as *The Company of Wolves* or *The Dream of a Beast*. In Jordan's text, when the little girl who interrupted a moment's pleasure is put back to bed by her father, she mentions bits of her dream that the narrator does not report.[38] Just before, she said she dreamt about him.[39] Back to his own room, the father realizes that his daughter is experiencing an unconscious feeling of desire for him. It can lead her to give in to the manoeuvres of a dangerous seducer, ready to "wolf" her down… The essential theme of "Little Red Riding Hood" is finally taken up by the dream of the narrator whose transformation makes him a typical representation of the male in its most instinctive nature.

Indeed, in *The Dream of a Beast*, the man, the father and the wolf are one. The lycanthrope exemplifies the different components of the male being who can show violent, destructive tendencies, but also adopt an empathic, protective behaviour. Bettelheim emphasizes a significant element about "Little Red Riding Hood":

> All through the tale, no father is mentioned, which is most unusual for a fairy story of this kind. This suggests that the father is present, but in hidden form. The girl certainly expects her father to rescue her from all difficulties, and particularly those emotional ones which are the consequence of her wish to seduce him and to be seduced by him. What is meant here by "seduction" is the girl's desire and efforts to induce her father to love her more than anybody else, and her wish that he should make all efforts to induce her to love him more than anybody else. Then we may see that the father is indeed present in "Little Red Cap" in two opposite forms: as the wolf, which is an externalization of the dangers of overwhelming oedipal feelings, and as the hunter in his protective and rescuing function.[40]

---

38   "Matilde whispered parts of her dream to me as I carried her to bed" (Jordan, *The Dream of a Beast*, 97).

39   "I was dreaming of you, she murmured" (*Ibid.*, 94).

40   Bettelheim, *The Uses of Enchantment*, 221.

These two parts are played by the protagonist of Jordan's story: he is a sensible, reasonable, protective father, but also a coarse and bestial lover. Like Jekyll-Hyde, the fictional character created by Stevenson one century earlier, he experiences inner struggle between good and evil, human and animal. The honourable English doctor can repress his baser instincts which make him have a debauched life by devoting his time to scientific research; but the duality of his nature leads him to make a drug which gives free rein to his profound antithetic personality. After drinking his beverage, he becomes a grotesque creature who is able to fulfil his most dubious desires. Progressively, the respectable citizen is replaced by his demonic double. In the end, he is a prisoner of the other's body and cannot be his old self again. Like *The Strange Case of Dr Jekyll and Mr Hyde*, *The Dream of a Beast* is focused on division, paradox and ambivalence which rule over human beings. Such a specificity is referred to by the lycanthrope when he answers Rosaleen who does not know if she should consider him as a man or a wolf:

> Are you our kind, or their kind?
>
> - Not one kind or the other. Both.
> - Then where do you live? In our world, or in theirs?
> - I come and go between them. My home is nowhere.

It all depends on whether sexual instinct is at work or not.

As young Matilde's bedroom is protected from any intrusion, Rosaleen's room is on the contrary invaded by an entire company of wolves. One after another, the beasts crash through the glass panes into the place. Toys and fragments of glass cascade onto the floor and shatter. This wild penetration destroys the world of childhood. It mirrors the liberation of the girl's repressed fantasies. Rosaleen herself is ultimately transformed into an animal, which implies that she is sexually prepared to accept her desires and live as she wants to live.

***

In his *Morphology of the Tale*, Vladimir Propp shows that there are basic structural elements that typically occur within fairy tales. These "functions" can be classified in a specific order in each story. For example, an initial peaceful situation is troubled by a magical trickery, which is solved by deliverance and final repair.[41] This specificity shows the close connection between the tale and the dream. Both of them gather extraordinary events. *The Dream of a Beast* is a hybrid text which, in Jordan's literary career, links up the collection of short stories that was published before and the novels that follow it. It relates an initially realistic situation – an ordinary Irishman's personal experience – which is imperceptibly drifting to the fantastic. The transition between the real and the unreal is blurred, the two worlds are mixed up by fiction in a large, undifferentiated space. The reference to "the beast with two backs" in the narrator's sleepy mind makes him slip into a dream in which he himself becomes a beast. The metamorphosis, characteristic of the fairy-tale universe, shows the man's fundamental difficulties, existential dilemmas and anxieties. *The Dream of a Beast* asserts that the sexual act depends on animal nature, that it can mean an attack, cause fear and arouse devouring fantasies in the depths of his being. Like the satanic Beast of the Apocalypse, described in the thirteenth chapter of the last book of the Bible, the characters of *The Dream of a Beast* are associated with number 13 insofar as their names start with the thirteenth letter of the alphabet, whether it is the narrator's wife, Marianne, his daughter Matilde or his colleague Morgan. This is a bad sign, a counterpoint to Blake's poem quoted as an epigraph, "Auguries of Innocence". The story contrasts with the virtue exhibited in the title of the poem. It can only explore the darkest areas of the human soul and is thus part of the heritage of traditional fairy tales. *The Dream of a Beast* is a turning-point in Neil Jordan's literary work. The latter's interest in fairy tales, confirmed by his friendship with Angela Carter and their collaboration for *The Company of Wolves* extended his sphere of activity and opened new perspectives. From then on, his work is based on founding texts, such as fairy tales, but also *The Metamorphosis* or *Dracula* in order to create his own floating, dreamlike, mysterious world where man's profound preoccupations are not ignored, where the reader meets with fragile, hesitant, tormented characters, full of contradictions,

41 Vladimir Propp, *Morphology of the Folktale* [1928] (Austin: University of Texas Press, 1968), 35 ff.

uncertainties and sufferings... This is the work of an artist who knows that "nothing is obvious, univocal and absolutely simple: man, like God, is *absconditus*, body and soul, beast and angel, a middle way between two infinites, equally distant from the alpha and omega, because everything is in-between".[42]

42 « Rien n'est évident, univoque et absolument simple : l'homme, comme Dieu, est *absconditus,* à la fois âme et corps, ange et bête, moyen entre deux infinis, également éloigné de l'alpha et de l'oméga. Car tout est entre les deux » (Jankélévitch, *L'Ironie,* 117). My translation.

The Fictitious Fulfilment of Oedipal Desires: *Sunrise with Sea Monster*

Ut pictura poesis: "a poem is like a painting", according to Horace, because "the mind is less keenly struck by what the author confides to the ear than by what he puts under his eye".[1] The theorists of the Italian Renaissance took up this formula, but reversed its meaning. With them, the referent is no longer the image, but the language: a painting is like a poem. It tells a story. Literary and pictorial arts have always engaged in a fruitful collaboration, a fertile dialogue. It indicates something of the creative dynamism and intense degree of cross-fertilization there is between these two artistic disciplines.

Neil Jordan's novel is entitled *Sunrise with Sea Monster* in England, but it was published in the United States as *Nightlines*. The American title, as interesting as it may be,[2] does not take into account the union of literary and pictorial arts. Indeed, *Sunrise with Sea Monsters* is a painting by William Turner (1845), exhibited at the Tate Gallery in London. A bright yellow – a colour that fascinated Turner throughout his life – dominates on this canvas. The painter used it in particular for his skies, as in the present case. *Sunrise with Sea Monsters* shows two fish in pink hues, with a piece of net and a red and white float. Fishing was one of Turner's favourite pastimes. It allowed him to take advantage of the particular lights of the English coasts. Moreover, the painter excelled in this activity. One of his colleagues, George Jones, testifies: "He would show me all the fish he caught and ask me if they were big enough to eat or if he should throw

---

1   Horace, *Epistles. Book II and Epistle to the Pisones ('Ars Poetica')* (Cambridge: Cambridge University Press, 1989), 72.

2   It is worth noting that John McGahern's first collection of short stories is also entitled *Nightlines* (1970).

them back into the water".[3] Several of Turner's paintings and watercolours attest to this passion: *Trout fishing in the Dee, Sunset at Sea with Gurnets, Fishermen at Sea* or *Sunrise with Sea Monsters.*

The descriptive, elaborate titles of Turner's work often specify the time of day. They fix an ephemeral duration, a luminous event, such as sunrise or sunset. They also reveal a detail that is difficult to read, because many of the artist's paintings, including the one that interests us here, blur the viewer's gaze. This option for confusion and imprecision is claimed by the painter himself. In doing so, Turner refers to the aesthetic theories of the eighteenth century, which assign an expressive emotional power to illegibility. Many images are sublime precisely because they are indecipherable. This characteristic is heightened by the painting's dazzling explosion of light, a luminous phenomenon to which Turner paid extreme attention. He introduced a radical change in the depiction of the sun. His compositions eliminate all the mediations that previously kept observers at a distance. The latter are not protected from the radiance anymore. Turner's paintings aim to show this dazzle and produce a realistic effect, the viewer's vision being subjugated by sunlight.

Neil Jordan uses the title of Turner's painting, because he is accustomed to shooting through the eye of a camera, and places an essential importance on visual aspect. This is characteristic of his literary fiction. The final episode of the novel where "the night's blanket of peaceful blue" gives way to "a veil of soft rose light across the empty sands", upon which the protagonist discovers, "outsize and majestic, a hooked creature from some lower depths, shuddering occasionally in the morning breeze",[4] seems to extend Turner's pictorial scene in words. It makes Jordan "a painter in poetry",[5] a colourist capable of harmonizing a range of tones that reinforce the way his story is offered to the eyes of his readers in order to make them spectators.

---

3   Anthony Bailey, *Standing in the Sun: A Life of J.M.W. Turner* (London: Pimlico, 1998), 86.

4   Neil Jordan, *Sunrise with Sea Monster* (London: Vintage, 1996), 173.

5   In his critical essay "Salon of 1846", Baudelaire sees in Victor Hugo "a painter in poetry" (« un peintre en poésie ») and in Eugène Delacroix "a poet in painting" (« un poète en peinture ») (Charles Baudelaire, *Œuvres complètes* [Paris : Gallimard, Bibliothèque de la Pléiade, 1976], 673).

However, Jordan's choice to use a pre-existing title is ambiguous: the presence of another work in his own makes it impossible to say precisely to which it refers. It probably refers to both. Thus, the reader, whose curiosity is heightened by this borrowing, is invited to grasp an interpretative key and to see to what extent the text justifies the title. As a rule, quotation titles refer to previous literary works. In this case, however, Neil Jordan borrows the title of his novel from an artistic work outside the field of literature. This option reflects the transversal, even transgressive aspect of his artistic production, which is not limited to a specific domain. A quotation title has a strong connotative value. It is an index of culture which, like an epigraph, brings to the text the indirect guarantee of another work, but also the prestige of spiritual heritage. Among the whole range of the artists of the past, Neil Jordan chooses a father figure who does not overshadow him, since both of them do not operate in the same discipline. Moreover, he shares with him a certain number of common points, in particular an interest in fishing scenes and in the different lights on the shore. By borrowing his title from Turner, Jordan articulates his novelistic production on visual arts in which he is also involved. Moreover, as he is free to choose his "fathers", he gives himself "the consecration and anointing of a prestigious filiation".[6] This theme of filiation pervades the novel: it can be seen in the spiritual influence exerted by Turner over Jordan, but also in the ambivalent relationship that links the young narrator to his father.

It is worth noting, however, that the title of Jordan's novel is not absolutely identical to that of Turner's painting. There is no literal reproduction. As such, it can be considered as parody, which is defined by Linda Hutcheon as "a form of imitation characterized by repetition with critical distance, which marks difference rather than similarity".[7] The title of the novel is slightly different from the title of the painting in its semantic orientation. *Sunrise with Sea Monsters* becomes *Sunrise with Sea Monster*: the last word, in the plural in the painting's title, referring to the sharp-toothed fish depicted on the canvas, is taken up in the singular in the novel's title to

---

6   Genette Gerard, *Paratexts: Thresholds of Interpretation* (Cambridge: Cambridge University Press, 1997), 160.

7   Linda Hutcheon, *A Theory of Parody. The Teachings of Twentieth-Century Art Forms* (Chicago: University of Illinois Press, 1985), introduction, 6.

describe "this outlandish shape" (*SSM*, 174), which refers not only to the monstrous sea creature washed up on the beach, but also to the narrator's father, who, after his disappearance, comes back to haunt the filial psyche in a dreamlike scene: "I'd fished him from the sea somehow, dragged him from one element to the other with an invisible line" (*SSM*, 174). In the novel, the sea monster is none other than a metaphor for the father. Moreover, the description of the monster on the beach, with "eyes bulging and distended, tulip-mouthed, on its forehead a curved and perfect horn" (*SSM*, 173) echoes an earlier passage in the story where the narrator describes his father as "a large horned monster" (*SSM*, 54). The father is portrayed as a frightening, fantastic animal, like a unicorn or a chimera. This specificity testifies to the undeniable subjectivity of the narrative, which is taken over by the son and him alone. The way in which the latter describes his father is significant: in Bruno Bettelheim's words, when the boy feels threatened by his father, he feels hostile, wants to replace him in the mother's heart, and "projects the father into the role of the fearsome monster".[8] The narrator's words thus reveal a singular psychic structure, namely the fulfilment of an oedipal desire.

***

Donal Gore, the narrator of *Sunrise with Sea Monster*, is inside the narrative and recounts the story in the first person. His presence cannot be overlooked. He is the focal character of the plot. Events are subjectively reported by himself. Since his point of view is relatively constant, the story can be considered as adopting a narrative system of fixed internal focus. It absorbs his own restrictions, ignorance and prejudices, and mostly relates the fundamental opposition between his father and himself. Such a Manichean perspective determines the structure of the novel and reflects a confrontation between two generations, with their conflicting interests and different worldviews.

It is very significant that Donal Gore insists on highlighting what makes him different from his father, Samuel, even as far as physiognomy

---

8   Bruno Bettelheim, *The Uses of Enchantment. The Meaning and Importance of Fairy Tales* (New York: A. A. Knopf, 1976), 177.

is concerned: the father has blue eyes, grey hair, a pale creamy complexion, whereas the son has brown eyes, dark hair and olive skin (*SSM*, 11, 37). This claimed dissimilarity also applies to their psychology, their political ideas or sexual practices.[9] Thus, father and son, reduced to silhouettes or even caricatures, obviously constitute two antithetical categories. Each of them seems to exist as a "negative" of the other.

This dual relationship is amplified by the fact that Donal is an only child; moreover, he is motherless. The presence of a third person – mother, grandparent, brother or sister – would ease the tension and weaken the hostility between the two protagonists. On the contrary, the narrator's loneliness increases the close competition between himself and his father, and turns their relationship into a duel, since a murderous desire is expressed. This reaction is linked to the mother who is doubly lost for the son: not only on the incestuous oedipal level, but also because of her death. Nevertheless, the place left vacant by her is about to be occupied by another woman. Because he makes his father responsible for this loss and interprets this new family configuration as a betrayal, the protagonist manifests a parricidal desire that is part of a dynamic of rupture and emancipation. This is the reason why he joins the Irish volunteers on the side of the Republicans during the Spanish Civil War.

***

The narrative of *Sunrise with Sea Monster* follows an initiatory pattern. At the beginning of the story, Donal is awaiting his execution in a Spanish jail. This is the opportunity for him to look back at his past, his family roots, childhood and adolescence. This trip abroad provides a field of experimentation during which he changes, acquires maturity and experiences a rebirth, which allows him to return to the starting point. Indeed, on the orders of the Irish government, Donal is released by Hans, a German officer who organizes his repatriation. In exchange for his release, he agrees to become a mediator between the Nazi regime and the radical wing of the IRA. Upon his return, convinced that he is acting as

---

9   Sexuality is practised within the exclusive institutional framework of marriage for the father and in a much freer and more relaxed way for the son.

a double agent, he informs the Irish authorities of this arrangement and agrees to give them regular reports. In return, his protection is assured by the team of Soames, a close associate of the head of government.

Donal Gore is actually nothing but a liar, a snitch and a traitor. He is an anti-hero. What's more, his return to his country excludes him from heroic paths since, as Marthe Robert points out, only "the exile who knows no return is promised for that very reason to the highest destinies".[10] Unlike the traditional hero who breaks definitively with his native environment to become a man without family or ties and to accomplish exploits in distant lands, the protagonist in this case is only temporarily exiled to finally return to Ireland and, moreover, to his father's house. This return to the father is not, however, a return to the chains, for the protagonist has matured somewhat during this absence. He has been able to settle his accounts with his father by an introspective work that leads to the desire to see him again. Indeed, the young man has changed, even if the setting he finds remains the same:

> I get off the boat in Dun Laoghaire and try not to feel familiar which is difficult, seeing nothing has changed. The buses are the same green, smoke hangs in the air like a cloud of its own, the train that takes me out to Bray chugs with the same old languor. I tell myself that I have changed and all else hasn't, but even that isn't true. The old self folds round me like a comforting cloak. I want to see him, the old devil, I realise. (*SSM*, 79)

To tell his story, the narrator lets his memories emerge. The movement of return is not only traceable in space, but also in time, which is confirmed by John Wilson Foster's statement that "the fiction writer's preoccupation with place is a preoccupation with the past without which Irish selfhood is apparently inconceivable".[11]

10   « L'exilé qui ne connaît pas de retour est promis pour cela même aux plus hautes destinées » (Marthe Robert, *Roman des origines et origines du roman* [Paris: Grasset, 1972], 89).

11   John Wilson Foster, "The Geography of Irish Fiction", in *Colonial Consequences: Essays in Irish Literature and Culture* (Dublin: The Lilliput Press, 1991), 142.

In *Sunrise with Sea Monster*, the period between the time of the narrative and the time of the story told is about thirty years, from 1915 to 1945, the date of Hitler's death mentioned at the end of the story. Without being really determined, the narration takes place after the story. This is the condition of the emergence of memory, and return to the past.

The retrospective narrative – in the past tense – is an analepsis which is alternately connected to the main narrative – in the present. This free alternation of the past and the present is based on a regular order, as if this parallel established causal relations between diegetic periods, the present being explained by the past.

Published in 1994, the novel was written by a 44-year-old writer. The diegetic period chosen by Jordan corresponds, roughly speaking, to the youth of his father, or even grandfather. How can such a choice be interpreted? Does it correspond to the narrator or author's fascination with the past? To their difficulty to dissociate from it? Does it reflect a desire to better understand his father, to identify with him by immersing himself in his life, by imagining his environment, his relationship with his own father? Or is the choice of this period merely justified by its historical richness? Indeed, the global and national events of the time are sources of particular interest to Neil Jordan, whether it be the First World War, the 1916 Dublin insurrection, the Irish War of Independence and Civil War, the Spanish War or the Second World War. In any case, the son's assumption of the narrative gives form and meaning to the father's path. Thus, in his novel, Jordan opts for a double return to the past since, in addition to the diegetic scope that extends over three decades establishing a temporal distance between the beginning of the story and the time of the narrative, another significant temporal distance also separates the time of the narrative from the time of Jordan's writing.

"I remember my father" (*SSM*, 2), begins Donal Gore, evoking the fishing scenes shared with him: "we would lay nightlines, in our rare moments of tranquillity, on the beach below the terrace where our house was" (*SSM*, 2). This activity is indicative of a dive into the deep waters of the past. In the psychoanalytic sense of the term, to fish is to proceed to a kind of anamnesis, to extract elements from the unconscious, not by a directive and rational exploration, but by letting spontaneous forces play and gathering their fortuitous results. The unconscious is a vast, dark ocean where riches are hidden that anamnesis and analysis bring to the surface, as fishermen catch fish into their nets. Moreover, symbolically, water "is what binds; it is the source of being [...] the communion of the saints".[12] It facilitates the memory process of the narrator who, like the aquatic mirror, generates a double image, a splitting, in this case between the past and the present. According to Bachelard, water causes an emergence of the past: "It seems well that one attributes a double sight to the quiet water because it shows us a double of our person [...]. So much fragility and so much delicacy, so much unreality push Narcissus out of the present".[13]

In the main narrative, the idleness of the incarcerated protagonist, anguished by his announced death, leads him to a work of memory reconstruction:

So we stand there, tough, resilient and apparently bored.

I remember my father. (*SSM*, 2)

The blank space which can be identified in the textual typology between these two sentences, is the sign of an ellipsis, a change from one narrative to another. Gérard Genette considers ellipsis as one of the four component parts of narrative rhythm. Jumping forwards or backwards, which are the classical processes of prolepsis and analepsis, are useful devices for a writer when playing with the time scheme of the story. Similarly, a few pages down, the analeptic narrative is interrupted again and the first narrative takes up where it left off, with the help of a deictic adverb establishing the present time, as if nothing had suspended it:

---

12   « L'eau est ce qui lie, c'est la source de l'être [...], c'est la communion des saints » (Jean Rousset, *Forme et signification* [Paris : José Corti, 1962], 186).

13   « Il semble bien qu'on attribue une double vue à l'eau tranquille parce qu'elle nous montre un double de notre personne [...]. Tant de fragilité et tant de délicatesse, tant d'irréalité poussent Narcisse hors du présent » (Gaston Bachelard, *L'Eau et les rêves* [Paris : José Corti, 1942], 34-35).

> The wind blew from the Head, my uncles strained to accommodate my father's height and only when we were seated inside, next to my tall, dark-suited father (...) did it strike me how fully gone she was.
>
> Now that the sun has whatever meridian it needs ... (*SSM*, 23)

It is worth noting that the father, either a young man or an old man, is always there to operate the junction between the two narratives. He is mentioned at all strategic points, from the first to the last sentence. His ubiquity in the text is indicative of his invasion of the filial imaginary and his immense power.

***

This power is often imposed by significant metonymies. As they are returning from the beach where they have set fishing lines, the narrator focuses on his father's feet, which seem insensitive to what they are treading on and whose characteristics make them superior to his own, as the comparatives attest: "We would walk back along the ribbed sand, my feet splayed to save them discomfort, his firm, set flat across the scallops, bigger, harder, infinitely older. Shoes in one hand, shovel in the other" (*SSM*, 3).

In the same way, when the father has a tense exchange with his son about remarriage, his gesture reveals a hold that escapes him:

> Hands gripping the green baize card-table, the veins already bulging blue with the signs of age, eyes all avoidance. I am marrying, he told me, because it will be the best thing for all of us. How? Father, I asked him. Don't gall me, he said, you know how [...]. This place hasn't been a home for fourteen years. And have you informed the lady? I asked him and his hands shook, as if at an insult. (*SSM*, 14-15)

The father's hands seize the first object they can reach to avoid grabbing the neck of the insolent son and strangling him. The magnifying effect on certain parts of the father's body, such as the foot or the hand, focuses the narrative lens in a very visual way on symbols of power. In this respect, it is revealing that such metaphors and metonymies multiply once the father's wedding is evoked. Indeed, it seems that Rose's arrival, by imposing a triangular structure on the household, reactivates oedipal feelings in the young man. This new "family" leads Donal to realize his unconditional love for his mother and feel jealousy and betrayal towards his father. Doesn't he refer to him as his rival when he himself has an affair with the woman who is bound to become his stepmother?

The reactivation of past events is explained by a desire to resolve a crisis, to get rid of painful memories. There is something cathartic about his speech when Donal denounces the instrument of censorship that oppresses him: "I pointed out [...] a kestrel flying by with a mole in its claws. Do you remember, I asked him, you did the same for me?" (*SSM*, 122) The story stigmatizes the paternal authoritarianism that generates an undeniable anguish, a castration complex, a permanent feeling of insecurity in the son who locks himself in stubborn mutism. Facing his father, Donal shows silent resistance. His attitude is part of a Joycean heritage and makes him similar to Stephen Dedalus, the protagonist of *The Portrait of the Artist*, who confesses:

> I will try to express myself in some mode of life or art as freely as I can and as wholly as I can, using for my defense the only arms I allow myself to use – silence, exile, and cunning.[14]

Like Joyce's protagonist, Donal remains silent when he is asked to reinforce his father's determination to marry Rose, a woman much younger than him:

> I need your support, he said. Just tell me I'm right.
>
> I stood there and said nothing. There was an obscenity at the heart of it I couldn't quite fathom. She is half your age, I wanted to say. Don't ask me to make your mind up for you, and I remembered what he said when he put me to bed the night she died. We'll make do, he said, won't we? There was the same question there, the need for reassurance. We didn't make do, I thought. (*SSM*, 15)

This extract shows the stubbornness of the insubordinate son whose attitude suggests more than it says. Donal avoids direct expression. His words are hushed, repressed, held back. He proves to be an adept of reticence, an obstinate silence that is significant and can be more confrontational than

---

14   James Joyce, *Portrait of the Artist as a Young Man* [1904], in *The Portable James Joyce* (Harmondsworth: Penguin, 1983), 519.

an exchange of insults, especially following a dispute: "He talked and I maintained my silence. About the day, the way it went, how we should do these things more often. We should, I lied, then walked in silence with him home" (*SSM*, 49).

This passive attitude destabilizes the father and allows the son to start on the path to emancipation. It covers their relationship with an undeniable charge of hostility and extreme coldness: the silence in the house is described as "a congealed pall of the unspoken" (*SSM*, 20). The bond between the two men is devoid of any sign of intimacy, conviviality, warmth. Donal longs for freedom, for escape into a different world, hence his constant concern to choose what is most likely to displease Samuel. He volunteers to take part in the Spanish war on the side of the Republicans because he sees this initiative as one of the best ways to irritate his father, a former minister of the Free State government. The latter is not fooled: "You are leaving, he said, because you hate me, not because of any nebulous political ideas [...]. You hate me because I am simply me, your father" (*SSM*, 56-57).

Donal develops behaviours in complete opposition to him for the sole purpose of bringing to a peak his hostile feelings towards his father. Such rebellion betrays resentment, even if the adoption of ideas or attitudes contrary to those of the father still somehow constitutes a link that binds them. Moreover, the Spanish war gives Donal the opportunity to leave the country and its emblematic representative. It is an open door to the world. Here again, Donal adopts an attitude systematically contrary to that of his father's behaviour: the restricted, insular paternal environment is opposed to the broadened horizon of the narrator who, in his attraction to elsewhere, discovers another country and builds relationships with foreigners.

During this counter-identifying stage, the young protagonist isolates himself in a purely masculine universe where he lives with his fellow men, in a state of indifferentiation, sometimes giving in to homoerotic leanings. Indeed, Donal has a very ambiguous relationship with the German officer Hans who, in the context of their spying activities, gives each of them an assumed name taken from the famous film *Gone with the Wind*, thus making their relationship some kind of romance:

> [Hans] stands too close to me in the darkness, swaying slightly.
>
> 'Scarlett', he says.
>
> I ask him what he means.
>
> 'An apparent name, for your apparent function'.
>
> He walks slowly towards the bed.
>
> 'And I shall be Rhett'. (*SSM*, 75-76)

The organization of Donal's libido passes through the homoerotic experience already lived with his classmate, Mouse. Here again, this choice contributes to making him the anti-portrait of his father. Indeed, the latter is strongly attached to the traditional family values advocated by the Irish authorities of the time, and considers it unthinkable not to conform one's conduct to them.

His hostile feelings lead Donal to fear that his father will castrate him as punishment. This is manifested in the narrative by the man's ghostly presence lurking in the shadows. Like a persecuting competitor, the father haunts the son with his continuous visits:

> The piano became my way to her, till one night a shadow crossed the moonlight over the keys and I felt the hair stipple on my back. I stayed still, my hands holding the dying notes until the shadow moved to my left and I heard the cough behind me and realised it was him. (*SSM*, 24)

The father's hold is played out in its most classic form: the refusal of separation. Even when he is physically absent, the father remains a nuisance: he is always present by his formidable authority. The father, or more exactly his spectre, regularly returns to haunt the filial psyche. He pursues the son and traps him, mainly when the latter engages in sexual behaviours reprobated by the father's morality.

The nightmare is the realization of a repressed desire. If the dream is the achievement of desire, the father, by opposing the son's desire, transforms dreams into nightmares. The filial anguish, which accompanies this realization, takes the place of censorship. It indicates that the rejected desire is stronger than the ban, that it has been realized or was bound to be realized in spite of paternal condemnation. This awareness is a source of guilt

for the son whose fear opposes desire while merging with it in the unconscious. The opposites embodied by the father who accomplishes the work
of the psychic censure and reveals himself to the son as moral conscience
are mixed together. The father thwarts his son's desire, punishes the trans-
gressor and generates his anxiety.

The father's ghost is uncanny and strangely disturbing. It is presented
as one of the demonic images defined by Northrop Frye in *The Anatomy
of Criticism*: "They belong to a world that desire totally rejects: the world
of the nightmare and the scapegoat, of bondage, pain and confusion".[15]
There is something evil about this black shadow, the bearer of trouble, and
it is significant that the father is associated with a demonic figure. Indeed,
when he refers to him, the inspirer of his nightmare,[16] Donal mentions "the
old devil" (*SSM*, 79), a symptomatic term for Freud, according to whom
"the devil is a duplicate of the father and can act as a substitute for him".[17]

The devil, according to its Greek etymology – *diabolos* – is the one
who divides and disunites. Isn't the father precisely diabolic insofar as he
constitutes an obstacle to the harmonious unification of the son? Moreover,
significantly, his name – Gore – relates him by anagram to the ogre, this
voracious giant, linked by etymology to an infernal divinity who devours
children in traditional fairy tales.[18] Besides, the description of the father

15   Northrop Frye, *The Anatomy of Criticism* (Princeton: Princeton University Press,
      1957), 147.
16   Jorge Luis Borges, in one of his lectures, confirms the idea that a demon causes
      the nightmare: "The root <of the English word 'nightmare'> would be *niht mare*
      or *niht maere*, the demon of the night. Samuel Johnson, in his famous dictionary,
      says that it is question here of the Nordic mythology – we would say today of the
      Anglo-Saxon mythology – which considers that the nightmare is produced by a
      demon; what would be a replica or, undoubtedly, a translation of the Greek *efialtes*
      or the Latin *incubus*" (Jorge Luis Borges, *Conferences* [1979] [Paris: Gallimard,
      1985], 42).
17   Freud, *The Uncanny*; "A Seventeenth-Century Demonological Neurosis", 289. For
      Donal's father, "the embodiment of satanic guile" is none other than another father,
      that of the nation, namely Eamon De Valera (Jordan, *Sunrise with Sea Monster*, 35).
18   The name 'Gore' also refers to the Gore-Booth sisters, Eva and Constance. Both
      Anglo-Irish and Protestant, like the father of the narrator of *Sunrise with Sea
      Monster*, they were politically and socially committed to the people, much to the

as a hybrid creature – half-man half-beast – does not fail to recall the fairy-tale universe, as it assimilates him to the monsters of mythological legends or to the strange creatures of Turner's paintings. Mentioned right from the title, the sea monster merges with Donal's father who holds such power that his human nature is singularly blurred. Firmly established in his ministerial job, Samuel Gore earns a comfortable living, occupies a stable position of authority, and an imposing physical place not only in society, but also in his home.

While the son depicts himself – very subjectively – with human features, he characterizes his father by dehumanizing him under a form that is not only animal and monstrous, but also mineral and material: the father's body "seems more impervious than granite" (*SSM*, 84). His features, described as marbled, enhance their enigmatic aspect: "The candles gave my father's face the gaunt look of church statues" (*SSM*, 111). Seeing a statue in the father is making a tombstone of him. It may reveal an oedipal desire for his death. The image, reactivated in a repetitive mode – "my last glimpse was of him, tall, statuesque" (*SSM*, 54) – makes him a true statue of the Commander, in other words the emblem of a murdered father. The man's impressive rigidity, the prestige of his stature, the stability of his upright position characterize the father whose features are recurrently described as inhuman: "I looked at him in the back seat, his face as gaunt as the stone walls that surrounded the stone fields, his beard the same limestone grey" (*SSM*, 149). The posters of the father's face, visible throughout the city during the election campaign, end up melting and blending with the walls on which they are stuck: "his face on the posts of the promenade urinal became gradually indistinguishable from the concrete" (*SSM*, 42). This paternal characterization, emphasizing statuary and marmoreal aspects, may be linked to the father's ubiquity in the text; the man is omnipresent from the first to the last page, which makes him the cornerstone of the narrative.

It must not be overlooked that such metaphors and comparisons are identifiable in the son's discourse which, in an argumentative perspective, clearly aims to highlight the absence of humanity of the character described,

---

chagrin of their friend W. B. Yeats, who would have preferred to see them live an artistic life in their large estate of Lissadell, County Sligo.

together with an obsessive distancing between the two of them. Through the evocative power of borrowed images, they contribute to make a striking representation of the father, in accordance with the son's intention. If the father's body is compared to a concrete wall, it is to better underline his role as an obstacle to the fulfilment of desire. As Michael Kenneally points out, "fathers are often depicted as the immediate barriers to the individual's progression".[19] The narrator's father gets in the way of his child, imposes his demands and puts himself in the same position as those in charge of a dictatorial power. The latter often claim to be the "fathers of the nation" and perceive citizens as irrational children who must be educated with authoritarianism. In the midst of Spain at war, the young protagonist has before his eyes a significant setting: "Both Mussolini and Franco flap against their wooden supports in the wind, [...] painted with the same monumental rigidity" (*SSM*, 1). Symptomatically, the same metaphors apply to fathers and dictators.

***

When Donal returns to his father's house, he has acquired the male sex role and has become his own master. His host, Samuel, is also very different, reduced to a state of helplessness, confined to a wheelchair. His weakening makes him a vulnerable character, whereas the son, on the contrary, is getting stronger. In the symmetry of antipodes, the balance of power is diametrically reversed: the father now appears to be the weak link in the chain. The phallus representing authority is now reduced to a meaningless sign. This symbolic castration of the father is, moreover, nothing but an allegory of parricide. By a counter-current effect, a reversal of roles, the son, previously dominated by his father – "I could see him *standing* above me"[20] – can, in turn, seize phallic power and enjoy superiority, as attested by his vertical position, as he is standing behind his father who is miserably curled up in his wheelchair: "I *stood* for a while,

19   Michael Kenneally, ed., *Cultural Contexts and Literary Idioms in Contemporary Irish Literature*, Irish Literary Studies 31 (Totowa, NJ: Barnes & Noble Books, 1988), introduction, 5.
20   Jordan, *Sunrise with Sea Monster*, 9. My emphasis.

with my arms on his shoulders".[21] The same verb, meaning verticality –
stand – is used, but its subject has changed. Through the irony of fate, this
permutation highlights the cyclical aspect of life and the phenomenon
of retrogression, which can be seen in the old man's loss of autonomy.
Consequently, the antagonists do not erase their differences, but only
swap their places.

After having proved to be an authoritarian father throughout his life,
Samuel Gore is humiliated, struck down with paralysis which prevents him
from standing up. Deprived of his power, the patriarch's universe is severely
restricted. Like a sphinx in the process of crumbling, he can neither express
nor feed himself. His son now perceives him as an ordinary old man, close
to death: "Come on father, I think, where is that barely suppressed rage,
those perfectly chiselled sentences, those austere denials of my right to be?"
(*SSM*, 84) The public and powerful man whose portrait was plastered on
all the walls of the city is now reduced to painfully opening his mouth in
order to be fed with mashed vegetables. The symbolic paternal function is
failing, its representative degraded, ridiculed, reduced to an infantile stage.
The narrative compares him to "a great immobile child" (*SSM*, 94), which
makes him a man without consistency; he is "like an obedient doll" (*SSM*,
155), a real puppet, that is nothing more than an instrument at the mercy
of others, in this case Donal and Rose, his symbolic parents who resume
their affair as soon as the son returns home.

The parable of the lost son[22] is ironically revised here. Like the young
man in the gospel, Donal leaves for a distant country. Determined to break
all ties with his past life, he lives in precarious conditions and eventually
makes the decision to return to his father in a process of sincere repent-
ance: the prodigal son's confession "I am no longer fit to be called your
son" (v. 21) is echoed in Donal's words to his father: "I've done you wrong"
(*SSM*, 134). This return is a sign of resurrection: the one who was lost is
found again, hence the father's joy in the gospel: "Let us have a feast to cele-
brate the day" (v. 23). He runs to his son to embrace him tenderly, whereas
Donal's father does not show the slightest sign of emotion. Incapable of

21   Jordan, *Sunrise with Sea Monster*, 98. My emphasis.
22   The Gospel according to Luke (15/11-32).

rising to his feet or uttering a word, he remains absolutely cold and indifferent. The father of the gospel kills the fatted calf for his son's return. On the opposite, the mood is not so festive in the house of Donal's father and the feast remains very reasonable: "Rose stood up, put on a blue smock and began to feed him, looking truly like a housewife. I watched as she held his jaw down with one hand, fed him mashed vegetables with the other" (*SSM*, 85).

In the gospel, the son who "was dead has come back to life" (v. 32), whereas Samuel Gore, who was alive at the time of his son's departure, is almost dead when Donal returns: "I touch his face, and he still doesn't turn. The skin is cold and waxen as if he could be dead. But a dead man does not breathe" (*SSM*, 81). Here again, the scene can be read as a parodic counterpoint, "a form of imitation characterized by ironic inversion".[23]

This paternal weakening redistributes the roles. The parental couple has changed: it is now Rose and Donal who act with Samuel as if he were their child. The father is no longer in a position to intervene as an interdicting authority that blocks access to the satisfaction naturally sought. Incest is therefore no longer prohibited. Once back home, Donal has sexual relations with Rose again, although she has become his stepmother.[24] The

---

23   Hutcheon, *A Theory of Parody*, 6.

24   This situation is a source of guilt for Rose, hence Donal's ironic remark one drunken night when he quotes a poem in front of her:

"Oh Rose, thou art sick", I tell her.

- "On the contrary, I am very well", she said.
- "It was a quote, another rose".
- "I know. The invisible worm" (*SSM*, 91).

Although the text does not explicitly signal its reference, the poem here evoked is William Blake's "The Sick Rose": "O rose, thou art sick! / The invisible worm / That flies in the night, / In the howling storm, / Has found out thy bed / Of crimson joy, / And his dark secret love / Does thy life destroy". To this 'evil' from which the flower of the poem suffers answers Rose's guilt relative to the affair she has with Donal, a deep and secret love, a reflection of the penultimate line: "dark secret love". Through this intertextual link, the poet's reputation as a visionary and prophet is confirmed insofar as his verses perfectly illustrate Rose's destiny.

young protagonist can act freely, "just as if" he were his father. Doesn't he take his place when he goes to bed with his father's second wife? "The son, writes Freud, seeks to replace the father in all respects; he therefore seeks to replace him in his desires, to desire what he desires".[25] As René Girard states, this desire is "essentially mimetic, because it models itself on a model desire; it elects the same object as this model".[26] In this case, it is an "incest of the second type",[27] that is to say copulation of related persons with a third party, father and son sharing the same partner, which is truly emblematic of the father-son mirror, as an object desired by both. The son has indeed become the mirror of his father, that is to say a man. If he returns home, it is precisely to let his old man know that they are now on an equal footing, that identification is effective, that he is "like him" and thus has access to the mother.

Donal's desire for Rose is primarily a desire to recreate the symbiotic unity with his own lost mother, as he himself acknowledges: "I wished to reinvent the mother I had lost perhaps" (*SSM*, 30). His attraction for the woman superimposes two objects: the body of his mother and that of his stepmother. Both stand for perfection, as evidenced by their flawless quality: Rose's "sweet presence" (*SSM*, 123) echoes the mother's "perfect cheek" (*SSM*, 12). Rose is clearly portrayed as the surrogate mother, the alter ego of the genitrix. In contrast to the father, who is icy and refuses to share, the mother is the giver of life and comfort, the provider of warmth and security. She is the *Alma Mater,* a deified object of filial admiration, the first object of love. She is gentle, listening, receiving, assisting, and has all the qualities that the father seems to lack. It is worth noting that she is probably described as perfect *because* the father is imperfect; she is perceived as irreproachable *because* the father's attitude is reprehensible.

Indeed as long as the father stands as an obstacle between the narrator and his (step)mother, he prevents the former from enjoying the exclusive

---

25   René Girard, *La Violence et le sacré* (Paris : Grasset, 1972), 251.

26   « Ce désir est essentiellement *mimétique,* <car> il se calque sur un désir modèle ; il élit le même objet que ce modèle » (René Girard, *La Violence et le sacré* [Paris : Grasset, 1972], 217).

27   The formula "inceste du deuxième type" is from Françoise Héritier: *Les deux Sœurs et leur mère. Anthropologie de l'inceste* (Paris: Odile Jacob, 1994), 233.

attention of the latter, and maintains him in the throes of his oedipal conflict. As a result, the son experiences a feeling of jealousy and hatred towards his father and wants to push him aside. It is a virile protest in the context of the castration complex. Once Samuel Gore can no longer interfere and prevent his son from transgressing the law by sleeping with his own wife, he incites him to fulfil his desires and get rid of him once and for all:

> I laid out the things for his breakfast [...] then wheeled him to the table. And I was bringing the fork towards his mouth when I heard the sound of nails scraping off a wooden surface and realised his hand was moving.

> It was moving towards the sugar-bowl, like a stiff crab, the veins standing out against the mottled skin. I looked at his eyes and saw them staring back at me with that sad intensity, his mouth pursed with the effort. I held my breath and watched the hand cross the acres of board to reach the bowl and grip it. I tried to speak, tried to encourage him but no sound came out. Then I saw the hand shake with a heroic inner fury and the bowl was overturned, the sugar spread in a neat arc beneath it. The eyes seemed to well up with tears then. Don't worry, father, I managed to say, you tried, and reached out a hand to his face, but he almost imperceptibly jerked it away. I could see the mouth then pursing with a further effort and followed the line of it, down his twitching shoulder to his wrist to his hand, gripped crablike as before but now with one finger extended, tracing a line in the spilt sugar. One unsteady stroke downwards then two more to reach the centre of the first. It was a K, traced with all the awkwardness of a child at kindergarten. Then another downwards stroke and another with a stroke to meet at the base. IL. He then repeated the L, began to form another letter but I already knew what it would say. Kill me. (*SSM*, 131)

The symbolic incest being accomplished, the murder of the father is bound to follow in order to complete the oedipal situation concretely. However, the fatal blow is not carried out, as if the pathetic sign of the father to finish him off[28] thwarted all aggressiveness. The parricide is only fantasized: the son cannot bring himself to kill his father, to annihilate

---

28 In the above quotation, the crab, mentioned twice, is a fitting metaphor for the disabled father, on the one hand, because, like the crustacean, the old man uses an oblique gait, a roundabout way to achieve his ends; on the other hand, because the crab, the zodiac sign of Cancer, corresponds to the summer solstice, the beginning of the downward movement of the sun, which is a sublimated symbol of the father, according to Freud.

the symbol of repression, the incarnation of the forbidden. Freud seeks to unravel this motif in *Totem and Taboo*. In this essay, the *Urvater*, the prehistoric father, the chief of the primitive horde, the holder of all goods, including females, an intransigent and inflexible legislator, is killed by his sons, who are castrated or expelled from the group. The dead father's body becomes the foundation of the social link by introjection of the forbidden at a meal during which it is eaten and "incorporated" by his sons:[29]

> It is by putting an end to the primitive horde and by putting to death the father of the horde that the sons paradoxically give birth to the *Urvater*: of all-powerful ancestor, he becomes indeed this psychic value. They thus invent, by their initiative, this father of the identification that they can absorb, in a totemic meal which marks the entry in *Kultur*.[30]

In a surreal dreamlike scene, such a totemic meal is related in the last pages of *Sunrise with Sea Monster*. It is a meal of reconciliation, of thanksgiving, a Eucharist in the etymological sense of the term. It also seals a new covenant.

***

As his son refuses to comply and kill him, the father seizes the opportunity to put an end to his life when he, Rose and Donal leave for the west country. In Lisdoonvarna, Samuel is to consult a healer. Donal, as for him, must welcome Hans who is to disembark from a submarine. He goes to the coast at nightfall, accompanied by his father who covers him, but the scene turns into chaos: Hans tries in vain to reach the shore, while Soames and his men are ambushed in the attempt to arrest him. Shots are exchanged. In the general confusion, Samuel, left in his wheelchair at the water's edge, mysteriously disappears. The investigations remain pointless. With Donal, Rose searches for him in vain, waits for days, and finally gives up and leaves the scene.

---

29   In this respect, Freud located the beginnings of the Oedipus complex at the origins of human society, and postulated that all religion was in effect an extended and collective form of guilt and ambivalence to cope with the killing of the father figure (which he saw as the true original sin).

30   Sigmund Freud, *Totem and Taboo* [1913] (London: W. W. Norton, 1962).

Then, Donal revives him – "I resurrected my father" (*SSM*, 166) – and joins him on the beach where he puts down his nightlines: "The moon was full [...]. The tide was low" (*SSM*, 171). Here again, the episode echoes a biblical text, more precisely the epilogue of the gospel according to John,[31] those chapters where Jesus, whose resurrected body also remains unaccounted for, manifests himself on the seashore to his disciples. The men have been fishing in vain all night long. Early in the morning, Jesus urges them from the beach to cast the net again: when they return, "they could not haul the net aboard, there were so many fish in it".[32] It is undoubtedly in memory of this miraculous sign that Donal specifies: "I said a prayer for fish then, the kinds of fish he would have been proud of" (*SSM*, 172). At sunrise – a symbol of resurrection – Donal notes that he has caught seven fish,[33] including a large, unidentified sea monster which, in a blurring depiction characteristic of Turner's painting, is quickly superimposed on his own father: "I'd fished him from the sea somehow" (*SSM*, 174). And Samuel Gore mysteriously appears, haloed in light, like a divine creature: "Then he looked up at me and walked forwards, the beard and the grey hair fringed by the sun behind him [...]. I reached forwards, touched his real sleeve and felt the salt water there" (*SSM*, 174). The gesture is reminiscent of that of Apostle Thomas who is told by risen Jesus, whose body still bears the stigmata of his crucified wounds: "Reach your hand here and put it into my side. Be unbelieving no longer, but believe".[34]

Like the disciples and their master who eat the fruit of their catch, Donal and his father cook the big fish and share it: "The unfamiliar filled my mouth, flesh that was hardly flesh, fish that was no known fish, taste that was somewhere beyond the bounds of sensation" (*SSM*, 176). This meal is

---

31   Chapters 20 & 21. "The appearance of Sam Gore is drawn from the memories of Donal, be that via sleep or inebriation (...) in an attempt to reconstruct his father's presence from the void within himself", as Val Nolan puts it (Nolan, *Neil Jordan: Works for the Page*, 120). This spectral apparition is one more example of religious influence on Jordan's worldview.

32   John 21:6.

33   The number seven is symbolic. At the time of the miraculous catch, the disciples are also seven.

34   John 20:27.

a sign of spiritual union. It becomes communion with God and prefigures the Eucharist, a meal in which all participants receive their share. It also recalls the Last Supper, the meal to which Jesus invited the twelve to offer his body as a sign of love. Did He not say: "I am the bread of life. Whoever comes to me shall never be hungry"?[35] This meal indefinitely feeds those who take part in it. Its abundance is a source of mystery, as Samuel tells his son when he is surprised to see that there is still so much to eat:

> The fish would never diminish, he told me, it would provide its meat until everything was said. We were there in a continual present, until there were no mysteries left. Then he could go back to that greater mystery. (*SSM*, 179)

The final episode of the novel, which brings father and son face to face in a surreal meal, is marked by mysticism and religiosity. The guests can eat to their hearts' content, without fear of running out, just like Jesus's disciples or the faithful participating in Eucharist. This sacrament, which commemorates the death and resurrection of Jesus, is a memorial and a sign of victory over death. To remember Him is to be nourished by Him and vice versa. Mysteriously, Donal feeds on the flesh of the fish, but also, symbolically, on his father's body, just as the bread is transformed into the body of Christ through transsubstantiation. But while bread is the essential staple food for every human being, it is somewhat ironic that the flesh of a sea monster becomes the father's body eaten by the son. Here again, there is something parodic about the scene.

***

Once fed with his father's body, Donal literally assimilates him and assumes his identity: "I slept in his room that night. In the hope of discovering some secret life he lived while the house slept, of dreaming a dream he dreamt, of hearing him talk in his sleep, I wasn't sure". (*SSM*, 137)

From then on, Donal is a man, the specular image of his father. His initiation has honoured his promises of an eternal possibility of renewal. This mystical rebirth is symbolized by the last scenes in which water is the main factor: the protagonist, having gone through a baptism of renewal,

---

35   John 6:35.

stands on the beach from which the sea has withdrawn.[36] This space is the final stage of his itinerary, the symbol of the borders of his inner world, where the *doxa* claims that everything merges – land, sea and sky – and where the fusion of generations takes place.[37] As Turner's painting also illustrates, the beach at low tide is the place of all possibilities, a vast expanse favourable to the appearance of the sacred. The erasure of all boundaries leads to the evocation of the infinite. Paradoxically, the emptiness produced by the mist or the dazzling light is a sign of unlimited fullness. Between the individual and eternal immensity, the lost unity is restored. The ordeal of the stranger followed by a return to his roots is presented as a conquest of self-awareness. In a final and hallucinatory scene, father and son talk over a meal, from dawn till dusk, from sunrise to sunset. The conflict is overcome, the relationship appeased. In a blinding rite of passage, regeneration takes place: the old man is incorporated so that the new man is born. The son is now his own father; he has succeeded in integrating the past into his history, as witnessed by the mystical illumination, heralding the advent of a new era.

36   Throughout the novel, Donal is near the sea, whether he is in Bray (County Wicklow, on the coast south of Dublin), Barcelona, Dun Laoghaire or Lisdoonvarna (County Clare, on the west coast of Ireland).
37   "That sea was our element, after all" (Jordan, *Sunrise with Sea Monster*, 181).

PART III

On the Fringe of Literature: Scripts and Screen Adaptations

CHAPTER 5

Troubles Never Come Singly: *The Crying Game* and *Breakfast on Pluto*

Neil Jordan's literary work cannot be studied without taking into account the scripts he wrote, particularly for the films which consolidated his fame. This is the case with *The Crying Game*.[1] Indeed, this original script can be considered as a fully fledged literary text, as illustrated by its presence in *A Neil Jordan Reader*. This volume, published in the U.S. in 1993, includes the complete screenplay for *The Crying Game*, the collection of stories *Night in Tunisia*, as well as the novella *The Dream of a Beast*.

Written for the cinema, a script contains the words of a film, together with the screen directions of the characters and events. It describes what is to be seen on the screen; it makes sense with respect to production and is supposed to be followed by acting, as a musical score is used for performance.

The story of *The Crying Game* takes place in Northern Ireland in the early 1980s. The violence and political problems of those days, euphemistically known as the Troubles, offend and question the young Neil Jordan whose first films – *Angel* (1980) and *The Crying Game* (1992) – arise out of this conflict.

"The Crying Game" initially refers to a song released in 1964 and performed by Dave Berry. The choice of this quotation title recalls the words of Neil Jordan himself who reckons he was so intimidated by the great literary figures of his country that he preferred to draw on the source of his generation's popular songs.[2]

---

1 *The Crying Game* won an Oscar for Best Original Screenplay in 1994.

2 "When I started writing I felt very pressured by the question: How do I cope with the notion of Irishness? [...] how to write stories [...] without being swamped in the language and mythology of Joyce? ... The only identity, at a cultural level, that I could forge was one that came from the worlds of television, popular music and

And yet *The Crying Game* is part of literary heritage, as it echoes Irish classics. A clue which makes it possible to establish an intertextual connection is provided by the way Jody, whose eyes are blindfolded and hands and feet are bound, is informed of the situation by Peter Maguire, one of his kidnappers:

> You're being held hostage by the Irish Republican Army. They've got one of our senior members under interrogation in Castleraigh. We've informed them that if they don't release him within three days, you'll be shot. You'll be treated as our guest until further developments. Have you anything to say?[3]

The word – "guest" – is somewhat ironical here insofar as it is generally used for a visitor who is shown friendly and generous behaviour and is made to feel welcome. In this instance, even if the guest is not manhandled, he is nevertheless a hostage. The word used here is reminiscent of Frank O'Connor's short story "Guests of the Nation" (1931).

This story takes place in the context of the wars that split Ireland into two camps from 1919 to 1923. Frank O'Connor himself took part in the civil war on the side of the Republicans against the Free State. His insubordination led him to refuse to obey the orders he considered as unfair. Captured, he was a prisoner in a camp where he wrote his story. In "Guests of the Nation", two British soldiers make friends with their Irish kidnappers. They discuss existential, political and religious problems, play cards, drink tea and joke together. Suddenly, the guards are given the order to shoot the prisoners as a reprisal for the deaths of two Irishmen killed by the other side. As they have no other choice but to do their "duties" and obey their commander, the Irish activists walk to the peat bog with the two Englishmen at night, shoot them dead and bury their bodies on the spot. The story illustrates the cruelty and absurdity of war as the soldier from the other side is not always an enemy.

---

cinema which I was experiencing daily" (Kearney, ed., *Across the Frontiers – Ireland in the 1990s* (Dublin: Wolfhound Press, 1988), 196-197).

3   Neil Jordan, *The Crying Game, A Neil Jordan Reader* (New York: Vintage International, 1993), 182.

In the same vein, in the late 1950s, Irish playwright Brendan Behan, who was remanded in jail for terrorist activities, wrote *The Hostage*, a play whose action is set in a Dublin brothel. The house is patronized by prostitutes, homosexuals and casual sailors. The owner and the caretaker of the place, who used to fight together for Ireland, are about to welcome their "guest",[4] a young British soldier kidnapped in Northern Ireland. The latter is held hostage by IRA activists to prevent the execution of a young Irish Republican who is bound to be hanged in Belfast Jail on the following day. Leslie, the blindfolded soldier, arrives between two IRA men to be confined in this whorehouse where no one would think about searching for him. He "fraternizes"[5] with Teresa, the skivvy of the place, who gives him some tea and cigarettes, but also a medal of the Virgin and ultimately, her whole body. When Leslie hears he is going to be executed in retaliation, he reacts with his teenage innocence:

> SOLDIER: They're going to shoot me?
>
> MULLEADY: I'm afraid so.
>
> SOLDIER: Why?
>
> MONSEWER: You are the hostage.
>
> SOLDIER: But I ain't done nothing.
>
> OFFICER: This is war.[6]

Ironically enough, he is accidentally killed by his fellow countrymen who come to release him and the Irish boy is hanged in Belfast. In spite of the tragic contextual reality, the play is not militant, but profoundly human. As a critic puts it:

> Brendan Behan has hatred for the political forces who divide and subject Ireland. But for the people, even if those people are the instruments of antagonistic political forces, he has only love and understanding.[7]

4   "Everything's ready for the guest" (Brendan Behan, *The Hostage* [1958], in *The Complete Plays* [London: Methuen & Co., 1988], 134 & 168).

5   "What's that girl doing, fraternizing?" (*Ibid.*, 188).

6   *Ibid.*, 206.

7   Ulick O'Connor, *Brendan Behan* (London: Coronet Books, 1970), 198.

The Hostage partakes of the farce and melodrama. Its dialogues, often peppered with comical songs, make the most of language, in this instance a hotchpotch of cockney, standard English and Irish slang.

These three texts are linked by the focus on their "guests", explicitly referred to as such. The prisoners are remanded in a hostile environment by antagonists who do not wish them any harm, but are themselves the hostages of a vicious circle which imposes them to act according to the army they belong to. As one of the characters puts it with fatalism: "this is war". Such a terse phrase reminds the ones who would tend to forget it that all of them are belligerents. *The Crying Game* can be approached in the context of this literary heritage.

Frank O'Connor depicts a world which illustrates that violence is very often a male feature, particularly when it is combined with war. According to Caroline Magennis, who wrote *Sons of Ulster*, an essay dedicated to masculinities in the contemporary Northern Irish novel, there is a specificity in this part of the UK:

> The mode of masculinity that has been most often presented as representative of Northern Ireland is that of paramilitary groups and their members, where masculinity is inextricably tied to violence and issues of national struggle.[8]

Magennis highlights the exclusive masculinity of the warring factions of the conflict[9]:

> The figureheads of the main political parties are all men and those engaged in violence appear to be almost exclusively male [...]. The public faces of Protestant and Catholic paramilitaries are men ... The people who talk about religion and the Church are men. The politicians are men ...[10]

This exhibited masculinity is damaged by Behan's shady and colourful characters whose behaviours contrast with the military austerity imposed

---

8   Caroline Magennis, *Sons of Ulster. Masculinities in the Contemporary Northern Irish Novel* (Oxford, Bern, Berlin...: Peter Lang, 2010, introduction), 7.
9   Magennis's theory is however to be qualified insofar as some women also took part in the conflict and were even imprisoned in Armagh for example.
10   Magennis, 9

by the context. It is even more demolished by Neil Jordan's film and script *The Crying Game* in 1992.

The story starts with the ambiguous relationship between Fergus, an IRA activist, and his hostage, Jody, a Black British soldier. Unlike the other kidnappers, Fergus is not rough with his prisoner: he is the only one who pulls off the hood to feed him. Fergus and Jody call each other by their first names; they talk about girls and sports, and treat each other with courtesy.[11] They share cigarettes, exchange smiles and jest about their looks. Jody admits that Fergus is quite handsome "with the killer smile and the baby face".[12] He shows him some photos of his girlfriend, Dil, a pretty Black girl, which leads Fergus to remark: "You make a nice couple".[13] On the following day, Jody gives his kidnapper the pictures, together with Dil's address, and asks him to get in touch with her in case he should be killed so that she knows he kept thinking about her.[14]

The relationship between the two men turns into homoerotic flirtation when Fergus leads Jody outside to urinate. Handcuffed, the hostage cannot make the necessary gestures to do so: he implores his kidnapper to unzip his fly and take his "piece of meat" out.[15] Back in the house, both of them laugh about this comical situation, thank each other and exchange overpolite remarks, such as "the pleasure was all mine".[16] Their roars of laughter infuriate Peter Maguire, the leader of the group, who sharply scolds Fergus and finally asks him to execute the prisoner. Like in O'Connor and Behan's texts, the kidnapper is reluctant to kill the hostage he has befriended.[17] He lets him run away, but Jody is accidentally hit and run over by a Saracen tank of his own army. Like *The Hostage, The Crying Game* shows that some cruel events can be governed by a strange irony of fate.

---

11   "Nice to meet you, Fergus.

My pleasure, Jody" (Jordan, *The Crying Game, A Neil Jordan Reader*, 192).

12   *Ibid.*, 185.

13   *Ibid.*, 190.

14   "Just tell her Jody was thinking –" (*Ibid.*, 200).

15   "It's only a piece of meat" (*Ibid.*, 193).

16   *Ibid.*, 194.

17   Jody even considers Fergus like a friend: "You're my friend" (*Ibid.*, 204).

As he is considered to have neglected his duties, Fergus must disappear and take refuge in London. Haunted by Jody's memory, he goes to the Metro Bar and meets with Dil, Jody's girlfriend, but remains silent about what happened in Ireland. After a few days during which they prove to be romantically and sexually interested in each other, they spend the night together. Dil turns out to be a man. It comes as a shock for Fergus who obviously ignored that the Metro Bar is actually a pub patronized by gay men, transvestites and transsexuals. He does not drop Dil for all that. The latter, falling in love, claims to be ready to do anything for his sake: at his request, she agrees to have a haircut, to wear Jody's clothes and even to become a boy again. Indeed, Fergus strives to protect her from his former "friends" who have picked up his trail; and vice versa, his own life is saved by Dil who does not hesitate to kill Jude, the threatening member of the IRA, when she confronts him. Fergus takes responsibility for the crime, is tried for murder, sentenced to several years' imprisonment, but is regularly visited by Dil, who shows so much love and gratitude to him.

The film is a variation on the old saying 'know thyself'. Indeed, its main theme is self-discovery resulting from the revelation of unsuspected identity components. A man's attraction for a woman who proves to be a man confirms that the person you fall in love with is not always the one you initially thought. With such a motif, a film like this is quite bold and daring, particularly in Ireland in the early 1990s. It turns stereotypes upside down, and may still offend and upset some people today. Be that as it may, *The Crying Game* is a highly original, experimental work of art which enhances paradox, difference and multiplicity.

***

As a matter of fact, the literary representation of the Troubles has been changing over time. In the 1970s and 1980s, sectarian violence between communities was approached in a realistic manner by writers who were not unbiased: Brian Moore, Bernard MacLaverty, Benedict Kiely or Seamus Deane considered that Northern Irish reality, complex though it is, could be mirrored by fiction. In the 1990s, a new generation of writers dealt with the Troubles obliquely. Their distant, ironic, postmodern approach questioned the presuppositions of realistic representation, reappraised the metanarrative with suspicion and envisaged history as pure fiction. This is the view taken by Eoin McNamee, Colin Bateman, Glenn Patterson or Robert McLiam Wilson, to name just a few. Neil Jordan might fall into this category.[18]

The myth of heroic violence, traditionally exploited to paint nationalistic sentiments in the rosiest of colours, is destroyed by Neil Jordan's work which deals here with gender trouble against the background of the Northern Irish Troubles. *The Crying Game* debunks the simplistic views which keep everyone within the limits of a precise, conventional identity. Postcolonial and postmodern identity complexities deconstruct the traditional nationalistic approach of the manly warrior and destabilize the usual representations of sex and gender. As skin colour does not accurately determine nationality, sexuality cannot systematically be assimilated to gender. Characterized by paradox, Jody and Dil sow confusion in the mind of Fergus, an IRA member attached to the rules and conventions of Catholic nationalism. As Eibhear Walshe puts it in *Sex, Nation, and Dissent in Irish Writing*, the fact that gender does not match sex perturbs the traditional representation of sexual division: "A lesbian and gay presence within any national literature *troubles* privileged formations of what traditionally constituted 'woman' and 'man'".[19] Fergus's identity crisis involves the rejection of masculinity as a usual emblem of paramilitary republicanism. The desire he feels for Jody and his identification with him – since he finally takes his place – lead him to re-appraise his own political and sexual identities. Contrary to what stereotypes convey, masculinity is unstable and negotiable.[20] It does not express itself in an act of war, but in a love story which is supposed to be long-lasting, as Dave Berry's song 'The Crying Game' puts it:

18   With the exception of Neil Jordan, all of the writers mentioned here were born in Northern Ireland in the 1960s.

19   Eibhear Walshe, *Sex, Nation, and Dissent in Irish Writing* (Cork: Cork University Press, 1997), 2.

20   The unstable and negotiable nature of masculinity is the central issue of Todd W. Reeser's essay, *Masculinities in Theory. An Introduction*, which aims to provide a response to the question: what is masculinity and how does it work? (Malden, MA and Chichester: Wiley Blackwell, 2010).

> I know all there is to know about the crying game
>
> I've had my share of the crying game
>
> First there are kisses, then there are sighs
>
> And then before you know where you are
>
> You're sayin' goodbye [...]
>
> Don't want no more of the crying game.

Enough tears, sufferings and misfortunes: such is the script conclusion in the face of sectarian violence which tore the British Isles apart, hence the choice of this theme song. Its interpretation by Boy George at the end of the film is significant insofar as it implicitly prolongs the motif of ambiguousness and cross-dressing. Indeed, the English artist, still very popular when the film was released, was also famous for his make-up, eccentric clothes and androgynous style.[21]

The Crying Game intermingles collective and individual histories, particularly through its main character Fergus who is present throughout the film. His name is not chosen by chance: it refers not only to a character in Behan's play,[22] but also to an Ulster hero in Celtic mythology. In this instance, the name of Fergus, suggestive of greatness and power, fits the protagonist who works for a united Ireland. His participation in the conflict gives him the opportunity to get involved, but also to lose his innocence. It makes him "grow" in many respects, all the more so as he goes through some troubles, a polysemous word with which the script plays. Indeed, the protagonist's inner troubles are coming on top of the national Troubles. Chaos, disorder and agitation are rampant not only in his environment, but also in his emotional life and personal relationships.

As an Irishman in London, Fergus is an outsider, just like Jody in Ireland. He is identified as a member of a minority and is made inescapably

---

21   The film opens in a funfair with the Percy Sledge song "When a Man Loves a Woman" (1966), which, with hindsight, proves to be somewhat ironical. It ends with Boy George singing the final version of "The Crying Game". These two songs allude to the protagonist's evolution throughout the story.

22   In Brendan Behan's play, the IRA volunteer who is in charge of keeping watch over the hostage, tells Teresa: "You can call me Fergus" (Behan, *The Hostage*, 227).

'other': he is "not English", as Dil points out when they first meet.[23] Similarly, the foreman of the building site on which he works emphasizes his Irishness by stereotypically calling him "Paddy".[24] Fergus's marginal status is confirmed when he realizes his possible sexual orientation. He is then confronted with another aspect of his identity, which, once more, makes him "different". Progressively, Fergus comes to understand that gender has nothing to do with sex, and that he may not meet the standards himself. This questioning first sows confusion and agitation in his mind, but the trouble is gradually assumed to be finally soothed at the end of the film, when he shows great devotion to Dil. From then on, it seems to matter little that the loved one is a male or a female.[25]

London is depicted as the place where such a lifestyle is possible: the city allows Fergus not only to escape the oppressive trap of his sectarian environment, but also to free himself from the imperative categories of gender. This normative dimension, which determines identities in two exclusive categories, is denounced by the queer approach which expands the line of thought first outlined in 1990 by Judith Butler in her founding essay, *Gender Trouble.* This book criticizes the processing of dividing humankind into sexes, not only for its oppressive binarity, but also in its claim to make sex a relevant indication of the divisions of the social world. In the same vein, Neil Jordan's script and film question these patterns, which establish two distinct, antagonistic groups, and refer to a social connection marked by power and domination. The criteria on which the conflict is based – nationality, social class, denomination and political stance – can be envisaged by analogy with other sorts of domination, that is, sex and gender. As a result, it is difficult to separate the queer dimension of the script from its political strategies. According to French theoreticians Bereni, Chauvin, Jaunait and Revillard, in the 1970s, tackling gender by analogy with the social class amounted to using the main conceptual key of the political fights of the time.[26] Gender then became an important collective

---

23　Jordan, *The Crying Game, A Neil Jordan Reader*, 209.
24　"Do it on your own time, Paddy" (*Ibid.*, 235).
25　"I'd do anything for you, Dil" (*Ibid.*, 263).
26　'Dans les années 1970, penser le genre en analogie avec la classe revient à mobiliser la principale "clé conceptuelle" des luttes politiques de l'époque, facilitant ainsi

issue which made liberation necessary. As a matter of fact, gender overlaps with race, class and sexuality. Different kinds of discrimination are related to one another, not only under the form of comparison, but of intersection too.[27] Intersectionality is a word used by American scholar Kimberlé Crenshaw in an inquiry about coloured women from the most underprivileged sections of the population in the U.S.[28] By extension, intersectionality designates the political thought concerning the situation of individuals who simultaneously suffer several forms of domination or discrimination.

According to Crenshaw, all individuals are at the intersection of several social relationships. And yet, they are often reduced to one particular component. This is exemplified in *The Crying Game*: each character is determined by one single characteristic, and therefore limited to that precise aspect of their identity – their nationality, skin colour or sexual orientation: Fergus is "Paddy" on the building site in London;[29] Jody is openly called "nigger" in Ireland[30]; as for Dil, she hears "scrag-eyed dyke cunt"[31] from the mouth of a vulgar man who only sees a transvestite in her. A multiplicity of traits is condensed into a single one which is taken as a target. When these insults are viewed together, they prove that individuals and social groups – minorities in most cases – are confronted with similar challenges, hence the solidarity among these three characters. The fact

---

l'érection du genre en authentique enjeu collectif nécessitant une "libération"' (Laure Bereni, Sébastien Chauvin, Alexandre Jaunait and Anne Revillard, *Introduction aux Gender Studies. Manuel des études sur le genre* [Bruxelles: De Boeck, 2008], 191).

27 'Le genre s'articule à d'autres rapports de domination, non plus sous la seule forme de la comparaison, mais aussi sous la forme de l'intersection, c'est-à-dire de la simultanéité ou de l'intrication des formes de domination de race, de classe et de sexe' (*Ibid.*, 191-192).

28 Kimberlé Crenshaw, 'Mapping the Margins: Intersectionality, Identity Politics, and Violence against Women of Color', *Stanford Law Review* 43/6 (1991), 1241-1299.

29 "Do it on your own time, Paddy" (Jordan, *The Crying Game, A Neil Jordan Reader*, 235).

30 "I get sent to the only place in the world they call you nigger to your face [...] (*He imitates a Belfast accent*) Go back to your banana tree, nigger" (*Ibid.*, 191).

31 *Ibid.*, 218.

remains that such derogatory remarks isolate, marginalize and, at worst, make monsters of the ones to whom they are addressed.

And yet, for Neil Jordan, the monster is not the cross-dresser who is fooling everybody, but the radical activist who, in the opening scene of the film, lures Jody into a trap to make his kidnapping easier. Once the latter is at her mercy, Jude proves to be pitiless: she is the only one who hits him. Later, she picks up Fergus's trail and pesters him for the resumption of his terrorist activities. Throughout the film, whether she is the naïve blonde who charms males on the fairground, the typical IRA nationalist in her Aran pullover in the den of detention, or the elegant black-haired business-woman in the smart districts of London, Jude is depicted as a dangerous, monstrous woman.[32] "I wrote Jude quite consciously as a monster",[33] admits Neil Jordan, for whom any work of fiction seems to have a monster among its characters. Obviously, the emblematic female personification of Ireland is here seriously harmed: indeed, the only biological woman in the film is a monster and the one "good" woman is a man, a feature which was considered as offensive and misogynistic by some feminist critics.

The challenge of stereotypes is recurrent in Neil Jordan's work. It is no matter of chance if, in 2006, he made *Breakfast on Pluto*, a film based on the novel by Patrick McCabe with whom he wrote the script. The motif of gender trouble in the background of the Northern Irish Troubles is also in the heart of McCabe's novel. The inner tumult of the protagonist Patrick, who is called Pussy when he dresses as a woman, becomes intermingled with the terrorist attacks of the paramilitaries of both sides. Patrick is at the wrong place and the wrong time, and therefore, unfairly treated by "the other side". He is longing to "journey to Mars and visit the stars finding our breakfast on Pluto", hence the title of the book, which is also a quote from a song. Travelling among the planets, Pussy no longer needs to live in bondage, no longer depends on anything, whether it be the natural forces of gravity or the strict patterns of social behaviour. His body is free. This is why he finds pleasure in humming 'Breakfast on Pluto', the lyrics

---

32   Jody is clear-sighted when he tells Fergus: "Don't leave me with her, man. She's dangerous..." (*Ibid.*, 186).

33   Marina Burke, *Film Ireland* 34 (April/May 1993), 18.

of which describe his dream of another place, where his looks and tastes will not be severely tested:

> Go anywhere,
>
> Go anywhere without leaving your chair
>
> And let your thoughts run free
>
> Living within all the dreams you can spin
>
> We'll visit the stars and journey to Mars
>
> Finding our breakfast on Pluto!

This song by Don Partridge (1969) refers to everyone's capacity to forget and come out of one's body to escape vexations, humiliations and sufferings. Such extracorporeal experiences are fights for survival. In its lyrics, this song, like 'The Crying Game', refers to the dream of an ideal place, anywhere out of the world, on Mars, Pluto, on the Moon, in the clouds or among the stars. Sad and lonely, the protagonist, whose pride is hurt, wants to fulfil his dreams, fly high in the sky and leave his worries here below. And indeed, no one can deny that the Northern Irish Troubles must look pathetic when they are considered from another planet.

The dream of being catapulted into an astral journey derives from the wounds of this character who is alone with his thoughts. Pussy is kept out of things and his marginal situation is metaphorically described by his bitter remark: "You'd just be feeling like dog's dirt upon a pavement, with well-dressed people standing over it and going: 'Who on earth left that horrible mess there?'"[34]

Pussy is a good pupil, but his high-pitched voice, his gift for imitating female stars and his tendency to wear earrings and sequined miniskirts inevitably make him a scapegoat. He gives a very clear-headed analysis of his situation: "As time went on, it became abundantly clear that I wasn't exactly growing up to become Mr 'Most Popular Adolescent Boy' around the town!"[35]

34   Patrick McCabe, *Breakfast on Pluto*, 72.
35   *Ibid.*, 20.

As an illustration of the pattern of intersectionality, when he stays in London, Pussy's Irish nationality makes him the classic culprit: he is arrested by British policemen for planting a bomb in a pub. Therefore, he is not only abused for his passport – "You facking Irish facking filth"[36] – but also and above all for his sexual orientation: "You fucking queer! [...] hooring nancy queen".[37] However, there are some who stand up for him and, consciously or not, accentuate the unsettled nature of his gender: "*He's* my girlfriend".[38] Patrick-Pussy is a man, but when he wears women's clothes, he shows he can assume not only the gender, but also the female sex, thus vouching for the fact that masculinity is nothing but a cultural construction. His ambivalence calls into question the binary heterosexual premise, and ignores the very concept of categorization in every way – gender, sexuality, religion or politics. When his friend and lover dies in a terrorist attack, Pussy remarks:

> There are those who say it was the IRA and others the UDA and then some who say it was the two of them together. I didn't know, and didn't fucking care. All I knew was that dear old Dums was gone![39]

The protagonist is above prejudices, above any kind of firm positioning. Although the novel was published in 1998, the year when the Belfast Agreement was signed, the Troubles are considered of secondary importance. Pussy repeatedly witnesses acts of senseless violence which cause the deaths of many people around him, but he does not take any side in all that. There is renewed tension in the province, "a night never seemed to pass without '*Clear the area!*'",[40] but Pussy is "much too preoccupied with [his] own personal revolution to be bothered with anything so trivial".[41] It is undeniable that this novel and its screen adaptation are much more focused on individual issues than on the Northern Irish problem. Pussy

36   *Ibid.*, 69.
37   *Ibid.*, 105.
38   *Ibid.*, 50.
39   *Ibid.*, 33.
40   *Ibid.*, 71.
41   *Ibid.*, 22.

describes him/herself as "an ordinary transvestite prostitute, not the slightest bit interested in politics at all!"[42]

Symbolically, the focus of the text on the glamorous style of the transvestite protagonist is essentially justified as a rejection of sanctimoniousness, etiquette and traditional, formalistic barriers. It can also be interpreted as a way of denouncing the misrepresentation of Northern Irish history and its distorted versions spread by biased media and political propaganda. Therefore, *The Crying Game* and *Breakfast on Pluto* are subversive on more than one account: on the one hand, their characters exemplify the idea that sexuality does not always work in perfect harmony with gender; on the other, the representation of the Troubles, which tries to encompass the complexity of the conflict, is here questioned by (script)writers who distance themselves from events and ideologies. McCabe and Jordan give up trying to depict reality as such, as there are always manipulations and (mis)interpretations anyway.

The Crying Game and *Breakfast on Pluto* were not written to help the reader develop a deeper understanding of the conflict in Northern Ireland. Their goal is not to examine the sociopolitical roots of violence, which are out of reach anyway, all the more so as many prejudices have been circulating for a very long time. These texts must be considered as rewritings which take up the sectarian stereotypes of that troubled period in order to destroy them once and for all. The Irish intellectual Seamus Deane mentions this intricate process by which a community, attempting to discover its 'true' identity, often begins with the demolition of the false stereotypes within which it has been entrapped.[43] To do so, it has to carry out a cathartic operation that consists of awakening entrenched hatreds in order to eradicate them definitively. This work on the past is essentially justified within a community that struggles to be clearly defined. Where are the communities concerned by the conflict in the search for their identities? Are they able to determine precisely what defines them, and to establish specific features which make them unique? Is their position ambiguous

---

42   *Ibid.*, 151.
43   T. Eagleton, F. Jameson & E. Said, *Nationalism, Colonialism and Literature*, Minneapolis: University of Minnesota Press, 1990, introduction by Seamus Deane.

or ambivalent? Like Fergus and Pussy, don't they feel uneasy? Are they struggling to make themselves heard and understood?

By giving a queer dimension to their stories, Neil Jordan and Patrick McCabe show that they want to deal with the Troubles from a human angle, without any partisan approach. By endowing their protagonist with a gender which does not correspond to their sex, they erase dividing lines and open new perspectives. They recall that the belligerents, before being identified as Irish or English, are first and foremost men and women. Whatever their sexual orientation, they are united by common humanity. As can be seen from their works, they refuse to be trapped in preconceived ideas, prejudices and stereotypes, whether they are political, religious or sexual.

Without adopting a particular stance, Jordan and McCabe point to new possibilities on the horizon. They destroy the numerous frontiers of Northern Irish society which separate Catholics from Protestants, Unionists from Nationalists, but also the rich from the poor or boys from girls. *The Crying Game* and *Breakfast on Pluto* invite us to recognize that any frontier is oppressive, that dualism often leads to duel. They subvert normative presuppositions and denounce any act of violence, whether it is imposed by inextricable sociopolitical situations or restrictive corporal norms. The texts explore the possibilities of revisable identities, and try to convince us, readers, that "the facking maniacs"[44] are not always the ones we thought.

44   McCabe, *Breakfast on Pluto*, 165.

CHAPTER 6

From the Page to the Screen: *Interview with the Vampire, The Butcher Boy* and *The End of the Affair.*

In the 1990s, over a period of five years, Neil Jordan made three films adapted from the literary works of English-language writers: *Interview with the Vampire* (1994), *The Butcher Boy* (1997), *The End of the Affair* (1999). He co-wrote the scripts of the first two with the novelists, that is, Anne Rice and Patrick McCabe,[1] but was the only scriptwriter of the third film, as the author of the novel, Graham Greene, had died a few years earlier.

These film adaptations prove, if need be, that Neil Jordan's interest is not restrictive. Indeed, they are inspired by novels written by an American woman in 1975, an Irish fellow countryman in 1992, and a well-known postwar English writer. It is significant that these three distinctive texts drew Jordan's attention to such an extent that he devoted several months to writing the screenplays and making the films.

Given that the change from one medium to another necessarily entails a certain number of differences, it is interesting in this instance to compare each book and film in order to assess the gap between them, but also to understand why Jordan made screen adaptations of these precise texts and, last, to show the extent to which components of these literary works echo his own favourite themes.

***

When Anne Rice published *Interview with the Vampire,* the book was such a success that she wrote other books in the same vein (without

---

1   Anne Rice receives sole script credit, although Neil Jordan made extensive contributions to it.

playing on words). As a result, this novel is the first volume of *The Vampire Chronicles,* which are made of ten books published over three decades.

Interview with the Vampire starts in San Francisco: Daniel Malloy, an incredulous reporter, hears the confidences of a mysterious man, Louis, who claims to be a vampire. All night long, he records the story of his life: his pact with the vampire Lestat, his initiation, the first ecstasies, the thirst for blood, then his doubts and heartbreaks, his illusory search of brotherhood, his confrontation with his peers and his incurable loneliness that has gone with him for centuries.

The novel is divided into four parts determined according to the location of the action. The first one takes place at the end of the eighteenth century in New Orleans where Louis, the rich owner of a plantation, suffering from depression, meets with Lestat who makes a vampire of him and becomes the guide of his soul. Horrified at the discovery that he has to kill in order to survive, Louis thinks of parting with his mentor that he has come to hate. The latter turns a child, Claudia, into a vampire in order to keep Louis with him. Like a family, the three of them live together for years in Louisiana, until Claudia realizes that she will never grow up, that her eternal child's body will never allow her to lead a fulfilling woman's life. She conceives such a violent feeling of hatred for Lestat that she gets rid of him with Louis's assistance.

The second part narrates Louis and Claudia's travel in Central Europe, the birthplace of vampirism, where they inquire about their origins and start looking for other creatures of their kind.

After years of wandering throughout the world, they stay in Paris where the third part takes place. There, they meet with their peers. Louis is fascinated by one of them, Armand, the manager of the *Théâtre des Vampires.* This company is a cult whose members take a strong aversion to the two vampires from the New World, because they consider they are guilty of a major crime: they killed a fellow creature. As Armand and Louis become attached to each other, the company, influenced by the uncompromising Santiago, disapproves of the creation of a vampire-child and lets Claudia die by exposing her to sunlight which burns her to ash. Louis takes his revenge by destroying the theatre and beheading the actors before leaving Paris with Armand.

In the fourth and last part of the book, Louis returns to New Orleans. He knows he is going to see Lestat again. And indeed, the latter, who has become a miserable outcast, gets by in a graveyard. Louis is invited to stay with him, but goes to San Francisco where he meets the reporter. At the end of the interview, as dawn is breaking, Malloy, mesmerized by Louis's story, tells him:

> It was an adventure like I'll never know in my own life! (...) If you were to give me that power! The power to live forever! (...) Make me a vampire now!
>
> - This is what you want? Louis whispered. This ... after all I've told you ... is what you ask for?[2]

Louis lets himself be persuaded, sinks his teeth into the young man's neck, but does not let him die and disappears at sunrise. The reporter loses consciousness, then opens his eyes, picks up his cassettes and tape recorder and runs to his car to move away from this worrying place.

The film seeks to recreate the strange and fascinating atmosphere of the novel, by playing on the aesthetic side through spectacular scenes, magnificent decors, historical costumes and entrancing music.[3] The shadowy lights of flames accentuate the claustrophobic atmosphere. The cast of good-looking men – Brad Pitt, Tom Cruise, Antonio Banderas – contributes to the resounding success of the film which gave such a boost to the sales of the book that it became a bestseller twenty years after it was published.

Yet Neil Jordan was not necessarily intent on appealing to public opinion. On the whole, the film is faithful to Anne Rice's novel, reproducing a large part of the dialogue. Nevertheless, the adaptation also takes some liberties with the original work, particularly to highlight the visual effects of some striking scenes, for example when Lestat sinks his teeth into Louis's neck, both of them rise in the air in an ecstatic, orgasmic experience and float for a while. As blood flows from the wound, Lestat drops Louis into the waters of the harbour. Other significant differences are worth noting: Louis mourns a brother in the novel, a wife and a child in the film. A status of husband and father makes him a heterosexual man established

2   Anne Rice, *Interview with the Vampire* (1976), 305-306.
3   Haydn, Haendel, Mozart.

in a conventional life, whereas the book depicts him as an eternal teenager whose sexual orientation is uncertain. Indeed, he can easily fall under the spell of a man, particularly if the latter is young and charismatic, as can be seen from his attraction for Lestat or Armand. The love Louis feels for Lestat changes into passionate hatred in the novel, a not so obvious feeling in the film, which is, generally speaking, not as violent as the source-text, although blood flows profusely too.

At the end of the film, the reporter admits he would give anything to become a vampire, which infuriates Louis. When he regains consciousness, he runs to his car, starts up the engine and drives to the Golden Gate Bridge. Lo and behold, Lestat is there, sitting next to him in order to drink his blood and turn him into his new vampire companion.[4] This final twist is presented as an evil pact implied by the soundtrack and the Rolling Stones's song – 'Sympathy for the Devil' – the first words of which are:

> Please allow me to introduce myself
>
> I'm a man of wealth and taste
>
> I've been around for a long, long year
>
> Stole many a man's soul and faith.

This allusion to the devil is one of the few in the film, whose religious discourse is strangely absent. This is a major difference between the text and its screen adaptation. The novel describes the questioning of Louis, a Roman Catholic whose soul is tormented by the possibility of being a fiend: "Am I damned? Am I from the devil? Is my very nature that of a devil? I was asking myself over and over".[5] Louis has the power to pass on his features, which he suspects to be diabolical; he is called a devil by those who curse him before dying; as a result, Louis wonders whether he is damned or not. Overcome by doubt, he enters the New Orleans cathedral where his body suddenly goes into spasm:

4   In the novel, Louis sinks his teeth into Malloy's neck and spares his life.
5   Rice, *Interview with the Vampire*, 69.

> I looked up and saw myself in a most palpable vision ascending the altar steps, opening the tiny sacrosanct tabernacle, reaching with monstrous hands for the consecrated ciborium, and taking the Body of Christ and strewing Its white wafers all over the carpet; and walking then on the sacred wafers, walking up and down before the altar, giving Holy Communion to the dust. I rose up now in the pew and stood there staring at this vision. I knew full well the meaning of it.
>
> God did not live in this church; these statues gave an image to nothingness, *I* was the supernatural in this cathedral. I was the only supermortal thing that stood conscious under this roof! Loneliness. Loneliness to the point of madness. The cathedral crumbled in my vision; the saints listed and fell. Rats ate the Holy Eucharist and nested on the sills.[6]

Then, Louis has an apocalyptic vision of a funeral procession, the coffin of which carries Lestat's body. He quotes the Bible: "And now art thou cursed from the earth, which hath opened her mouth to receive thy brother's blood from thy hand".[7] Louis's fate is sealed by the divine condemnation of the fratricide Cain who, unable to find peace, mourns for his unfortunate immortality and now has before him no longer Lestat's mortal remains, but his own brother's: "darkness gathering – behind me, across from me, and now above me".[8] Louis suffers such feelings of guilt that he confesses his murders to a priest: "I am not mortal, father, but immortal and damned, like angels put in hell by God. I am a vampire",[9] but his listener does not believe him and considers he is just a provocative heathen. As a result, Louis concludes: "I sank my teeth into his neck".[10]

This very dark scene is missing from the screen adaptation. As the murder of a cleric, together with sacrilegious acts and blasphemous words would indisputably be opportunities for spectacular pictures, Neil Jordan decided not to include them in the film. How can this choice be explained? Is it due to his religious upbringing, to a deliberate wish not to provoke outrage or angry responses from the church authorities, or offend the sensibilities of some members of the audience?

6   *Ibid.*, 131.
7   *Ibid.*, 132. Quotation from Gen. 4:11.
8   *Ibid.*, 133.
9   *Ibid.*, 134.
10   *Ibid.*, 135.

The myth of the vampire is delicate because it has to do with the dogma of transubstantiation, which explains why the Catholic Church ignored this creature. Indeed, as the Church, from its origins, had accepted all kinds of ghosts, witches, demons and evil spirits, it refused bloodsuckers. In the eighteenth century, a written document from Pope Benedict XIV forbade exorcisms against vampires, who were considered as the products of pure fancy. The Church showed reserve and worries about vampires who shake the essential *raison d'être* of Christendom.

As he transfuses the blood of fertility, the vampire is both the great comforter and supreme saviour. His bite gives eternal life to those who drink his blood. As a result, he has certain similarities to the Son of God. Did not Christ say: "Whoever drinks my blood possesses eternal life"?[11] The vampire is a creature whose existence is not indebted to the divinity, whose power defies humankind. But is the vampire's capacity to generate creatures like himself satanic? The question preys on Louis's mind. The myth of the vampire is a perverse, blasphemous version of a myth of creation which takes us back to the origins of the world according to the Book of Genesis.

In Rice's novel, the vampire himself narrates his own story, just like the monstrous creature in Mary Shelley's *Frankenstein*. These narrators are in revolt, as can be seen from the way they give vent to their bitterness and satisfy their desires for personal revenge.

Revolt is also a feeling experienced by Anne Rice herself: as she was writing *Interview with the Vampire*, her 6-year-old daughter had just died of leukemia. Born into a Catholic Irish-American family, Rice revolted against God: if He existed, how could He tolerate such events? She was in the depths of despair when she wrote this novel. The myth of the vampire establishes a link between her experience of loss and mourning and there is most probably something cathartic about it. In 1998, Anne Rice drew closer to the Catholic Church but, ten years later, distanced herself again from this institution which, according to her, did not warmly welcome the homosexual community. As she supported her openly gay son's activism, she claimed to be an independent believer. Rice's changing moods are mirrored through Louis's religious questioning and fundamental melancholy.

11   John 6:54-55.

By the same token, Neil Jordan's Irishness and Catholicism show through the film. As any adaptation, his movie is a fully fledged work whose complexion is determined by the artist's personality, opinions and ideologies. As a matter of fact, the religious discourse is not as present in the adaptation as it is in the original text. Unlike the writer, the film-maker is not in revolt against God. Maybe he sees in the violation of a tabernacle and the scattering of holy hosts eaten by rats an act of violence too closely associated with the writer's personal history. Besides, contrary to a certain number of Irish artists of his generation, Neil Jordan never shows any hostility to the Catholic Church. He does not even blame it whether in his films, books or interviews. Although, in the 1990s, this institution was the target of scathing attacks from the media, public opinion and the artistic world, following the revelations of evil deeds within the clergy, Neil Jordan deliberately steers clear of this debate.[12]

Another aspect through which Jordan's point of view is perceptible concerns his choice to delete the second part of the book. This is here another major difference between the text and its screen adaptation. Indeed, the latter leaves aside Louis and Claudia's trip to Central Europe, which is only rapidly evoked through a few clichés. True, adapting a five-hundred-page novel into a two-hour film is a difficult task. Some drastic cuts inevitably have to be made, but it is worth trying to understand why this part was deleted, as if the protagonists travelled directly from New Orleans to Paris.

Here again, the second part contributes to giving the novel a satanic element. During the transatlantic crossing, the ship is struck by a strange "fever". There are marks on the throats of the sick passengers. Louis realizes then that "there would be no rest in damnation, could be no rest (...); what consolation it would be to know Satan".[13] With Claudia, he reaches the Carpathians where the natives believe that the dead wander among them and suck blood from the living people at night. In a miserable inn, the two protagonists meet Morgan, an English tourist whose wife Emily has just passed away during their wedding night. Morgan lets them see

---

12   As Val Nolan puts it: "Jordan's portrayal of Catholicism's (...) spiritual aspects in his fiction can often be surprisingly sympathetic" (Nolan, *Neil Jordan: Work for the Page*, 33).

13   Rice, *Interview with the Vampire,* 149.

her body and curses God: on her throat, there are two puncture wounds, engraved in the skin, which is the evidence that a vampire is loitering in the vicinity. Morgan is all the more in desperate straits as the local population wants to drive a stake into Emily's heart, cut off her head and burn her corpse. In front of Louis, he bursts out: "French, English, we're civilized men. They're savages!"[14] With a crucifix offered by the inn-keeper to protect him, Louis walks at night to the ruins of a gothic castle where he meets with the vampire who killed the woman, fights against him and manages to eliminate him.

Considering the region where the second part of the book takes place, together with the details about the means to get rid of those evil creatures, Rice's novel calls up all sorts of vampire paraphernalia. And yet, it never mentions the names of Dracula or Bram Stoker. The film, on the contrary, actually alludes to the director's fellow countryman and even mentions its hero's name, although it only briefly evokes the characters' trip to Central Europe. Indeed, talking to Malloy, Louis acknowledges he found "nothing in Europe, except rumours, nonsense about garlic, crucifixes, stakes through the heart.

> - So there are no vampires in Transylvania? No Count Dracula?
> - Fictions, my friend. The vulgar fictions of a demented Irishman".

As Bram Stoker's compatriot, Neil Jordan is familiar with the figure of the vampire.[15] Besides, the two writers have affinities. It is significant that the film mentions the name of Dracula, which is immediately associated with the theme of vampirism. Lord Ruthven, the hero of Byron-Polidori's *Vampire,* which was published before Stoker's novel, could have been mentioned, but the reference would not have been so clear because the text is not so well-known.[16] A second veiled reference to Dracula can be spotted at the end of the film when Louis, back to New Orleans in 1988, goes to a movie theatre to watch sunrises that he cannot enjoy in reality any more: in a fine example of *mise en abyme,* a short extract from

---

14   *Ibid.,* 164.
15   The myth of the vampire is reexamined in Neil Jordan's film *Byzantium* (2012).
16   However, Ruthven is the name given to the villain in *Byzantium.*

Murnau's film *Nosferatu* is shown within the film. Obviously, unlike the novel, Jordan's screen adaptation pays a glowing tribute to Dracula.

The Irish cultural heritage can be spotted not only in these references or allusions to Bram Stoker's vampire, but also in the promise of immortality that is combined with it. According to Celtic mythology, there is a mythical land where time does not end with death. The place is peopled with creatures whose indestructible bodies remain young and healthy. It is the land of eternal youth, *Tyr Na Nog*. Dorian Gray, Oscar Wilde's hero, seems to be a part of it insofar as time has no hold on him. Doubtless, there are similarities between Louis and Dorian Gray. Indeed, both of them are caught in a trap after making a thoughtless wish without realizing that some time they would have to pay the price. Both of them are at the mercy of a harmful Mephistophelian corrupter. Both of them live in a fantastic world: they sell their souls in exchange for eternal youth. The Faustian myth is debunked. In a disillusioned voice, Louis says: "I had now lived in two centuries, seen the illusions of one utterly shattered by the other, been eternally young and eternally ancient, possessing no illusions".[17] Dorian and Louis are weary sensualists, damned heroes who break scandals, but also sully, tarnish and destroy the ones who come across them. They have a lot in common: the taste for youthful beauty, for sin and contravention, but also their unintentional murders and incapacity to ease their minds. Their seductive beauty conceals a dark satanic side. Under their virtuous exteriors, there is something vicious about them. Like Dorian, Louis cannot stand the evil other in himself. The motif of the double plays an essential part in *The Picture of Dorian Gray* as in *Interview with the Vampire*. The double is the symbol of dualistic opposition; it is the mirror image, the mask and portrait: after drawing the curtains, Dorian is face to face with himself, until he becomes the reflection of the canvas, then the horrible thing which he observes with disgust.

Louis does not look like Dracula or Lestat; he is not such a bad fellow. He is a new kind of vampire, an ingenuous, romantic one, both good and evil. Confronted with a moral dilemma, he keeps his human conscience. Louis is a sensible and sensitive being who loves and suffers because he is

17   Rice, *Interview with the Vampire*, 129.

deeply unsatisfied. As a pathetic, unhappy narrator, he wins the reader over because he can also prove to be a likeable character. His behaviour could be due to his split personality, his vicious id and helpless self.

***

Vampires can be considered as superheroes, fallen angels or vulgar butcher boys. Francie Brady is not as bloodthirsty as Louis and Lestat, but he brings chaos and death to an innocent family. *The Butcher Boy* (1997) is a film by Neil Jordan adapted from Patrick McCabe's novel, which was published five years earlier.[18]

"The Butcher Boy" is first and foremost a song by The Clancy Brothers and Tommy Makem (1961) which relates a tragic love story: "its all about a woman hanging from a rope all because this butcher boy told her lies".[19] Francie's mother keeps listening to this song, an obsession which could possibly play a part on her final decision to kill herself.

The butcher boy is Francie Brady, the young protagonist who after giving up school prematurely works in a slaughterhouse where he cuts up, packages and carries meat. He also becomes a butcher, in the vilest sense of the word when, in a killing frenzy, he murders and eviscerates Mrs Nugent, the mother of his schoolmate Philip.

The story takes place in the early 1960s in a fictional little town of Ireland, Carn, the name of which is suggestive of meat, carnality and carnage.[20] The film renders the outdated atmosphere of those days very well: the characters' haircuts, clothes and glasses, the few cars in the streets, the national specificities, particularly the weight of the Catholic Church on society, but also the international context of the Cold War, with references to Kennedy and Khruchtchev, to the Cuban missile crisis, the threatening extension of the Communist world or the fear of a nuclear war.

18 In the three adaptations treated in this chapter, the titles of the films are exactly the same as the titles of the books which inspired them.

19 Patrick McCabe, *The Butcher Boy* (London: Picador, 1992), 46.

20 *Carn* is the title of Patrick McCabe's first novel. It refers to a small, imaginary town which is supposed to be a microcosm of the Irish nation (Patrick McCabe, *Carn* [London: Picador, 1989]).

Francie Brady is a typically Irish red-haired teenager. The son of an alcoholic father and a depressive mother who finally commits suicide, he tells his own story in the first person. This unique point of view traps the reader who has no other choice but to share the hallucinations of the narrator whose deranged mind cannot distinguish reality from his fantasy world. As the narrative progresses, Francie's paranoiac delirium intensifies to such an extent that it leads to murder.

The Nugents are back in Carn from England where they spent a few years. This family is the opposite of Francie's: there is order, affective stability and material well-being in the house. One day, Mrs Nugent, who pays attention to whom her son is mixing with, rings the Bradys' doorbell to complain about Francie who stole Philip's comic books. Straightaway, she attacks and insults the Brady family, as Francie narrates with his own words:

> Nugent started on about the pigs. She said she knew the kind of us long before she went to England and she might have known not to let her son anywhere near the likes of me what else would you expect from a house where the father's never in, lying about the pubs from morning to night, he's no better than a pig. You needn't think we don't know what goes on in this house oh we know all right! Small wonder the boy is the way he is what chance has he got running about the town at all hours and the clothes hanging off him it doesn't take money to dress a child God love him it's not his fault but if he's seen near our Philip again there'll be trouble. There'll be trouble now mark my words!
>
> After that ma took my part and the last thing I heard was Nugent going down the lane and calling back *Pigs – sure the whole town knows that!*[21]

This bestial metaphor triggers off obsessional delirium which leads Francie to identify himself with a pig. In order to avenge his humiliated family, he breaks into the Nugents' house, leaves his excrement in the middle of the living-room, turns the whole place upside down and writes PIG in big letters on the walls. He does not miss an opportunity to threaten and harass Mrs Nugent whenever he meets her. On his ultimate visit, more delirious than ever, he applies the know-how acquired in his job to murder her as he does with an animal at the slaughterhouse.

---

21   Patrick McCabe, *The Butcher Boy*, 10.

The representation of Irish people under the traits of pigs is based upon the caricatures of some English magazines of the colonial period. Flann O'Brien exposes this racist stereotype in *The Poor Mouth*, a novel he first wrote in Irish in 1941.[22] In an unspecified past, a Gaelic-speaking family lives in the west of Ireland, in an isolated cottage where humans and animals share bed and board. There is a very strong smell in the house because of the presence of Ambrose, a pig so huge that it cannot get out of the place. When the English government decides to pay a sum of two sterling pounds a year for each child who gives up Gaelic to speak English, Mr O'Coonassa, whose household counts more pigs than children, has the idea of dressing up all his piglets in clothes to make them look like kids and qualify for the award. In order to persuade his wife, he justifies his brilliant idea:

> Our sow Sarah has a great crowd of a family at present and they have vigorous voices, even though their dialect is unintelligible to us. How do we know but that their conversation isn't in English. Of course, youngsters and piglets have the same habits and take notice that there's a close likeness between their skins.[23]

On his visit, the British inspector who does not feel like venturing into the end of the smoky, smelly cottage, contents himself with questioning the eldest child who mumbles a couple of English words, and writes down that the twelve O'Coonassa children have command of the language. The text sarcastically exploits the cliché of the Irish pig that was so popular in the Victorian press.

Taking the metaphor literally, Francie Brady considers that since he is called a pig, he will behave like one. As in *Interview with the Vampire*, his human nature recedes before turning to brutal savagery. Both films describe the descent into hell of a social outcast who is plagued by his obsessions and left to his own devices.[24] Abandoned in turn by his mother,

---

22   Flann O'Brien, *An Béal Bocht* (Dublin: An Preas Naisuinta, 1941).

23   Flann O'Brien, *The Poor Mouth* [1941] (London: Paladin, 1988), 36.

24   The numerous night scenes in the two films mirror the protagonists' descent into hell. It is also significant that both Louis and Francie burn down their houses: on the one hand, the fire refers to the eternal flames of Gehenna, but on the other, it can also be interpreted as the characters' desire for getting rid of unpleasant

his father and his uncle, then disowned by his best friend, Francie is sent to a reform school where the only character who seems to be benevolent with him proves to be a paedophile priest. Then he is given electric shock treatment and is locked up in a psychiatric hospital for several decades. The first sentence of the narrative shows that he is not fully aware of what he went through: "When I was a young lad twenty or thirty or forty years ago I lived in a small town where they were all after me on account of what I done on Mrs Nugent".[25]

Society is depicted as being unable to help Francie. It is hostile, merciless towards the one who proves to be different. Although religion is ubiquitous, particularly through holy pictures, statues, crucifixes, prayers and processions, it does not turn out to be helpful either. If they are not paedophiles, the priests take an interest in Francie only when he claims that the Virgin Mary appears to him. Similarly, public authorities, doctors,[26] nurses, teachers, neighbours, friends and relatives prove to be unable to give the mentally disturbed young man any support. Ireland as a whole is represented here as "the old sow that eats her farrow", as Joyce put it in *The Portrait of the Artist*.[27] This is why Francie, who is first an innocent victim, becomes a monstrous predator, like the vampire Louis.

Irish identity is implicitly questioned by the novel, which was published at the end of the twentieth century. As the values of the past have been rejected, what foundations can Irish society rely on? The pictures of a huge nuclear explosion mushroom cloud of post-apocalyptic desolation in a town reduced to ashes probably hint at the destruction of the past, but there is no promising future on the horizon. What is going to rise from

---

memories and keeping their distance from a situation that has developed into a real infernal mess.

25   McCabe, *The Butcher Boy*, 1.

26   Francie is not properly treated for his trouble by the medical profession. Hospital psychiatrists are portrayed as incompetent, just like the family doctor who, in the book as in the film, is compared to Dracula: "I wasn't expecting Roche so I got a bit of a shock when I looked up and seen him standing there staring at me. Who the fuck did he think he was. Count Dracula?" (*The Butcher Boy*, 105).

27   James Joyce, *A Portrait of the Artist as a Young Man* [1915], in *The Portable James Joyce* (London: Penguin, 1983), 470. Joyce certainly did not choose the metaphor by chance.

these ashes? The film shows Francie's fantasies in this end-of-the-world atmosphere where wasp-faced extraterrestrials emerge, sitting astride some grotesque mounts like parodies of the Horsemen of the Apocalypse. Chaos and desolation invade Francie's universe. In the last scene of the novel, he is walking in the snow, crying at the gates of the hospital, whereas the film closes with a more optimistic touch: Our Lady hands a flower to him, a snowdrop whose white colour blooms at the end of winter like an indication of better days.

Apart from a few exceptions, the film is faithful to the novel. A close relation between them can be noted. It must be borne in mind that the script is the fruit of a close collaboration between the film-maker and the novelist who are not only compatriots, but also members of the same generation. Therefore, they share common memories of the Irish society of the 1960s and could easily agree on several points, particularly the visual elements to be highlighted in the screen adaptation.

On the whole, however, the film is not as dark as the novel, maybe because of the protagonist's casual attitude, which is emphasized by the soundtrack. The songs of Frank Sinatra, jazz or cavalry tunes, but also the overture to 'William Tell' by Rossini provide the adaptation with a light, playful, superficial atmosphere which contrasts with the seriousness of the subject. This burlesque gap is relevant: indeed, the grotesque chases, shot to the sound of a band with great shouts of joy, mirror the hero's schizophrenia and irresponsibility. Francie proves to be cheerful when he spreads panic and devastation.

Another marked contrast can be noticed when the Holy Mass is turned into a vulgar match by a patient of the mental home. The circularity of the host shown by the priest at the Elevation is parodically superimposed on the shape of the ball which scores a goal:

> When we went to Mass what does he do when the priest is holding up the Eucharist. <Walter> stands up and shouts at the top of his voice – Good man yourself! Now you have it – *run!* Into the back of the net with her! By Christ this year's team is the best yet![28]

28   McCabe, *The Butcher Boy*, 155.

The liturgical ritual is belittled here by a process of debasement which is closer to a schoolboy prank than to iconoclastic fury. In this field, once again, Neil Jordan distinguishes himself from the novelist. His film is not as virulent as the book in the way religion and clerics are represented. True, in the film, Francie is irreverent towards statues[29] but, unlike the protagonist of the book, he does not utter blasphemous remarks, nor does he commit any sacrileges. For example, in the novel, he and a priest visit the reform school where he will have to stay for a few weeks: "I pointed to Our Lady. She's in a bad way I said to him, she needs to suck a zube".[30] Later, he breaks statues deliberately and when he serves mass, parodies the rite by twisting the usual phrases irreverently:

> I'd carry the cruets and stuff and off we'd go me and Father Sullivan like two big whispers moving along the corridor to the chapel rustle rustle. Domine, exaudi orationem meam, he'd say with the hands outspread. I was supposed to say Et clamor meus ad te veniat. Et fucky wucky ticky tocky that was what I said instead. But it didn't matter as long as you muttered something. Father Sull never listened anyway.[31]

The young narrator stresses the transformation of the words – what he is supposed to say, and what he says instead – for parody would pass unnoticed if the initial text was not identified.

The fundamental difference between the text and its screen adaptation is in the abuse of paedophile priests, which is depicted in detail by the novel and only hinted at by the film. Francie is far from being innocent, but he minutely describes the lecherous habits of Father Sullivan whose nickname – Tiddly – shows his small capacities:

> What does Sull do only plant this big slobbery wet kiss right on my lips. (...) Sit up here he said and slapped his knees. So up I went. What does Tiddly do then only take out his mickey and start rubbing it up and down and jogging me on his knee. Then his whole body vibrates and he bends away over I thought he was going to break off in two halves.[32]

---

29   "Fuck off!" (McCabe, *The Butcher Boy*, 137).

30   McCabe, *The Butcher Boy*, 69.

31   McCabe, *The Butcher Boy*, 76.

32   *Ibid.*, 79.

These two halves reveal the character's duplicity. The ingenuousness of the description makes the situation all the blacker and shows again, in a burlesque contrast, how the spiritual is replaced by the lowest temporal. The narrative alternates Francie's descriptions of paedophile and masturbatory scenes with the priest's demonstrations of guilt:

> Tiddly just crumpled up like a paper bag and lay there hiding his eyes and saying no (...). Tiddly says dear God I'm sorry Francis (...). I said nothing and just sat there with my mickey snoozing on my thigh smoking fags and reading about Matt <Talbot> and all the saints. Blessed Oliver Plunkett! Chopped in quarters! For fuck's sake![33]

The detail about his own bare flesh implies that the narrator is also naked and has probably been sexually abused by the priest.[34] The narrative deliberately allows some doubt. Two pages further, a similar scene is repeated:

> Then the next time he starts this breathing into my ear. He said I smelt like St Teresa's roses and he'd give me as many Rolos as I wanted if I told him the worst bad thing I ever did. I told him things about the town but he kept saying no no worse than that and I could feel his hand trembling under me. No matter what I told him it still wasn't bad enough. No he says you must have something worse than that something you are afraid to tell anyone something you are so ashamed of you don't want anyone in the wide world to know about. I told him to stop I didn't want him to do it I didn't want him to say it anymore. But he wouldn't stop. I could barely hear him but he was still saying something you could never forgive yourself for a terrible thing Francis a terrible thing please tell me I said stop it! But he wouldn't then I heard ma again it wasn't your fault Francie I got a grip of him by the wrist I just grabbed on to it and sank my teeth in he went white and cried out No Francie!, I said *stop it don't ever say it again!*[35]

These dialectics of the 'worse' correspond to the priest's craving to hear a salacious confession. And yet, there is nothing sexual about Francie's worst action: the thing he is "so ashamed of" is linked to his feeling of

---

33   *Ibid.*, 80.
34   Later, Francie tells his friend Joe what happened: "Joe kept going back to the other thing so in the end I told him and what does he say then he says Francie he didn't really do that did he? I said what are you talking about Joe he *did* didn't I just tell you?" (97). What does "that" refer to: the priest's masturbation or sexual abuse?
35   *Ibid.*, 82.

guilt as a son: he broke his promise to watch over his mother and proved unable to protect her and prevent her death. This is why, confronted with this painful reality, he gets angry and reacts aggressively with the priest who involuntarily reminds him of these terrible events.

The film neglects these scenes. It is content with showing Francie lying on a sofa near the priest who leans over him to have a word in his ear, whereas the audience can easily guess what the man's hand is doing under his cassock. The priest is masturbating, but does not commit any act of indecency with the teenager. Here again, the scene is treated in a flippant way and could even be considered as situation comedy if the subject was not so risqué. Anyway, the young protagonist of the film is neither traumatized nor even upset by the man's objectively unacceptable schemes, all the more so as he is not strictly speaking his victim, as there does not seem to be any sexual abuse.

As Neil Jordan himself says, he wants his film to show how powerful the Catholic Church was in twentieth-century Irish society:

> My films are always on the dividing line between fantasy and reality. It is most probably the fruit of my Catholic education (...). In *The Butcher Boy*, I wanted to portray the strange atmosphere of the Ireland of my childhood. It was a poor, isolated country; it was also very naïve, superstitious and paranoiac. Everything was under the control of the Catholic Church which chose the clothes you had to wear and even seemed to make people's beds.[36]

Even if he takes a critical look at the Catholic Church of his early days, Neil Jordan does not turn out to be an apostate in his artistic production. He does not seem to have any scores to settle with the Church, unlike many other Irish writers of his generation, including Patrick McCabe

---

36   My translation. « Mes films jouent toujours aux frontières de la fantaisie. Ma fascination découle moins de la culture irlandaise mais elle doit être plutôt le fruit de mon éducation catholique (...). J'ai voulu rappeler, à travers *Le Garçon boucher*, l'ambiance bizarre de l'Irlande de mon enfance. C'était un pays pauvre et isolé, plein de naïveté, de paranoïa et de superstition. L'Eglise catholique contrôlait tout. Elle déterminait les vêtements et semblait même faire le lit des gens » (Marcus Rothe, « Neil Jordan remonte aux sources rêvées de son enfance », *L'Humanité*, 6 mai 1998).

who shares his personal opinion about what he considers as the harmful influence of this institution on society. Neil Jordan remains out of this sphere. Nevertheless, it would be a mistake to consider him as a faithful member of the flock: his engagement as a film-maker with Catholicism is not uncritical. This is obvious in the casting as the Virgin Mary of singer Sinéad O'Connor, who is known for her controversial and provocative relationship with the Church. Did not she tear in two a picture of Pope John-Paul II in a popular TV show in the early 1990s to protest against the Church which, she argued, was guilty of abusing its power?[37]

Neil Jordan's choice to cast Sinéad O'Connor in this role can be interpreted as his subscribing to her personal initiative, although the script of the film never passes any judgement on the religious institution or its representatives. Obviously, Neil Jordan is much more interested in the 'fantasies' and 'strangeness' of those days, to take up his own words. He portrays some uncanny scenes without trying to denounce any culprits in the real world. His adaptations of *Interview with the Vampire* and *The Butcher Boy* show his interest in atypical characters who live on the fringe of society, in hybrid creatures who prove to be different and surreal, while still anchored in the human condition. All of these characters plunge into a strange world, into an extraordinary atmosphere which is a constant theme for Neil Jordan whose work is closely akin to the novels he adapts for the screen.

***

The third adaptation of a literary work – *The End of the Affair* – shows once more that everyday life and the irrational can be closely interwoven. The novel of the same title, written by Graham Greene in 1951, relates an adulterous love story between the narrator, Maurice Bendrix, and Henry Miles's wife, Sarah. The plot is set in London during the Second World War. In June 1944, the house where Sarah and Maurice spend the night together is damaged by a bomb. Bendrix is knocked out, lying unconscious

---

37   This act of provocation was performed in a broadcast of *Saturday Night Live* on the American TV channel NBC on 3 October 1992.

in a pool of blood, under a door which has been blown up. Sarah thinks he is dead. Distraught, she immediately kneels down and prays:

> Dear God, make me believe (…). I will believe. Let him be alive, and I *will* believe. Give him a chance (…). I love him and I'll do anything if you'll make him alive (…). I'll give him up for ever, only let him be alive with a chance.[38]

When Maurice miraculously comes back, Sarah realizes that her prayer has been answered and that her wish must be respected. She puts an end to their affair without giving any explanations to her lover who, as an atheist, would not understand them. Progressively, she draws closer to spiritual values and comes to profess her faith – "I believe in God" – a short time before she dies of a lung infection in February 1946.

The protagonists are affected *a contrario* by the events of history. Indeed, the air raids and bombings, particularly the Blitz which ravaged London, are associated with happy days for the lovers. On the contrary, the year 1945, which celebrates victory and liberation, is tainted by sadness, suffering and depression, insofar as both of them are haunted by their memories without being able to come to terms with the fact that they have split up.

The novel is a conversion story. There is something autobiographical about it, not only because the Protestant author converted to Catholicism when he was 22, but also because he had an adulterous relationship with a married woman.[39] Graham Greene's whole work depicts ambiguous unorthodox characters such as Bendrix, a man jealous of his mistress who "deceives" him with God. Seeing the latter as his rival, he expends a lot of efforts to win back his lover, but in vain. Although he considers himself as fundamentally atheistic, he speaks to God at the end of the narrative. There are elements of prayer and settling of scores in his words:

> You've taken her, but you haven't got me yet. (…) I don't want Your peace and I don't want Your love. I wanted something very simple and very easy: I wanted Sarah for a lifetime and You took her away. With Your great schemes You ruin our happiness like a harvester ruins a mouse's nest: I hate You, God, I hate You as though You existed.

---

38 Graham Greene, *The End of the Affair* [1951] (London: Vintage, 2004), 76.

39 Greene, who was a married man, made no secret of his affair with Catherine Walston, wife of aspiring Labour Party politician Harry Walston.

> (...). O God, You've done enough, You've robbed me of enough, I'm too tired and old to learn to love, leave me alone for ever.[40]

Spiritual quest, conflict between faith and doubt, salvation through betrayal are Graham Greene's favourite themes. His protagonists often try to snatch others from the way they do not want them to take. There is an atmosphere of tension in his books and films. For Greene, like Neil Jordan, is not only a novelist, but also a film-maker: he made screen adaptations and wrote scripts, including a classic of the *film noir, The Third Man* in 1949.

The mysterious atmosphere of *The End of the Affair* probably influenced Neil Jordan when he wrote his own novel *The Drowned Detective* a few years later. Indeed, in both texts, the male protagonist is haunted by a woman's ghost. This woman, in her lifetime, is shadowed by a detective whose objective is to dig up anything about her and struggle with her secret life. In Greene's novel, Bendrix has to steal her diary to discover the truth. He learns then that if she refuses to see him, it is not because she is involved in other affairs with new lovers, but because she made a promise to God and endeavours to honour it in recognition of her granted request.

Like Jordan's two previous cinematic adaptations, *The End of the Affair* is focused on the considerable effects that words can have when they are taken literally. The speakers do not anticipate the potential consequences of their wishes made in the heat of action. By calling the Bradys pigs, Mrs Nugent does not think about the import of what she is saying on Francie's behaviour. With this insult, she signs her own death warrant. In *Interview with the Vampire*, Louis, at death's door, expresses the wish to give himself body and soul to Lestat. These words seal his fate forever. Finally, in *The End of the Affair,* Sarah, who is also confronted with death, implores God to spare her lover's life; she promises to mend her ways and give up this adulterous affair in exchange. Taken at her word, she considers she has to honour her solemn commitment and actually breaks up with Bendrix, although her commitment is based on a mistake, her lover being only injured. Sarah however shows total abnegation in the respect of her deal, but

---

40   *Ibid.,* 159-160.

when Bendrix discovers the truth, he refuses to sacrifice what he considers as their common interest.

This is one of the differences between the novel and the film. In the book, Bendrix and Sarah meet twice after eighteen months' silence. First, they have lunch together at a restaurant; the second time, they have a conversation in a London church. The reunions are limited to verbal exchanges. In the film, they go to Brighton where their affair starts again. For Neil Jordan, the seaside resort is a magical place where everything is possible, where people can express themselves freely and joyfully, as the funfair on the pier suggests.[41] During that stay, Bendrix informs Sarah that he would like to have a child with her. He thinks she is going to leave her husband, but learns from the latter a few days later that the woman they love is seriously ill and that there is no hope for her. Her life expectancy is only six months. As a result, any plans for the future are now out of the question. At Henry's request, Bendrix moves into the couple's house where the two men watch in turn over the dying woman. In the novel, Henry and Bendrix live under the same roof only after Sarah's death.

The eternal triangular relationship – husband, wife, lover – which could be appallingly trite, is here worthy of interest on account of the complexity, ambivalence and psychological depth of the characters whose evolution can be followed as the story progresses.

Sarah is initially described as a woman of easy virtue – "Any man could have her"[42] – but she makes a complete break with her past life and becomes a believer, if not a saint. She gives vent to her heart's enthusiastic impulses in her diary, invokes God with Augustinian echoes: "But, dear God, what shall I do with this desire to love?"[43] She is clearly torn between her physical desire for a man and her promise to God. The pages of her diary dated 1944 are written by an unhappy woman bound with a "stupid vow",[44] a woman revolted by the fact that her lover will be unable to understand her radical decision. But, with time, Sarah seems to feel progressively serene. The last pages, written in 1946, show that in spite of her serious illness, she

41   Some scenes of Jordan's films *Mona Lisa* and *Byzantium* are set there.
42   *Ibid.*, 150.
43   *Ibid.*, 74.
44   *Ibid.*, 84.

is at peace with her conscience: "I wasn't afraid of the desert any longer because You were there".[45] After her death, she answers the prayers of the ones who have known and loved her. Implored by Bendrix, she helps him get out of danger when he is tempted by a young woman, by sending her own mother between them; she cures Lance Parkis, the detective's son, of violent stomach-aches; last, Richard Smythe, a rationalist speaker who had conversations about God with Sarah, goes to her and pays tribute to her body when he hears about her death. He steals a tuft of her hair on which he falls asleep. He suffers from a skin disease which ravages a part of his face. In the following morning, his face is totally cleansed. Smythe states the facts over the phone with Bendrix, the narrator:

'Nobody treated my face. It cleared up, suddenly, in a night.'

'How? I still don't ...'

He said with an awful air of conspiracy, 'You and I know how. There's no getting round it. It wasn't right of me keeping it dark. It was a ...' but I put down the receiver before he could use that foolish newspaper word that was the alternative to 'coincidence'.[46]

What some interpret as miracles[47] are only coincidences for others. And Bendrix goes on: "I tried to summon up all my faith in coincidence (...) and I thought with a sense of weariness, how many coincidences are there going to be?"[48] Upset, entertaining doubts about his own atheism, he comes to wonder "whether a faith cure is possible".[49]

As for Sarah's husband, Henry, he is depicted as a man totally devoted to his position as a top-ranking civil servant. He has no physical desire for his wife, but shows a lot of respect for her, even if he suffers from the

45 *Ibid.*, 90.
46 *Ibid.*, 157.
47 Such events that cannot be explained according to the laws of nature and are considered to be acts of God are interesting and puzzling for Neil Jordan who made a film precisely titled *The Miracle* in 1991, but also for Graham Greene who witnessed Padre Pio's stigmata in a monastery in Southern Italy.
48 Graham Greene, *The End of the Affair*, 157-158.
49 *Ibid.*, 160.

situation. Their relationship is based on the implicit. Although he is aware of her extramarital affairs, he never judges her. He is described as a frustrated homosexual, particularly when he invites his dead wife's lover to sleep in his house, then to stay with him. He obviously longs for being on very intimate terms with a man, as he recognizes himself when he confesses to Bendrix: "I look forward to these evening walks of ours (...) They are the only things I do look forward to".[50]

And yet Bendrix, the narrator of a great part of the story, is far from being a likeable character. In his affair, he harasses and torments Sarah, and proves to be quarrelsome with her. He feels humiliated for being abandoned without any explanations and reacts like a selfish male chauvinist, eager for sensual pleasures: "if I could have her once more – however quickly and crudely and unsatisfactorily – I would be at peace again: I would have washed her out of my system, and afterwards I would leave her, not she me".[51] He is full of hatred and jealousy, sticking stubbornly to his desire for revenge. This is why he tries to catch Sarah in a trap by hiring a detective to tail her, whereas Henry quickly gives up this ridiculous idea. As a result, the latter is furious when he learns Bendrix's initiative: "Can't you see that what you've done is – monstrous?"[52]

Bendrix knows that Sarah was secretly baptized when she was a child, that "she caught belief like a disease", that she had "fallen into belief like <she> fell in love".[53] And yet, he persuades Henry not to organize Catholic funerals, in spite of the pressures of those who have been next to her in her last days. He remains unchanged in his rejection of religion and arrogantly sticks to his principles. To God in whom he sees only a rival, he makes outraged, nearly laughable remarks which prove his need to dominate: "Sarah was mine, not Yours. You didn't own her; I owned her (...) It was I who penetrated her, not You (...). It's just a coincidence that nearly brought her back at the end to You".[54]

---

50   *Ibid.,* 160.
51   *Ibid.,* 19.
52   *Ibid.,* 52.
53   *Ibid.,* 121.
54   *Ibid.,* 282-283.

The three protagonists of the film are pretty faithful to the novel models, although Greene's Bendrix is more detestable than Jordan's. As for secondary characters, they are less numerous in the screen adaptation than in the original text. Indeed, the rationalist speaker, Richard Smythe, does not appear in the film. His name is given to Father Crompton who becomes Father Smythe, in whom Bendrix sees Sarah's new lover, which fuels his hostility to the clergy. The priest's distinctive features are not as negative in the film as in the book. In the latter, the clergyman is described as "ugly, haggard, graceless, rigid, bitter, ridiculous, grim-looking and self-important". Generally speaking, the characterization is stronger in the novel than in the script. Besides, the marks that spoil Smythe's looks in the novel are transferred onto Parkis Junior in the film: the child is cured by Sarah who, despite the repulsive aspect of his ailment, does not hesitate to give him a tender kiss. This is the only miraculous cure of the film, whereas there are three of them in the novel.

The End of the Affair is a ghost story with metaphysical undertones. It questions the existence of God and the intervention of supernatural powers in our lives. Humankind – who is at the mercy of the forces of evil, among them, war – is offered a possibility of redemption. Men and women remain torn between sensuality and spirituality, between the world of carnal desire and the one from on high. In the direct tradition of Saint Augustine, whose name is mentioned in the novel,[55] man cannot count on his reason to get to know his Creator, since he is corrupted by original sin. This is why he has to submit to the transcendent authority by his belief in the grace granted by God.

In spite of a certain number of obstacles and temptations, Sarah takes the path to the Christian faith, whereas Francie and Louis take a different one. The former drifts off because of his mental disorders, the latter turns to a dangerous road in the wake of an unpleasant encounter. Louis's transformation into a vampire takes place in a graveyard where the statue of an

---

55   After Sarah's death, Father Crompton tells Henry and Bendrix at dinner: "St Augustine asked where time came from. He said it came out of the future which didn't exist yet, into the present that had no duration, and went into the past which had ceased to exist. I don't know that we can understand time any better than a child" (149-150).

angel follows him with a sidelong look to mean that the young man wanders from the straight and narrow and takes a road which may lead him to ruin. The three screen adaptations by Neil Jordan are focused on the eternal issues of good and evil: some protagonists take the path to conversion, while others the way to perversion.

***

Adaptation is an adjustment which transforms an existing work. In this instance, the transition from a book to a film is a change from the written to the shown: the interpretative appropriation of a text is followed by a representation through a visual medium. Resorting to the camera inevitably displays divergences. In this instance, Neil Jordan develops, deletes and transforms some parts of the texts. His aesthetic choices may change the initial meaning. They mirror his own personal reading of the books. His adaptation is in line with what he is, what he understands and believes, as his approach to religious issues show. It also comes up to the audience's expectations which are different in 2000 from what they were in 1950: as Graham Greene's novel enhances Sarah's generosity of spirit in the way she keeps her promise, the adapted version emphasizes the irony of fate since the young woman learns the imminence of her death when she is about to go back to Bendrix.

On the whole, although adaptation does not necessarily mean faithfulness, these three examples show a close relationship between the film and the book. They do not take excessive liberties with the texts, whether Jordan participates in the writing of the script or not. They extend them, and follow their letters and spirits as much as possible. Neil Jordan is particularly aware of the importance of faithfulness, perhaps because he is a writer himself. And yet, when the words, context or intention seem too dark to him, he does not hesitate to add a few hints of humour.[56]

56   As a young vampire, Claudia, who slits the throats of her preys in the middle of the ornate living-room, is scolded by Lestat who seems to be only annoyed to discover some bloodstains on sofas and carpets: "Not in the house!" he cries out, furious. Likewise, in *The Butcher Boy,* the scenes where Irish housewives, cramped in their raincoats, are gossiping and commenting upon Francie's doings are quite humorous.

Paradoxically, Neil Jordan does not adapt his own literary fiction for the screen, but prefers working from other writers' texts. Why these three novels? Jordan's interest seems to lie in characters who first lead an ordinary life, then plunge suddenly into chaos and the extraordinary. This specificity characterizes Jordan's literary work. Indeed, there are meeting points between these film adaptations and his own written work: the oral character of the narrative, its supernatural universe, its gothic décor and hidden truths are recurring themes in his literary fiction. Similarly, the protagonists of these films have a lot in common with the characters of his books, oscillating between life and death, haunted by ghosts, transformed into monsters, preys to homoerotic leanings or incestuous tendencies, they are in search of God or ponder over metaphysical issues. These convergences account for Neil Jordan's particular interest in these novels that he could have written himself.[57] He would certainly have liked writing them. And yet, is not he somehow the "author" of these books insofar as he adapted them and created a new work out of them?

57   Michel Charles expands on the idea that a literary text is written by the renouncement of possible texts (Cf. Michel Charles, *Introduction à l'étude des textes* [Paris: Seuil, 1995]).

CHAPTER 7

Shade: A Beheaded Actress's Narrative

In his work published in 1973, *The Anxiety of Influence*, Harold Bloom views literary history from the angle of the Oedipus complex and bases his theory of influence upon the notion of inter-generational conflict. According to his approach, any young writer lives in the shade of a famous precursor, and is thus like a son, oppressed by a castrating father. The young writer is so much on the defensive that he distorts his precursor's work: he re-envisions, re-evaluates and revises it when he writes his own text, in a bid to overcome his "anxiety of influence". His text is a response to a previous one. This implies that he has to negotiate with the authority of his predecessor who somewhat becomes the author of his own work, like a ghost who suddenly comes back to life, as Harold Bloom contends through the notion of *Apophrades*:

> *Apophrades*, or the return of the dead; I take the word from the Athenian dismal or unlucky days upon which the dead returned to reinhabit the houses in which they had lived.[1]

Ghosts proliferate in the second work: the ghosts of undeveloped potential texts, the ones who are reactivated from other texts, but also the ghosts who are more or less deliberately summoned. These ghosts are referred to as shadows by Irish literary critics and theorists. Indeed, Benedict Kiely acknowledges: "What I am trying to offer are the random thoughts of a would-be novelist trying to practice under the *shadow* of James Joyce".[2] Dermot Bolger remarks: "Frequently Joyce and others are *shadows* that newer Irish writers

---

1   Harold Bloom, *The Anxiety of Influence. A Theory of Poetry* [1973], 2nd edn (Oxford and New York: Oxford University Press, 1997), introduction, 15.
2   Benedict Kiely, ed., *James Joyce, the Artist and the Labyrinth* (London: Ryan Publishing, 1990), 42. My emphasis.

are trying to avoid being pushed under".[3] Augustine Martin notes: "Our own modest tradition has fallen under the immense and crippling *shadows* of Joyce and Yeats".[4] As for Neil Corcoran, he justifies the title of his essay in the following way:

> [Today's] literature is 'after Yeats and Joyce', [...] that is to say, a literature always to some degree *shadowed* by the achievements of these un-ignorable turn-of-the-century writers.[5]

In this book published in 1997 – *After Yeats and Joyce* – Neil Corcoran quotes the novelist Ferdia MacAnna for whom *Ulysses* is the nightmare of many contemporary writers, to such an extent that some of them renounce to compete with Joyce and finally decide to give up writing.[6] MacAnna cites the case of Neil Jordan who, in the late 1990s, after publishing a book of short stories and two novels, "turned from writing to film-making in the attempt to cast off the long *shadow* of Joyce".[7] A few years earlier, indeed, Jordan had explained: "When I started writing I felt very pressured by the question: how to write stories without being swamped in the language and mythology of Joyce?"[8]

In retrospect, no one can deny that – although he stayed in the background for several years – Neil Jordan did not put an end to his literary career, since he wrote five novels after the publication of Corcoran's essay.[9] Besides, two

---

3   Dermot Bolger, ed., *The Picador Book of Contemporary Irish Fiction* (London and Basingstoke: Pan Books, 1993), viii. My emphasis.

4   Augustine Martin, *Bearing Witness. Essays on Anglo-Irish Literature*, ed. Anthony Roche (Dublin: UCD Press, 1996), 83. My emphasis.

5   Neil Corcoran, *After Yeats and Joyce. Reading modern Irish Literature* (Oxford and New York: Opus Oxford University Press, 1997), preface, vii, viii. My emphasis.

6   "*Ulysses* is the nightmare from which Dublin is trying to awake [...]. Many contemporary writers choose not to read it" (Ferdia MacAnna, "The Dublin Renaissance", *The Irish Review* 10 (Spring 1991), 18; quoted by Neil Corcoran, *After Yeats and Joyce*, 123).

7   Corcoran, *After Yeats and Joyce*, 123. My emphasis.

8   Richard Kearney, ed., *Across the Frontiers – Ireland in the 1990s* (Dublin: Wolfhound Press, 1988), 196-197.

9   *Shade* (2004), *Mistaken* (2011), *The Drowned Detective* (2016), *Carnivalesque* (2017) and *The Ballad of Lord Edward and Citizen Small* (2021).

of them quote Yeats in their epigraphs.[10] It is the case of *Shade*, a novel published in 2004. It is evident that Neil Jordan, then aged 54, who is no longer a young writer, is deliberately in line with a cultural heritage and feels able to write his own fiction without suffering from any particular anxiety, without feeling overshadowed by famous predecessors. It is certainly no matter of chance if the significant word *shade* is the one he uses as the title of his novel published after a long silence. Indeed, *shade* or *shadow* are words also used by Yeats himself when he refers to ghosts.[11] The term is echoed by the epigraph, an excerpt from a poem written in memory of the poet's deceased friends, Eva Gore-Booth and Constance Marciewicz: "Dear shadows, now you know it all".[12] The word is to be understood as the representation of the soul, or the spirit of the dead to which mythic imagery attributes an underground other world which is not widely sundered from our own, according to Yeats.[13] The latter always proves to be puzzled by this mysterious state which follows death, as his poem "Byzantium" shows:

> Before me floats an image, man or shade,
>
> Shade more than man, more image than a shade;
>
> [...]
>
> A mouth that has no moisture and no breath
>
> [...]
>
> I call it death-in-life and life-in-death.[14]

10   *Carnival* and *Shade*. At the beginning of *The Past*, Neil Jordan's first novel, there is an epigraph in the first edition which has been removed from the following ones. This epigraph – "Eternity is passion" – is the first line of the eighth section of Yeats's poem "Supernatural Songs", from the 1935 collection *A Full Moon in March*. It is also worth noting that Jordan's 1999 film *In Dreams* borrows its title from the epigraph to Yeats' 1914 volume *Responsibilities* ("In dreams begins responsibility").

11   "The shade of the departed appearing at times" (William Butler Yeats, *Writings on Irish Folklore, Legend and Myth* [London: Penguin, 1993], 48).

12   W. B. Yeats, "In Memory of Eva Gore-Booth and Con Markiewicz", *The Winding Stair and Other Poems* [1933], in *Collected Poems* (London: Macmillan, 1989), 263.

13   "In Ireland this world and the other are not widely sundered" (William Butler Yeats, "Tales from the Twilight", from the *Scots Observer* [1890], in *Writings on Irish Folklore*, 58).

14   W. B. Yeats, "Byzantium", *The Winding Stair and Other Poems* [1933], in *Collected Poems* (London: Macmillan, 1989), 280. It must be borne in mind that 'Byzantium' is also the title of a film by Neil Jordan (2012).

This breathless mouth mentioned by the poem recalls the female narrator in Neil Jordan's novel.

In 1900, Nina is 3 years old. She lives in Baltray House, a large country estate near the mouth of the river Boyne, with her parents, Mr and Ms Hardy, wealthy Anglo-Irish industrialists. Nina is a whimsical little girl whose imagination runs wild. She creates her own separate universe, imagines stories and regularly talks to her doll Hester, but also to a mysterious secret friend, a ghostly presence that she and no one else can see. She strikes up a friendship with two children of labourers who live across the river, Janie and her somewhat deranged brother George. The threesome extends with the arrival of Gregory, Nina's half-brother whose existence she ignored so far. These four youngsters become inseparable and make a solid quartet whose members start having love affairs together. When George and Gregory are preparing to go to the front in 1914, Nina gives herself to both of them in turn, as if she wanted to consolidate the bonds between them.[15] On the battlefields of the Dardanelles, the two boys watch over each other. Meanwhile, Nina puts an end to her pregnancy with her maid's help, hastily buries the foetus in her shawl and, as she feels misunderstood by her parents, embarks for England where she starts a career as an actress.

Back to Ireland, George, disfigured and psychologically scarred by the war, is confined to a mental hospital. As for Gregory, he settles in London and becomes Nina's manager until they fall in love with the same man and part ways. Nina becomes a film actress and rises to fame in Hollywood.

---

15   Incest is crossing the boundary *par excellence*. Horace Walpole's *The Castle of Otranto* or Matthew Gregory Lewis's *The Monk*, among others, show that it is a recurrent theme in Gothic novels. Incest breaks sexual taboos, violates family structures and is therefore one of the biggest crimes committed in these novels. Some critics, such as Claire Kahane, establish a link between incest and the motif of terror which is peculiar to the genre. And yet *Shade* differs from the traditional Gothic stories insofar as incest does not inspire horror to those who are involved in such relationships. Indeed, Nina is not an outraged victim. She starts an affair with her half-brother on her own initiative and is consequently somewhat responsible for her fateful destiny. Similarly, Gregory is no butcher, tormentor or executioner: he is neither dedicated to evil nor really guilty. Besides, his homosexuality contributes to challenge the archetypal male predatory protagonists of traditional Gothic novels. The same is true of George's disability.

After the Second World War, she returns to Ireland and decides to live in her family's big house, deserted since her parents' deaths. As she thinks she can become friends with George again, Nina gets him out of the hospital and employs him as a gardener. It is while digging that George unearths Nina's shawl in which he discovers the remains of an unborn child. He feels betrayed and decides to take his revenge[16]: he strangles and beheads the woman he was in love with, and dumps her body in the septic tank of the estate.[17] Nina then watches her life flash by, as in a film of which she would be the actress and spectator. This is how she narrates the events which have led to her murder, together with her passage from life to death, while remaining a silent observing shadow.[18] Disembodied, her voice from the beyond makes her an omniscient narrator:

> How can I explain my eye that is bloodless, fleshless, my sight that is constant? [...] How am I everywhere and nowhere? [...] I am your perfect narrator, inhabit then and now, dance between both, am nothing but my story. [...] Being I have and substance none.[19]

---

16   When he comes back from the battlefield, George is disfigured, hideous and monstrous. He behaves like a wild beast, just like other creatures from Neil Jordan's fiction, the titles of which explicitly refer to a beast or a monster (*The Dream of a Beast* and *Sunrise with Sea Monster*). It is worth noting that these uncanny creatures are always male. In *Shade*, Nina's murder by George can be interpreted as a parody of *Beauty and the Beast* which has already been mentioned before. In the fairy tale, the Beast, freed from the magic spell by a woman's love, can have a future with her. In Jordan's novel, the Beast – George – cannot get rid of its monstrous look (although Nina obviously forgets it) and behaves savagely by slaughtering her. Another echo of the fairy tale concerns the father-daughter relationship which is also diverted here. Indeed, unlike Beauty who is in love with her father, Nina leaves her father and breaks up with him once and for all, to the latter's utter despair.

17   In ancient Rome, the first Christian martyrs, once killed, were frequently thrown away in the sewers of the city, as Callista, the protagonist of John Henry Newman's novel, shows (*Callista. A Tale of the Third Century* [1857] [London: Kessinger Publishing, 2008]).

18   Narratives by voices from beyond the grave are characteristics of other Irish novels, such as Samuel Beckett's *Malone Dies* (1951), Flann O'Brien's *The Third Policeman* (1967) or, more recently, Mike McCormack's *Solar Bones* (2016).

19   Neil Jordan, *Shade* (London: John Murray, 2004), 96-97.

Nina has access to pure knowledge without any material contact. In her observation of the world, she only sees her own reflection, her own ghost who has been lurking there since the beginning.[20] From the first to the last page, the narrative alternates eras and points of view in order to depict a rough, chaotic, entrancing, supernatural environment. After the funeral of Nina whose body cannot be found, the river, swollen with heavy rains, melts with the waters of the sea, the tank overflows and releases its contents.

Nina's expulsion from the tank in which she was trapped is a symbolical rebirth. Freed, she can be born again at the end of the narrative once she knows the truth and the reasons why she was killed. Passing from life to death gives access to knowledge, as the epigraph puts it: "Dear shadows, now you know it all". Yeats's words imply that death is a gate to the fundamental knowledge of the mysteries of existence.[21]

20   This ghostly reflection can be related to the motif of the double which generates an uncanny feeling. Nina's partnership with her doll or with her imaginary friend shows her dual personality which is reminiscent of the *Doppelgänger* of fantastic Gothic tradition. This is a specificity of Neil Jordan's work in which the motif of the double is omnipresent. In *Shade*, Nina forms an association with her neighbour Janie, with her friend George; she also matches with Gregory, then with Jonathan. The theme of the double is also exemplified by the parts Nina plays on stage: each character – Rosalind, the Colleen Bawn and Orinthia – being in turn her *alter ego*.

21   And yet, it is not what the poem writes, since the quote is followed by: "now you know it all / All the folly of a fight / With a common wrong or right". The "folly of the fight" refers to the commitments undertaken by the two sisters, Constance Markiewicz and Eva Gore-Booth, who dedicated a great part of their lives to the common people to whom they did not belong: Eva Gore-Booth was a feminist poet, Christian mystic and social reformer. In 1897, she moved to Manchester where she campaigned among textile workers for women's emancipation; she became editor of *Women's Labour News* and in 1914 joined the Women's Peace Crusade. Constance Markiewicz, née Gore-Booth, was a republican socialist. She joined Sinn Fein, fought in the 1916 Rising, as an officer of the Irish Citizen Army, but her death sentence was commuted because of her sex. She became the first woman elected to the House of Commons (1918) but did not take her seat. She was the Minister for Labour in the first Dail Eireann, rejected the Anglo-Irish Treaty, and fought and was imprisoned during the Civil War. Their friends William Butler Yeats deplored that they did not stay in Lissadell, the family's property, to give vent to their artistic gifts.

The poem is in tune with the novel it opens, considering the motifs of shadows, of women's untimely deaths or more generally destruction, the universe of the Big House being doomed to end. The theme of knowledge, brought out by the quotation, is also essential in the novel, the narrator of which describes herself as omniscient, as the first two words of the narrative put it: "I know". (*S*, 3)

Access to knowledge is also a central motif in the Celtic legend of the Boyne, the novel being set on the mouth of the river. Formerly there was a well, shaded by nine magic hazel-trees. These trees bore crimson nuts, and it was the property of the nuts that whoever ate of them immediately became possessed of the knowledge of everything that was in the world. Only divine salmon had this privilege: living in the well, they swallowed the nuts as they dropped from the trees into the water, and thus knew all things, and appear as the "Salmon of Knowledge". All others, even the highest gods, were forbidden to approach the place. Only Boann dared to disobey this fixed law. She came towards the sacred well, but, as she did so, its waters rose up at her, and drove her away before them in a mighty, rushing flood. The waters made the Boyne, to which Boann gave its name. The end of the novel, which describes the rise in the water level, the flood and the narrator drifting away with the stream makes Nina a manifestation of the mythological character.[22]

Celtic myths resonate in the novel, not only through the symbolic nature of water, but also through the traditional ritual practice of the severed head, which acquires the property of a magic cauldron, the typical container of regeneration in the Otherworld. Nina's death and decapitation make her a metamorphosed creature who, as in Celtic mythology, keeps her ability to think and speak.[23]

Nina, whose head is dropped in a tank, is at home without really being there. As a result, she is perfectly *unheimlich*, a word used by Freud

---

22   Boann's story confirms the Celtic custom to personify rivers. Furthermore, it is significant that the estate of the protagonists is located on the mouth of the river: the confluence was considered as a sacred area.

23   In the Mabinogion, Bendigeit Vran's head, after being cut off, goes on talking with the men he used to lead. His mouth encourages them and helps them arrive safe and sound at the end of their journey.

to describe the uncanny, a phenomenon which combines the strange with the familiar. The root *Heim* (home) is preceded by the privative prefix *Un-*. Nina is part of the house, but has no hold on it, her presence being only ghostly. "Many people experience the feeling [of the uncanny] in the highest degree in relation to death and dead bodies, to the return of the dead, and to spirits and ghosts",[24] writes Freud in his essay. A bit further down, he remarks: "Dismembered limbs, a severed head [...] have something peculiarly uncanny about them, especially when they prove capable of independent activity".[25] How shall we not see an "independent activity" in the way Nina takes charge of the narrative from the bottom of an isolated tank?

This female character talking from the dark recalls Beckett's universe, particularly the play *Not I* where a lit mouth is the only part of the anatomy which is visible to the audience. A disembodied mouth pours out without stopping:

> tiny little girl [...] powerless to respond ... like numbed ... couldn't make the sound ... no sound of any kind ... no screaming for help for example ... [...] all silent as the grave ... no part of her moving ... shut out the light ... no feeling of any kind ... [...] but the brain still ... still sufficiently ... in control ... under control ... [...] all dead still ... sweet silent as the grave ... [...] gradually she felt ... her lips moving ... [...] mouth on fire ... stream of words ... [...] and can't stop ... no stopping it ...[26]

Neil Jordan is familiar with this play since he made a film adaptation of it. This fourteen-minute stream-of-consciousness monologue came out in 2001, three years before he published *Shade*. It is highly likely that he already planned to write a novel whose dead narrator would only be a mouth talking from the dark beyond. Questioned about the symbolism of the mouth in this short film, Neil Jordan gives an interesting answer, considering the novel which was then in preparation:

24 Sigmund Freud, *The Uncanny (Das Unheimliche)* [1919] (London: Penguin, 2003), 239.
25 Freud, *The Uncanny*, 243.
26 Samuel Beckett, *Not I* [1972], in *The Complete Dramatic Works* (London and Boston: Faber & Faber, 1986), 378-380.

> It looks like a cave, it looks like a vagina [...]. It definitely looks like a birth canal [...] it looks like somewhere where you'd be born out of, somewhere where you might die.[27]

The magic properties of the human head are enhanced in Celtic myths, and prolonged in Christian tradition, in which, likewise, death is not the end. A martyr's head can be venerated: in Drogheda, the town close to Nina's family estate, in Saint Peter's church, Saint Oliver Plunkett's head is on display in a shrine.[28] Nina takes Gregory there when they first meet, the latter suspecting the former to aim at frightening him.

Such ghastly details are not out of place in this environment. It must be borne in mind that the story is set on the mouth of the Boyne, a river of myths and legends. The ghosts of kings, monks, combatants and pillagers sweep over the surface of its waters. The river banks, strewn with medieval castles and ruined abbeys provide a specific décor which is perfectly in line with the story. Such an environment comes on top of some criteria which are peculiar to Gothic fiction and can be spotted in the novel. Just like Melmoth, for example, Nina, in spite of her death, somehow 'revives' to enjoy exceptional powers and lead "a posthumous and preternatural existence".[29]

These specificities are however sometimes twisted for indeed most Gothic novels are tales of mystery and horror, intended to chill the spine. They have familiar presences and happenings: a young innocent lady is kidnapped by a wicked tyrant and held in the underground of a wild and desolate place. And yet, here, the female protagonist is neither young nor

27   Carole Zucker, ed., *Neil Jordan: Interviews* (Jackson: University of Mississippi, 2013), 155.

28   Catholic archbishop and martyr, Oliver Plunkett reorganised the Irish church and imposed stricter discipline. His resolution in 1671 of a long and bitter dispute between the Franciscans and the Dominicans in favour of the latter further soured relations, and members of the Franciscan order were to give evidence against him at his trial. Plunkett was the main Irish victim of the Popish Plot. Arrested in 1679 and taken to London after an abortive trial in Dundalk, he was charged with high treason for allegedly plotting a French invasion. Despite his clear innocence, he was convicted and was hanged in 1681. Plunkett was beatified in 1920 and canonised in 1975.

29   Charles Maturin, *Melmoth* [1820] (London: Penguin, 2000), 381.

innocent; in her lifetime, she even turns out to be scheming and manipulative. By the same token, her murderer proves to be cruel, but his violent behaviour is justified by his mental weaknesses. Last, in this instance, the heroine is not imprisoned in a medieval castle or a ruined abbey, but a vulgar septic tank. Obviously, the novel takes up the whole apparatus of Gothic fiction to twist it all the better, as in a grotesque parody. It resumes and updates the specific elements of a tradition with ironic detachment. What has been dubbed Neo-Gothic is discernible here, as Chris Baldick acknowledged in 1992:

> In principle and in practice it is perfectly possible to have a Gothic story set in the author's own time, provided that the tale focuses upon a relatively enclosed space in which some antiquated barbaric code still prevails.[30]

Is not a septic tank a perfect "enclosed space"?[31] This symbolic grave is located in the garden of an Anglo-Irish couple's big house.[32] The property, surrounded by a wild desolate seascape on the estuary of a river is the ideal topography for a strange story. It fuels a need to escape out of reality which is a feature of Celtic imagination. Along the edge of the real world, particularly on coastlines and estuaries, Celtic territories are liminal and partly ghostly.[33] "Ireland is a country formed from ghosts",[34] according to Neil Jordan whose fiction is rooted in the heritage of a genre

---

30 Chris Baldick, ed., *The Oxford Book of Gothic Tales* (Oxford and New York: Oxford University Press, 1992), introduction, xv.

31 Neil Jordan admits he is particularly interested in containment, as it is exploited by his compatriot: "There is something about the way Beckett confines actors which is very interesting" (Rockett Emer and Rockett Kevin, *Neil Jordan. Exploring Boundaries* [Dublin: The Liffey Press, 2003], 275).

32 "For a variety of reasons, the Anglo-Irish were intrigued by the supernatural, fairies and the afterlife" (Welch Robert, introduction to Yeats, *Writings on Irish Folklore*, xix).

33 Joep Leerssen, *Remembrance and Imagination: Patterns in the Historical and Literary Representation of Ireland in the Nineteenth Century*, Field Day Monographs 4 (Cork: Cork University Press, 1996), 190-191.

34 Zucker, *Neil Jordan: Interviews*, 98.

which is characteristic of Irish literature.[35] Claude Fierobe's essay *Les Ombres du fantastique* shows the persistence of "this organic relationship between the Gothic and Ireland".[36] Isn't the evanescent figure of Dracula perceptible against the church where Nina's funeral is held *in absentia*? The intertextual allusion is a way to recall that the one of whom they are about to honour the memory is both present and absent:

> The church's spire sits behind [Gregory's] head like a conical hat, the fuchsia hedges of the little lane sprout either side of his shoulders like a bat's wings or a pantomime witch's cloak. The wind blows from the river, ruffles the water, darkens the grasses like a cosmic chuckle.
>
> The dead are laughing. An empty coffin, an incense-burner wafted over an absent corpse, why wouldn't they be? But it's a forced laugh, the awful throaty wheeze of a joke badly told. (*S*, 114)

Nina belongs to the community of the living dead or the undead, which is the initial title considered by Bram Stoker for his famous novel. This term is originally applied to vampires only, but it progressively refers to many other supernatural creatures and the heroine of *Shade* is one of them.

Nina Hardy shares many features with Bram Stoker's female protagonists. On the one hand, her name associates her with Mina Harker, one of the characters in *Dracula* but, on the other, she is also reminiscent of "the Lady of the Shroud" who, like her, "is not dead in the real conventional way":

> We can only die once! Is that so? What about my Lady of the Shroud? [She is] subject to some laws, though not in exact accord within those which govern human beings. [...] What wonderful power or knowledge she must have to be able to move in such strange ways as she did? [...] Locks and bars, even the very seal of death itself, seemed unable to make for her a prison-house. With such freedom of action and movement, going when she would into secret places, what might she not know that was known to others?[37]

---

35   « cette relation organique existant entre le gothique et l'Irlande » (Fierobe Claude, *Les Ombres du fantastique. Fictions d'Irlande* [Dinan: Terre de Brume, 2016], 85).

36   Fierobe, *Les Ombres du fantastique*, 10.

37   Bram Stoker, *The Lady of the Shroud* [1909] (London: Wordsworth Editions, 2010), 111/113/86/138.

Like the Lady of the Shroud, Nina has supernatural gifts. Her death is followed by a sadly cold, stern and horrible existence, during which she narrates her story. The smallest details of what she lived are now known to her since she has become omniscient.

The confusion between life, death and rebirth contributes to make her an extraordinary being, stemming from old fantastic legends. Swept out of the tank by the floodtide in the wake of heavy rainfalls, Nina acknowledges:

> I am the river now, the seaweed my hair, the barnacles my bed, the long slow womanly weight of water dragging me towards the house when the tide flows, away from it when it ebbs. (*S*, 316)

Released by the tides that expose the septic tank to the brine, Nina Hardy is drifting along with the current, like a water snake. It is probably meaningful that her name is an anagram of 'hydra', this monstrous creature of the Lernean marsh, whose heads immediately grow again when one of them is cut off. Heracles has to sever the hydra's only immortal head to manage to get rid of it.

Anagrams – from the Greek 'writing back or anew' – transpose the letters of a word to form a new word. In a series of notebooks, Ferdinand de Saussure expounds his private theory that Latin poets concealed anagrams of proper names in their verse. The first thirteen lines of Lucretius's *De rerum natura* are an invocation of the goddess Venus, and Saussure finds in them three anagrams of the name Aphrodite, who was her Greek equivalent.

Is the presence of the name Hades – the dismal divinity who rules over the Underworld – in the title of the novel, *Shade,* the fortuitous product of coincidence or an intentional act of the part of the novelist? Like Nina whose body is abandoned in a dark underground space, Hades lives in a prison where the departed are trapped. The dead are doomed to stay forever in the land of the shades. In the depths of the abyss, without strength, without light, deprived of materiality, they are the pale reflections of their former selves.[38]

---

38   In Homer's *Odyssey*, in his descent into hell – his *Nekyia*, Ulysses cannot embrace his mother because she is only a shadow.

According to the anagrammatic rule, there is a shift from *shade* to *hades*, as if Neil Jordan wanted to emphasize the infernal nature of Nina's situation. There is doubtless more than meets the eye in the text through this keyword on which it is focused. Like Nina whose body is hidden in the ground, the theme-word is concealed in the text. Anagrams are "words upon words", as the title of Starobinski's essay puts it.[39] As they dislocate the letters of a word, they mirror the disruption of the chronological order of the narrated events, but also reflect the protagonist's dismembered body. Therefore, they perfectly fit in the fantastic which is "always a break in the acknowledged order", according to Roger Caillois.[40]

Words are not chosen by chance, particularly in a title. They show that different strata can be superposed and significant devices deciphered. They can revive "the ghost in the text".[41]

And yet, one question remains: do anagrams result from the author's intention or do they leave him offside and prove that what the text writes is more important than what the writer meant? If we cannot really prove that the transposition of letters is intentional, we can however notice, on the one hand, that the protagonist of *Shade,* like many other characters of Neil Jordan's fiction, willingly creates anagrams.[42] Obviously, the writer himself enjoys playing with words.[43]

On the other hand, it is worth mentioning that the process can be observed in one of the first Irish Gothic novels, *Carmilla* by Joseph Sheridan Le Fanu: "She called herself Carmilla? asked the General. Aye, that is Millarca. That is the same person who long ago was called Mircalla".[44] Carmilla, alias Millarca or Mircalla, is a vampire, an undead survivor that

---

39   Jean Starobinski, *Words upon Words: The Anagrams of Ferdinand de Saussure* (Yale: Yale University Press, 1980).

40   « Le fantastique est toujours une rupture de l'ordre reconnu » (Roger Caillois, *Au Cœur du fantastique* [Paris : Gallimard, 1965], 161).

41   Haroldo de Campos, "The Ghost in the Text (Saussure and the Anagrams)" [1976], in *Novas: Selected Writings* (Evanston, IL: Northwestern University Press, 2007).

42   "George, Eorgeg, Egg Roe, ogre, Gregory" (Jordan, *Shade*, 5).

43   For example: "Andy, Ynad, Nyad, Dany" (Jordan, *Carnivalesque*, 43).

44   Joseph Sheridan Le Fanu, *Carmilla* in *In a Glass Darkly* [1872] (Ware: Wordsworth Classics, 1995), 296.

keeps on reincarnating and repeating the same exterminating gestures. Her name and its anagrams show the same woman under the guise of another. Like the Lernean Hydra, Carmilla reappears endlessly and disappears for good only once her head is cut off, her corpse burned and her ashes are scattered on a river. The fantastic in Le Fanu's books combines Irish legends with the tradition of the Gothic novel, and obviously, Neil Jordan is one of his faithful heirs. As a result, it is to be supposed that he is most often quite aware of what he writes.

The novel ends with a symbol of liberty: a woman in the water, moving along with the tides. This image seems like a haunting metaphor in Neil Jordan's artistic output: indeed, it resurfaces in the film he made a few years after the publication of *Shade*. Carried along by the sea, Nina gives way to Ondine who appears in the eponymous film.

Ondine is a young woman caught by the nets of Syracuse (alias Colin Farrell), a handsome fisherman and reformed drinker. The latter gives assistance to the strange nymph (Alicja Bachleda) and wonders if she is not a selkie, a seal of Scottish folklore that can shed its skin and transform into a human being. Interviewed about the sources of *Ondine*, Neil Jordan once again admits that he had been inspired by Yeats's work, and more particularly by the tale "The Lady of Gollerus", in which "a fisherman pulls a woman from the sea, marries her, and she goes back to the sea, eventually".[45]

Henceforth, there is absolutely no doubt that the shadows of famous Irish men of letters are so regularly referred to in Neil Jordan's work that they tend to become one of its specificities. Obviously, this source of inspiration does not cause anxiety: Jordan acknowledges this influence and deliberately forges connections with the figureheads of local and universal cultures.

***

45   "The reason I talked about Yeats with regard to 'Ondine' is because Yeats collected fairy tales. Early on in his career he had a book called *The Irish Fairy and Folk Tales of Ireland*. [...] One of these fairy tales he collected was called 'The Lady of Gollerus', and it was about a fisherman who pulls a woman from the sea, he marries her, and she goes back to the sea, eventually" (Zucker, ed., *Neil Jordan: Interviews*, introduction, xxiv).

Shade is shadowed not only by the works of Yeats, Stoker or Beckett. The Gothic universe is one aspect of the novel. As the protagonist is an actress, the parts she plays cannot be ignored. In Neil Jordan's first novel – *The Past* – Rene, the narrator's mother, appears on stage in many towns of Ireland during her pregnancy. Her performance of the leading role in *As You Like It* attracts a lot of attention: "The first critic said that Rene's Rosalind would make Shakespeare enjoyable even to those whose reading had never gone beyond a train timetable" (*TP*, 224). Lili, who went with her on this tour, remembers:

> We did botched-up versions of the comedies, *Measure for Measure, As You Like It,* we did all the old staples, *The Colleen Bawn, The Workhouse Ward* (...). But no matter what story each of them told, the same story always told itself through them. Which was love, I suppose. (*TP*, 214)

As You Like It and *The Colleen Bawn* are plays in which Nina Hardy also wins fame. These plays, respectively written by Shakespeare and Boucicault, migrate to Jordan's fiction since, first mentioned in *The Past,* they reappear in *Shade.* These references contribute to the construction of a fictional world in continuity with the actual world. The works staged and played by characters produce an *effet de réel* – or reality effect – that underpins the verisimilitude of the narrative. They are means of cultural exchanges and make sense in the way they correspond to the novel they are included in. Therefore, we the readers are invited to read the inserted plays so as to identify the way they connect with *Shade.* The presence of a literary text within another one calls upon the intertextual notion of *mise en abyme.*[46] A book read by a character can be considered as a mediator

---

46 *Mise en abyme* is a French expression originally used in heraldry to describe a small shield set within a larger shield bearing the same device. Equivalent formal devices have long been used in both literature and the visual arts, the obvious examples being the play within a play in Shakespeare's *Hamlet* and Velazquez's *Las Meninas.* The expression *mise en abyme* was given a new currency by the French novelist André Gide (1869-1951), who defined it as the representation within a work of art of that work's structure. *Mise en abyme* is frequently used by the writers associated with the *nouveau roman,* and a similar self-reflexivity is typical of much postmodernist fiction.

of the dialogue with the global library. Therefore, a relation of comment, transformation or quotation can be established between framed and framing books.[47]

The plays staged by characters in *Shade* are as many enclaves bearing several similarities to it. They can be considered as "mirror books",[48] in which characters discover their own stories or read what the future has in store for them. These protagonists have split personalities in front of the mirror held out by the text they read, as they can "become" part of the book. Isn't Nina's personality divided when she leaves the family house in order to *become* Rosalind,[49] when she joins a company in England and claims her name is Rosalind? (*S*, 231). Her identity is blurred by a confusion between the real and the fictitious. As young Nina considers her doll and an imaginary friend like living children, once an adult, she plays Rosalind so well that she completely identifies with her. She says:

> I remember Rosalind as a series of colours, a riot of smells, a host of stratagems, an intelligence I could never have matched, but once inside her I was glad to be that luminous mind, that well of kindness, that ironic affectionate muse. (*S*, 162)

Shakespeare's pastoral comedy is staged by the four children in the garden of the big estate during the summer holidays: Nina plays the part of Rosalind, Janie is Celia,[50] Gregory Orlando, and George is the clown Touchstone. The latter is in love with Rosalind who loves Orlando. Rene and Nina's performances of Rosalind on stage are significant: each

47 « La présence d'un livre dans la fiction semble inviter le lecteur à le mettre en relation avec ce roman qu'il est en train de lire. Un livre représenté porte en lui un programme narratif potentiel [...] mais aussi un texte et un contenu sémantique qui peuvent, actualisés, interférer avec des éléments du livre représentant » (Joëlle Gleize, *Le Double Miroir. Le livre dans les livres de Stendhal à Proust* [Paris : Hachette, 1992], 18).

48 Henri Mitterand mentions "livres-miroirs" in his essay, *Le Roman à l'œuvre. Genèse et valeurs* (Paris: Presses Universitaires de France, 1998), 54.

49 In a letter to her father, Nina writes: "So I will change myself, my home, my life, I will become someone other than your little Nina, become Rosalind, become Cordelia, become Lady Macbeth, who knows" (Jordan, *Shade*, 265).

50 Like Celia in *As You Like It*, Janie plays a minor part in the novel.

of them is torn between two men. The light-hearted gallantries of the play mirror the love relationships in *Shade* and *The Past*. There is convergence and unity between the texts. Therefore, it is not impossible that the Shakespearian heroine's whimsical personality influences the desires and behaviours of the ones who play her part.

For Rene and Nina, Shakespeare's comedy takes part in the construction of their personage characterization. It contributes to their education and training. It plays an active part in the service of the novel, for it fuels their imagination of young actresses whose dreams come true, like the character they are on stage. Each of them assumes the identity of the daughter of the duke in exile. Playing the part of Rosalind nurtures their fights, their revolts and desires.

When George, though psychologically scarred, leaves the hospital, he goes back to Baltray House in the middle of the night. In the garden where he used to find true happiness, he has a go on a swing and spontaneously quotes a line from the comedy: "If a hart do lack a hind / Let him seek out Rosalind".[51] The wordplay on *hart* and *heart* – a cliché of Shakespeare's drama – imposes the idea of a love game as the interface of hunting. This activity targets the beloved's heart, referred to as a royal hart, by homophony. By way of a hart, the hunter George chases Nina and finds it difficult to control the impulses of his heart, but he also has certain similarities to "a horn-beast"[52] for he feels cuckolded. Betrayed, George kills Nina in a moment's madness. Like Touchstone, he is just a fool who suffers inferiority complex and painfully realizes that he has always been reduced to a pathetic role:

> It was a fool's tale, he knew [...]. He had always been the fool and had dragged his fool's tale with him, ignorant of its secrets, unaware of its plot [...]. He cried, from the awful realisation, somewhere deep inside him, that all those years could have been different. (*S*, 309-310)

Rosalind, disguised as Ganymede, is no game but a huntress. This dressing-up allows her to organize a love hunt and be a part of it. She inspires Nina

---

51   Jordan, *Shade*, 299; William Shakespeare, *As You Like It*, III, ii, 97-98.
52   Shakespeare, *As You Like It*, III, iii, 45.

who is also very good at taking initiatives. Nina's position, hidden in a tank, is comparable to her model's, concealed in a man's disguise: both of them watch from the outside and enjoy their lovers without turning up. In order to justify her behaviour with George, Nina could make Rosalind's words her own about the way to manage a bashful lover:

> [I] would now like him, now loathe him; then entertain him, then forswear him; now weep for him, then spit at him; that I drave my suitor from his mad humour of love, to a living humour of madness, which was, to forswear the full stream of the world, and to live in a nook merely monastic. And thus I cured him.[53]

Nina thinks she can "cure" George by making him work in her garden and getting him out of his "monastic nook", that is his long stay in a hospital room. Nevertheless, the state of innocence cannot be restored, and George's illusions are well and truly destroyed. Love and madness have gone hand in hand since the dawn of time.

There is surely a convergence between framed and framing books. Both of them treat the same motifs – desire, conflict, violence and sacrifice. Not only are they linked, but they also respond to the characters' experiences. This connection establishes a literary dialogue between the two works.

As in a mirror, which shows her the image of the dramatic heroine she plays, the protagonist of the novel can see in advance what her destiny has in store for her. The same can be said for the part Nina plays afterwards.

*****

At the beginning of the nineteenth century, in County Limerick, a young woman from the countryside is killed at her lover's instigation so that she does not hinder his plan to marry a rich heiress. This grim event, which made the front page of Irish newspapers, inspired Gerald Griffin's novel *The Collegians*.[54] The title of the novel is justified by the fact that the traitor of the story and his best friend are students at Trinity College Dublin. Before the murder, the good match slips away and the young man from a good family resolves to marry the peasant woman, but it is too

---

53   Shakespeare, *As You Like It*, III, ii, 407-413.
54   Gerald Griffin, *The Collegians* [1829] (London: Atlantic Books, 2012).

late: his zealous friend, in charge of the nasty job, has already carried it out. Stricken with remorse, the culprit has to go to court and stand trial.

In 1860, the Irish dramatist Dion Boucicault wrote a play titled *The Colleen Bawn*,[55] which is adapted from *The Collegians.* As the event on which the play is based is a tragedy, Boucicault wrote a melodrama and gave the story a happy ending. Indeed, Myles na gCopaleen manages to thwart the murder attempt perpetrated by Danny Mann. As for the accomplice, Hardress Cregan, he agrees to marry the peasant girl Eily O'Connor and to overcome the social differences that separate them. This popular play was a success and a sensation in the towns and villages of Ireland where it was staged. There is nothing surprising that Nina attends a rehearsal of this melodrama in Laytown:

> There was a girl on a raised wooden stage, lamenting her undoing at the hands of a gentleman. There were painted flats behind her depicting a thatched Irish cottage in a landscape of bog. I watched the girl, and despite her stiff gestures and her mannered delivery was soon engrossed in her story, her impending death in the unseen lake behind the cottage. And I thought this was a use to which I could put this useless body of mine. (*S*, 197)

As the leading role is available when the actress has to take a break at the end of her pregnancy, Nina jumps at the opportunity to join the touring company. From Liverpool, she writes to her friend:

> Dear Janie,
>
> I am in Liverpool, moving towards Wales [...]. Sister Catherine said acting would never be remotely appropriate for a [...] girl, but here I am, acting the part of the Colleen Bawn, Eily O'Connor, not Rosalind by any means but sufficient to the day the evil thereof. Eily is thought to be drowned in a lake by the hunchback Danny Mann, but comes back to life by the good graces of Myles na gCopaleen, Myles of the Ponies, if you don't remember your Irish which I for one hardly do. (*S*, 239)

Later, in Brighton, a film director suggests that Nina plays in a silent film, *The Real Tragedy of the Colleen Bawn.* To shoot it, he takes her to London.

---

55   Dion Boucicault, *The Colleen Bawn or the Brides of Garryowen* [1860] (London: FB&c. Ltd, 2018).

This is how she becomes famous. It can be noticed that Nina speaks *about* the play, but does not cite it. Unlike Shakespeare's comedy, Boucicault's melodrama is never taken up in the novel. There is textual copresence but on a different scale. In this case, an explicit intertextual practice is at work: the name of the Colleen Bawn is mentioned indeed and the story is briefly summarized. And yet, this intertextual connection is not literal insofar as *Shade* never quotes the play.

However, there are many connections between the two works. Jordan's novel echoes Boucicault's play. Both stories are Gothic. Characterization rests on a quartet of protagonists made of two males and two females.[56] The beautiful girl, wooed by two men who are divided on everything, gives herself over to youthful romances without considering social differences and ends up being (nearly) drowned by a vengeful murderous dropout. Nina however views Eily's story with humour and detachment, maybe because she is like her, torn between two lovers. She seems to believe that the twentieth century in which she lives is more civilized than the previous one. And yet, the destiny that is in store for her is worse than Eily's: as the latter is saved from drowning at the last minute, Nina dies for good, killed by her former lover, like the girl who inspired her part. Nina's performance and involvement in the spectacular sensation scenes of the play gives her a foretaste of her own destiny. Beyond the intertextual connection, the story of the Colleen Bawn forecasts the tragic outcome of the framing narrative. As the play heralds Nina's destiny, it can be considered as the sub-plot of the novel.

***

In London, Nina is weary of being a film actress, her parts in movies being too artificial:

> Mr Shaw effected my release, came to the studio one winter's morning on a quasi-regal visit, to view the source of this new phenomenon that was filling the picture houses, promising me a play that was like those pictures, one hundred percent talk [...]. I played Orinthia in *The Apple Cart*, to everyone's approval [...]. His septuagenarian affection proved as thrilling as that of any nineteen-year-old and his jealousy

---

56   Each character of the novel has his/her counterpart in the play: Nina/Eily, Gregory/Hardress, George/Danny, Celia/Anne.

even more compulsive. He followed the production to London and for two hundred and fifty-eight days plied me with advice on performance, diction, deportment and style. I was to be the last of his intellectual romances, he warned, so I must humour his ardour.[57]

The publication date of *The Apple Cart* (1929) and the detail on the playwright's approximate age make it possible to deduce that the scene is set around 1930. Here again, an Irish play is present within the novel. It is not quoted, however, but only mentioned by its title and the names of its author and its main protagonist staged by Nina. *The Apple Cart* is neither a tragedy nor a comedy; it is not a melodrama either, but "a political extravaganza" which owes its title to the expression "upsetting the apple-cart". The apple-carts that Shaw upsets here are the ones of monarchy and democracy. The two-act play is a parable about modern parliamentary democracy. Its plot concerns a monarch – Manus, king of England – who is assaulted by his elected cabinet. They feel that the king is too meddlesome and threaten to resign if he does not sign an ultimatum, which in effect would strip him of his authority and turn him into a powerless figurehead. Either way, the king would be doomed, without a cabinet or without power; his dilemma is the play's catalyst. What follows is political debate, as many sides and problems are discussed and revealed. Added to the commentary on politics is a brief interlude on marriage and adultery, in which Magnus faces his grand mistress, Orinthia. This pretty, capricious woman throws a jealous fit because she does not want to be the monarch's favourite any more, but his official wife, that is the queen.

This part perfectly suits Nina Hardy who also proves to be scheming and demanding. Her affair with two men of different births mirrors the dilemma of Magnus, torn between his lawful wife Jemima and his mistress Orinthia. The social difference between the two women is metaphorically referred to by the latter who sees herself as a goddess in comparison to the queen:

---

57 Jordan, *Shade*, 276. True, Bernard Shaw took a keen interest in cinema, all the more so as some of his plays were adapted for the screen: for example, *Pygmalion* (1938) became *My Fair Lady* in 1964.

ORINTHIA: "Heaven is offering you a rose, and you cling to a cabbage!"[58]

Rivalry in love requires to get rid of one of the two:

MAGNUS: But my wife? The queen? What is to become of my poor dear Jemima?

ORINTHIA: Oh, drown her.[59]

As in the novel, drowning and decapitation are the methods used to send someone to kingdom come:

MAGNUS: They bring us papers we sign. You have no time to read them. But I am expected to read everything. I do not always agree; but I must sign: there is nothing else to be done. For instance, death warrants. Not only have I to sign the death warrants of persons who in my opinion ought not to be killed; but I may not even issue death warrants for a great many people who in my opinion ought to be killed.

BOANERGES <sarcastic>: You'd like to be able to say 'off with his head!', wouldn't you?

MAGNUS: Many men would hardly miss their heads, there is so little in them. Still, killing is a serious business.[60]

The motif of decapitation is shared by the two texts, although it is mentioned in different tones:

ORINTHIA: I believe you would sign my death warrant without turning a hair.

MAGNUS: That is true in a way.[61]

Ironically, these words mouthed by Orinthia and Magnus could literally be taken up by Nina and George. The part of the mistress in Shaw's play puts Nina in second place. It could make her realize what George experienced because of her flippancy. For indeed, the *mise en abyme* of plays staging a character torn between two loves is reminiscent of the dilemma Nina is confronted with. The parts she plays reflect her own

---

58   Bernard Shaw, *The Apple Cart* (Leipzig: Bernhard Tauchnitz, 1932), 149.
59   Shaw, *The Apple Cart*, 155.
60   Shaw, *The Apple Cart*, 70.
61   Shaw, *The Apple Cart*, 146.

story and warn her against the risks of being involved in two love affairs simultaneously.

The plot of the play is a mirror held out to prompt the actress to be on her guard and incite her to clear-sightedness, if not introspection. As in Molière's or Shakespeare's dramatic works, the *mise en abyme* reveals a secret truth. It is supposed to be an eye-opener and give the audience food for thought. With such echoes, the sub-plot gives depth to the narrative. The introduction of some characters from the dramatic universe who can be considered as the twins of the framing work's protagonist shows to what extent literature mirrors human realities. The autotelic or self-centred nature of a work of art fuels questions about existential issues.

The title of the novel – *Shade* – refers not only to the invisible presence of the beheaded narrator, but also to the shadows of Neil Jordan's father figures: Yeats, Stoker, Beckett on the one hand, Shakespeare, Boucicault and Shaw on the other. Apart from the Bard of Avon, these literary predecessors are from the same land as his. Jordan's fiction is indeed "the scene of an intertextuality in which Ireland is itself read".[62] The author deliberately establishes connections with founding texts and invites his readers to (re) discover them. He is thus part of a cultural heritage which highlights the motifs of identity and difference, the same and the other, continuity and break-off, or the articulation between the past and the present.

62   "Irish literature is the scene of an intertextuality in which Ireland is itself read" (Corcoran, *After Yeats and Joyce*, vi).

CHAPTER 8

Mistaken: Division, Duplication and Usurpation

In January 2011, a short time before the publication of *Mistaken*, Neil Jordan stated in an interview:

> The bundle of emotions I talk about in this novel, I know them very well, it's more of a kind of nagging suspicion, a sense that you haven't really lived your own life, that you haven't lived the life that you should have. This is about a very real sense of loss. [...] I suppose the reason one uses fiction, if fiction exists, is because you can have these different personae and these characters have an independent life through which you then filter all kinds of personal stuff. That seems to be the nature of the game... Of course Kevin and Gerry are both absolutely a part of me.[1]

The protagonists' spatiotemporal universe is roughly speaking Neil Jordan's, as some narrative clues confirm: indeed, Kevin and Gerry are teenagers in the 1960s, youngsters in the 1970s and 50-year-old men in 2000. References to films, singers, rock bands, concerts and news items make it possible to date the related scenes.[2] Architectural buildings can also be used as clues or milestones: "I saw the metal spire where the Pillar used to be, vanishing into the haze above" (*M*, 37). This large, pin-like monument, erected in 2003 and located on the site of the former Nelson's Pillar on O'Connell Street in Dublin, is a meeting-point where most of the plot is set. Such references allow readers to find their bearings in time, but also

---

1   Helen Brown, "*Mistaken*: Neil Jordan Interview", *The Telegraph* (14 January 2011).

2   For example, the narrative mentions *Blue Hawaii* with Elvis Presley (1961), *Brides of Dracula* with Christopher Lee (1960) or *2001: A Space Odyssey* (1968) (Neil Jordan, *Mistaken* [London: John Murray, 2011], 33, 100). Rock stars Manfred Mann or David Bowie in "Ziggy Stardust" are also referred to, as well as Fleetwood Mac's concert at the Roundhouse in Dublin in 1970. Last, Charles Manson is mentioned too. This notorious criminal was convicted of murder and conspiracy to commit murder for the deaths of seven people in 1971.

in space. Indeed, topographical descriptions are so minute and accurate that readers can closely follow the character's journey:

> I turned right at Bakers Corner and headed up Kill Avenue towards Foxrock Church. [...] The car turned right then, on to the dual carriageway, left again on Leopardstown Road, past the racecourse and traced a route I could never have followed myself, through the industrial parks and the new hotels. (*M*, 15)

This cartography is so detailed that it gives us the impression of following the indications of a GPS system. Besides, the titles of the 82 chapters of the novel are all place names. Most of the time, they refer to a specific place in Dublin, a street, a park, a pub or a store. Perhaps a veiled reference to Leopold Bloom's peregrinations throughout the city in *Ulysses* can be perceived here. What is striking is the way in which this rigorous accuracy contrasts with the confusion between the two protagonists.

The motif of mistake, displayed right from the title of the book, is also mentioned in the first sentence of the narrative: "I had been mistaken for him so many times that when he died it was as if part of myself had died too" (*M*, 1). The novel starts with the funeral of Gerald Spain, a 50-year-old writer at Deansgrange cemetery, in the suburbs of Dublin. There, Kevin Thunder, the narrator, meets with Emily, the deceased's daughter. He had known the girl when she was a child, before he became estranged from her father. The novel is the story Kevin tells Emily. It goes back over the lives of the characters up to this funeral day.

Kevin grew up in Clontarf, a coastal suburb on the north side of Dublin, in Marino Crescent. Bram Stoker, creator of *Dracula*, had once inhabited the house next door.[3] This detail has fuelled the boy's fertile imagination. Repeatedly, Kevin is mistaken for somebody else: he gets a scolding from a bus driver who claims he did not pay the fare, from a retailer who recognizes a shoplifter in him, and from the owners of a gaming room who throw him out like a delinquent. Similarly, a boy he has never seen before mentions some adventures they are supposed to have shared; some girls he meets for the first time go around with him and allude to the attitudes he adopted in the past. As a result, Kevin reaches the conclusion that he must

---

3   It must be recalled that Neil Jordan himself lived there.

have his spitting image in this town. He finally spots this boy: he is called
Gerald Spain and lives in Ranelagh, a residential area on the south side of
Dublin. When they first meet, Kevin goes to Gerald's aid, as the latter is
involved in a brawl. He experiences the sensation of confronting himself
through a mirror. This symmetrical exchange is described with chiasmus:

> I found myself looking at myself [...].
>
> "He thought I was you".
>
> "He thought you were me" [...].
>
> He was me, somehow [...].
>
> "You for me and me for you" [...].
>
> I was his height. His hair was my length. His face was mine. (*M*, 72, 160).

The fool's game which consists in pretending to be someone else initially
delights the participants, but it soon makes them feel uneasy, because the
deception can have unexpected effects: "there's a deceit going on, and (...)
once started, it doesn't stop, does it?" (*M*, 300). Darragh, a fragile girl,
has to pay for this mistake which leads to her confinement in a mental
hospital. The two boys are caught up in their hoax, which creates an identity crisis in the narrator who suffers from inferiority complex and life by
proxy. Indeed, the women with whom he has affairs think they are dealing
with Gerry, and not with himself. Therefore, Kevin has no love life of his
own: "'Dear', she said, and I had never been called that and I found it un-
accountably touching" (*M*, 319). Kevin is never loved for who he is. Apart
from his parents, no one seems to consider him. He is partly responsible
for this situation insofar as he never tells the truth when he is mistaken
for Gerry. He proves to be the victim of his own game and reaches a
distressing conclusion: "[I am] just a shadow. I never had any particular
life" (*M*, 375). Sartre's essay, stolen in a bookshop by Gerald's future wife
has a symbolical import when its title – *Being and Nothingness* – is transposed to the boys: Gerald is a brilliant being, a celebrated writer, whereas
Kevin is *néant* insofar as he is completely dependent on Gerald: "My real
name was zero, zilch, a blank [...]. I became nothing, a human absence"

(*M*, 352). One of them being in the light, the other remains in the dark. Mistaken identities create mirror effects and reversed images.

When Gerald Spain publishes his first texts under the pen-name Kevin Thunder, he justifies this choice by the following remark: "Being you for a time was a release" (*M*, 149). This notion is mentioned by Neil Jordan himself. In an interview, he says that in his early days, he had to write fiction to be an artist, because he could not be a film-maker:

> The culture I grew up in, the only creative endeavour that was open to an Irish person was literature... Irish people didn't make films [...]. So when I began to make films I experienced this huge release, it was like somebody else was doing this thing, somebody unIrish. It was like there was this different person inside me that I had thought I would never be.[4]

As a matter of fact, Neil Jordan did not choose a pen-name for his books and films, but this acknowledgement emphasizes the dichotomy which separates his twofold artistic career and the schizophrenic effects generated by such an ambivalence. Regardless, Jordan seems to be able to write on the myth of the double by experience.

Gerald and Kevin continue their investigations to try to discover why they look so much alike and finally learn that they are twin brothers, born of the union of a foreign clown and a circus entertainer.[5] The latter left them in the care of nuns who had them adopted. Such a rational explanation turns the fantastic universe of the narrative towards the uncanny, as defined by Todorov. According to him, the uncanny is experienced upon encountering something that is at once both strange and familiar. It is the supernatural explained: the laws of reality remain intact and permit an explanation of the phenomenon described. Strange facts are a specificity of Jordan's world, as the recurring adjective "strange" in his narrative testifies. This repetition echoes Shakespeare's play *The Comedy of Errors* which is also focused on twin brothers:

---

4   Helen Brown, "Neil Jordan: Interview", *The Telegraph* (14 January 2011).
5   Cissy Hassett, the twins' natural mother, is not at all touched by the reunion: when Kevin meets her, she does not show the least sign of emotion and, as a circus artiste, seems to be much more afflicted by a lion cub's death and its mother's sadness, a configuration which is yet comparable to hers.

> And, which was *strange,* the one so like the other,
>
> As could not be distinguish'd but by names.[6]

This play is referred to by Gerald at the end of the novel, in a letter he writes to Kevin:

> We are twins, as in any fable of separation and confusion, and reconciliation, I can only hope, in the end. Shakespeare wrote one of them, I remember, two matching sets of separated twins, but that was a comedy, and while we have had our moments, I don't imagine either of us would call our mutual experience comic (*M*, 382).

Neil Jordan's novel could have been titled "The Tragedy of Errors", the confusing state being based on a mistake due to the fact that they are duplicates of each other. Each of them is imperfectly characterized as long as they are not brought together in unity, for this is the way they perceive themselves: "We were two halves of the same soul" (*M*, 4). When Kevin speaks about his brother with Emily, he admits: "He said to me near the end that he'd only led half a life. And that makes two of us" (*M*, 88). The twins are like their city: they form a unit split in two. The north and south sides of Dublin, in which each of them has lived, are separated by the "river that cuts like a knife through its middle" (*M*, 116). In this respect, it is significant that Kevin migrates to the reunified city of Berlin. Such a specificity recalls the fantastical story told by Aristophanes in Plato's *Symposium:*

> Our ancient nature was not what it is now, but of another kind [...]. The form of each human being as a whole was round, with back and sides forming a circle, but it had four arms and an equal number of legs, and two faces exactly alike on a cylindrical neck; there was a single head for both faces, which faced in opposite directions, and four ears and two sets of pudenda, and one can imagine all the rest from this [...]. Well, they were terrible in strength and force, and they had high thoughts and conspired against the gods [...]. They tried to storm Heaven in order to displace the gods.
>
> Zeus said: "I'll now cut each of them in two" [...]. When their nature was divided in two, each half in longing rushed to the other half of itself and they threw their

---

6   William Shakespeare, *The Comedy of Errors*, I, i, 51-52. My emphasis.

arms around each other and intertwined them, desiring to grow together into one
[...]. They were unwilling to do anything apart from one another.[7]

As a result, each human being is only a part of a whole in search of its
complement – the *symbolon*. When someone meets their half, they identify, unite and become one flesh. In the speech of Aristophanes, the two
halves of the androgynes are separated because of themselves: the fault
lies with them. In *Mistaken*, on the contrary, the two brothers are not responsible for this split.

The novel is an integral part of the context in which it was published.
Indeed, the first decade of the new millennium in Ireland is marked by the
revelation of numerous scandals within the Catholic Church. Among them,
it was exposed that, throughout the twentieth century, many unmarried
women who could not afford to raise their children were forced to abandon
them to nuns who left them to adoptive parents. *Philomena* relates the story
of a mother searching for the son that was taken away from her fifty years
before. This film by Stephen Frears came out in 2012, one year after the
publication of *Mistaken*.[8] That very year, the United Nations Committee

7   *The Dialogues of Plato* (vol. II), *The Symposium*, "The Speech of Aristophanes", 189c-
     193c, translated with comments by R. E. Allen (New Haven, CT and London: Yale
     University Press, 1994), 130-132.

8   *Philomena* is a British drama film directed by Stephen Frears. London-based jour-
     nalist Martin Sixsmith has lost his job as a government adviser. He is approached at
     a party by the daughter of Philomena Lee. She suggests that he write a story about
     her mother, who was forced to give up her toddler son Anthony nearly fifty years
     before. Though Sixsmith is initially reluctant to write a human-interest story, he
     meets Philomena and decides to investigate her case. In 1951, Philomena became
     pregnant after an encounter with a man at a county fair, and was sent by her father
     to Sean Ross Abbey in Roscrea in Ireland. After giving birth, she was forced to work
     in the convent laundry for four years, with little contact with her son. The nuns
     gave her son up for adoption without giving Philomena a chance to say goodbye.
     She kept her lost son a secret from her family for nearly fifty years. Martin and
     Philomena begin their search at the convent, then in the United States, when they
     discover that most of the children were sold for £1,000 each to wealthy Americans.
     Back to Ireland, Martin goes to the convent and argues with an elderly nun who
     worked there when Anthony was forcibly adopted. He accuses her of lying and
     denying the chance to finally reunite the son with his mother. Martin demands

Against Torture alleged that the conditions within the Magdalene laundries and the exploitation of their labourers amounted to human rights violations. In response, the Irish government set up a committee to establish the facts of the Irish state's involvement with those laundries. Following an eighteen-month inquiry, the committee published its report which found that more than 11,000 women had entered laundries since 1922. These "fallen women" had to work without being paid. Symbolically, they were supposed to cleanse their sins and repent, modelling themselves upon Mary Magdalene in the gospels. These revelations inspired Peter Mullan's drama film, *The Magdalene Sisters*. The living conditions in those institutions were so hard that they killed some young children. This was proved by the discovery of a mass grave near a convent. Such an event created a shock wave in public opinion. Here again, it is noteworthy that Neil Jordan does not express a personal opinion on such abuses.[9] The scandal is only alluded to. When Kevin knocks at the door of a religious institution, the sister is hesitant to let him in: "We don't want any bother, she said. We've had trouble enough from journalists" (*M*, 281), a defensive response that Kevin justifies in Emily's presence:

> Think of it from her perspective [...]. There are lost generations out there, bent on revenge.
>
> Are you one of them?
>
> No [...]. I've been lucky. (*M*, 294)

This remark could be formulated by the author himself. Obviously, Neil Jordan does not feel resentful towards religious communities. There are quite a few metafictional remarks like this in the narrative, in which readers can, to some extent, recognize in the characters who express them the writer's spokespersons. For example, one of them acknowledges: "Maybe I can't do accuracy" (*M*, 251) or "If you use the third person singular, speak

---

an apology, telling her that what she did was un-Christian, but is speechless when Philomena instead chooses to forgive her of her own volition.

9   The narrator contents himself with a caustic remark on "Christian Brothers, the name being the only Christian thing about them" (Jordan, *Mistaken*, 68). The nuns, however, who could have been criticized, are not at all.

of yourself as he, invent a name, a character, a mask, you find yourself speaking with a different voice, revealing parts of yourself that otherwise would lie hidden" (*M*, 171-172). When Gerald, sinking into alcoholism and drug addiction, stops writing, Kevin takes over to narrate their story in a long letter to his niece Emily:

> I am the writer, after all, who now types on that old-fashioned thing I bought him, who resuscitates memories – the swans on the Tolka river, the tulips in Fairview Park, the vampire, all of that. But memories are unreliable, and strangely pleasurable, one can wallow in them, invent a detail. Sometimes an afternoon goes by and I look at two typed pages and wonder, whose life was that? (*M*, 408)

"If all men were twins, there would be nothing else but mistakes", states the protagonist of a Japanese novel.[10] The twins' fate is seldom happy because their existence is considered as a perversion of natural law. Human beings are supposed to be unique, and they erase all manner of differences insofar as they were "born twice". Twins are the fruit of extraordinary "dionysiac" strangeness, if not monstrous doubles, as René Girard puts it:

> The entire everyday world is caught up in the whirl producing a hallucinatory state that is not a synthesis of elements, but a formless and grotesque mixture of things that are normally separate. [...] An attempt is made to classify the monsters; but despite their initial disparities they end by resembling one another; no stable difference really serves to separate them [...]. A fundamental principle, often overlooked, is that the double and the monster are one and the same being [...]. There is no monster who does not tend to duplicate himself or to "marry" another monster, no double who does not yield a monstrous aspect under close scrutiny.[11]

The recognition of a monstrous double arouses the violent reaction of Loretta, a young woman who is pregnant from an affair she had with Gerald during his trip to the United States. The latter asks his brother to fly to New York City, pretend to be him and meet Loretta in order to convince her not to keep the child. But things go wrong when Loretta

10   Yasunari Kawabata, *Kyôto* in *House of Sleeping Beauties and Other Stories* [1987] (London: Vintage International, 2017), 248.

11   René Girard, *Violence and the Sacred* [1972] (London and New York: Continuum, 2005), 169-170.

discovers the pretence. In the cramped staircase of her cellar, incandescent with rage, she physically attacks Kevin:

> She hit me across the face [...]. She struck me again and again and began a kind of ballet of slapping, with the palm, the backhand, the fist. I had to step back before the onslaught [...]. She threw her face down towards me [...] drawing a spout of blood from my open lips. And she drew her head back then to do it better this time, and I grabbed her widow's knot of hair in my fist, pulled her face around so she couldn't do it again. She jerked her head back, fiercely this time, and we both would have tumbled down that metal staircase had my other hand not grabbed her black kimono and pulled her back to me. Her breasts stroked my chest and I could feel her winy breath in my face. Then she swung the glass towards me in a long arc and I ducked, missing contact with the glass though not the ejaculation of wine.
>
> My hand swung after hers and the momentum of her misplaced strike turned her body clockwise. I had slammed my fingers round her knuckles and both of our hands continued the movement and slammed the glass into her throat. So you could say we both did it. The glass shattered at the bone of her chin and what remained on the stem sliced a half moon into the skin below. There was a low gurgle from her, the taste of vintage wine in my mouth and suddenly an enormous geyser of blood. I wouldn't have thought her starved frame could have contained so much. It sprayed over me in gouts that must have been pumped by her dying heart [...]
>
> The blood pumped from her open throat on to my lips, it mixed with the wine in a salty, leathery bile. [...] one hand grabbed my collar, the other my hair [...]. She hung on to me with that extraordinary vigour [...]. And her hand, though it never relaxed its terrible grip, began to achieve a kind of stasis, fixed itself into an arthritic knot and after a diminishing series of shivers, went totally still.
>
> She was dead then [...] and I had killed her. (*M*, 348-350)

The erotic proximity of the bodies, together with the spurt of blood from one protagonist's throat to the other's mouth recalls Count Dracula's operating mode with his preys. This connection implies that Kevin, haunted by this father figure, has now become a fully fledged vampire. When he was a child, his fertile imagination led him to believe that the old lady next door was Dracula's housekeeper, because her house used to belong to Stoker. The boy, who mixes up the writer and his character, is convinced that his neighbour *is* Count Dracula and therefore grows up in the shadow of a vampire. The latter is an inner voice which imposes itself upon him, whispers in his ear and intrudes on his privacy to such an extent that he cannot escape from it. This invisible presence creeps into his life night and day. It appears under the features of a pervert who avidly watches the boy after his sea bathing and craves for his blood. The pedophile vampire suggests an immoral act, a forbidden erotic union, a criminal offence. There is a malicious shift when Kevin, in his sleepless nights, considers himself as this strange creature:

> The sense of that vampire was back [...] there was the sense of something still awake in this house of sleeping strangers, something wide-eyed and observant that never slept. And it took some time for me to realize, in the creaking darkness, that this someone was me. (*M*, 100)

This new identity is confirmed by the narrator's behaviour with Loretta at the end of the novel. After having sex with her, he examines the sheets:

> - You're bleeding, I said.
> - I know, she said.
> - You're not pregnant.
> - And you're not Gerald. (*M*, 345)

The stain provides a foretaste which incites "the false Gerald" to shed more blood in order to assuage his vampiric thirst. This scene is comparable to the second chapter of *Dracula,* in which Jonathan Harker cuts himself as he is shaving. The cut bleeds a little, and the blood trickles over his chin, which causes "a sort of demoniac fury"[12] in the Count's eyes. Blood calls for blood. Loretta's remark – "you're not Gerald" – implicitly means: who are you then? The fact that this stranger is her lover's duplicate qualifies him as an uncanny creature such as a vampire, which can be transformed into something or someone else. Like other books and films by Neil Jordan, *Mistaken* is the story of a human being who plunges into vampirism. This is a specificity of the artist who acknowledges: "I like to

---

12   Stoker, *Dracula,* 30.

take stories that have a realistic beginning; that start from the point of realism and go to some other place that is surrealistic".[13]

After Loretta's murder, the two brothers go their separate ways. Gerald, horrified at the unpunished crime perpetrated by Kevin, lets him know that he does not want to see him again. Their similarity turns into dissimilarity: Gerald is depicted as a pallid, long-haired overweight man who drinks too much and looks unwell, whereas Kevin has "that permanent tan of the upper classes"; he runs four miles a day and lives on "a diet of line-caught salmon and goji juice" (*M*, 384). Unlike the former, whose "hair was long and greying", the latter "had done that trick with the shaven head, so that one didn't know where incipient baldness began and ended" (*M*, 373). At the beginning of the novel, the two brothers are described as absolutely identical, but they are very different at the end. The protagonists' characterization is based on a categorical opposition so that none of them can be studied separately. Each of them is determined before all by the way he contrasts with the other: each is able to assert himself only by being the other's negative.

By the same token, their social status is opposed too: the one who has lived an opulent life is ultimately reduced to renting a small room, whereas his brother who was raised by a working-class couple is now a member of the upper class. This permutation is emphasized when Gerald, who lives apart from his wife, and racked by despair, takes his brother's place by settling in a room let by Kevin's father, 14 Marino Crescent. The old man mixes up the two boys who both give him support. Being the adoptive father of one of them, he somehow becomes the other's surrogate father, until Gerald's death, an event which leads back to the beginning of the narrative. One of the brothers, a professional writer, has to die for the other to start writing. Once the story is told, Kevin seems to be disorientated, as the title of his last chapter suggests, "Nowhere". Unlike the preceding chapters, the titles of which are accurate place names, the ultimate section refers to emptiness with which the protagonist, deprived of his "half", is now confronted.

***

13   Zucker, *Neil Jordan: Interviews*, 66.

The plot of the novel is set in the second half of the twentieth century, but it never mentions the Northern Irish problem. True, the story takes place mostly in Dublin, but the city was also concerned by terrorist attacks. Besides, the Republic took part in the peace process and signed the 1998 agreement. The narrative, however, never refers or even alludes to this context. And yet, usually, Neil Jordan does not turn a blind eye to national political issues: some of his films are anchored in the very real and traumatic events of the Northern Ireland troubles.[14] In the late 1960s, his generation was inevitably marked by such sectarian violence and its disastrous aftermaths. In his review of Cathal Black's film *Wheels*, in 1978, Jordan notes that the most prominent screen "landscape" of his country was that of the Northern Ireland troubles, with its bombed-out streets, gutted hotels, barricades and burnt-out buses. He himself experienced threats, terror and intimidation. He says: "I've never really seen things in black and white when it comes to Irish politics, which is why I prefer to examine things from the personal",[15] although he considers that "most Irish people wind up jaded and a bit confused about the whole thing".[16]

Here again, there are a lot of misunderstandings and misinterpretations. As a result, it is legitimate to wonder about the allegorical significance of the novel: for an Irishman of the Republic, isn't the citizen of Northern Ireland a twin brother? Aren't Kevin and Gerald the emblems of blood-brothers separated by force of circumstance, by the vagaries of life and history? Sometimes they get closer, sometimes they become estranged from one another, torn between decisions taken in their stead. They did not have their say and have never been consulted. This is why they do not blame each other for anything personal: they are the victims of authorities who made radical decisions for them. There is incalculable damage; bloodshed is inevitable. The imaginary figure of the vampire could be interpreted as the bloodthirsty instigator of revenge and retaliation who always requires more sacrifice. If the fantastic genre is attractive for an Irishman who witnessed this violence, it may be because it is connected to the morbid state

---

14   *Angel, The Crying Game* and *Michael Collins*.
15   Zucker, *Neil Jordan: Interviews*, 122.
16   *Ibid.*, 61.

of conscience which produces images of terror, nightmare and delirium. As the Gothic novel initially mirrored the fears of privileged classes who went against the general trend, the strange universe described here may reflect a whole generation's anxieties, caused by an alarming political situation, the embers of which are still likely to be rekindled.

When Ghosts Cling to the Living

A Necrophilic Romance: *The Drowned Detective* or the Magic Spell of the Cello

On 19 April 2013, Neil Jordan, who had had cruciate ligament surgery the previous week, had a walk in Dublin City centre. He was using a walking stick, and attempting to cross the pedestrian crossing at the top of Dawson Street when a bus suddenly came around the corner and drove at him in an "aggressive manner". Jordan claimed that he tried to get out of the way of the bus and fell to the ground as a result. He suffered personal injuries, was hospitalized and seriously inconvenienced: "I couldn't move out of my house for about a year and for another two years I was kind of incapable – my movement was very restricted so I had to stop making films".[1] This long immobility was for him the opportunity to start writing again: *The Drowned Detective* and *Carnivalesque* were published during that convalescence. This may be the reason why the protagonists of these novels walk so much.

During the three previous years, on the contrary, as he was the creator and executive producer of *The Borgias*, a historical fiction drama television series filmed in Hungary and produced in Canada, Jordan moved a lot. Once in a plane, he met a private detective and questioned him about his job which exerted great fascination over him. These encounters and experiences lay the foundations of his 2016 book *The Drowned Detective*, which is not really a detective novel after all.

The "drowned detective" is Jonathan, an English expatriate who lives in a former Soviet Republic with his wife Sarah and their daughter Jenny. Although the chronotope of the plot is not clearly specified, it is quite

---

1   Caoimhe Fox, "From Captain America's to Hollywood and back. Interview with Neil Jordan", *Books Ireland* (May/June 2016), <https://booksirelandmagazine. com/interview-neil-jordan/>.

obvious that the story is set in a time contemporaneous with the publication date of the novel, as shown by the references to Putin,[2] electronic cigarettes (*DD*, 14), transgendered protests (*DD*, 159) or modern technologies, such as the GPS or Google Maps (*DD*, 129, 18). As for the place, the story unfolds in a city of Central Europe, cut in the middle by a river which can be crossed by a bridge the pillars of which are decorated with angels. According to a legend, once the bridge was built, the sculptor realized he had forgotten to carve out the eyes of his figures and jumped into the river to kill himself. Therefore, the stone angels are blind or eyeless and cannot watch over the river. This architectural specificity allows the reader to recognize the *Margit hid* or Marguerite Bridge, a major road of Budapest which links the western and eastern banks of the Danube. Indeed, huge stone statues of the spirits of strength, represented by angels, adorn the pillars of this bridge. They were sculpted by Frenchman Martial Thabard who never plunged into the water to put an end to his life. On the contrary, he lived several years after the *Société de Construction des Batignolles* built this bridge in 1871. This clue about a unique architectural work allows the reader to conclude that the story is set in the capital city of Hungary.

This hypothesis can be confirmed by the narrative which mentions Hungarian words,[3] typical local names – Istvan, Ferenc (*DD*, 77) – or refers to a book purchased by Sarah, the 1946 autobiography of a Jewish Hungarian writer, Bela Zsolt, *Nine Suitcases* (*DD*, 82). It is worth pointing out that Budapest is minutely described by the author, because he is familiar with the city. Indeed, Jordan worked in Hungary, Romania and in the Czech Republic from 2010 to 2013. Although some details are borrowed from cultural specificities of neighbouring countries,[4] the décor of the story is mostly inspired by the Hungarian capital.

***

The river that cuts the city in two, together with the bridge which spans it and connects Buda and Pest play a prominent part in the plot. Indeed,

2   Neil Jordan, *The Drowned Detective* (London: Bloomsbury, 2016), 237.
3   *Erzelmi* (*Ibid.*, 103).
4   Romanian words can be picked up indeed: *Vulcanizace* (*Ibid.*, 2), *Lecturi Psihice* or *Gelozie* (*Ibid.*, 5).

at the beginning of the novel, Jonathan jumps from this bridge and dives into the water to save a young woman from drowning, an operation he repeats at the end of the story to rescue his own daughter. One of the first details the reader is given about this protagonist is not that he drowns, but that he *is drowned*. Jonathan is swamped with work and worries due, on the one hand, to his professional missions complexified by his corrupt environment, but also, on the other, to his private life since he is jealous of his colleague who has an affair with his own wife. Considering these troubles, the novel could have been titled "The Drowning Detective". And yet, it is called *The Drowned Detective*, as if the story was narrated by a man who had died in the water. Repeatedly, particularly after taking home the woman he saved, Jonathan acknowledges: "I felt I was drowning" (*DD*, 91, 93). That desperate woman who was pregnant from an affair she had with Grigory, her music teacher who abandoned her, jumped into the river to drown herself, just like the sculptor of the legend. Once rescued, she leads a sullen life in a small apartment of the old town, the furniture of which is limited to a mattress on the floor, a sofa and a cello on which she endlessly plays Bach's Suites. These touching, melancholy melodies spread throughout the narrative.

The Cello Suites were composed around 1720 when Johann Sebastian Bach served as *Kapellmeister* in Köthen. They were rediscovered in the early twentieth century by Pablo Casals who recorded them *in extenso*. As he regularly visits the young woman who rapidly becomes his mistress, Jonathan is also "drowned" in the Cello Suites, not only because she works at them every day, but also because he hears them at home too: one day, rummaging in an old box, Sarah comes across a CD of the Suites performed by Casals and keeps listening to it. As a result, Jenny studies and plays them on her violin. Bach's music is such a considerable attraction that from the first to the last page of the novel, the Cello Suites are mentioned no less than seventeen times.

***

In the detective agency where he works, Jonathan receives Mr and Mrs Pavel who are in search of their daughter, Petra. She disappeared without trace twelve years before as she was staying in a resort by the Black Sea.

Her parents, exasperated with the idleness of the police forces, consulted a clairvoyant, Gertrude, who, from a photograph of the girl, told them that Petra was somewhere in the city, in a small room she could not leave. Jonathan, the narrator, gathers as much information as he can and lets his colleague know that he wants to lead an investigation into the case:

> You can't be serious.
>
> But I can, I told him.
>
> Why? he asked.
>
> Because, I told him, as I held up the Polaroid, I have a daughter that age.
>
> Her blonde hair and her hopeful eyes. The girl I knew absolutely nothing about.
>
> Because, I told him, this face will haunt me forever if I don't. (*DD*, 12)

The use of the verb "haunt" in the last remark implies that supernatural events are bound to happen in what follows.[5] From Gertrude's words, Mr Pavel understands that Petra is held prisoner in one of the many brothels of the city where she may be forced to prostitute herself. The end of the novel shows that he sees nothing else but a sex object in her. Indeed, the detectives discover later that the girl has not gone missing, but fled her father to escape his inappropriate behaviour. The steps of the detectives take them first to a whorehouse where a Petra works, but she is not the girl they are trying to find. They wonder if it would not be useful to check the identities of the occupants of the city morgue first.

During those days, Jonathan regularly returns to the young cellist's apartment. Three visits are reported: on the first occasion, he allows himself a tender gesture and strokes her cheek.[6] On the second, he can see that she is bleeding: he helps her go to the bathroom and washes her dress as she is having a shower. She informs Jonathan that she has lost a child, kisses him and asks him if they will be friends or lovers.[7] On his third visit, she

---

5   The theme of characters haunted by ghosts who are constantly preying on their minds is the major motif of Neil Jordan's film *In Dreams* (1998) which is focused on the paranormal, the subconscious and clairvoyance.

6   *Ibid.*, Chapter 10.

7   *Ibid.*, Chapter 17.

talks about Grigory, but also questions him about his wife.[8] Each time they meet, the young woman plays Bach's *Suites for Cello Solo.*

One day, Jonathan calls on her again, but she is not at home. He falls asleep on her bed and has erotic dreams.[9] After a conversation with Frank, his colleague and wife's lover, he plans to make peace with Sarah and buys a bracelet of black natural pearls for her. He walks to the opera house and again meets the young cellist who is rehearsing on stage.[10] She thinks the present is for her, fastens the jewellery on her wrist, kisses him and tells him: "There now. We're cursed" (*DD*, 150). Jonathan realizes he has to put an end to their relationship: he writes a farewell letter and leaves it in the apartment of the young woman whose name he still does not know. "As I made my way down the stairs, it gradually began to build. A constriction in my chest, a sense of panic, a sudden sense of loss, as if someone or something had died" (*DD*, 165). In the street, Jonathan can feel the woman's presence behind him. She catches up with him, slips her arm under his, and says:

> It felt so different with you. With us. You were my twin [...]. You want to forget me, I understand that. But the thing is, I met you in another life. There's another world, where this never dies. And it has all happened before [...].
>
> - With who? I asked. And stupidly, I thought of grammar. I should have said "with whom".
> - You know who, she said. He lives on the other side. And you must take me there.
> - Why? I asked, stupidly again.
> - Because, she said, and her logic seemed impeccable, I cannot go there alone. (*DD*, 167)

They take the metro together, reach the other bank of the river and walk to Grigory's house where Jonathan leaves her. "As I rounded the corner, I heard the crack of splintering glass. Was she the stone-throwing type? I wondered. But I thought it best not to look back" (*DD*, 169). Then Jonathan picks up Gertrude, the clairvoyant, to go to the morgue where they meet Istvan, a detective colleague. With the missing girl's photograph, Gertrude points at the drawer number 11 and opens it: on the

---

8   *Ibid.,* Chapter 22.
9   *Ibid.,* Chapter 26.
10 *Ibid.,* Chapter 29.

metal tray, they can see the body of Petra Pavel, the missing woman, who proves to be the cellist as well. Deeply disturbed, Jonathan asks a member of the staff:

> How long has she been here? [...]
>
> - Close to three weeks now.
> - Where was she found?
> - Floating in the river.
> - A suicide? I asked.
> - Most likely. No one has claimed the body. (*DD*, 178)

Jonathan realizes that only a few moments passed between his latest encounter with the young woman in the street and his morgue visit, that their relationship had started precisely three weeks before, once he saved her from drowning. Therefore, if she died on that very day, how has she been able to be next to him since then? There is a turning-point here: things change dramatically and become inexplicable. The story, which has so far been realistic, is no longer. Jonathan wonders if what happens to him is real or if it partakes of a dream or an illusion. His hesitation between belief and disbelief of the supernatural is properly fantastic according to Todorov's definition: "The fantastic is that hesitation experienced by a person who knows only the laws of nature, confronting an apparently supernatural event. It occupies the duration of this uncertainty".[11]

From then on, Jonathan is plunged – drowned – in doubt: are such strange events pure fancies? In order to explain the phenomenon and fit the pieces of the jigsaw together, he takes Gertrude to the bridge from which he jumped to rescue Petra. Next, he takes her to the girl's apartment and notices that the dust is several weeks old there:

> There was a sofa there, with no cello perched upon it. And maybe there had never been a cello [...]. Maybe I came in alone, wet from the river, maybe I had found this place, this empty hell or heaven. Maybe I had drowned. Maybe I was dead. (*DD*, 184-185)

11   Tzvetan Todorov, *The Fantastic: A Structural Approach to a Literary Genre*, trans. Richard Howard (London: Case Western Reserve University, 1973), 25.

The adverb "maybe", emphasized by its anaphoric recurrence, bears the mark of the characteristic hesitation of the fantastic genre. It maintains the combination of the natural and supernatural. When Jonathan would be tempted to believe that this is all a dream, he is confronted with pieces of evidence which prove quite clearly that it cannot be a dream, which reactivates his questioning: "There was the mattress on the bare boards, with my envelope lying on the sheets. Someone had opened it" (*DD*, 185). When, on the bridge, he wonders how he has been able to climb such a high parapet three weeks earlier – "It seemed impossible. Maybe I hadn't" (*DD*, 189) – there she is, next to him, like a lively angel from the bridge, with whom she shares her connection with stone, her name being Petra:

> The angel is like you, it cannot see.
>
> She let her hair fall over her eyes as if she didn't want to see either.
>
> And I know, she said, you want to end it all. [...] But I will have my say before I go. [...] The cello suites [...] I learned them all and played them and will keep playing them if there is anything for me where I am about to go. When you start something the way you did, when you make promises the way you did, you have to realise it never ends. I have a child now that can't be born so I'm an unfinished thing, the way those angels are unfinished things. You taught me that too. The man forgot to make the eyes.
>
> She was talking to someone else, I realised. To the first cellist in the opera orchestra. [...]
>
> Stupid historical fact, she said. And she jumped.
>
> [...] She vanished into the mist that obscured the brown river. (*DD*, 189-190)

The bridge is a transition between two banks. Symbolically, it can be perceived as a gate which gives access to strange phenomena, which makes it possible to change from human to supra-human states. In *Nosferatu,* the silent film based on *Dracula* and directed by F. W. Murnau (1922), the protagonist is sent to Transylvania by his employer, an estate agent, to visit a new client, a Count who proves to be a vampire. He rides on a coach to the Count's castle, and is left a few yards from it by local men who, frightened by the mere mention of the Count's name, do not want to venture onto the castle estate. He then leaves the familiar world to enter off-limits areas. This change is referred to on a significant title card: "As soon as he crossed the bridge, he was seized by eerie visions". The bridge is not only a way to pass from one bank to another, but also to cope with adversity. As a medium between two worlds, it connects life and death. Once again, there are echoes of Bram Stoker's work in Neil Jordan's. As a matter of fact, both protagonists are called Jonathan and their experiences are quite similar: they leave England with professional ends for the Carpathians where they are haunted by the living dead. "Between Transylvania, an archaic country, and England, a civilised state, the distance is the one that separates the nightmare from the wake", as a critic puts it.[12] Once the bridge is crossed, Jonathan Harker becomes Count Dracula's prey, just like Neil Jordan's Jonathan, who has no surname, finds himself at the mercy of Petra, a strange creature who might be a ghost from the other world.

On a rainy night, she suddenly appears in Jonathan's house, like Stoker's "Lady of the Shroud", with wet hair, a deathly pale face and a mouth filled with mud. On the following day, Jonathan goes back to the morgue, kisses Petra's body and whispers: "let me go" (*DD*, 206), as if *she* was the living one and he the dead one, longing to rest in peace. After all, who is the ghost in this story? Petra, Jonathan or both of them? Did the young woman return to the bridge to kill herself after being rescued by Jonathan? Did he drown as he was saving her? If this is the case, his wife and daughter's return to England would be more understandable. By the same token, Jonathan's presence at the airport at the end of the story could be interpreted as a symbolical representation of his "last great journey".

Unless they died together ... Anyway, all of these questions remain unanswered, like so many others: how can Jenny progress in her interpretation of the Suites thanks to the advice of Petra who never taught her? Why is the pearl bracelet on her arm, since the young woman kept it? Is it a coincidence if Jenny's doll is called Petra? Is this toy equipped with extraordinary powers? Is it an anthropomorphous object, an android with a life

---

12   « Entre la Transylvanie, pays archaïque, et l'Angleterre, état civilisé, la distance est celle qui sépare le cauchemar de la veille » (Jean-Luc Steinmetz, *La Littérature fantastique* [Paris : Presses Universitaires de France, 1990], 94). My translation.

of its own? Why does Jenny claim she saw Petra at the bottom of the water when she falls into the river?[13] There are blanks in the story which leave characters – together with readers – in a state of uncertainty. Could those events be explained by the narrator's possible mental disorder – overexcited imagination, neurosis or any other psychological pathology? Should a look at magic be taken to find some clues? The narrator's limited, subjective point of view does not allow the reader to know more than what Jonathan himself perceives and relates. He is a detective, and his wife an archeologist; in other words, both of them are experts in the art of investigating and digging up hidden truths. And yet, they prove to be unable to answer the question: "Did I live or imagine what happened with her?" (*DD*, 238) Because of this uncertainty, readers are not given any explanation of the phenomena described. They remain in mysterious vagueness and are therefore free to interpret the text as they wish. And there are quite a few possible explanations.

After Petra's rescue, it is noteworthy that she addresses only one person – her lover and music teacher. The man obviously haunts her, but she is determined to pester him too. On the contrary, Jonathan has a social life: he meets and talks with many different people. As a result, we can imagine that the young woman died that night, that most of the story is focused on a man who cannot come to terms with the fact that he did not manage to rescue her. Besides, Jonathan had strained relations with his wife; he tried to save a young woman from drowning, but she died; this loss plunged him into grief. He considers himself as responsible and guilty of her death, tries to deny it and finds himself progressively alienated and possessed by the deceased woman whose haunting presence in his mind becomes an obsession. It is impossible for him to turn his back on this lost object. He then begins to suffer from bouts of melancholy. Traditionally, melancholy is one of the four humours of Hippocratic medicine in Greek antiquity. Etymologically, it is an abnormal state attributed to an excess of "black bile" and characterized by depression. This humour is materially symbolized by the dark, dirty waters of the river into which the protagonist dives:

13   "She's down there and she doesn't want us to go" (*Ibid.*, 253).

> I hit the water as if I was cracking a sheet of ice. And then there was brown, foaming, oily liquid flooding my nostrils, from them to the roof of my mouth. I would have vomited, if I could have. I could see nothing but darkness. (*DD*, 36)

The melancholy subject is drowned in "black bile" which is accompanied by great erotic tension. And this may be another way of justifying the title of the novel. Indeed, as he leads an investigation into a missing woman not to be haunted by her face forever, a hidden truth resurfaces: his marriage is no longer satisfying and his adulterous fantastical relationship with a woman's ghost is tinged with guilt. Jonathan and Petra's relation is hypnotic, "the devotion of someone in love to an unlimited degree".[14] According to Freud:

> From being in love to hypnosis is evidently only a short step. The respects in which the two agree are obvious. There is the same humble subjection, the same compliance, the same absence of criticism, towards the hypnotist just as towards the loved object. There is the same absorption of one's own initiative.[15]

The protagonist denies the young woman's death; she is just moving and talking in his dreams. Jonathan is in a trance, like the children of the German legend of the Pied Piper of Hamelin. The latter is a rat catcher hired by the town to lure rats away with his magic pipe. When the citizens refuse to pay for this service as promised, he retaliates by using his instrument's magical power on the children, leading them away as he had the rats. Likewise, Jonathan is under the spell of Petra's cello, the music of which paves the way for fantastic seduction. After leaving his colleague, he walks on the streets and narrates:

> The bridge loomed up before me, with the giant blind angels guarding the river below. I turned right and walked across it and felt a fresh wind from the water underneath. [...] I walked on [...]. I crossed between the bumpers to get to the other side, and walked up the stone steps underneath the metal arch and found myself on the promenade. [...] I turned into the warren of streets beyond and heard music again and recognised the sound of a cello, rich and dark. I walked underneath a cement

---

14   Sigmund Freud, *Group Psychology and the Analysis of the Ego* [1922] (New York: W. W. Norton, 1975), 97.

15   *Ibid.*, 199.

passageway and found myself in one of those old courtyards, which I didn't recognize at first. But the cello sounded from somewhere above, languorous and familiar. And I crossed the courtyard and found the same stone steps and realized I was at the building that she had led me to last night, but that I had approached it from the other side [...]. I began climbing the stairs, following the resonant sound [...] I knew I was back at her door [...]. I placed one finger on the door.

It was unlocked and it opened with a slow creak of wood. The cello came through, richer and fuller. It was as if whomever was playing it had hit a more intense vein of emotion. Or maybe the door had been impeding the sound. It swung open, wide enough for me to walk through. And she was there on the sofa, the broad wooden shape between her knees, drawing on the bow.

She allowed the bow to scrape to a slow halt when she saw me. [...]

Hello, she said.

- You remember me?

- I remember. (*DD*, 62-64)

Jonathan is guided by "the cello winding its spell" (*DD*, 49). Each time he meets the young woman in her apartment, she plays the Suites, as if the music was a way of luring him into her nets, a power that is not denied by the narrator:

The sound this time was like a summons, authoritative and plangent at once. [...] Here we go again, I thought, someone's calling me. [...] I began walking towards the source. [...] I just followed the sound. I would lose it traversing a bank of houses, then turn down another street and there it would be again. And I found myself at the entrance this time, with the river of sound flooding the arch with its tiled ceilings, tracing its arabesque round the balconies inside. And I walked, of course, up the steps, towards the open door and she was inside, playing, in a white summer dress appropriate to the heat of the day.

- Hello again, she said without breaking the stride of her bow. Have you come to tell me something?

- What could I tell you? I asked. (*DD*, 88-89)

Once again, Jonathan does not seem to be able to resist the call. Two days later, he watches his wife go away among the pedestrians:

> She turned left, down that warren of small cobbled streets, and I heard the cello playing and I stopped and let her disappear. She was on her way to pick up Jenny, and I was on my way, following that sound.
>
> Again, the arch with the ceramic tiles, the courtyard, the balconies above. The stone steps, leading up into a mouth of darkness, and the bowed sound echoing round. There was something oriental about that space, a touch of fantasy [...]. Again, my echoing feet on the stairs [...]. I walked up slowly, as if I wanted to delay the moment. Again, the door was half-open and it creaked as it let me inside.
>
> And she was sitting on the couch, again, that woman-shaped instrument between her knees. (*DD*, 113-114)

Of course, there is something deeply erotic in the girl's position. The instrument itself can be seen as a sexual substitute. The narrator's description reveals his desire to be like the cello, "between her knees". No wonder he later imagines he makes love with her:

> I dreamt of an entanglement of limbs in brown soupish water. Hair like green weeds drifting over my face. A woman naked under a pink ski mask, the open black O of her mouth, into which I was sinking. (*DD*, 133)

In this place that he himself considers as "a touch of fantasy", Jonathan gives vent to his most exuberant dreams about Petra. This *idée fixe* recalls Edgar Allan Poe's uncanny story "Ligeia", whose narrator admits:

> Now, then, did my spirit fully and freely burn with more than all the fires of her own. In the excitement of my dreams [...] I would call aloud upon her name as if, through the consuming ardour of my longing for the departed, I could restore her to the pathway she had abandoned upon the earth.[16]

In both of these stories, the men, whose minds are haunted by "posthumous" heroines, are defined by the duplicity of their conscience: if life is

---

16   Edgar Allan Poe "Ligeia" [1838] in *Tales of Mystery and Imagination* (London: J. M. Dent & Sons, 1952), 164.

a dream, then death is the awakening, and the dreamer – the living man –
coexists with an evanescent partner, a "dead woman in love"[17] who makes
him his victim.

As long as she is not buried, Petra goes on leading an existence halfway
between life and death. She is able to appear among the living and haunt
them. This is why she keeps showing herself for more than three weeks, the
time elapsed between the rescue of her drowned body and her funeral. From
the bottom of the river, she is also seen by Jenny when the latter is saved
from drowning by her father who jumps once more, thus reiterating the
initial traumatic event. Nevertheless, once Petra's body is buried, Jonathan
is freed from the spell and released from the effects of the magic cello. To
make sure that the deceased's remains are well and truly left in a precise
place where she will rest in peace forever, Jonathan and his colleague Istvan
attend the funeral in a small village in the countryside: "There was a bell
ringing, a mournful toll as we walked down the cracked pathway of dried
mud, cigarette ends and scattered beer cans. For some reason, I thought
of the road to Emmaus". (*DD*, 236)

This reference to the Gospel of Luke which reports that Jesus appeared,
after his death and resurrection, before two of his disciples while they were
walking on the road to Emmaus implies that it is possible to go on seeing
the dead and talking with them. The episode emphasizes that their experience is neither a dream, nor a hallucination or an imaginary vision, but a
physical apparition of the risen Christ. The Jesus who reveals himself to
the two disciples is not a ghost or a spirit, but a real human being. He is
not only back from the dead, but also living in a different way. This is the
reason why his companions cannot recognize him or catch hold of him.

In view of Neil Jordan's Judeo-Christian culture, it is likely that the
mention of this biblical episode is coupled with an allusion to the theological meaning of the text which considers that death does not have the
last word.

***

17   "The Dead Woman in Love" (« La Morte amoureuse ») is a short story written by
      Théophile Gautier in 1836. It tells the story of a priest who falls in love with a beau-
      tiful woman who turns out to be a vampire.

As it is often the case in the writer's fiction, the story ends with very visual scenes, pictorial or cinematographic images. The city is in a state of chaos: riots break out and there is violent fighting between black balaclavas – which cover the faces of the police officers – and coloured balaclavas worn by transgender demonstrators. Jonathan happens to be among them at the wrong moment:

> I heard sudden footsteps on the bridge. But with the mist around, I could see nothing other than the huge hawsers and the steel ropes that clung to them, vanishing into a blur. Then out of the haze I saw three coloured balaclavas running towards me, with bright pastel-yellow dresses beneath them. [...] Their dark mouths were open in a scream of panic and I ducked sideways to avoid them. (*DD*, 190)

This scene immediately calls to mind *The Scream* by Edvard Munch (1893), the painter of metaphysical anxieties. This picture shows a bridge on which a lonely character can be seen in the foreground. He looks terrified by a traumatic event. His mouth is wide open, maybe because *he* screams. And yet, he puts his hands over his ears as if he did not want to hear other voices screaming, perhaps the silhouettes in the background. The Norwegian painter, who was himself confronted with many deaths in his lifetime, was obsessed with his powerlessness in front of the unavoidable, hence an artistic work haunted by desperate ghostly faces. Jonathan goes on: "Faces loomed out of the mist, towards me and away, like ghosts. And that's what ghosts should do, I thought, they should appear and disappear and not cling to the living" (*DD*, 191). Gertrude enjoins him to "finish that business, whatever it is [...], the dead business. Otherwise they whisper, they murmur, they don't know they're dead" (*DD*, 210).

During this scene on the bridge, Jonathan listens to what Petra still has to tell him, then suddenly sees her jump into the water: "I watched her fall [...] she vanished into the mist that obscured the brown river" (*DD*, 190). And yet, this time, he does not dive to rescue her, as if he had finally realized that he was not in love with a woman, but a chimera. Petra is a temptress, a fallen angel, a prey to the demon of analogy. Once more, she jumps into the water, pretends to be drowning and incites the man to save her, considering that he did it before, but Jonathan is careful not to respond impulsively again. He is not as distraught as before and proves to have the situation much more under control at the end of the novel.

The repetitive scene of the desperate act of a woman who jumps into the river until she manages to take her own life is reminiscent of Alfred Hitchcock's film *Vertigo*. There are certain similarities between the film and *The Drowned Detective*. It is highly likely that Neil Jordan, who proves to be a devotee of the famous film-maker, was more or less consciously influenced by this "vertiginous" descent into hell.

Vertigo tells the story of Scottie (alias James Stewart), a former police detective in San Francisco. He is hired by an acquaintance, Gavin Elster, as a private investigator to follow Gavin's wife, Madeline (Kim Novak). The latter is behaving strangely and obviously wants to die. Scottie tails her to the art museum where she gazes at the *Portrait of Carlotta*. She never seems to be there and identifies herself with her great grandmother Carlotta, the woman in the picture, who committed suicide when she was cast aside by the wealthy married man she loved. She had been his mistress and bore his child. Madeline has however no knowledge of this. The film is shot according to Scottie's subjective view. The camera's eye is his own. His interest in Madeline progressively turns into obsession. He finds her very attractive, and she him. One day, Scottie tails Madeline to Golden Gate Bridge, Fort Point. When she leaps into the bay, he does not hesitate to dive and rescue her. In her flat, he stays with her, dries her clothes and tells her: "The Chinese say that once you've saved a person's life, you're responsible for it forever." When Madeline reiterates her suicide attempt and, this time, manages to plunge to her death, Scottie breaks down, becomes clinically depressed and catatonic. He frequents the places that she visited, often imagines that she is there. Haunted by her ghost, he notices women on the streets who remind him of her despite their different appearances. His love for her is so strong that it breaks the dividing line between the past and the present, between here and there, between life and death. He dates Judy, asks her to change her clothes and dye her hair so that she resembles Madeline. One night, he notices her wearing the necklace portrayed in Carlotta's painting. Scottie understands he has been the victim of a conspiracy: he realizes that Madeline and Judy are the same person, that Judy was Gavin's mistress before being cast aside, just as Carlotta was. Judy confesses that Gavin paid her to impersonate a "possessed" Madeline.

Like Hitchcock's mystery film, *The Drowned Detective* is a fantastic story which, from a natural situation, becomes supernatural. Its themes are related to psychoanalysis insofar as the unconscious is allowed free expression. The fantastic is structured like a fantasy, like a scenario which represents the fulfilment of an unconscious desire, according to Jean Bellemin-Noël.[18] If love goes on after death, this desire re-creates this comforting love and involves all of our senses. It implies the acceptance of losing the loved object in order to find it again. Indeed, the mourning process is achieved once the subject manages to safeguard his/her love of the object, together with his/her love of life. Spiritually speaking, as the western world nowadays tends to deny death and dodge the issues of grief and mourning, the readers are also invited here to view our human condition as it is, and realize that it is possible to keep a strong attachment to the dear departed whose presence remains, though in another form. Maybe there is something beyond the visible world after all.

18   « Le fantastique est structuré comme un fantasme, c'est-à-dire comme un scénario qui figure l'accomplissement d'un désir inconscient » (Jean Bellemin-Noël, « Notes sur le fantastique », *Littérature* 8 (décembre 1972), 20). My translation.

CHAPTER 10

Through the Looking-Glass: The Marvellous World of *Carnivalesque*

As he already did in *Mistaken* six years before, Neil Jordan takes up the motif of the double or doppelgänger again in *Carnivalesque* in 2017. This is a typical theme of fantastic literature, as Poe, Maupassant or Dostoyevsky's works show. And yet, as the phenomenon can be explained by the protagonists' twinship in *Mistaken*, which makes the novel uncanny, the characters' replica in *Carnivalesque* remains irrational and mysterious throughout the narrative. As a result, the novel belongs to another genre: the marvellous.[1] It invites the reader to admit the existence of unlikely events and supernatural characters, to plunge into an extraordinary universe which is not subject to the laws of nature. This world can be reached through the looking-glass since, like Lewis Carroll's famous heroine, Andy has access to this "wonderland" through a mirror. According to Todorov, "mirror" and "wonder" are closely related: "the mirror is there whenever the characters must make a decisive step toward the supernatural".[2] In fantastic fiction, the mirror is often a spatiotemporal dividing line: it is both a transitory period, together with a gate from the natural to the supernatural.

Right from its title, *Carnivalesque* refers to the world of entertainment. At a funfair, Andy, a young teenager, escapes his parents' notice and ventures into the hall of mirrors. In the heart of the maze, he is hypnotized by the many selves staring back at him. Sometime later, one of those selves walks out, emerges and rejoins his parents, leaving Andy trapped inside the glass. A duplication process is at work. As Carroll's Alice is "very fond of

---

1   Tzvetan Todorov, *The Fantastic: A Structural Approach to a Literary Genre*, trans. Richard Howard (London: Case Western Reserve University, 1973), 46-62.

2   *Ibid.*, 121.

pretending to be two people",[3] the role play is here concretely implemented insofar as Andy and Dany, from one individual, *become* two people.

From then on, the chapters of the narrative alternate the story of the former Andy, the genuine one – now Dany, his anagram – who starts a new life among the Carnies, with the story of his substitute, his spitting image, the new Andy, the bogus one, who inhabits his life as an ordinary teenager in a house which is not his own. Two stories develop in parallel: James and Eileen Rackard, unaware of the subterfuge, are unsettled by their son's transformations and attribute them to his puberty. Andy used to be very close to his mother, but becomes stand-offish and even proves to be cold with her: he does not call her "mum" or "mummy" anymore, but "mother"; he fails to understand things which seemed clear before; he now communicates as little as possible and retreats into mysterious isolation. His mother is worried when she notices that he is fascinated by scores of rats swarming in the holes of uprooted trees. She deplores that her son is so different from what he used to be. She has got the feeling that his body is possessed by a stranger. When Andy goes around with Carmen in the dunes, both of them are attacked by clouds of insects which frighten the girl, but have no effect on him. On his mother's initiative, the teenager consults a psychiatrist who concludes that Andy does not need a therapy, but that Eileen does.

Dany, as for him, integrates into the world of travelling Carnies. The latter are depicted in the novel like fabulous creatures whose specificities are inspired by mythological stories. They are here supposed to stem from the ancient Tuatha Dé Danann, the mythical pagan tribe of gods of old Ireland. According to the legend, following the successive invasions of the island and their eviction by the Gaels, they take refuge in an underground kingdom where they keep their influence on the supernatural. Ireland is thus split in two by an upper world and a lower one. According to the novel, some of them live at the surface of the ground and organize funfairs under the guise of Carnies. They travel a great deal from place to place, but also down the ages since time and death have no hold on them. Scattered by the Great Famine in the nineteenth century, they try to recreate their community in popular forms of entertainment – funfair, circus, carnival – which allow them to give vent to their magic powers through shows of force, feats of contortion, so many miracles, marvels

---

3	Lewis Carroll, *Alice's Adventures in Wonderland* [1865] (Paris: Flammarion, 1970), 92.

and outstanding achievements braving death. The young boy ushered into this world wonders if he is not a Carnie himself, considering the affinities he has with this community. Indeed, he does not know that the transitional space between his former life and his new life – "The Burleigh Hall of Mirrors" – bears the name of a travelling salesman who, in a travesty of the Annunciation, had mysteriously predicted his birth for his mother who was in despair then because she could not have a child…

Carnivalesque entertainment disrupts values and turns the hierarchical scale upside down, as precisely as a mirror: monstrous anomalies become fascinating objects; the laws of gravitation are challenged, the spatiotemporal dimensions upset. It turns order into disorder; it has a subversive specificity symbolized by reversed symmetrical reflections.[4] In addition, the mirror which holds Andy prisoner also reverses the words pronounced on the other side. Therefore, the young protagonist finds it difficult to introduce himself to Mona, an acrobat who asks him for his name:

> 'Andy', the boy said. But his name didn't come out as Andy. Because he was in a mirror now. It came out as Ydna, which he realized, with a growing sense of unease, was Andy, only backwards.
>
> 'Ydna', the girl said. 'That's an odd name'.
>
> And the boy tried again. He spoke carefully this time, enunciated what he knew were the vowels and syllables.
>
> 'Nyad'.
>
> 'That's even less of a name. That's a girl thing, a kind of nymph'. […]
>
> 'Dany'.
>
> 'Dany. At least that sounds like a name. Nice to meet you, Dany'.[5]

---

4   Likewise, after going through the looking-glass, Alice is puzzled in front of a book in which "'it's all in some language I don't know,' until she realizes: 'Why, it's a Looking-glass book, of course! And if I hold it up to a glass, the words will all go the right way again." (Lewis Carroll, *Through the Looking Glass and What Alice Found There* [Oxford: Macmillan, 1871], 18-19).

5   Neil Jordan, *Carnivalesque* (London: Bloomsbury Publishing, 2017), 14-15.

For this reason, Andy loses his name and becomes Dany. As a result, he is in a state of uncertainty about himself and questions his personal identity. Throughout his experience among Carnies, Dany is confronted with the impossibility of giving an answer to the question "Who am I?", just like Alice who, when asked "who are *you*?", pathetically replies: "I – I hardly know".[6] Like her, Dany agrees to answer to a name which is not his own, widening the gap between referent and signifier. His identity quest even leads him to have doubts about his human nature, as the narrative – "the thing that was not Andy" (*C*, 6, 7) – or a direct question puts it: "what kind of carnie are you?" (*C*, 198). Here again, this question echoes the one Alice has to answer: '*what* are you?'[7] ... The Carnies' land is a wonderland whose entry is marked by a loss of bearings and identity crisis. This new world gives rise to a strange feeling of split personality, and raises a number of questions. Like Alice in *Wonder*land, Andy watches in *wonder*ment the specificities of this unusual carnivalesque place and keeps *wonder*ing about them. Every sense of the word *wonder* is used by the text. When Andy enters the Burleigh Hall of Mirrors, he notices that there is something strange about the name of the place: "Burleigh who, he *wondered*, Burleigh what?"[8] Prisoner of the mirror, being nothing else but a reflection, "he *wondered* had he actually become a ghost",[9] and later: "He began to *wonder* himself – was he a Carnie now?"[10] Going through the looking-glass raises a whole series of questions about the nature of this new world which remain unanswered.

It is the same for Alice, whose questions show her desire to know more about her situation down the rabbit-hole: "I *wonder* if I shall fall right through the earth!"[11] or "I *wonder* what Latitude or Longitude I've got to?"[12] and the narrative goes on: "she thought they were nice grand words to say",[13] just like Dany who, as a good pupil, is fond of using learned

6　　Carroll, *Alice*, 140.

7　　Carroll, *Alice*, 152.

8　　Jordan, *Carnivalesque*, 3. My emphasis.

9　　*Ibid.*, 12. My emphasis.

10　　*Ibid.*, 131. My emphasis.

11　　Carroll, *Alice*, 84. My emphasis.

12　　Carroll, *Alice*, 84.

13　　Carroll, *Alice*, 84.

vocabulary: "He was good at school and enjoyed thinking of terms like gravitational pull and centrifugal force" (*C*, 1).

The new world is obviously a cause for concern. It is not as *wonder*ful as it looks. It has nothing to do with the real world, and yet does not destroy it. The words used to describe it imply the coexistence of two worlds, the real one being not fundamentally challenged by it: Alice considers wonderland as "curiouser and curiouser",[14] whereas Dany's words emphasize its abnormality. This universe is depicted as "strange, magical" or "mysterious" (*C*, 3, 4). Besides, the boy says he is "confused", "puzzled" or "amazed" (*C*, 7, 8, 15), which is the sign that his former being lives on. The myth of the double is not only present in his metamorphosis into two beings – Andy/ Dany –, but also in his own split since the "real" boy has not forgotten his former life. Moreover, he also experiences another temporality: at the end of the novel, he looks at his own tombstone on which are carved not only the dates of his birth, but also of his death.

This motif of the replica of the original is taken up each time mirrors are mentioned. The reflection of distorting mirrors allows Dany to see himself as tiny or huge, to watch his face stretched down to his waist, his hands lengthened so much that they can touch the ceiling. These changes of size and proportion recall Alice's metamorphoses: the girl is either too big to get out of the rabbit's house or so small that she nearly drowns in her own pool of tears. Such physical transformations also remind us that the protagonists are growing teenagers.

Obviously, Dany's adventures among the Carnies are reminiscent of Alice's in Wonderland. Many contemporary writers, such as Jorge Luis Borges and Alberto Manguel, have attested to Lewis Carroll's influence on their work. Neil Jordan could acknowledge it as well. The latter's interest in the supernatural, but also in mathematical logic, in wordplay[15] and in the realm of childhood and fairy tales, proves that he has a lot in common with his famous predecessor. It is worth pointing out that this influence is perceptible in some other aspects of Neil Jordan's work, particularly

---

14   Carroll, *Alice*, 58.
15   The anagrams in *Carnivalesque* – Andy/Dany, Andrew/Wander... – recall Alice's numerous plays on words in *Alice's Adventures in Wonderland* or *Through the Looking-Glass*.

in his films: for example, in *The Company of Wolves*, one of the two sisters, significantly called Alice, wears a white dress, just like Lewis Carroll's heroine; she lets herself slip into dreams, which are finally closer to nightmares, considering the uncanny creatures she meets. Such details are the film-maker's additions since they do not appear in Angela Carter's original text on which the film is based.[16]

And yet, if some features of *Alice's Adventures in Wonderland* or *Through the Looking-Glass* are hinted at in *Carnivalesque*, there is another influence which plays a prevalent role here.[17] To the question about his cultural and aesthetic influences, Neil Jordan has answered by mentioning great Irish writers and William Butler Yeats in particular.[18] As the present study confirms, Jordan often quotes his famous countryman and repeatedly refers or alludes to his poems. Here again, *Carnivalesque* uses an excerpt from a poem by Yeats as an epigraph. Besides, the novel is also inspired by local mythological legends collected and published by the poet.

Born to an Anglo-Irish Protestant family, Yeats discovered another world peopled with fairies and supernatural creatures through his conversations with Catholic farmers, servants or fishermen. With Lady Gregory, he wrote down their stories which had so far been passed down from generation

16   Unlike Neil Jordan in his film, Angela Carter does not give a name to her young protagonist in the short story "The Company of Wolves". The latter is described as "the little girl" or "this stubborn child". Furthermore, she wears a shawl the red colour of which symbolizes her menses.

17   Among the texts which influenced Neil Jordan in *Carnivalesque*, Angela Carter's novel *Nights at the Circus* (London: Chatto & Windus, 1984) could also be quoted. The novel focuses on the life and exploits of Sophie Fevvers, a woman who is – or so she would have people believe – a Cockney virgin, hatched from an egg laid by unknown parents and ready to develop fully fledged wings. At the time of the story, she has become a celebrated aerialiste, and she captivates the young journalist Jack Walser, who runs away with the circus and falls into a world that his journalistic exploits had not prepared him to encounter.

18   Mario Falsetto: "Who were some of the cultural and aesthetic influences on you?" Neil Jordan: "Well, I come from Ireland, so William Butler Yeats, James Joyce, and Samuel Beckett, basically. It was a writer's culture; it always has been" ("Conversation with Neil Jordan" in Zucker, ed., *Neil Jordan. Interviews* [Jackson: University Press of Mississippi, 2013], 3).

to generation by word of mouth and thus got into a specific imaginative world.[19] He reexamined the stories of the mythical Irish past and became one of the founders of the Irish Literary Revival through publications of articles on local folk tales and legends or essays such as *The Celtic Twilight*.

In this age-old cultural heritage, the Otherworld is mainly inhabited by the "little people" of mythical beings from ancient Ireland. The latter were said to have retreated in forts or underground, in the depths of fields surrounded by ditches, under hills or at the bottom of lakes in order to protect themselves from foreign invaders, colonizers or superheroes. According to another tradition, they are "fallen angels who were too good to be lost, too bad to be saved, and have to work out their time in barren places of the earth".[20] Their typical features, described by Yeats, are taken up in *Carnivalesque*: the young protagonist, trapped inside the mirror, can see "a small squat version of himself" (*C*, 4) running away. This *alter ego* often sits on the ground to watch hundreds of rats coming out of the roots of pulled down trees. "Those old roots, buried in the ground for a hundred or so years. [Rats] would grow their own colonies, wouldn't they?" (*C*, 82) his worried mother tells her husband, who asks: "Is colony the word for a collection of rats?" (*C*, 83) It is worth mentioning that Yeats, in one of his essays, points out that "at Howth, for instance, ten miles from Dublin, there is a fairies' path whereon a great *colony* of other-world creatures travel nightly from the hill to the sea and home again".[21] The odds are that the use of this word in the novel is not accidental. Magical creatures certainly hide behind these rats. Indeed, they are able to change their appearance at will and assume another aspect in order to do their wrongs.

Another feature is that fairies are immortal, according to Yeats.[22] In many folktales, they are old and wrinkled, but do not die. One of the first things Dany notices about Mona who, at first sight, is "a girl" (*C*, 13), is her old age, as a revealing sign shows: "Her hands were small and strong

---

19   In this project, Yeats and Lady Gregory are also inspired by Lady Wilde's and Douglas Hyde's works.

20   William Butler Yeats, *Writings on Irish Folklore, Legend and Myth* [London: Penguin, 1993], 24.

21   Yeats, *Writings on Irish Folklore*, 60. My emphasis.

22   "In Ireland, we say fairies are immortal" (Yeats, *Writings on Irish Folklore*, 10).

and indescribably ancient. They had criss-crossing lines, not so much lines as indentations" (*C*, 17). Besides, her outdated language confirms that she is "as old as the hills"[23]: Mona, who witnessed the Great Famine, uses old expressions. When she is about to release Dany from the mirror trap, she warns him: "'I can get you out of there', she said, 'but you have to realise that once I do, it will be nose to the grindstone, all the way. [...] Shoulder to the wheel'" (*C*, 15).

Yeats remarks that the little people can set their hearts on a mortal being, take him/her to work for them, and leave a fairy-child or changeling instead. This substitute looks like the one they have stolen but is not human.[24] *Carnivalesque* is inspired by these local traditions: it uses the word "changeling"[25] a couple of times and quotes as an epigraph one of Yeats's poems titled "The Stolen Child": "Come away, O human child!"[26] The poem is an invitation to escape from reality to the Otherworld of Irish legends and myths, to the universe of the Celtic Twilight, hence the calls of the fairies who incite the child to join them in a refrain at the end of each stanza:

23   They sometimes disclose their age, often in comparison with a nearby forest or hill. This could be related to the Irish phrase *chomh sean leis na cnoic* – 'as old as the hills', an anglicisation used commonly to indicate old age.

24   Yeats, *Writings on Irish Folklore*, 180.

25   Jordan, *Carnivalesque*, 54, 140, 143. The American writer Keith Donohue also offers his take on the changeling motif through a fantasy work entitled *The Stolen Child*. He portrays a community of wild children, the changelings, living in the woods on the fringes of the town, who take turns in exchanging their lives with that of children from the area, effectively becoming these boys and girls and growing up in their stead. The novel revolves around Henry Day, a 7-year-old who is abducted by the changelings and thus becomes part of their group as Aniday, while another changeling takes his place as Henry. The readers follow both of them as they are growing up (or not), through parallel and alternating chapters narrated by the two protagonists. In an attempt at re-enchanting the world, Donohue thus uses the motif of fairy abduction to evoke the issues of child identity and of belonging (Keith Donohue, *The Stolen Child* [New York: Nan A. Talese], 2006).

26   William Butler Yeats, "The Stolen Child", *Crossways* [1889], in *The Collected Poems of W. B. Yeats* (London: Papermac, 1982), 20-22.

Come away, O human child!

To the waters and the wild

With a faery, hand in hand,

For the world's more full of weeping than you can understand.[27]

"The Stolen Child" appeared in 1886 in a magazine when Yeats was 21, and it was republished in 1889 in his collection *The Wanderings of Oisin and Other Poems*. It depicts a human boy lured away by the fairies, in the landscape of Co. Sligo – Yeats's birthplace, but also Jordan's. These otherworldly beings invite the child to follow them, ride the wind, float along with the current and lead an idle, carefree life on the moor, in the open air, in wild lands, far away from sad and narrow-minded human beings.

The poem depicts the Otherworld as a universe characterized by its youth, benevolence and *joie de vivre*. Fairies frolic about, dance on the peaceful waters of the lake, "leap and chase the frothy bubbles" of the river, then jump in pools among the rushes "where the wandering water gushes from the hills above Glen-Car". These fresh waters contrast with the bitter tears shed by humans. The child is invited to faraway places. A new life without worries is offered to him. First, he hesitates to leave his parents' cottage, "the kettle on the hob", and "the oatmeal-chest", but finally makes up his mind to reach the Otherworld, as the last refrain puts it:

For he comes, the human child,

To the waters and the wild

With a faery, hand in hand,

From a world more full of weeping than he can understand.

As soon as he favourably responds to the fairies' call, the child is no longer referred to as 'you', but 'he' to emphasize his distance from the world he

27   Yeats, "The Stolen Child", 20.

has chosen to leave. The end of the poem reverses the viewpoint, invites the reader to 'the other side' to enhance the interaction between the natural and the supernatural. The motif of the child abducted by fairies is typically rooted in local cultural heritage. Otherworldly beings have no offspring, but only children kidnapped from our world who belong to the first fairy who touches them. In the poem, the young boy is therefore the property of the fairy with whom he goes "hand in hand". Similarly, Mona's setting Dany free from the mirror allows her to make him her assistant. Straight away, she makes him hold the rope and heave her up so that she can grip the trapeze bar far above him. The rope is a way for her to keep in touch with the ground; it is a kind of umbilical cord, a connection between this world and the other. Here again, such a feature echoes the "old Gaelic account of a magician who threw a rope-ladder into the air and then sent climbing up it all manner of men and beasts".[28] Yeats comments: "It reads like an allegory to explain the charms of folk- and fairy tales: a parable to show how man mounts to the infinite by the ladder of the impossible".[29] Indeed, many tales mention people spinning and spiralling upwards, a recurrent movement in Yeats's work.[30]

The line of the poem quoted as an epigraph – "Come away, O human child!" – helps readers identify the text as being borrowed from another one and sets their interpretative skills in motion. If the connection is precisely established and the source-text recognized, the understanding is all the better because, as Genette puts it, the function of one of them cannot be perceived and appreciated without having the other in mind or to hand.[31] Indeed, the novel can be fully understood only if its doubleness is taken into account and if the link is established with the poem and its cultural context.

28   Yeats, *Writings on Irish Folklore*, 68.

29   Yeats, *Writings on Irish Folklore*, 68.

30   Yeats's collection *The Winding Stair*, his poem 'The Gyres' or his essays – *A Vision* and *The Celtic Twilight* – develop this motif of the winding stair, particularly inspired by Blake and Swedenborg.

31   « On ne peut percevoir et apprécier la fonction de l'un sans avoir l'autre à l'esprit ou sous la main » (Gérard Genette, *Palimpsestes* [Paris : Seuil, 1982], 31). My translation.

And yet, the free, cheerful life on large wild areas that the child of the poem is going to lead has seemingly nothing to do with the one in store for Dany: indeed, the latter is first trapped in the reflection of a mirror, then shut up in a horse-drawn caravan and last, imprisoned in the reduced, artificial space of a funfair. Dany's confinement contrasts with the freedom of the boy in the poem. Besides, unlike the latter, who chooses a carefree life of pleasure and leisure, Dany is not the master of his own fate: he is not the one who makes the decision and finds himself recruited into a place where he is bound to slave away. As a result, the novel both imitates and transforms the poem to which it refers. Therefore, the process can be considered as parody, that is, according to Linda Hutcheon's definition – which has already been quoted here – "a form of imitation, but imitation characterized by ironic inversion [...]. Parody is, in another formulation, repetition with critical distance, which marks difference rather than similarity".[32] The novel takes over the poem, establishes a similar situation, but also a diverging element. Jordan's approach can somehow be considered as the changeling of Yeats's viewpoint. It highlights a postmodern, ironic use of a modern text. This "ironic inversion" perfectly fits the carnival sense of the world which, according to Bakhtin, symbolically upsets social order and hierarchies:

> All the symbols of the carnival idiom are filled with this pathos of change and renewal, with the sense of the gay relativity of prevailing truths and authorities. We find here a characteristic logic, the peculiar logic of the 'inside out', of the 'turnabout', of a continual shifting from top to bottom, from front to rear, of numerous parodies and travesties, humiliations, profanations, comic crownings and uncrownings.[33]

By definition, parody is carnivalesque and subversive. It upsets the original text, supplants its authority and introduces an alternative. Like the hall of mirrors, parody displays a reversed image. In *The Celtic Twilight*, Yeats writes that "the fairies' magic presents the world upside down".[34]

---

32   Linda Hutcheon, *A Theory of Parody. The Teachings of Twentieth-Century Art Forms* (Chicago: University of Illinois Press, 1985), 6.

33   Mikhail Bakhtin, *Rabelais and His World* [1965] (Bloomington: Indiana University Press, 1984), introduction, 11.

34   W. B. Yeats, *The Celtic Twilight*, 30.

And indeed, isn't this the way acrobats perceive the world in their achievements?

> Mona was gravitationless, <Dany> realised now, barely human, and had to remind herself to catch the arms of leotarded youth, swinging upside down on the trapeze bar, on the other side of the vertiginous top. (*C*, 130)

This magical, marvellous universe is the realm of the upside down. It is particularly in keeping with carnivalesque spirit, which is characteristic of mirror-like parody. These combinations confirm the etymology of the word, parody being a song (*ôdè*) performed close by or out of tune (*para*). As a result, *Carnivalesque* can be read as the descant of *Alice's Adventures in Wonderland*.

In Jordan's text as in Carroll's, there is a connection with another world, but communication is established through the dream in the case of Alice, unlike that of Dany. Wonderland has an air of cruelty, but the conflicts there are nothing more than debates and battles of wit. True, Alice meets with a queen who gives orders to behead whoever annoys her, but nobody is ever executed. Her threats are never followed by actual deaths. Although the orders come from the top of hierarchy, they remain mostly unsatisfied, thus showing the limits of desire. In *Carnivalesque,* on the other hand, many acts of violence lead to murder. Father figures are brutally slaughtered and the ultimate funfair ends in a blood bath. Obviously, Neil Jordan's marvellous world is not funny at all. His novel can be read as a hallucinatory tale in which violence is expressed freely. It can also be considered as an allegory of adolescence, since the protagonist, who is no longer a child and not yet a man, struggles to discover who he really is in a strange new world. Besides, he leaves his family home once and for all, unlike Alice, who wakes up on her sister's knees and symbolically remains a little girl growing up in a loving and caring environment. Such differences confirm the parodic feature of *Carnivalesque*.

In traditional folktales, the kidnapped creature is not abandoned to its sad fate, but lives among pleasures and festivities. The same goes for "the stolen child" in Yeats's poem. On the contrary, Dany is very sad when he thinks nostalgically of his mother: "If she missed him the way he missed her she must be hurting terribly, he realized" (*C*, 87). The boy "sees" his mother once again, but posthumously. As the dividing line between the natural and the supernatural is often blurred, it is hard to know where the one between life and death is drawn. The last but one chapter of the novel relates a scene in a small graveyard. There, Dany witnesses his mother's grief and sorrow. She is weeping, kneeling by the marble slab which reads: "James and Andrew Rackard, dearly beloved of Eileen". Surprised by the sight of his whole name, he wonders what anagram Mona would have made of that: not Dany, not Ynad, but *wander,* a word in keeping with his new condition as a wandering soul:

> There was a robin, flitting between the buried gravestones [...]. He performed a warp and found himself inside that robin, in that carnie way [...] He took a leap on to her hand. [...] 'Mother', he whispered. He saw her surprised eyes, looking down at the feathered interloper on her ring finger. And a tear finally willed itself from her grey eyes. It fell and touched his robin's breast. [...] He would wander [...], but could always return to her [...] And he would be there [...] And she would find sleep then, and he would be there.[35]

By the transmigration of the soul, Dany is a messenger from the Otherworld – possibly the world of the dead – which is evoked from biblical, mythological or quite simply poetical views. Writing his codex, one of the characters, Walter, is interested in the Carnies' origins:

> There was an Eden from which carnies fell. A mirror of the biblical one, and as with mirrors, the question once more arises, what was the real and what was the reflected? [...] There simply was a place, a state, a paradise. He tries out a string of names, Avalon, Hy-Brasil, Tir na nOg, but settles on the one that carnies favoured, the Land of Spices. And there Walter allows himself some relief from Miltonic bombast, into the quieter measures of George Herbert:

> Softness, and peace, and joy, and love, and bliss,

> Exalted manna, gladness of the best,

---

35   *Ibid*, 276-277. The anagram Andrew/Wander is significant. It is worth mentioning that the epigraph of the novel is a quotation from Yeats's collection of poems *The Wanderings of Oisin*. The verb is also used to describe the visitors' movements at the funfair: "people *wander*ing through the carnival ways" (Jordan, *Carnivalesque*, 12; my emphasis).

Heaven in ordinary, man well dressed,

The milky way, the bird of Paradise,

Church-bells beyond the stars heard, the soul's blood,

The land of spices; something understood.[36]

These lines are taken from "Prayer", a poem by George Herbert (1593-1633), an Anglican priest who professed his fervent faith through his metaphysical verse. The motif of this Elizabethan sonnet, with its compact style and unexpected imagery, is "a heart in pilgrimage",[37] in religious meditation. It shows that the sacrifice of Jesus on the cross is a victory which justifies jubilation. The extract quoted in *Carnivalesque* is the end of the poem, more precisely the third quatrain and final couplet. In those lines, the world above seems to be down on earth: the borders between the earthly and celestial worlds are fading. The reference to this new environment is based on the Scriptures. "Exalted manna" echoes the celestial food mentioned in the Book of Exodus. After they had left Egypt, the Israelites follow Moses and Aaron in the wilderness and complain to them because they are short of food:

> Then the Lord said to Moses, "I will rain down bread from heaven for you. The people are to go out each day and gather enough for that day." [...]. In the morning there was a layer of dew around the camp. When the dew was gone, thin flakes like frost on the ground appeared on the desert floor. When the Israelites saw it, they said to each other, "What is it?" For they did not know what it was. Moses said to them, "It is the bread the Lord has given you to eat". [...] Each morning everyone gathered as much as they needed [...]. The people of Israel called the bread manna. It was white like coriander seed and tasted like wafers made with honey [...]. The Israelites ate manna forty years, until they came to a land that was settled; they ate manna until they reached the border of Canaan.[38]

---

36   Jordan, *Carnivalesque*, 163-164. The last line is taken up in the title of Kate O'Brien's novel *The Land of Spices* [1941] which relates the life of a religious community of nuns and repeatedly refers to this poem and its author.

37   Jane Falloon, *Heart in Pilgrimage. A Study of George Herbert* (Bloomington, IN: Author House UK, 2008).

38   Exod. 16.

The "exalted manna" comes down from the sky, whereas prayer ascends towards God in Herbert's poem. On the contrary, in Jordan's novel, the Carnies live on a dew produced by human emotions, particularly on the benches of the circus big top. For its magical properties, they collect this substance oozed by the fright and excitement of the audience, some members of whom have little sense of hygiene. Such crude, ordinary details provide ironical counterpoints to the biblical episode. There is a wide gap between the food directly sent by God to the Israelites and the Carnies' food, which is produced by the vulgar audience of carnival entertainments. The precious providential gift is here transformed into human secretion. The theological value of manna, which heralds the "bread of life" or "body of Christ" offered by Jesus as a sacrifice in the gospel according to John,[39] is here debunked and belittled by a parodic process of debasement.

Similarly, "a form of imitation characterized by ironic inversion"[40] can be noticed in the mention of "the land of spices" in the last line of Herbert's poem. This line refers to the fourth chapter of *The Song of Songs* in which the bride is compared to "a garden locked up" distilling oils and fragrances:

HE: How beautiful you are, my darling! [...]

How delightful is your love, my sister, my bride!

How much more pleasing is your love than wine,

and the fragrance of your perfume

more than any spice! [...]

You are a garden locked up, my sister, my bride;

you are a spring enclosed, a sealed fountain.

---

39   "Your ancestors ate the manna in the wilderness, yet they died. But here is the bread that comes down from heaven, which anyone may eat and not die. I am the living bread that came down from heaven. Whoever eats this bread will live forever. This bread is my flesh, which I will give for the life of the world." (John 6:49-51).

40   "Parody is a form of imitation, but imitation characterized by ironic inversion" (Hutcheon, *A Theory of Parody*, 6).

> Your plants are an orchard of pomegranates
>
> with choice fruits,
>
> with henna and nard,
>
> nard and saffron,
>
> calamus and cinnamon,
>
> with every kind of incense tree,
>
> with myrrh and aloes
>
> and all the finest spices. [...]
>
> SHE: Awake, north wind,
>
> and come, south wind!
>
> Blow on my garden,
>
> that its fragrance may spread everywhere.[41]

In Christian interpretation, the bride is the Church or the believer's soul in search of Christ. In the novel, the land of spices refers to the lost paradise, the garden where Carnies used to live on local mildew until they were expelled by the Dewmen. In accordance with the parodic process, their means of subsistence contrasts with the fruit and flowers mentioned by the biblical text. The Scriptures are given a meaning which is not the one they are supposed to have. Here again, parody establishes a mirror effect in which the repeated image is reversed. In addition, it ironically distorts the intentions of the canon by suggesting that the Scriptures depict an ideal which is not appropriate to our contemporary lives. Parody distinguishes itself from religious quotations but nevertheless keeps referring to them. Paradoxically, it contests a model that it takes up, renews and illustrates. Parody both incorporates and challenges that which it parodies, which makes it a postmodern form in which the dialogical relation between identification and distance is permanent.

In her book dedicated to *A Theory of Parody*, Linda Hutcheon takes into account the imitative and transformative compositional elements

---

41   *The Song of Songs*, chapter 4.

of the device. In parody, alterity is recognized, assimilated and replaced. Parody simultaneously refers to two enunciative acts, two contexts of utterance: the present one and a previous one, the familiar one and an unusual one in a subversive goal. Linda Hutcheon seems to detect a tradition of parody in Ireland which would be due to the position of the nation on the periphery of a dominant culture:

> Parody becomes the mode of the 'ex-centric', of those who are marginalized by a dominant ideology. Parody has been a favorite postmodern literary form of writers in places like Ireland or Canada working as they do from both inside and outside a culturally different and dominant context.[42]

According to this postmodern view, parody sets up an inter-discursive relationship, made of identification and distance between the dominated and the dominant, between the periphery and the core. Parody is based on an ironic view of life which characterizes Irish literature from Sterne and Swift to the most contemporary writers, via Beckett or Joyce. Neil Jordan is part of this heritage. Parody is an insolent device which is fundamentally double and divided: it combines tradition with novelty, the familiar with the unusual, in humorous, recreational, ironic and subversive purposes. This subversion of authority is carnivalesque in the sense given to the word by Bakhtin: carnivalization describes the penetration or incorporation into everyday life of specific features of carnival – the disruption of values, the turning upside down of the hierarchical scale – and its shaping effect on language and literature. The carnivalesque element is characteristic of burlesque and mock-heroic parody. According to Bakhtin, the device is liberating, dynamic and subversive. It disrupts authority and introduces alternatives. Moreover, it ignores all kinds of borders, in the present case, the one between the sacred and the profane. With the introduction of carnivalesque features, any kind of formal, dogmatic culture becomes debunked and demystified in an ironic way. In postmodern parody, wide is the gap between the story and the initial subject which is transformed to such an extent that it is inverted. On

---

42   Linda Hutcheon, *A Poetics of Postmodernism. History, Theory, Fiction* (New York and London: Routledge, 1988), 35.

the ironic model of the mirror image, the device conforms to the prior text in order to transform it better. This is what Vladimir Jankélévitch calls "ironic conformity".[43] In a chapter of his essay dedicated to irony, the French philosopher shows that ironic conformity pretends to adopt other people's opinions in order to discredit them. Ironic conformity is the stratagem of the Trojan horse: it consists in getting in on the inside to better turn everything upside down. The cunning lies in "the contrast between a form which grammatically conforms" to the other writer's discourse – such as the quotations from Herbert's or Yeats's poems or the allusions to *Alice in Wonderland* – and "an intention that can be imagined as subversive",[44] like the inversion of conventions. Between the restrictiveness of conformity and the openness of irony, there is some kind of interference, of resistance, an assertion of distinctiveness, a willingness not to go on moving forward with a model, which clearly means that mythological legends and the stories of the Old Testament, as appealing as they may be, cannot be credited today.

43   « conformisme ironique » (Vladimir Jankélévitch, *L'Ironie* [Paris : Flammarion, 1964), 110). My translation.
44   « le contraste entre une forme grammaticalement conforme au propos de l'autre et une intention qu'on devine subversive » (*Ibid.*, 114). My translation.

PART VI:

As Everything Ends with a Song

"Drink, to the obliteration of all distinction!"[1] and Sing *The Ballad of Lord Edward and Citizen Small*

Neil Jordan is a cultured man. As he is always eager to know more about Irish history, he is a regular reader of biographies, including the ones of great men who sank into oblivion. For example, he read Thomas Moore's *Life and Death of Lord Edward Fitzgerald*,[2] and the latest biography devoted to this historical figure, *Citizen Lord* by Stella Tillyard.[3]

Born in London in 1763, Lord Edward Fitzgerald was an Irish aristocrat. He descended from King Charles II, the twelfth child of James Fitzgerald – first duke of Leinster, twentieth Earl of Kildare – and Emily Lennox, daughter of the Duke of Richmond. He was brought up at Carton House, the family estate in County Kildare, and then at Frescati, the idyllic bathing lodge at Blackrock outside Dublin. In 1773, his father died and his mother soon afterwards married William Ogilvie, who superintended her children's education. In order to improve his career prospects, young Edward purchased a lieutenancy in the British army and set sail for America to fight in the War of Independence. At the battle of Eutaw Springs in South Carolina, he was seriously wounded and left for dead on the battlefield. After the fighting, scavengers usually searched the fallen bodies for scraps and valuables. One of them, a runaway slave, Tony Small, stripped

---

1   Neil Jordan, *The Ballad of Lord Edward and Citizen Small* (Dublin: The Lilliput Press, 2021), 236.

2   Thomas Moore, *The Life and Death of Lord Edward Fitzgerald* (London: R. & T. Washbourne, 1831). Between 1807 and 1834, Thomas More also wrote ten volumes of his *Irish Melodies* which was a great success. He fitted the old tunes of Irish ballads to English words. The misfortunes of his nation were thus sung in British salons. Perhaps Neil Jordan had the idea of making his novel a ballad under his influence.

3   Stella Tillyard, *Citizen Lord* (London: Chatto & Windus, 1997).

him of his boots, then realized that the man was still breathing. This presented him with a dilemma: would he ignore the body in front of him or risk losing his own freedom by drawing attention to the wounded man? Sympathetically, Tony got by as best he could to feed him, nurse him and, after three days, managed to set him back on his feet again. In recognition of his help, Lord Edward freed Tony, brought him back to Europe and employed him as a personal assistant who could lead a decent life at his side.

In 1783, Lord Edward became an Irish parliamentarian; he was elected MP for Athy, but soon got bored and restive. His spirit of adventure incited him to sail again for America with his "faithful Tony". In Canada, he accomplished a long journey and fraternized with Indians. In a subsequent expedition, he was formally adopted at Detroit by Mohawk clans, and made his way down the Mississippi to New Orleans, whence he returned to the British Isles. Revolted by the inequalities among human beings and inspired by the French Revolution, he joined the Society of United Irishmen and journeyed with Arthur O'Connor to Hamburg and Paris where his fluent French gave him instant access to revolutionary proceedings. Following the example of Wolfe Tone, he did his best to obtain French assistance for an insurrection in Ireland, the aim being the establishment of an independent republic founded on human rights and the equality for all men, regardless of religious affiliation. Lord Edward became a master strategist in the military organization of the Society which was banned by British authorities. Influenced by the tenets of French Revolution, he embraced radical politics, gave up his seat as an MP, ostentatiously renounced his titles and declared himself a fully fledged republican, *le citoyen Edouard Fitzgerald*. His peers from the Ascendency turned their backs on him. From being a loyal servant of the British Empire, Edward Fitzgerald thus became a rebellion leader. In May 1798, on the eve of the intended uprising, he was betrayed, arrested and seriously wounded in a desperate attempt to escape. He was conveyed to Newgate Prison, Dublin where he was denied proper medical treatment. His wound became infected and mortally inflamed. Lord Edward died at the age of 34 on 4 June 1798 as the rebellion raged outside. His incapacity to take part in the rising is one of the many reasons why the insurrection failed. This fascinating story aroused Neil

Jordan's interest and curiosity, and prompted him to gather more material on the subject. He says:

> I knew so little about Lord Edward, in common with pretty most people in Ireland (...). I did a tremendous amount of work in research into the Irish War of Independence proper, but the earlier period kind of slipped away. I found that intriguing. I began to write a few things out and I began to think about writing a novel and I was really in two minds about it because of all the cultural appropriation issues and all that, and initially I thought I don't have any position or right to write on this man's life.[4]

It is easy to get some information about Lord Edward's life: in addition to the biographies that are devoted to him,[5] a considerable collection, made of an extensive correspondence and all kinds of historical archives, is available at the National Library of Ireland in Dublin. As he was doing research and working on his preliminary draft, Neil Jordan consulted these "Fitzgerald papers" and discovered something striking: while the details of Lord Edward's life are well-documented, very little is known of Tony Small. This sharp contrast gave him pause: why not make Tony Small the narrator of the novel, an eye-witness devoid of any ideological prejudices who just reports events according to what he can see, hear and understand? Neil Jordan made up his mind to portray Lord Edward as the man he was and Tony Small as the man he could have been. As a result, *The Ballad of Lord Edward and Citizen Small* weaves together elements of speculation, fact and imagination: some of the attributions made to public figures are exact; others are fictional. The real is thus re-imagined in such a way that the discourse of fiction is a patchwork, made of different elements, most

---

4   'Neil Jordan Talks *The Ballad of Lord Edward and Citizen Small* with Damien O'Reilly on RTE Radio1' (25 February 2021). <https://www.rte.ie/culture/2021/0225/1199336-reviwed-neil-jordans-new-novel/> These issues are transferred into the mouth of his narrator Tony who, right from the start of the narrative, remarks: "I wonder what gives me the right to tell his story" (Jordan, *The Ballad*, 3).

5   In his acknowledgments, Neil Jordan mentions a third biography: Ida Ashworth Taylor, *The Life of Lord Edward Fitzgerald 1763-1798* (London: Hutchinson & Co., 1903).

of which are borrowed from reality.[6] This discourse is mixed, alternate: although it introduces recognizable signs that refer to the outside world, its status remains fictional. *The Ballad* has the special feature of being a hybrid novel whose protagonists come from the real world and have the name of people who really existed. Yet, these names do not keep their full referentiality in fiction. A historical personage's name does not refer to the actual man: 'my Lord' or 'Ned' no longer describe historical Lord Edward, but a plausible fictional character.

In his acknowledgements, at the end of the book, Neil Jordan mentions the biographies which were useful to him in order to "fictionalize" Lord Edward and Tony Small. It is thus interesting to draw a parallel between these texts and Jordan's novel so as to spot meeting points.[7] Besides, *The Ballad* also refers to a few fiction books which, on the one hand, give rise to reflections about the ideologies and prejudices of the eighteenth-century western world and, on the other, leads us to think about the issues of our twenty-first century. This literary dialogue, together with the specificities of *The Ballad of Lord Edward and Citizen Small* are the subject of the present chapter.

***

Historical documents and biographies have a lot in common with Neil Jordan's novel. These meeting points deal not only with Lord Edward's

---

6   « le discours de fiction est en fait un patchwork ou un amalgame plus ou moins homogénéisé d'éléments hétéroclites empruntés pour la plupart à la réalité », according to Gérard Genette in *Fiction et diction* [1979] (Paris: Seuil, 2004), 58.

7   There are hardly any discrepancies between the biographies and Neil Jordan's novel. Surprisingly, another Irish novel telling the same story of the relationship between Lord Edward and Tony Small was published one month before Neil Jordan's: Laura McKenna's *Words to Shape My Name* (Dublin: New Island, 2021) is a historical fiction book on the same topic. The story starts in 1857 in a London cemetery where Miss Harriet Small is handed a bundle of papers. In this narrative, her father – Tony Small – recounts his life. From being a slave in America, he became an Irish aristocrat's friend and personal assistant. One remembers Colm Toibin and David Lodge both delivering books on Henry James in 2004. Lodge comments upon these literary coincidences in an essay published two years later, *The Year of Henry James*.

feat of arms or involvement in the Society of United Irishmen, but also with his travels, his taste for recreational activities and his love life. Indeed, Lord Edward fell in love with Georgina Lennox, his English aristocratic cousin, who finally married another suitor. In recoil from a frustrated love and disgusted at the cold realities of the English marriage market, Lord Edward re-joined the British army as a commander and set sail for Canada in 1788. With Tony, he traversed the country, practically unknown to white men, from New Brunswick to Quebec where he discovered and admired the Iroquois worldview and lifestyle. His travels throughout the Canadian interior brought him into contact with Joseph Brant, a Mohawk military and political leader who warmly welcomed him. Lord Edward's friendships with native Americans – Joseph Brant – and African Americans – Tony Small – convinced him of the validity of the eighteenth-century concept – the universal brotherhood of men. These encounters made him realize that human companionship was possible across the barriers of colour, class and nationality. After his epic trek from Canada, down to Louisiana, once back to England, he was offered a lieutenant-colonelcy, but accepting it required absolute political loyalty to the then Prime Minister, the second William Pitt. That was a step too far for a principled Irish Whig. Edward's refusal opened a breach with the English side of his family. He put an end to his army career and returned to his seat in the Irish Parliament.

During a stay in London, Lord Edward met Elizabeth Linley, a celebrity singer and the wife of the dramatist Richard Brinsley Sheridan. He embarked on a passionate affair with her. Together, they had a short-lived daughter, but Elizabeth died soon after of consumption. Heartbroken, Lord Edward went to Paris where he attended the debates of the Convention and met with Thomas Paine, the international advocate of the French Revolution. He showed himself more and more republican and influenced by revolutionary tenets, and finally embraced the cause of an Irish independent republic. While in Paris, he became enamoured of an elegant young lady whom he chanced to see at the theatre, Stephanie Sims, who received the pet name "Pamela", after Richardson's fictional heroine. Pamela Sims was allegedly the natural daughter of Madame de Genlis and the King's cousin, Louis-Philippe duc d'Orléans. As he was then *persona non grata* in his milieu, including a part of his own family, Lord Edward married Pamela in the strictest privacy in December 1792 and took her to Ireland where they had three children.

For seventeen years, from the battle of Eutaw Springs in September 1781 until his death in June 1798, during the second half of his short life, Lord Edward never parted from the man who saved his life, his loyal Tony. Indeed, the latter went with him to England, Spain, France or to the New World, took him to shows or society dinners in London or Dublin; Tony was also a go-between in Lord Edward's love correspondence; and now and then, he even collected him from the brothels where he sought comforting to bring him back home in a sorry state. In the late eighteenth century, Tony Small became a frequent sight around Dublin where coloured men were few and far between. The sight was all the more unusual as he had a wealthy local aristocrat by his side. Both of them gave people something to talk about, and sing about.

In those days, ballads were extremely fashionable in Ireland. Some of these long poems serve as instruments of resistance to the occupying forces; they sing the exploits of local heroes and describe political events, particularly the Irish rebellion and French expedition.[8] As a result, Lord Edward and the United Irishmen are the subject of some of them. That is why – and this is one of the specificities of *The Ballad of Lord Edward and Citizen Small* – the structure of the novel is modelled on that of ballads, which are generally made of six verses. Indeed, the narrative is divided into six sections, each of which is subdivided into chapters, which sometimes take up the titles of traditional popular ballads, such as "The Croppy Boy", "The Kilmainham Minnit" or "The Shan Van Vocht". These poems tell local stories of the late eighteenth century and therefore mirror Lord Edward's life: "The Shan Van Vocht" is the embodiment of her nation, a poor old woman who shares her confidence in the United Irishmen's victory;[9] "The Kilmainham Minnit" is a ballad written at Newgate Prison where Lord Edward passed away. It tells the *danse macabre* of a notorious

---

8   Indeed, there are many ballads relating to the 1798 rebellion: "The Heroes of '98, Boolavogue, The Boys of Wexford, The Minstrel Boys, The Wearing of the Green, The Wind That Shakes the Barley".

9   *An tseanbhean bhocht* = the poor old woman.

criminal whose legs moved involuntarily in convulsive movements as he hanged as if he was dancing minuet. As for "The Croppy Boy" – an allusion to the Irish and French revolutionaries who wore their hair cropped short, a fashion to which Lord Edward willingly submitted – it is a ballad about an Irish rebel who, on his way to battle, stops in at a church to make a confession. After he has told his story, confessed his sins and outed himself as a rebel, the shrouded "priest" reveals himself to be an English soldier who arrests the young man and takes him away to be executed.

The cultural context of the Irish ballad, whose content is generally controversial and revolutionary, permeates the universe of the story. As the title shows, the narrative is presented in the form of a sung and danced poem which tells the unusual story of two men that are totally unalike. "His ballad will be mine too" (*BLECS*, 3), Tony says straightaway to make it clear that both of them are united by a close relationship. In the novel, the faithful companion is himself the subject of a popular ballad, as he can hear from children's mouths in Dublin streets:

> You maidens so pretty in country and city
>
> Come hear my ditty about Tony Small
>
> That Indian fella in orange and yella
>
> Black as an umbrella or an old cannonball. (*BLECS*, 128)

Tony is *the other* par excellence, an exotic creature, a curio. The Irish only consider his skin colour and identify him with an African, if not an Indian, although he comes from America. "We are their theatre" (*BLECS*, 129), ironically notes Lord Edward to justify the infatuation of children who cannot help touching Tony's clothes. Maybe the remark also implicitly refers to the fancy of his own mother, Lady Emily, who commissioned a portrait of the coloured man by the artist Thomas Roberts. On the painting, Tony Small is dressed by a London tailor in orange jodhpurs, a yellow satin waistcoat, a big white leather belt and gilt mules, hence the details mentioned in the ballad devoted to him. On the "Portrait of Tony Small – Ireland 1786", the model is posing in this oriental getup next to a young horse and a small dog, in the artistic tradition of those days.

Another original aspect of Neil Jordan's novel is that the story is recounted by the escaped slave. This specificity gives the narrative an impartial standpoint, insofar as Tony Small observes Lord Edward's universe innocently since he is not familiar with it. Indeed, Tony relates the facts according to what he can see and hear, but he is well aware that he does not always get what they mean. He cannot always understand what is going on since he has never been introduced to the mysteries and secrets that his Lord shares with his peers. Tony is unable to say more than he knows and does not suggest conjectures: why would an African-American emancipated slave wish to play a part in an Irish rebellion against England? He could not care less about United Ireland. Nevertheless, more than anyone, he knows the consequences of resistance and rebellion and, as a result, worries about the man he strives to protect.

As a devoted servant, Tony is commissioned to go from Dublin to London where he is supposed to hand cigar boxes to a man he has never met before. Hindered in his mission, he allows himself a break and discovers pamphlets by Thomas Paine in some of the boxes. He somehow reads them, intuitively notes that "Mr Paine's words seemed dangerous" (*BLECS*, 230) and quickly realizes that his lord is involved in a high-risk business. "There were secrets. I felt the pang of exclusion. Others knew something I didn't. It was something to do with those ships, I knew […]. My Citizen's companions were in need of ships" (*BLECS*, 272, 275). This "pang of exclusion" is all the more unpleasant as it affects Tony not only as a character, but also as a narrator. Indeed, the reader, conscious of the historical part played by Lord Edward, has more information than the narrator and thus understands the meaning of the reported events. The reader knows that there is something brewing, whereas the narrator, who does not have the benefit of hindsight, wonders about these secret schemes without being able to find answers to his questions. By a process of dramatic irony, Tony is maintained in "the pang of exclusion": he is kept out of the triad author-reader-narrator, since he is the only one who cannot get the implications of the situation he reports. And when Tony speaks to Lord Edward in order to gather information, he is none the wiser: "To know nothing is the sweetest life, he told me, as old Erasmus said".[10]

---

10   Jordan, *The Ballad*, 275. The reader can also be kept out of the triad insofar as

The narrator's ignorance is obvious from the very start: on the battle-field of Eutaw Springs, Tony Small first spots "a fool" who proves to be "an officer" in a red uniform, breathing his last. The latter, who is "hardly more than a boy" (*BLECS*, 7, 8, 10), says he is Irish and can be called "Ned"; he implores him not to leave him alone there. Tony hesitates, but finally nurses him and goes with him to Charleston where the perked up Irishman introduces himself to two soldiers. In other words, it is only after eighteen pages, which narrate several days of the story, that the protagonist's identity is disclosed: "Lieutenant Lord Edward Fitzgerald of the 19th Regiment of Foot" (*BLECS*, 25). These delaying tactics reveal not only the narrator's ignorance, but also his generosity since he helps a complete stranger, good Samaritan-like.

Tony is fully aware of facts only at the end of the story which is set much later. By then, he had time to gather more information. Indeed, the last pages of the book relate the fire which actually broke out in London Drury Lane theatre in the night of 24th February 1809, more than ten years after Lord Edward's death. This retrospective narrative suggests that the period between the time of the narrative and the time of the story told allowed the narrator to fill in the blanks and get some explanations that he did not have before. Besides, it gives Tony the opportunity to disclose the ending in advance. Some prolepses bridge the gaps and exceed the knowledge of the protagonists. It is indeed by anticipation that complementary information is given, introduced by formulas which refer to the narrator's later experience, such as: "All it would lead to would be the Newgate cell and him waiting in it with Major Sirr's lead ball in his gut, waiting to dance the Kilmainham Minnit" (*BLECS*, 110).

As a narrator, Tony Small is only a witness. His name, ironically given by his slave trader as a reference to his imposing height, proves to be appropriate in this instance, because it reveals his limited perspective. His subjective and restrictive point of view, in the first person, does not give him access to his master's thoughts and feelings. As a result, the latter, always watched from outside, remains mysterious. Even if some of his traits are

---

(s)he does not know anything about the lives of the protagonists before they met on Eutaw Springs battlefield.

sometimes revealed, Lord Edward acts in front of us, readers, without our being admitted to know his inner "truth". The narrative is thus organized on a dichotomy between Tony Small's internal point of view and Lord Edward who is always described from the outside. Perhaps it is this incapacity to penetrate his master's mysteries that incites the narrator to establish a direct relationship with his narratee, as the use of the second-person pronoun shows. Who does Tony speak to when he says:

> You know the feeling when you're huddled beneath the canvas covers of the cases on the coach roof and the rain is sheeting down [...]? No you don't. And you shouldn't. Nobody should ever be acquainted with that feeling (*BLECS*, 93).

This direct means of communication attracts the attention of a narratee with whom the narrator establishes a close relationship, as if both of them were facing each other in this means of transport, out of the way of the others, including the author who finds himself expelled in turn. This person he is speaking to, who can just as well be each of us, readers, as a vague, anonymous interlocutor – unless the speaker is talking to himself – would almost be incited to respond. This is a typical eighteenth-century narrative process, as Sterne, Swift or Goldsmith's works testify. This is also a way for the reader not to lose sight that the story is set at that time.

On account of these specificities, the narrator's presence can never be ignored. Besides the fact that he is in charge of the narrative, Tony is a character who plays a part in the recounted events, but he is not the hero for all that. And yet, he proves to be as heroic as his master and friend. He tells not only the story of the man he follows, but also his own. And if the historical hero that is Lord Edward could distinguish himself by his extraordinary feats and courage, it is precisely thanks to Tony Small, who left no trace in archives, but is however of the stuff heroes are made of. By giving him a significant role in the narrative and making him a major protagonist in the story, Neil Jordan denounces Tony's unfair treatment by history.

Nevertheless, the choice to make an illiterate man the narrator of his novel goes against plausibility. Indeed, it is highly unlikely that Tony has enough vocabulary at his disposal to state the facts in accordance with the syntactic rules, without any malapropisms or language errors.[11] Surprisingly, in spite of his ignorance, he is able to express himself with ornaments and even to pepper his narrative with quotations. Indeed, his language takes up extracts from Shakespeare or Sheridan's works. After a transatlantic crossing, Tony disembarks in Liverpool and evokes "this sceptred isle", as a reference to the play *Richard II* in which England is described as "this royal throne of kings, this sceptred isle, this earth of Majesty, this seat of Mars..."[12] Similarly, when Lord Edward asks him what his heart tells him, Tony answers: "It tells me love has been a masquerader, my Lord, since the days of Jupiter",[13] which arouses his interlocutor's amazement: "You're quoting Sheridan, Tony?"[14] It is funny to note the huge progress made by this uneducated slave once he sets foot on the soil of old Europe.

True, there are some who see to his academic training. Repeatedly, in the novel, characters read and go to the theatre: they are in touch with existing literary works. These references contribute to the construction of a fictional world in continuity with the actual world. Here again the dividing line between fiction and reality is blurred. The works read or watched by characters are often referred to by authors' surnames and produce an *effet de réel* – or reality effect – that underpins the verisimilitude of the narrative. A book in a work of fiction is not only a material object but also a means of cultural exchange. It makes sense in the way it corresponds to the novel it is included in. Therefore, we the readers are invited to refer to the inserted literary texts so as to identify the way they connect with *The Ballad*.

---

11   Mehitabel Canning, one of Lady Elizabeth Sheridan's maids, mistakes "consumption" for "consummation", but also "elevate" for "alleviate" or "wound" for "womb" (Jordan, *The Ballad*, 216).

12   William Shakespeare, *Richard II,* II, i, 40.

13   Richard Brinsley Sheridan, *The Rivals,* I, i.

14   "And what does your heart tell you, Tony?

 - It tells me love has been a masquerader, my Lord, since the days of Jupiter.

 - Where have I heard that before?

 - *The Rivals*. Drury Lane.

 - You're quoting Sheridan, Tony?

 - He does see the humour in affairs of the heart" (Jordan, *The Ballad...,* 176).

The presence of the book within the book calls upon the intertextual notion of *mise en abyme*. A book read by a character can be considered as a mediator of the dialogue with the global library. Therefore, a relation of comment, transformation or quotation can be established between framed and framing books. This literary dialogue makes it possible to spot the effects produced by the reading activity and the *mise en abyme* of specific books.

Back to Europe with Tony, Lord Edward calls on his mother and stepfather, Lady Emily and William Ogilvie. The latter, a very cultured man, is intrigued by the story of this young enfranchised slave in whom he sees the *noble sauvage*. As a faithful disciple of Jean-Jacques Rousseau, in order to introduce him to reading, he gives him one of his books that he considers to be appropriate to the situation[15]:

> 'But if reading is your goal, you could do worse than begin with this'.
>
> He placed a volume in my hands.
>
> I read, hesitantly.
>
> '*The Life and Strange...*'
>
> The next two words defeated me.
>
> '*...Surprising Adventures...*', he said.
>
> '*...of...*', I had no difficulty with that.
>
> '*Robinson Crusoe*', he said, '*of York, Mariner*'.
>
> He smiled then, in that way of his, as if there was a joke I was not party to. (*BLECS*, 123)

With the help of Molly, Lady Emily's maid, Tony, who is unfamiliar with the written world, somehow manages to decipher and read Defoe's novel. In many respects, this text is linked to *The Ballad*, particularly because

---

15   Jean-Jacques Rousseau considered that his pupil could be schooled by *Robinson Crusoe*. He wanted him to start his education by reading Defoe's novel: « Puisqu'il nous faut absolument des livres, il en existe un qui fournit, à mon gré, le plus heureux traité d'éducation naturelle... Quel est donc ce merveilleux livre ? Est-ce Aristote, est-ce Pline ? Est-ce Buffon ? Non ; c'est *Robinson Crusoé* » (Jean-Jacques Rousseau, *Emile ou de l'éducation* [1762], livre III [Paris : Larousse, 1938], 148).

both of them are focused on the relation between two men of very different origins and cultures. A more detailed observation of the texts leads us to note that Lord Edward and Tony Small's first encounter recalls Robinson and Friday's. Indeed, in the embedding novel, a runaway slave, a coloured man, saves a White man's life on a battlefield. In the embedded novel, it is the opposite: a coloured man, dangerously pursued by assailants, manages to escape from them thanks to a White man's intervention.

The two narrating "saviours" interpret their spontaneous response as the sign of the Providence's mysterious ways, as the use of the word in their speech shows. Tony's remark – "Maybe providence had a hand in it" (*BLECS*, 10) – echoes Robinson Crusoe's: "I was plainly called by Providence to save this poor creature's life".[16] Both of them feed the wounded man, quench his thirst and can see a smile on his face in return. Friday, who owes his name to the day his life was saved, shows his gratitude to Robinson by a symbolical gesture: "He came nearer [...] kneeling down [...] taking my foot, he set it upon his head, which, it seems, was in token of swearing to be my slave forever".[17] This strange initiative is conjured up, though transformed, by Tony Small who remarks: "I could have put my own bare foot to his throat [...]. But I didn't" (*BLECS*, 8).

The helping hand forges a very tight bond between the two men who gradually live with each other in harmony, as the chiasmus in Tony's speech enhances: "And maybe that's what began it all. He became my charge and later I became his and we were tied together forever after for reasons I could never fully understand" (*BLECS*, 8-9). This feeling of everlasting affection is also present in Robinson's language: "he made every sign imaginable to me, of subjection and submission, to let me know that he would serve me as long as he lived".[18] Further on, he also accentuates the connection between them: "his very affections were tied to me, like those of a child to a father".[19] These symbolical family ties are also mentioned by Tony who notes the wounded man he nurses needed him "the way a child needs its father" (*BLECS*, 24). This emotional bond is mutual: "And I suppose I came to

16   Daniel Defoe, *Robinson Crusoe* [1719] (Paris: Hachette, 1886), 139.

17   *Ibid.*, 140.

18   Defoe, *Robinson Crusoe*, 143.

19   *Ibid.*, 145.

love him" (*BLECS*, 7), recognizes Tony who perceives their relationship as being as strong as the bonds of marriage. When Sally, the former slave who became a free woman, asks: "Will you marry me, Tony?", the latter smiles and shakes his head: "I seem to be wedded to my Lieutenant, I answered. Where he goes, I go" (*BLECS*, 49). Obviously, what binds them is indeed "something like love" (*BLECS*, 331).

This shared affection is justified by the fact that after rescuing Lord Edward from death, Tony himself has his own life spared thanks to him: he becomes a free, respected and esteemed man. To those who want to send him back to the chains of servitude and tie him to a tree, Lord Edward is firmly opposed: "This man is Tony Small, my nurse and my saviour. And he untied me as they took off their hats" (*BLECS*, 25). He publicly shows that he is deeply attached to Tony to whom he offers a free life.[20] Thus, Tony is not only Lord Edward's saviour, but he also recognizes his own saviour in him.[21] Each of them perceives "an angel of redemption"[22] in the other, for both of them have the opportunity to lead a second life thanks to the other's benevolence and generosity. This angelical, friendly nature reveals itself even posthumously – as often in Neil Jordan's fiction – when, after his death, Lord Edward's ghost reassures Tony by whispering in his ear that he is not responsible for his arrest and untimely death.

Tony and Friday are both recognized to be the faithful manservants of their masters.[23] They are distinguished however by a significant difference: Robinson notes with horror that his protégé eats human flesh. Determined to make his island a "civilized" place, he urges him to put an

20   "He's a free man, and he placed an arm around my shoulder" (*Ibid.*, 43).

21   "I had my own savior" (*Ibid.*, 59).

22   "You were my angel of redemption", Lord Edward tells Tony (29). On the following page, Tony remarks: "an angel called my name to wake me up" (30). Each of them is in turn the other's guardian angel. This is why the ladies of Lord Edward's family – his mother, Lady Emily, or his cousin and fiancée, Georgiana – ask Tony to keep a watchful eye on him (107/181). Furthermore, in the correspondence of the Fitzgerald papers, the word 'angel' is repeated again and again to describe Lord Edward. Obviously, he was adored by his family circle.

23   "my faithful manservant" (Jordan, *The Ballad*, 50) echoes Robinson's remark: "never man had a more faithful and affectionate servant than Friday was to me" (Defoe, *Robinson Crusoe*, 145).

end to his cannibalistic practices. His attitude perfectly mirrors the White man's conquest of the world, a major motif of Shakespeare's *The Tempest* in which the very name of Caliban, the salvage and deformed slave, is nothing else but the anagram of 'can(n)ibal'. Besides, it is probably no coincidence that during their stay in London, Tony goes with his master to Drury Lane theatre where this precise play is staged.

The Ballad of Lord Edward and Citizen Small refers to the eighteen-century theatromania which prevailed in Paris, London or Dublin, where the number of staged dramatic works were on the increase. In these cities, society life was governed by the rhythms of fashionable plays which swept across the social space. People were pushing to get into theatres. As the members of the elite had refined boxes in the dress, the lower classes watched the play at a distance, from the railing of the gallery. There, Cecil, Lord Edward's coachman, incites the young enfranchised slave to be careful of the show for "there's a blackfella like you in it, Caliban" (*BLECS*, 75). The play gives Tony the opportunity to compare, if not identify himself with the staged character: "All I had eyes was for that Caliban", he says (*BLECS*, 77).

And yet, Tony quickly notices that the connections established by others are not justified: Caliban is monstrous, vicious, brutal, "a born devil".[24] Doesn't he intend to kill his master whose daughter he tried to rape? Obviously, Tony has more affinities with Ariel, the faithful man-servant with a beneficent mind. And even if it is hard for him to make allowances between fiction and reality,[25] particularly when he wonders whether the slave goes with his master to Naples at the end of the play as he himself followed his own to Europe, he also notices that Lord Edward is nothing like Prospero. The latter is pretentious, domineering, full of himself. Besides, he is the symbol of expropriating invasion, just like Robinson who considers himself as a king or an emperor, requires to be called 'His Excellency' and claims to be "the lord of the whole manor",[26] that is the governor of the island in the name of England and Christendom.

---

24   William Shakespeare, *The Tempest*, IV, i, 188.
25   It is difficult for Tony to distinguish real persons from fictitious characters: he asks a Neapolitan workman if he has ever met Prospero or wonders how Friday managed to adapt himself to his new life in England (Jordan, *The Ballad*, 332).
26   Defoe, *Robinson Crusoe*, 102.

In his essay *Culture and Imperialism*, Edward Said demonstrates the huge part played by novels in the composition of imperial attitudes, references and experiences. He points out: "The prototypical modern realistic novel is *Robinson Crusoe*, and certainly not accidentally it is about a European who creates a fiefdom for himself on a distant non-European island".[27] Prospero and Robinson distinguish themselves not only by their conquering minds and mercenary ideologies, but also by their prejudices against others in whom they see only savages to subjugate in order to make them slaves. Caliban and Friday are considered as domesticated animals who are necessary for the White man to rule the world. In the cultural system of those days' western explorers, they are at the bottom of the hierarchy of beings, in everlasting servitude. *The Tempest* and *Robinson Crusoe* are typical examples of man's exploitation of one's fellow human being.

Lord Edward's worldview is quite different. Educated by a private tutor who was a disciple of Jean-Jacques Rousseau, he is an enlightened man who listens to his conscience. He lets himself be guided by reason, and not by the prejudices of the majority of people around him. He distinguishes the just from the unjust, and firmly believes in the equality and goodness of all men. His neighbour is not only his fellow citizen, but any human being, including the most distant one, who is entitled, as anyone else, to lead a free, healthy and happy life.[28]

The texts are inseparable from the contexts in which they are written. Their authors are most often in tune with their time and shaped by the society they live in. Shakespeare wrote *The Tempest* in an era of imperial growth in a country curious to know more about the native inhabitants of recently discovered lands overseas. *Robinson Crusoe* was written by a man who shared the ideas of his contemporaries about lower, primitive, barbarian races that needed to be civilized by colonial expansion. By the

27   Edward W. Said, *Culture and Imperialism* (New York: Vintage Books, 1994), xii.
28   His faith in the equality of men does not prevent him from regarding the tribes of the far-off lands as "savages", as he writes in his letters: "I really would join the savages, and, leaving all our fictitious ridiculous wants, and be what nature intended we should be. Savages have all the happiness of life, without any of those inconveniences or obstacles to it which custom has introduced among us" (<https://www.dib.ie/biography/fitzgerald-lord-edward-a3138>).

worldviews and ideologies they convey, these texts are not comparable with *The Ballad of Lord Edward and Citizen Small* which was written in a totally different context. True, the story is set in a pivotal period when slavery, although progressively challenged, was still a reality, but it must be borne in mind that the novel was published in 2021, that is to say over two centuries after the narrated events. Neil Jordan writes after decolonization, after the detailed examination and deconstruction of western representations of peripheral territories, after the analyses of Said, Fanon, Deane, Kiberd and so many others. He has a good knowledge of these intellectuals' postcolonial theories, all the more so as being an Irish citizen himself, he is well aware of the persistence of old clichés, those entrenched stereotypes taken up in the novel by the British midshipman: "What is Ireland like? [...] It's a rathole, a slave ship [...] an island of Calibans".[29] The resumption

29   Jordan, *The Ballad*, 63, 64, 88. Reinforced by the predominance of his industrializing nation and the power of his vast colonial empire, the Anglo-Saxon is convinced he belongs to a superior 'race'. According to this ideology, he supplies the standard degree of civilization. As he considers himself perfectly civilized, the 'other', whose initiatives and results are obviously not so glorious, is a foil to him and therefore perceived as a savage. Such an ethnocentric, more precisely Anglocentric approach perpetuates a simplistic dichotomous worldview, but it was nevertheless widely held in the past and particularly in the nineteenth century. Some magazines and newspapers of the time fuelled these prejudices and contributed to make them available. For example, some articles of the very serious *Anthropological Review* studied the "Gaelic Mental Characteristics" and noted that the Irishman was "deficient in depth of reasoning power, headstrong and excitable [...] with a propensity for crowding together". *Harper's Weekly: A Journal of Civilization* established three levels of civilization in which "the Irish-Iberian" is "different in physiognomy" and closer to "the Negro type" than to "the Anglo-Teutonic". As for *Punch* magazine, it regularly lampooned the Irishman as a monkey or a pig, particularly through John Tenniel's satirical cartoons. In his essay *Paddy and Mr Punch. Connections in Irish and English History*, Irish historian Roy Foster analyses and comments upon these cartoons and notes that the Irishman is always presented there "as stupid, feckless and idle – a stereotyping that had been very prominent and often noted since the first colonial interactions between Britain and Ireland" (London: Penguin, 1993, 171).

of such archaic language can be interpreted as a cathartic operation which consists in awakening old hatreds in order to eradicate them definitively.[30]

The relationship between Lord Edward and Tony Small is not one between master and slave, but rather master and disciple who prove to be friends. The former does not try to colonize bodies, minds and souls: he does not expend his energy to subjugate Tony or convert him to Christian faith. Instead of the discourse of the White man's superiority and the coloured man's savagery, inseparable from the contexts in which Shakespeare's play and Defoe's novel appeared, Neil Jordan substitutes the language of natural freedom and equality for all men. Like Rousseau, Lord Edward considers the Citizen as the founder of this freedom. He rejects social and political conformism, refuses isolation in his elitist milieu and sets himself the task of advocating tolerance in order to build a new world.

Lord Edward is an enlightened man who embodies the mind of his time.[31] He is an Irish citizen, but feels at home everywhere, including among the native tribes of America. He does not leave a national enclosure to shut himself into another. His life is made of free movement and mobility. As a citizen of the world, a 'cosmopolitan' – a word which is part of the revolutionary vocabulary – he obliterates all differences between human beings, cuts across borders and has faith in universal solidarity. And because

30   Taking up such sectarian stereotypes can be a way to destroy them for good. The Irish intellectual Seamus Deane mentions this intricate process by which a community, attempting to discover its 'true' identity, often begins with the demolition of the false stereotypes within which it has been entrapped. To do so, it has to carry out a cathartic operation which consists in awakening entrenched hatreds in order to eradicate them definitively. Such a process is the opportunity to look back and go over the events of a painful history, to settle one's score with old demons in order to exorcize them once and for all and make a fresh start (Cf. T. Eagleton, F. Jameson and E. Said, *Nationalism, Colonialism and Literature* [Minneapolis: University of Minnesota Press, 1990], introduction by Seamus Deane).

31   Lord Edward is enlightened, but is not for all that a member of the Enlightenment, the intellectual movement in eighteenth-century Europe. This group emphasized the importance of human thought and science rather than religious belief and even rejected theological and metaphysical explanations, whereas Lord Edward considers that "we are all God's creatures" (Jordan, *The Ballad...*, 59) which once more proves, if need be, that he remains faithful to Rousseau's principles.

cosmopolitanism is the opposite of colonialism, he plans, with the United Irishmen, to break the links between Ireland and England and to conquer his nation's independence by establishing a new political regime. His attitude to Tony, who embodies this involvement in freedom and equality for all, is the evidence of his absolute recognition of the "other".

Likewise, Tony is a universal citizen: he belongs to both sides of the imperial split and represents a salutary alternative to the sense of belonging to only one culture and one nation. Besides, he realizes that the notion of belonging is often illusory: when he thinks he is of Irish stock insofar as his father – he has never known – is called 'Mayo', like the Irish county, Tony notices, when he finally meets him in Louisiana, that he is completely mistaken: his roots are Hispano-Indian, his father being called after the day he was born, on 1 May – *primero de Mayo*. This piece of information reduces to nothing his pride to be a fellow countryman of his master who points out, tongue-in-cheek, that they have something in common:

> So, my dear Tony, we both got it wrong. But at least we laboured under the same illusion.
>
> - What is that illusion, my Lord?
> - The illusion of belonging. And you are still a mongrel. Like me. (*BLECS*, 75)

Though aware of his aristocratic lineage, Lord Edward cynically considers himself as a mongrel, which, under the influence of the French revolutionary mind, leads him to renounce his hereditary titles and feudal privileges, get rid of his uniforms and decorations, and introduce himself as "Citizen Fitzgerald".[32] At a convivial gathering in Paris, with some republican supporters of the cause, Tony reports:

> And as the whole table erupted into raucous wine-soaked cheers, Tom Paine leaned into my ear and begged me to share in the celebration. 'Drink, to the obliteration of all distinction'. So I drank. To the newborn citizen, who, I was sure, could still employ a manservant. (*BLECS*, 236)

---

32 "I do not like to be Lord Edward", he writes in a letter to his sister, Lady Lucy. The latter, after his death, writes: "He was a Paddy and no more; he desired no other title than this" (Angela Bourke, *The Field Day Anthology of Irish Writing* [New York: New York University Press, 2002], 59).

***

There are some who may consider that the character of Tony Small is idealized in the novel. Indeed, the young man is depicted with sentimentalism, in accordance with Rousseauistic principles. And yet, the odds are that historical Tony was confronted with many more formidable difficulties than the ones he mentions in his narrative. Similarly, Lord Edward is portrayed as a charismatic personality whose generosity and benevolence seem to hide any weakness or failing. This embellishment of the truth is to be connected with the motif of the ballad which gives structure to the novel. Sung, sometimes danced, these popular traditional poems show burlesque flippancy which contrasts with their revolutionary words.

In spite of this idealized picture, no one can hide the historical fact that Lord Edward and Tony Small offered each other a second life. For us, readers of the twenty-first century, this leads us to establish a connection with the realities of our present world. For three decades now, Ireland has been a country of refuge. Nowadays its population is a kaleidoscope of mixed cultures since one citizen out of eight was born abroad. Its identity, now hybrid and heterogeneous, has become considerably more complex. And yet, Ireland is also a nation where closed, selfish, intolerant attitudes can be observed, particularly in times of crisis.[33] No one can deny that some first or second-generation immigrants are good examples of successful integration, particularly when they fulfil high-rank functions,[34] but many of them are however still confronted with racist violence and discrimination. Published in such a context, a novel focused on a close friendship between a local aristocrat and a stateless man tossed by the vagaries of history and

33   In September 2019, a report from the EU's human rights agency warned that Ireland had a disturbing problem with racist violence and discrimination. Based on testimonies of coloured migrants, it highlighted worrying patterns of racist behaviour in Ireland where figures of harassment, discrimination and racism were significantly higher than in many other EU countries <https://www.irishtimes.com/news/polit ics/ireland-has-worrying-pattern-of-racism-head-of-eu-agency-warns-1.4032957>.

34   For example, Leo Varadkar, the son of Indian immigrants, was the Prime Minister of the Irish Republic from 2017 to 2020. Hazel Chu, whose parents are Chinese immigrants, was elected Lord-Mayor of Dublin in 2020.

considered as a beast of burden, if not a commodity, provides a source of inspiration.

By making Tony the narrator of the story, Neil Jordan increases the standing of the outcast and invites his blinkered readers who stick to their presuppositions to revise their opinions. Against a trend of history which is only interested in great men, the enfranchised slave's narrative can be considered as an alternative form related by a peripheral citizen who has no reason to remain out of history now. His voice rises from the margins and maybe that is why it is so typically Irish. It praises the ones who are able to obliterate all distinctions, to free others from their bonds, and welcome them without prejudices to offer them a second chance. This voice pays tribute to enlightened minds who do not hesitate to break the rules and customs in order to establish equality of men and show sympathy for the cause of peoples and the triumph of liberty.

Conclusion

> What causes [this work] to soar above endless other novels of what might other-wise be its kind? I would suggest, [the writer's] curious, near-visionary manner of seeing and way of writing; [...] his sympathy with the off-beat, with deviation; [...] He is aware of the monstrous, and makes a not wholly ironical bow to it [...]. Note particularly Irish attributes of [his], all of them to the fore in [his work]. His feeling for, acceptance of, and matter-of-fact though none the less terrifying treatment of the supernatural; [...] his sense of the illimitable majesty of death, and its train of incurable desolations.[1]

These words of Elizabeth Bowen about Joseph Sheridan Le Fanu could be transposed because they apply perfectly to Neil Jordan. The latter's work is indeed part of the heritage of nineteenth-century Irish writers – Le Fanu, but also Maturin and especially Yeats and Stoker. It belongs to the fantasy genre and shows a strong attraction to the gothic imagination, mixing the rational and the irrational, endowing characters with super-natural powers, and exploiting the themes of loss of identity, usurpation and vampirism. The eternal struggle between Good and Evil, the original anxiety that haunts man and his destiny, the paradoxes of our nature torn between contrary aspirations are all themes present in Jordan's work as in those of his illustrious predecessors. However, while being part of this tradition, Neil Jordan also knows how to distance himself from it, as shown by the recurrent use in his work of parody, which Gérard Genette conceives as "the playful transformation of a single text".[2] Indeed, it seems that the process is perceived by the writer as a game, in the same way as the fool's games, mirror images, puns or plays on words that are scattered throughout his fiction.

---

1   Allan Hepburn, ed., *People, Places, Things. Essays by Elizabeth Bowen* (Edinburgh: Edinburgh University Press, 2008), 174.

2   « La transformation ludique d'un texte singulier » (Gérard Genette, *Palimpsestes : la littérature au second degré* [Paris : Seuil, 1982], 164).

The work studied here, which could be described as "neo-gothic" with regard to the processes exploited and ironically diverted, diffuses a twilight atmosphere announcing a completion, whether it is the end of a day, the end of an experience or of a world. This particular temporality is accompanied by "liminal landscapes by essence",[3] such as coastal areas, deserted beaches or flooded territories whose demarcation lines are blurred by mists, water vapours or torrential rains. Such spatiotemporal specificities are in line with the viewpoints of narrators who are floating in daydreams. They illustrate that human life takes place on an indecisive frontier, at the limit of two worlds, that consciousness is a dividing line. Seized with vertigo, characters hesitate between two poles; they wonder about others and about themselves.[4]

The death of Nina, the protagonist of *Shade*, occurs on January 14, 1950.[5] From then on, the heavens open and, for weeks, pour a biblical flood.[6] Forty days later, the date of 25 February 1950 coincides with Neil Jordan's birth. The liberation of Nina, thrown out of her sinister burial place by the rising waters, refers implicitly to Noah's exit from his ark, but also to the author's coming into the world, all three of them getting ready to discover a new environment.[7] A subtle shift occurs from fiction to reality through

3   Marie Mianowski, *Post Celtic Tiger Landscapes in Irish Fiction* (London and New York: Routledge, 2016), 6.

4   From the first novel, *The Past*, to the latest, *The Ballad of Lord Edward and Citizen Small*, the questioning of the self – who am I really? – is recurrent.

5   "I know exactly when I died. It was twenty past three on the fourteenth of January of the year nineteen fifty" (Jordan, *Shade*, 3).

6   "The heavens open, the rain cascades […], each raindrop like a falling angel, the beatings wings of a dove" (Jordan, *Shade*, 313). The allusion to the biblical text is clear: when God sends the Flood on earth, "The windows of the sky were opened, and rain fell on the earth for forty days and forty nights" (Gen. 7:11-12).

7   There is a lot in common between *Shade* and the Book of Genesis: both books are composed of fifty chapters. Moreover, the child Nina and her friends consider their playground as the enclosure of paradise – "our garden of Eden" (Jordan, *Shade*, 318) – which adjoins muddy areas on the river estuary, an empty and vague space, the place of the original separation between land and water. In the novel, as in the biblical text, the garden is also the scene of the encounter between man and woman. It is also the place of lost innocence, of transgression, and of the fall leading to the estrangement from the place and separation from the father, before the forty-day flood.

the myth. This passage from the inside to the outside, heralding a new life, is part of the theme of transgression which, as this study illustrates, characterizes the entire work. Transgression pushes back the frontiers of the possible, abolishes the norms; it blurs any separation between life and death, between the natural and supernatural, but also between truth and fiction.

In the same way, characters split into two, depending on whether they open their eyes to the facts of the present or to a deeper reality, with unlimited horizons. Refusing to reduce our world to the visible, Neil Jordan's work oversteps the observable universe that surrounds us: it questions what goes beyond the existing,[8] wonders about the immaterial, as if it were necessary to be outside the world to understand it in any way. Exploiting the themes of darkness, uncertainty, hesitation and the existence of other worlds, it slides from the fantastic to the metaphysical.

Neil Jordan's work has an undeniable transcendent dimension. It is no matter of chance if it refers or alludes to the English baroque of the seventeenth century and its illustrious metaphysical poets. Indeed, Jordan mentions the name of George Herbert and quotes one of his poems in *Carnivalesque*;[9] he claims that John Milton's *Paradise Lost* was the most significant influence in his film adaptation of *Interview with the Vampire*;[10] similarly, many of his texts implicitly refer to a poem by John Donne, the leader of the metaphysical school, "Good Friday, 1613. Riding Westward". As a matter of fact, it is worth noting that throughout Jordan's work, the

---

8   "Metaphysics is the question that goes beyond the existing" (Martin Heidegger, "What Is Metaphysics?" [1929]).

9   The reader can refer to the end of the chapter in this book: "Through the Looking-Glass: The Marvelous World of *Carnivalesque*".

10   "Jordan has claimed that John Milton's *Paradise Lost* was the most significant influence in his adaptation of <Rice's> book. The story of the angels expelled by God after they participate in a rebellion tantamount to a palace revolt is well-known. Because of their abortive mutiny, the fallen angels cascade from heaven down into the dust of hell. With *Paradise Lost,* Satan assumes the stature of fallen beauty: 'splendor shadowed by sadness and death'; he is 'majestic though in ruin' (Mario Praz, 56). This description is perfectly embodied by Brad Pitt's incarnation of Louis" (Zucker, ed., *Neil Jordan. Interviews* [Jackson: University Press of Mississippi, 2013], introduction by C. Zucker, xvi-xvii).

privileged axis of the protagonists' movements is from east to west.[11] More than a geographical place, such a destination is a mythical, imaginary and supernatural point in space. This is a common element between Jordan's fiction and Donne's poem:

> Hence is't, that I am carried towards the West
>
> This day, when my Soul's form bends to the East.[12]

The poet deplores not being able to meditate properly on the ultimate sacrifice of Christ who died in the East, because he is busy riding west-wards to a friend's house:

> There I should see a Sun by rising set,
>
> And by that setting endless day beget.[13]

The rising sun refers to the Son of God lifted up on the cross[14] on which He also 'lies down' by dying there, thus opening the doors of eternal life – an "endless day" – to the human kind. In its evanescent fluidity, the setting sun metaphorically designates death and its mystery. As mentioned above, Elizabeth Bowen's statement about the "sense of the illimitable majesty of death, and its train of incurable desolations" is once again appropriate to Neil Jordan's fiction, whose main character is none other than Death itself. From the suicide narrated in the very first text published by the author to the confidence of Lord Edward's ghost who whispers in Tony's ear that he is in no way responsible for his death in the final pages of his latest novel, death is omnipresent and can be considered as the cornerstone of

11   In many of Jordan's texts ("A Love", *The Past, Sunrise with Sea Monster* or *Carnivalesque*), the protagonists leave the shores of the Irish Sea, in the east of the country, for the west coast, at the edge of the ocean, and in particular the health resort of Lisdoonvarna, in County Clare.

12   John Donne, "Good Friday, 1613. Riding Westward" in *The Metaphysical Poets* (Harmondsworth: Penguin Books, 1957), 87. The poet meditates on the death of Christ which took place towards the east, "behind his back". He turns his back to Christ who calls him to "turn around", to convert.

13   *Ibid.*

14   This connection is confirmed by the proximity of the terms *sun* and *son*.

the whole work. Death awaits the characters at the end of the shore, an intermediate zone between land and sea, a seemingly desolate territory where consciousness seems to open up, impregnated with the fabulous proximity of the Great Whole. Doesn't the ocean allow us to imagine God, according to a character in *The Past*?[15] Offshore, in maritime fogs, under dense, heavy clouds, mythical lands can be guessed: Avalon or Tír na nÓg – the Land of the Young People – have acquired the metaphorical meaning of distant places located beyond the borders of the known world. Ireland is an island on the fringe of mainland, an *Ultima Thule*, a land's end, on the threshold of the unknown. Its west coast is "the soul of Ireland",[16] its "spiritual heartland".[17] No wonder Jordan's fiction tends to look always towards the west. It is both sensual and spiritual; it gives food for thought about 'the other world', which makes Jordan a metaphysical poet. The movements of his characters in the same direction is highly symbolical: heading westwards is melting into another universe,[18] in order to watch, as in a dream, the daystar disappear into the waves. It is the situation of the one who wanted to follow the course of the sun, and who finds himself one evening, alone, in front of the shore, in a shady, abandoned place, without any other resource than to resign himself, to adapt and get used to it since, in the moment, one cannot go further. *There* is the end of the journey, the boundary of the earth, the edge of the abyss...[19]

15 "You imagine God to be a sea" (Jordan, *The Past*, 62).

16 Nolan, *Neil Jordan: Works for the Page*, 67.

17 *Ibid.*, 82.

18 Hence the colloquial expression *to go west*.

19 Etymologically, "Occident" refers to *occidere*, i.e. "to fall". There is therefore a risk of falling beyond the western fringe.

Bibliography

Fiction by Neil Jordan

The Ballad of Lord Edward and Citizen Small (Dublin: The Lilliput Press, 2021).
Carnivalesque (London: Bloomsbury, 2017).
The Drowned Detective (London: Bloomsbury, 2016).
Mistaken (London: John Murray, 2011).
Night in Tunisia and Other Stories [1976] – *The Dream of a Beast* [1983] – *The Crying Game* [1993] in *A Neil Jordan Reader* (New York: Vintage International, 1993).
The Past [1980] (Berkeley: Soft Skull Press, 2012).
Shade (London: John Murray, 2004).
Sunrise with Sea Monster (London: Vintage, 1994).

Selected Works on Neil Jordan's Literary Fiction

Books

McGuirk, Paul, *Neil Jordan: The Literary Fiction* (Leipzig, Germany: Limanaki Books, Amazon Distribution, 2016).
Nolan, Val, *Neil Jordan: Works for the Page* (Cork: Cork University Press, 2022).
Pernot-Deschamps, Marguerite, *The Fictional Imagination of Neil Jordan, Irish Novelist and Film-Maker: A Study of Literary Style* (Lewiston, NY: The Edwin Mellen Press, 2009).
Rogers, Lori, *Feminine Nation. Performance, Gender and Resistance in the Works of John McGahern and Neil Jordan* (Lanham, MD: University Press of America, 1998).

Articles

Brace, Marianne, 'Neil Jordan: The Writing Game', *The Independent* (14 January 1995).
Cherry, Kelly, 'An Art of the Heart: The Fiction of Neil Jordan', *Hollins Critic* 55/1 (2018).
Cotta Ramusino, Elena, 'Neil Jordan's *The Past*: A Journey in Time and Memory', in Sean Crosson and Werner Huber, eds, *Towards 1916–1916 and Irish Literature, Culture & Society* (Trier: Wissenschaftlicher Verlag, 2015), 145-153.
Fierobe, Claude, « Double jeu : *Confusion* de Neil Jordan », in *Les Ombres du fantastique. Fictions d'Irlande* (Dinan : Terre de Brume, 2016), 108-127.

Goarzin, Anne, « Jeux d'ombres et de lumière: révélations de l'image chez James Joyce, Neil Jordan et Paul Durcan », in Renée Dickason, ed., *Analyse d'images* (Rennes : Presses Universitaires de Rennes, 2003), 45-61.

Grassi, Samuele, 'Fathers in a Coma: Father-Son Relationship in Neil Jordan's Fiction', *Estudios Irlandeses* 3 (2008), 101-112.

Hopper, Keith, '"A Postcard from the Homeland": Neil Jordan's *The Past*', *Litteraria Pragensia* 22/44 (2012), 75-90.

Möller, Karin, 'Beast in the Barrier Zone: Transformations of Irish Politics, History and Myth in Neil Jordan's *Sunrise with Sea Monster*', *Humanetten* 6 (2000).

O'Brien, Harvey, 'Local Man, Global Man: Masculinity in Transformation in the Horror/Fantasy of Neil Jordan', in Ondrej Pilny and Clare Wallace, eds, *Global Ireland. Irish Literatures for the New Millennium* (Prague, Litteraria Pragensia, 2005).

Rogers, Lori, 'In Dreams Uncover'd: Neil Jordan, "The Dream of a Beast", and the Body-Secret', *Critique: Studies in Contemporary Fiction* 39/1 (1997), 48-54.

Schwall, Hedwig, 'Fictions about Factions: An Analysis of Neil Jordan's *Sunrise with Sea Monster*', *Nordic Irish Studies* 1 (2002), 31-50.

Williams, Niall, 'Time past; Imagine and Remember: A View of Neil Jordan's Novel *The Past*', *Gaeliana* 3 (1981), 165-170.

Works on Neil Jordan's Films

Pramaggiore, Maria, *Neil Jordan* (Urbana and Chicago: University of Illinois Press, 2008).

Rockett, Kevin & Emer, *Neil Jordan: Exploring Boundaries* (Dublin: The Liffey Press, 2003).

Zucker, Carole, *The Cinema of Neil Jordan: Dark Carnival* (London: Wallflower Press, 2008).

Selected Interviews with Neil Jordan

Fox, Caoimhe, 'From Captain America's to Hollywood and back. Interview with Neil Jordan', *Books Ireland* (May/June 2016).

McCabe, Patrick, '1916 I Think Impossible to Think about Without Thinking of Yeats and O'Casey', Public interview with Neil Jordan, 9th EFACIS conference, 5-7 June 2013, NUI Galway, in Sean Crosson and Werner Huber, eds, *Towards 1916–1916 and Irish Literature, Culture & Society* (Trier: Wissenschaftlicher Verlag, 2015), 229-253.

O'Reilly, Damien, 'Neil Jordan Talks *The Ballad of Lord Edward and Citizen Small* with Damien O'Reilly on RTÉ Radio 1' (25 February 2021).

<https://www.rte.ie/culture/2021/0225/1199336-reviwed-neil-jordans-new-novel/
> accessed 28 April 2021.

Toibin, Colm, 'The *In Dublin* Interview: Neil Jordan talks to Colm Toibin', *In Dublin* 152/29 (1982), 14-19.

Zucker, Carole, ed., *Neil Jordan: Interviews* (Jackson: University Press of Mississippi, 2013).

Selected Essays on Irish Literature and Culture

Brown, Terence, *Ireland. A Social and Cultural History 1922-2002* (London: Harper Collins, 2004).

Cahalan, James M., *The Irish Novel* (Dublin: Gill & Macmillan, 1988).

Cardin, Bertrand, *Miroirs de la filiation. Parcours dans huit romans irlandais contemporains* (Caen : Presses Universitaires de Caen, 2005).

Carlson, Julia, ed., *Banned in Ireland. Censorship and the Irish Writer* (London: Routledge, 1990).

Corcoran, Neil, *After Yeats and Joyce. Reading Modern Irish Literature* (Oxford and New York: Oxford University Press, 1997).

Cronin, Michael, *Across the Lines. Travel, Language, Translation* (Cork: Cork University Press, 2000).

Deane, Seamus, *Celtic Revivals. Essays in modern Irish Literature 1880-1980* (London: Faber & Faber, 1985).

——*A Short History of Irish Literature* (London: Hutchinson & Co., 1986).

——*The Field Day Anthology of Irish Writing* (Derry: Field Day Publications, 1991).

Eagleton, Terry, *Crazy John and the Bishop and other Essays on Irish Culture* (Cork: Cork University Press, 1998).

Fierobe, Claude and Jacqueline Genet, *La Littérature irlandaise* (Paris : Armand Colin, 1997).

Fierobe, Claude, *Les Ombres du fantastique. Fictions d'Irlande* (Dinan : Terre de Brume, 2016).

Foster, Roy, *The Irish Story: Telling Tales and Making It Up in Ireland* (Oxford: Oxford University Press, 2001).

Genet, Jacqueline, ed., *La Nouvelle irlandaise de langue anglaise* (Villeneuve d'Ascq : Presses Universitaires du Septentrion, 1996).

Gillis, Alan and Aaron Kelly, eds, *Critical Ireland. New Essays in Literature and Culture* (Dublin: Four Courts Press, 2001).

Goarzin, Anne et Stéphane Jousni, eds, *Voix et Langues dans la littérature irlandaise* (Rennes : Presses Universitaires de Rennes, 2003).

Harte, Liam and Michael Parker, eds, *Contemporary Irish Fiction. Themes, Tropes, Theories* (London: Macmillan, 2000).

Hunt Mahony, Christina, *Contemporary Irish Literature. Transforming Tradition* (New York: St Martin's Press, 1998).

Hyde, Tom, ed., *Fathers and Sons* (Dublin: Wolfhound Press, 1995).

Imhof, Rüdiger, ed., *Contemporary Irish Novelists* (Tübingen: Gunter Narr Verlag, 1990).

Kearney, Richard, ed., *Across the Frontiers: Ireland in the 1990s, Cultural – Political – Economic* (Dublin: Wolfhound Press, 1988).

Kiberd, Declan, *Inventing Ireland* (London: Jonathan Cape, 1995).

Lalor, Brian, ed., *The Encyclopaedia of Ireland* (Dublin: Gill & Macmillan, 2003).

Longley, Edna, *The Living Stream. Literature and Revisionism in Ireland* (Newcastle upon Tyne: Bloodaxe Books, 1994).

Maher, Eamon, ed., *Cultural Perspectives on Globalisation and Ireland* (Bern: Verlag Peter Lang, 2009).

Martin, Augustine, *Bearing Witness. Essays on Anglo-Irish Literature* (Dublin: UCD Press, 1996).

Mercier, Vivian, *The Irish Comic Tradition* (London, Oxford and New York: Oxford University Press, 1962).

Mianowski, Marie, *Post Celtic Tiger Landscapes in Irish Fiction* (London: Routledge, 2016).

Mikowski, Sylvie, *Le Roman irlandais contemporain* (Caen : Presses Universitaires de Caen, 2004).

Murphy, Neil, *Irish Fiction and Postmodern Doubt: An Analysis of the Epistemological Crisis in Modern Irish Fiction* (Lewiston: Edwin Mellen, 2004).

Ni Anluain, Cliodhna, ed., *Reading the Future. Irish Writers in Conversation with Mike Murphy* (Dublin: The Lilliput Press, 2000).

O'Carroll, J. P. and J. A. Murphy, eds, *DeValera and his Times* (Cork: Cork University Press, 1983).

Pétillon, Pierre-Yves, *L'Europe aux Anciens Parapets* (Paris : Seuil, 1986).

Pierce, David, ed., *Irish Writing in the Twentieth Century. A Reader* (Cork: Cork University Press, 2000).

Rafroidi, Patrick, *L'Irlande, Littérature* (Paris : Colin, 1970).

Smyth, Gerry, *The Novel and the Nation: Studies in the New Irish Fiction* (London: Pluto Press, 1997).

Welch, Robert, *Changing States. Transformations in Modern Irish Writing* (London: Routledge, 1993).

Welch, Robert, ed., *Irish Writers and Religion* (Gerrards Cross: Colin Smythe, 1992).

Literary Criticism

Bakhtin, Mikhail, *The Dialogic Imagination* (Austin: University of Texas Press, 1984).

Barthes, Roland, 'The Death of the Author' [1968], in *The Rustle of Language* (Berkeley: University of California Press, 1989).

Bloom, Harold, *The Anxiety of Influence. A Theory of Poetry* (Oxford: Oxford University Press, 1973).

—— *The Anatomy of Influence. Literature as a Way of Life* (New Haven and London: Yale University Press, 2011).

Borges, Jorge Luis, *The Total Library: Non-Fiction 1922-1986* (London: Penguin Publishers, 2007).

Compagnon, Antoine, *Literature, Theory and Common Sense (New French Thought),* (Princeton: Princeton University Press, 2004).

Dällenbach, Lucien, *The Mirror in the Text* (Oxford: Polity Press, 1989).

Eagleton, Terry, *Literary Theory: An Introduction* (Oxford: Basil Blackwell, 1983).

Eco, Umberto, *Interpretation and Overinterpretation* (Cambridge: Cambridge University Press, 1992).

Frye, Northrop, *The Anatomy of Criticism* (Princeton: Princeton University Press, 1957).

Genette, Gérard, *Paratexts: Thresholds of Interpretation* (Cambridge: Cambridge University Press, 1997).

—— *Palimpsests: Literature in the Second Degree* (Lincoln: University of Nebraska Press, 1997).

Hannoosh, Michele, *Parody and Decadence* (Columbus: Ohio State University Press, 1989).

Hutcheon, Linda, *A Theory of Parody. The Teachings of Twentieth-Century Art Forms* (Chicago: University of Illinois Press, 1985).

—— *A Poetics of Postmodernism. History, Theory, Fiction* (New York and London: Routledge, 1988).

Riffaterre, Michel, *Text Production* (New York: Columbia University Press, 1985).

Todorov, Tzvetan, *The Fantastic: A Structural Approach to a Literary Genre* (London: Case Western Reserve University, 1973).

Index

Reimagining Ireland

Series Editor: Dr Eamon Maher, Technological University Dublin

The concepts of Ireland and 'Irishness' are in constant flux in the wake of an ever-increasing reappraisal of the notion of cultural and national specificity in a world assailed from all angles by the forces of globalisation and uniformity. Reimagining Ireland interrogates Ireland's past and present and suggests possibilities for the future by looking at Ireland's literature, culture and history and subjecting them to the most up-to-date critical appraisals associated with sociology, literary theory, historiography, political science and theology.

Some of the pertinent issues include, but are not confined to, Irish writing in English and Irish, Nationalism, Unionism, the Northern 'Troubles', the Peace Process, economic development in Ireland, the impact and decline of the Celtic Tiger, Irish spirituality, the rise and fall of organised religion, the visual arts, popular cultures, sport, Irish music and dance, emigration and the Irish diaspora, immigration and multiculturalism, marginalisation, globalisation, modernity/postmodernity and postcolonialism. The series publishes monographs, comparative studies, interdisciplinary projects, conference proceedings and edited books. Proposals should be sent either to Dr Eamon Maher at eamon.maher@ittdublin.ie or to ireland@peterlang.com.

Vol. 5   Eamon Maher (ed.): Cultural Perspectives on Globalisation and
             Ireland
             ISBN 978-3-03911-851-9. 256 pages. 2009.

Vol. 6   Lynn Brunet: 'A Course of Severe and Arduous Trials': Bacon, Beckett
             and Spurious Freemasonry in Early Twentieth-Century Ireland
             ISBN 978-3-03911-854-0. 218 pages. 2009.

Vol. 7   Claire Lynch: Irish Autobiography: Stories of Self in the Narrative of
             a Nation
             ISBN 978-3-03911-856-4. 234 pages. 2009.

Vol. 8   Victoria O'Brien: A History of Irish Ballet from 1927 to 1963
             ISBN 978-3-03911-873-1. 208 pages. 2011.

Vol. 9   Irene Gilsenan Nordin and Elin Holmsten (eds): Liminal Borderlands
             in Irish Literature and Culture
             ISBN 978-3-03911-859-5. 208 pages. 2009.

Vol. 10   Claire Nally: Envisioning Ireland: W. B. Yeats's Occult Nationalism
             ISBN 978-3-03911-882-3. 320 pages. 2010.

Vol. 11   Raita Merivirta: The Gun and Irish Politics: Examining National
             History in Neil Jordan's *Michael Collins*
             ISBN 978-3-03911-888-5. 202 pages. 2009.

Vol. 12   John Strachan and Alison O'Malley-Younger
             (eds): Ireland: Revolution and Evolution
             ISBN 978-3-03911-881-6. 248 pages. 2010.

Vol. 13   Barbara Hughes: Between Literature and History: The Diaries and
             Memoirs of Mary Leadbeater and Dorothea Herbert
             ISBN 978-3-03911-889-2. 255 pages. 2010.

Vol. 14   Edwina Keown and Carol Taaffe (eds): Irish Modernism: Origins,
             Contexts, Publics
             ISBN 978-3-03911-894-6. 256 pages. 2010.

Vol. 15   John Walsh: Contests and Contexts: The Irish Language and Ireland's
             Socio-Economic Development
             ISBN 978-3-03911-914-1. 492 pages. 2011.

Vol. 27   Dawn Duncan: *Irish Myth, Lore and Legend on Film*
           ISBN 978-3-0343-0140-4. 181 pages. 2013.

Vol. 28   Eamon Maher and Catherine Maignant (eds): *Franco-Irish
           Connections in Space and Time: Peregrinations and Ruminations*
           ISBN 978-3-0343-0870-0. 295 pages. 2012.

Vol. 29   Holly Maples: *Culture War: Conflict, Commemoration and the
           Contemporary Abbey Theatre*
           ISBN 978-3-0343-0137-4. 294 pages. 2011.

Vol. 30   Maureen O'Connor (ed.): *Back to the Future of Irish
           Studies: Festschrift for Tadhg Foley*
           ISBN 978-3-0343-0141-1. 359 pages. 2010.

Vol. 31   Eva Urban: *Community Politics and the Peace Process in
           Contemporary Northern Irish Drama*
           ISBN 978-3-0343-0143-5. 303 pages. 2011.

Vol. 32   Mairéad Conneely: *Between Two Shores/Idir Dhá Chladach: Writing
           the Aran Islands, 1890–1980*
           ISBN 978-3-0343-0144-2. 299 pages. 2011.

Vol. 33   Gerald Morgan and Gavin Hughes (eds): *Southern Ireland and the
           Liberation of France: New Perspectives*
           ISBN 978-3-0343-0190-9. 250 pages. 2011.

Vol. 34   Anne MacCarthy: *Definitions of Irishness in the 'Library of Ireland'
           Literary Anthologies*
           ISBN 978-3-0343-0194-7. 271 pages. 2012.

Vol. 35   Irene Lucchitti: *Peig Sayers: In Her Own Write*
           ISBN 978-3-0343-0253-1. Forthcoming.

Vol. 36   Eamon Maher and Eugene O'Brien (eds): *Breaking the
           Mould: Literary Representations of Irish Catholicism*
           ISBN 978-3-0343-0232-6. 249 pages. 2011.

Vol. 37   Mícheál Ó hAodha and John O'Callaghan (eds): *Narratives of the
           Occluded Irish Diaspora: Subversive Voices*
           ISBN 978-3-0343-0248-7. 227 pages. 2012.

Vol. 69   Michel Brunet, Fabienne Gaspari and Mary Pierse (eds): George Moore's Paris and His Ongoing French Connections
ISBN 978-3-0343-1973-7. 279 pages. 2015.

Vol. 70   Carine Berbéri and Martine Pelletier (eds): Ireland: Authority and Crisis
ISBN 978-3-0343-1939-3. 296 pages. 2015.

Vol. 71   David Doolin: Transnational Revolutionaries: The Fenian Invasion of Canada, 1866
ISBN 978-3-0343-1922-5. 348 pages. 2016.

Vol. 72   Terry Phillips: Irish Literature and the First World War: Culture, Identity and Memory
ISBN 978-3-0343-1969-0. 297 pages. 2015.

Vol. 73   Carmen Zamorano Llena and Billy Gray (eds): Authority and Wisdom in the New Ireland: Studies in Literature and Culture
ISBN 978-3-0343-1833-4. 263 pages. 2016.

Vol. 74   Flore Coulouma (ed.): New Perspectives on Irish TV Series: Identity and Nostalgia on the Small Screen
ISBN 978-3-0343-1977-5. 222 pages. 2016.

Vol. 75   Fergal Lenehan: Stereotypes, Ideology and Foreign Correspondents: German Media Representations of Ireland, 1946–2010
ISBN 978-3-0343-2222-5. 306 pages. 2016.

Vol. 76   Jarlath Killeen and Valeria Cavalli (eds): 'Inspiring a Mysterious Terror': 200 Years of Joseph Sheridan Le Fanu
ISBN 978-3-0343-2223-2. 260 pages. 2016.

Vol. 77   Anne Karhio: 'Slight Return': Paul Muldoon's Poetics of Place
ISBN 978-3-0343-1986-7. 272 pages. 2017.

Vol. 78   Margaret Eaton: Frank Confessions: Performance in the Life-Writings of Frank McCourt
ISBN 978-1-906165-61-1. 294 pages. 2017.